06/2021

ALSO BY

HERVÉ LE CORRE

After the War

IN THE SHADOW
OF THE FIRE

Hervé Le Corre

IN THE SHADOW
OF THE FIRE

*Translated from the French
by Tina Kover*

Europa
editions

Europa Editions
1 Penn Plaza, Suite 6282
New York, N.Y. 10019
www.europaeditions.com
info@europaeditions.com

Translation by Tina Kover
Original title: *Dans l'ombre du brasier*
Translation copyright © 2021 by Europa Editions

*This work received the French Voices Award for excellence in publication
and translation. French Voices is a program created and funded by the
French Embassy in the United States and FACE Foundation.*

Library of Congress Cataloging in Publication Data is available
ISBN 978-1-60945-617-7

Le Corre, Hervé
In the Shadow of the Fire

Book design by Emanuele Ragnisco
www.mekkanografici.com

Jacket photo © RMN-Grand Palais / Agence Bulloz-RMN distr Alinari

French Voices Logo designed by Serge Bloch

Prepress by Grafica Punto Print – Rome

Printed and bound in Great Britain by Clays Ltd, Elcograf S.p.A.

CONTENTS

IN THE SHADOW
OF THE FIRE

THURSDAY, MAY 18TH

Night, and a too-bright moon that tinges their hair blue. They walk noiselessly, their shoes bound up in rags. There are three of them in this crumbling trench, lower legs eaten away by dense shadows, ankles twisting, lurching, stumbling, biting back curses, clinging to comrades visible even close up only as dark shapes. They have just passed within a hundred yards of a bivouac, its fire dying, a mere heap of embers. The sentry drowsing over his rifle. They'd held their breath, burrowing their heads into the raised collars of their shell jackets. From time to time there is another burst of artillery fire from the fortress of Mont-Valérien, like a rumble of distant thunder, or the rolling of funerary drums. A shell whistles in the blackness. Versailles is bombarding Paris blindly in an attempt to kill anyone who's awake. Behind them the explosions are like stifled coughs. The city huddles beneath the onslaught, trembling with fear and rage. Turning, the three men see the reddish glow of fire rising above the dark mass of the fortifications.

A horse whinnies in the distance, somewhere toward the Avenue de Saint-Cloud. A dog begins barking not far away and is silenced by a man's sharp command which, to judge by the animal's yelp of pain, is accompanied by a kick.

They are three soldiers of the Commune. 105th Federated Battalion.

The man at the front of the group is Nicolas Bellec. Sergeant. He was promoted last Saturday at the Fort de

Vanves[1] when it became necessary to replace the previous sergeant, who had had half his head taken off by a piece of flying
shrapnel. The eight comrades remaining out of the twenty alive
that morning had flattened themselves to the ground and
decided it then and there, wild-eyed, covered in blood and
brains, shouting through the din, "You're in command, Bellec!
For the love of God, get us out of here!" He'd hardly been able
to see them, huddled at the foot of a rampart beneath a hissing
onslaught of chunks of stone and steel shards as big as a man's
hand, glinting palely through the fug of dust and smoke. They
had retaken the fort two days earlier, clinging on despite the
storm of artillery shells unleashed by the Versaillais, until
General Wroblewski finally ordered the evacuation. Then they
had fled via the quarries of Montrouge, soot-stained and
bleeding and weeping tears of rage. So he was a sergeant,
because there had been no choice.

They had escaped through a breach in the rampart near the
Porte de Passy, slipping away from the command post set up
in the arrondissement's Hôtel de Ville. They had listened for
a moment to the discussions, the arguments, the curses, and
then they had removed themselves from the melee, from the
shoving and jostling and howls of treason, from the snarling
clashes over the fate warranted by the artillerymen who had
abandoned the fortifications since the bombardments began
two days prior. Nicolas had motioned to his two companions.
Adrien, the younger, a boy of perhaps sixteen at most, had
shouldered his haversack with some difficulty, encumbered as
he already was by his rifle, and the tall ginger-haired man by
his side, whom everyone called Red, had slung two large

---

[1] Vanves (and Issy): Forts defending southwestern Paris, conquered by
the Versaillais on May 9th and 13th. Strategically, they were the scene of
bloody combat. [All notes are the author's unless otherwise specified.]

leather pouches crosswise across his chest. Then the three of them had woven their way through the crowd of shouting, dithering men, dodging elbows and poorly aimed punches and wild gesticulations, and slipped without a word out into the cool night air.

The street was dark, deserted. Torches burned here and there, sooty flames dancing. They headed silently in the direction of a brazier, which cast a reddish glow on the silhouettes of the Federates grouped around it. They were murmuring, rubbing their hands together, huddled over the fire, their upper bodies gilded by the light like polished bronze busts. One of them coughed, then spat into the flames. Turning to Nicolas, he eyed their weapons and the kit strapped to their backs. He was a large man with a drooping mustache, his cheeks bristling with several days' worth of stubble. He was no longer young, and the night and the flickering gleam of the fire highlighted the deep lines on his face.

"Hello, Citizen. Where are you going with that gear?"

"We can't tell you anything. We just have to go."

"Then you don't pass. Nobody crosses this barricade. Nobody in, nobody out."

He gestured vaguely toward a levee built of earth mixed with cobblestones, atop which three carts had been tossed.

"Needs a bit more; we passed it without noticing," said Red.

The man scrutinized him, smoothing his mustache.

"Aren't you the joker. Suppose you teach me, eh? We could have used some wise guys like you in '48. They wouldn't have killed so many of us."

Nicolas laid a hand on Red's arm before the younger man could respond.

"It's not '48 anymore. That was revolution; this is war. Civil war, but war. There are at least twenty thousand infantrymen in the Bois de Boulogne and all the way out to Montrouge. You saw the bombardments yesterday. The marine artillery at Mont-Valérien is keeping a quarter of the city under fire. They'll enter Paris in two or three or four days, if nothing is done, and I don't think anything will be. So your barricade, Citizen, will be about as solid as a bale of straw in front of an oncoming train."

The man hung his head and sighed, and then a fit of racking coughs bent him double. He caught his breath with difficulty and spat on the ground. He remained silent for a long moment, his eyes on the barricade. All conversation around the brazier had ceased. The men looked at one another without really seeing each other in the flame-streaked night.

"We're waiting for a *mitrailleuse*. An eight-pounder, maybe, but we aren't sure. We're going to derail their train, as you say. Wisp of straw, grain of sand. We're going to jam their mechanism."

A new voice resonated in the shadows, borne on a gust of warmth and a spurt of flame.

"You're from the 105th?"

"Yes."

A man limped forward, leaning heavily on a twisted cane. He shook each of the newcomers' hands, bowing slightly.

"We wanted to march on the fort the other day to get you out of there, but La Cécilia[2] said we'd only get ourselves blown to bits, so—God help us—we didn't budge. Damned infuriating. One company set out anyway, against orders, but the shelling was so heavy they gave up after a couple of hours. Came back carrying their dead; didn't want to leave them lying there. What could the rest of us do?"

No one knew how to answer. The distant rumble of cannon fire spoke for them. The old revolutionary filled his pipe. His pupils sparkled in the glow from his match.

[2] La Cécilia: General of the Commune.

"We'll hold it, this barricade. We'll cling to it like a buoy in a flood. And it will blow up in their faces."

He shook his head, eyes still downcast, as if trying to make himself believe his own words. Nicolas couldn't think of anything to say in return. As a boy in Saint-Pabu, where he grew up, people had often told stories of sailors lost to storms at sea. Carried off with their buoys, vanished forever. Or washed up on the coast, greenish and swollen with water, like the ones he'd seen once after a terrible gale.

"We'll go down with it," the man with the limp replied. "You heard what our comrade said. They've got bands of assassins in the Bois . . . there won't be any quarter with them. All these infantrymen who broke ranks and ran from the Prusscos but feel brave enough now to come and gun down the common people. Sons of bitches and drunkards, all of them, just like their papas. The world's still in the hands of thugs. The Revolution won't make it this time."

The old man straightened, shrugging. He turned to face Nicolas and his two companions. With his back to the fire and the dark night pressing down on him, his face was lined with shadow and his eyes sockets seemed empty, like the face of a corpse, and Nicolas could see nothing but unfathomable sadness despite his bushy white mustache and the wide smile beneath it.

"Bah! That's for later, once I've kicked the bucket. We'll show those who come after us how we fought, teach them a thing or two, and then we'll try to outrun the bullets!"

Behind him, Nicolas heard Adrien exhale and set his haversack down on the ground with a dull metallic clunk.

"What are you lugging around in there?" demanded the man with the mustache.

The limping man came closer, leaning on his stick. He nodded, as if he'd understood.

"We can't tell you anything. We've got to go; it's late. I have a pass from General Dombrowski.[3] If you want to know more, you'll have to go ask him."

Nicolas rummaged in his jacket pocket and extracted a piece of paper, which he began to unfold.

"All right," the old man interrupted, holding up a hand. "Go ahead. Try to come back alive and in one piece."

As they passed near the fire, the sentries bade them farewell in low voices, wishing them courage, or luck, clapping them softly on the shoulders. Close to the barricade twenty or thirty more men slept, slumped uncomfortably or curled on the ground, grunting and snoring, tossing, groaning. The three had climbed over the levee, cobblestones rolling under their feet. They'd walked through debris and rubble scattered by the bombardments, down the middle of a street leading to the ramparts, without a single lantern now, not a flicker of light to guide their steps. The odor of poorly extinguished fires was suffocating. At one point they'd had to scale the remains of a demolished house, with its broken furniture and shreds of curtains scattered among the ruins. Farther along, the carcass of a dead horse, fallen between the shafts of a carriage, was beginning to reek, its belly swollen between its sprawling hooves. The bright whiteness of the moonlight was insolent, the façades of the houses rising from its bluish shadows like the walls of a gorge.

The ground here is strewn with mangled tree trunks and overturned stumps trailing naked roots, as if a monstrous plow has been at work. Mingled smells of wood, gunpowder, and

[3] Jaroslaw Dombrowski: Born in Poland (annexed by the Russian Empire) in 1836, killed on the Rue Myrrha in Paris on May 23, 1871, during combat with the Versaillais. Named a general of the Commune, he was one of the few senior officers, along with another Polish soldier, Walery Wroblewski, to have military training. The talent and bravery of these two men were universally recognized.

rotting flesh. The residue of battle. Here and there the shafts of carts jut out of the ground, axles broken across the back of a dead horse. Just now they shuddered at the sight of an arm rising from the embankment, caught bizarrely between the spokes of a broken wheel, the fingers of its large hand contorted like a giant spider brandished at the sky. They paused wordlessly and contemplated the remains, then looked around as if they might find the arm's owner staggering around amidst the carnage. Adrien asked if they were going to leave it like that, sticking out of the ground like a tree branch, but the two others started walking again without answering, so he followed, turning back to look at the macabre tableau until it vanished in the gloom.

They emerge from the cutting and stop to orient themselves, hunkering down, so still that they look like a trio of boulders thrown here during the destruction of battle. The Versaillais have withdrawn following their attack on the Porte d'Auteuil; in the distance, beyond the lake, the faint glow of three campfires is just visible. Ammunition wagons line the road all the way to the crossroads with the Allée de la Reine. There is no movement. No sound. It feels as if everything has suddenly frozen and fallen silent, the better to watch them approach. Traps set to spring have this kind of silence, this stillness of gaping jaws.

"Over there," whispers Red. "We've got to get to the lake. It's just before the waterfall."

They start walking again. The avenue unrolls beneath their feet like a wide, pale ribbon. Red has taken the lead. He knows the Bois like the back of his hand; when he was a little boy his father, to thicken the family soup, had hired himself out to park-strollers on Sundays with his small carriage, drawn by a nag saved from the slaughterhouse for a few francs. The horse, a brave and gentle old beast, had lasted four years before collapsing one June evening on the Pont de

Grenelle, its nostrils filled with blood. Red knows these woodlands and the routes through them by heart, every footpath and bridge. Despite the mess left by the battle, he orients himself now with the strange assurance of a blind man.

They cross the road and tramp back down into a muddy ditch. The clay clings to their shoes and pulls at them with greedy slurping sounds as if it wants to suck them downward and absorb them. They wrench their feet out of the muck again and again, breathing heavily, feeling fatigue weigh down their sacks. They catch sight of the gleam of firelight through the foliage and hear faint murmurs carried on the wind. Distant voices. A woman's laughter. They stop to listen more closely, then start moving again. Suddenly, Red leaps over the bank in two bounds and runs toward the trees. The two others follow him. They stumble into holes left by artillery shells and scale hillocks that smell of sulfur. Reaching the cover of the trees, they stop to gulp a bit of air. There are male voices speaking ahead, right in front of them, the speakers invisible through the thicket. They creep forward, hunching low, then freeze and drop to the ground when they spy the glowing bowl of a short-stemmed pipe and the silhouettes of two soldiers, rifles shouldered, standing around the bluish flames of a dying fire. Behind them is a battery, erected near a pier and its open-air café. This twelve-pounder has been bombing the whole arrondissement since yesterday. Two or three shells every hour. They get to their feet and advance again, step by step, not daring to breathe. The two infantrymen are a mere thirty meters away. The cannon reflects the moonlight with a cold, dull, animal gleam.

Nicolas and Adrien shrug off their sacks and set them noiselessly on the ground. They unsheathe knives and slip them into their belts at the small of their backs. Red has sat down to catch his breath. He has a large revolver in his hand. Adrien moves off and disappears into some sort of hollow, a ditch, maybe, or the crater left by an explosion. Nicolas has followed him but pauses at the edge of the clearing, trying to see where the boy has hidden himself. He can't see anything but a vast field dotted with enormous molehills and, farther away, the glimmer of water.

"Help me! Please, for God's sake!"

The voice rises up from ground level.

"Who goes there?"

One of the soldiers cocks his rifle and moves forward, his silhouette round-shouldered in the moonlit glare. His comrade doesn't move; he, too, grips his gun more tightly.

"Oh, God! It hurts!"

"Who the hell're you, hollering like that?"

The soldier pauses on an embankment, his rifle shouldered.

"I have a message for General Clinchant!"

Nicolas keeps his eye on the other infantryman, who has taken a few steps after his comrade. Adrien's voice, muffled in the depths of his hole, is that of a dying man.

"And just what have you got to tell the General? He's asleep, at this hour!"

"The . . . the Communeux . . . they're planning something . . ."

"What?"

"Finish him off," advises the soldier who lagged behind. "We can see if he's got a message on him afterward. Got to be careful with these people. He's already in his grave; what the hell does it matter?"

"But what if the general doesn't get his message; what if this carcass has something to tell him that's actually important?"

The man hops down into the hole. There is the sound of a groan. Then a muffled whine, like a child would make, or a dog. The other soldier moves forward in his turn, gun at the ready. He passes barely ten meters away from Nicolas, climbs the little hill, stands immobile for an instant, then leans over for a better look. Nicolas makes a leap for him but catches his foot in a rut and falls flat on his face. He hears the man cry out and, lifting his head, sees him aim his rifle and then topple backward, screaming again. Nicolas dashes to the edge of the dark pit and makes out a tangle of arms and legs, and then something black beneath them in which he sees the glint of Adrien's bright eyes. The boy clambers out from under the bodies of the two soldiers, his big knife still in his hand, covered with dirt and blood.

"It's no worse than cutting piglets' throats. They make less noise, is all."

They stand there, catching their breath and gazing at the two corpses sprawled on their backs. Adrien wipes his knife blade on his thigh, then spits on the dead men and sends a shower of dirt clods down on them with a kick. Nicolas tries to make out their faces but can only see their gaping mouths, their foreheads white in the moonlight. They hear Red whistle behind them, so they turn back toward him and find him standing near the pile of their gear, unmoving, rising from among the shadows like a ghost.

"Job's not done," he says. "Better deal with that cannon now."

They run toward the battery as best they can, stumbling and panting, and freeze in their tracks when a voice comes out of the blackness:

"Eh? That you, fellows?"

A man is sitting with a blanket over his head, leaning against a chest filled with cannonballs. He looks around and is about to get up when Red smashes him full in the face with the butt of his rifle. He goes down with a moan and is silent.

They open their sacks and get out their gear. A roll of cord, a keg of gunpowder, and an eight-inch artillery shell. Red loads the cannon, powder, barrel plug. Then he hefts the eight-inch shell and, holding it to his chest as carefully as if it were made of crystal, lets it slip backward into the tube. He has set the fuse to explode at ten kilos of pressure. Slowly, he straightens the backsight adjuster, and all three of them hold their breath until everything has settled. Then Nicolas packs the cannon with dirt and tamps it down and leaps away from it. Next, they unload another shell from which the fuse has been removed and replaced with a simple cork stopper. They set this beneath the two munitions chests sitting on an artillery caisson, then plant the cord in the shell and back away for twenty meters, unrolling it as they go. Then, for a few seconds they are still. They gaze back at the infernal device they have just created.

"Let's go," says Red.

They pick up their sacks. Adrien is already on the move, head hunched low.

"What about him?"

He points at the unconscious artilleryman.

Nicolas shrugs.

"Two days now he's been bombarding and killing us from a distance. Let's see how he likes a taste of his own medicine."

Red snickers behind him. He tosses him a box of matches.

"All yours."

The cord is already crackling. A blossom of phosphorous skitters across the ground. Red touches a flame to the breech, and they run, suddenly much lighter, bounding over holes and puddles, hurling themselves toward the shelter of the woods like frightened game. They reach a footpath, and at that moment the first explosion lifts them off the ground, knocking them to the dirt on all fours. They turn to watch a tree of dazzling flame rising toward the heavens, then the salvo of artillery fire hits like a punch to the gut and they hear the steel shards hissing through the woods, ripping and slicing off leaves and branches. A wave of heat stinking of gunpowder washes over them, and splinters and bits of wood catch fire and fall sizzling to the ground, dying in the mud at their feet.

Finally they turn their backs on this fireworks display of

their own creation and start running again. Already the bugles are sounding the alarm and there are cries in the distance. They run as fast as their legs will carry them. Adrien even finds enough breath to chortle, "That'll teach the bastards!"

They reenter Paris the same way they left it only a short while ago. No one at the bastions, not a single sentry. Two thousand men could get in before anyone noticed. Nicolas stops and turns, straining his eyes into the night, listening to the silence that seems so strange; hearing, maybe, the faint heavy footfalls of regiments marching to attack, the rumble of cart wheels on cobblestones. They could be right on their heels, thousands of them erupting from the trees like wolves, ready to swarm through Paris, a plague of iron and fire.

"What are you staring at?" demands Red. "Waiting for another explosion? Haven't you had enough?"

"Yes, sure, but—"

"Shush, then. They won't come tonight."

They can barely see one another, can't see anything in front of them. Anxiety and hope laden with exhaustion make their feet feel like leaden weights. They set off again, following the railroad tracks back to the barricade they left so recently, its guards still slumbering.

They pass the command post at the Hôtel de Ville again. There are still more than two hundred men there, national guardsmen with rifles over their shoulders, civilians in smocks or frock coats, and even lascars laden with cartridge bags, revolvers stuck in their leather belts, and a few women talking together in one corner. Everyone still shouting, still arguing. Gesturing passionately, jeering, belching, screaming themselves hoarse.

The stretch between La Muette and Point du Jour is deserted. There are no defenders here; the gunners have fled, the sentries abandoned their posts. The cannons stand untended, the embankments gutted. Fire and steel that seem to have sprung from the very bowels of the earth. No one dares venture into this hell brimming over. Dombrowski managed to push the enemy line back as far as Choisy before he was forced to give up, outnumbered and lacking reinforcements and ammunition. The cannon fire ceased around midday; the Versaillais withdrew most of their troops, but some infantrymen could be seen strolling peacefully in the Bois de Boulogne. They were camping beneath the trees there and a bit farther out. Their fires were visible in the dark of night. When the wind blew just right, they could be heard laughing, or singing.

"Tits exposed, legs unclosed!" bellows a corporal in one building, standing on a chair beneath a red flag nailed to the wall. "*Voilà* Paris! Nothing left for the Versaillais to do but roll on top of her like a poor bitch!"

"Just like my missus!" cackles a little man, spitting on the ground. "I'll give 'er to Monsieur Thiers; she'll shag 'im to death!"

Laughter all around.

A man tall and thin as a beanpole, wearing a military cap the wrong way round, the enormous bowl of his pipe bouncing off his chin, waves his bayonet around like a Villette butcher with a boning knife.

"What the hell are they playing at, up at the Hôtel de Ville? What about the Central Committee? We need reinforcements! And Delescluze? Trimming his beard in the mirror after a nice warm bath? Give me ten men and we'll go find them, these gentlemen, so they can come see for themselves, if they don't believe us. And we'll shoot every deserter we pass on the way there, and bring back ten battalions!"

"Well said, Citizen! To the Hôtel de Ville, everyone! *Vive la Commune!*"

Applause. Boos. Catcalls. A few fistfights break out. Shirt collars are grabbed, arguments shouted. The room rumbles with anger, and outraged pipe-smokers spit sparks. They howl with rage at the cowards who have deserted the ramparts, left the fortifications undefended, abandoned the cannons. They have seen Versaillais officers aim artillery shots by the light of phosphorous lamps.

"I'd have liked to see you there, under fire these past few days, by God! I was there—me! Carnage, it was. Anyone who didn't run was blown to bits. We were picking arms and legs and guts up off the street. Yes, sir! There was courage there every step of the way, fat lot of good it did!"

"Who's talking about courage? All we're lacking is ammunition! You open fire on three hundred, you end up with a hundred left. Then you look around for the rest and they've run off, mewling about how the officers know nothing and are leading them to slaughter! Without having fired a single shot! Running away like baby chicks! The cowards; they should be lined up against a wall!"

Two men seize each other by their tunic lapels, forehead to forehead, eyes boring holes into one another, then push each other away, suddenly weary, heads sagging, while around them the crowd heaves and shouts, a billowing tide of heads and shoulders.

Captains climb onto tabletops, trying to round up their men. "First company, 112th, with me!" They brandish their sabers and wave their caps, but there is too much noise, and they turn in all directions to harangue the raging men, to catch an eye or grab a lieutenant to relay their orders or browbeat a sergeant into falling in line. The mob laughs in their faces, shaking its fists and inviting them to go fuck themselves. Mouths twisting with fury and frustration bellow insults at them. They shout until their throats are raw: "85th, obey my orders, damn you! Assemble in the courtyard!" but the uproar cancels out their commands and drowns their authority in an ocean of confused anger.

Red pulls at Nicolas's arm. Adrien shoulders his haversack.

They leave the tumult behind and plunge back into the dark streets without speaking, occasionally picking their way through the rubble of bombed-out façades. After a while they spy a lantern suspended above the sign on a café door.

"Look there," Adrien says. "It's open."

Light glows faintly in the window, and when they step inside, they can make out five men huddled over beer mugs beneath oil lamps hung on the wooden beams, their military caps on the table in front of them. They talk in low voices, barely looking up at the new arrivals. Rifles lean against the wall in one corner. A woman alone at another table seems to be asleep, head slumped on her crossed arms, long gray hair tumbling about her shoulders. The bar is a wooden plank set atop three barrels. Overhead, two chandeliers make the shadows on the ceiling dance and the bottles gleam on the shelves.

"We're about to close," says a big, dour man with a shaved head, stepping out through a heavy curtain.

"We won't stay. Give us some wine and let us clean up a bit."

Nicolas places three coins on the plank.

"Out back, in the yard," says the man. "There's a pump. And keep your money. No charge here for the National Guard."

They wash their hands and faces without really being able to see what they're doing. The blood and mud have dried on their skin, so they rub hard, snorting and grunting.

"I'd give my rifle for a bath," says Adrien.

Red guffaws. "Good idea; that way you'll die clean."

"If Maman could see me now . . . she always insisted on a bath once a week."

"She'd smell you before she could see you. Give her time to get the water nice and hot!"

All three of them laugh, drying themselves with their shirt-tails. When they reenter the café, the five men are standing, rifles shouldered. In the middle of them is a disheveled woman, tall and well built. Her hands are bound in front of her. One of the guards approaches Nicolas. His eyes are cheerful beneath the visor of his cap.

"Sergeant Corvoisier, of the 212th. We're taking her to the Sûreté. Witnesses saw her yesterday signaling to the Versaillais with a lamp to guide their cannon fire. She had a map of the area on her."

The woman keeps her head down. One of the soldiers grasps her jaw and forces her to look up. Her right cheekbone is swollen, and there is a beard of dried blood on her chin. Her gaze is unfocused, her eyes darting in all directions as if she's looking for something. The soldier delivers a brisk slap to the back of her head.

"Eh, whore? Like to see us all shot or bayoneted, would you? They should have shoved that burning lamp right up your arse! But they'll make you talk down at the prefecture, sure enough. Cough up the names of your thug accomplices."

"Place is crawling with scum at the moment," says Corvoisier. "Spies and traitors. We spend all our time running after them. Even officers. A colonel the other day. The Sûreté conscripted us to do the job after the police disappeared. What brings you out here so late?"

"We're giving artillery lessons," says Red. "But they're a bit thick, so it's not going so well."

The sergeant's face splits into a wide smile.

"That wasn't you, was it? The fireworks display an hour ago, in the Bois?"

The three comrades nod.

"They think it'll demoralize the Versaillais," Nicolas says. "Harassing fire, the general calls it. He says Napoleon was chased out of Spain that way. Never rely on line battle tactics against a more powerful army. It's like a people's war. The enemy is everywhere, and these arseholes don't know how to get to them anymore. He also says that if the Central Committee would just listen to him, we could retake Issy and Vanves and reinforce the garrisons. And that we should use more artillery. Instead of that, we leave the ramparts open to fire and build barricades."

Behind his bar, the proprietor shakes his head in irritation.

"These barricades are nothing but cardboard. Décor for the Boulevard du Crime."

The men stare at him, astonished.

"You don't agree? This isn't the way to stop Versailles, and you know it! At a stretch they'll last just fucking long enough to hold the Faubourg Saint-Antoine for three days!"

He sighs, then continues:

"At any rate, the die is cast. Tomorrow, or the week after next, they'll enter Paris, and nothing and no one will be able to stop them."

Red steps closer and drains a glass of wine. "We'll see," he says.

Corvoisier's men murmur approvingly. "They don't know what they're getting into, attacking the people of Paris," says one of them.

The proprietor shrugs his shoulders. "You're young . . . and who knows, maybe you're right . . ." He reaches for clean glasses and serves them a round of drinks. They all start talking at once. They argue over the best way to hold a barricade, where to place the cannons. Grapeshot, crossfire. Ambush. Suddenly it all seems so easy. As if Thiers were leading a regiment of operetta soldiers against them. Nicolas lets them talk. The café owner listens to them, smiling sadly, a bottle of sweet wine in his hand. Adrien sleeps on a chair in the corner, mouth open, rifle propped between his knees.

Sergeant Corvoisier worriedly checks the time. Almost midnight. They'll have to go halfway across Paris to deliver their prisoner to the Sûreté. The Federates shake hands and clap one another on the shoulders, exchanging friendly *Comrade*s and *Citizen*s and promising to see each other soon on the barricades. And Versailles in a month, in the gardens of kings. Then the guards troop out of the café with a great flurry of farewells, pushing ahead of them the woman, who stumbles, hampered by the ropes around her ankles. The thumps of their boots on the cobblestones echo for a long time in the stillness.

Adrien wakes up and looks around the empty room, rakes a hand through his thatch of hair, then slaps himself twice on the cheek.

"Just how old are you, my lad, to be spending the night following these two around?"

"Almost eighteen."

The man smiles as he puts away his bottles. "And if that's true, I was born yesterday."

"What the hell does it matter how old I am? And I'm not following them around; I'm making myself useful!"

"He's the king of the jackknife," says Nicolas. "Fast and clean."

"I was a butcher's apprentice in Le Bourget, before the war. My old man and I killed half the pigs in the village; there was nobody better than us."

"And now you're butchering infantrymen."

"I don't get as much for it, but it's for the Commune, so it'll pay in the end!"

Red has picked up his sack. He signals to Nicolas that it's time for them to go. All three ready themselves, breathing heavily with the effort, fatigue weighing them down. The café owner accompanies them to the door, dragging his feet, looking suddenly dejected.

"Come again for a drink if you get the chance. You're good lads."

They promise to do so; no one believes it. An artillery explosion sounds somewhere in the north, near the Arc de

Triomphe, which makes them raise their faces to the blank sky. What were they saying? Ah, yes: *au revoir*. Until we meet again.

They get a bit lost in the maze of darkened streets, passing a few furtive bystanders who dart out of sight of the three national guardsmen. They walk past gutted buildings, their feet crunching on broken glass. Sometimes a collapsed wall reveals a stretch of green lawn with a private mansion tucked at the far end, shutters closed.

"We could get some sleep in there," says Adrien. "Wouldn't be as far to go, and it'd be a nice change from a straw mattress."

A ghost quarter. The houses that are still intact stand fast against them, locked tight and double-bolted. Heavy with a silence that seems to well up through the walls and out into the street like disdain. The bourgeoisie fled the city in late March, leaving behind a few servants to watch over their possessions, confident that the riots would be put down in a couple weeks, no longer than it took for the army to mass, and that they would return quickly to resume their parties and prosperity in silks and velvets. They dreaded the rabble's pillaging of their parlors, but it was the party of law and order whose cannonballs now crashed into their dining rooms and who ripped from the ruined walls the stern-faced portraits of their ancestors in their gilded frames.

Nicolas looks up at a building whose balconies are supported by carved caryatids. The roof is in tatters, beams jutting out. What will they be capable of when they have Montmartre and Ménilmontant within firing range? When they bombard buildings overflowing with human misery, the hovels of the poor? When they try to bury that most detested part of the population under the rubble of their own slums? He thinks of the battle the other day, at the Fort de Vanves. True war had been waged against them, total war, much more savage, more relentless than anything Badinguet and his staff of good-for-nothings had thrown at the Prussians. With a foreign nation, you ended up negotiating peace, signing surrender agreements or treaties. Among themselves, princes and generals, sometimes bastards sharing the same bloodline, always finished with polite words, doffing their feathered hats to one another. But when it came to fighting the people, no truce, no quarter. They massacred them, cut them to pieces, till there was nothing left but silence and terror.

He shudders. Nicolas Bellec, lowly sergeant in the National Guard, mind plagued by horrific visions. He shrugs his shoulders, shakes his head, shakes himself to banish the shivers running beneath his skin. His two comrades walk ahead of him, feet dragging, heads down, as exhausted as he is. He catches up with them, pressing on despite the fatigue, and the three of them fall into step, as clumsy and awkward as if they've all gone lame.

At the Quai de Passy, the breeze is cool and fresh, and they remove their caps to let their hair flutter and dry. Red closes his eyes for an instant and murmurs, "Feels nice, anyway. You could almost forget." The Seine flows past in the dark, sucking at the bank. A barge is moored at the foot of the Pont de Grenelle, serving as a dormitory for the barricade blocking the quay.

"Keep clear!" a man's voice shouts.

"Sergeant Bellec of the 105th. We have a pass."

They hear movement behind the high wall of cobblestones and overturned wagons. Three silhouettes are leaning on the parapet, rifles aimed. Two men emerge from a double bend and walk toward them. One of them holds a lantern high; the other points his bayonet at Nicolas, who has stepped forward, his mission order in his hand. The man skims the paper. He sighs, shakes his head. A half-unsewn epaulette says he's a lieutenant.

"What the hell are you doing out at this hour? General Dombrowski, right? A pass for a mission of the highest importance? And what were you doing? Gathering flowers at Versailles?"

"We blew up one of their cannons, in the Bois. And ammunition. And now we'd like to get a little sleep."

"Ah, that was you, that ruckus? A cannon? Only one? What was it?"

"A twelve-pounder. It was pointed toward the Porte d'Auteuil, hidden in the trees, and it had been shelling the ramparts and the quarter all day."

"Won't be that one that kills us, then—almost comforting, really."

The lieutenant lowers his lantern, letting it dangle from one hand, and hands Nicolas back his piece of paper. He gestures tiredly for them to pass. The swaying lantern casts its pallid glow on the jumble of the barricade, making it look like a heap of ruins. As they walk away, the lieutenant wishes them good night.

"I'm Grelier," he calls. "Lieutenant Augustin Grelier."

Nicolas turns and sees him leaning against a lamppost, his lantern on the ground. Nothing is visible of him but his gaunt face, a death's head set atop a living body.

"I tell my name to everyone I meet. The ones who survive might remember me and tell my parents what I did. They have a little farm at Roissy. It's a fair distance, but the road's good."

His voice has changed. It has become less abrupt, softer. As if the officer has cast off his rank. It's the voice of a young man, and in the explosion-dotted silence of this night, they can hear it quiver slightly.

"Stupid, right?"

"Bellec. Nicolas Bellec. From Saint-Pabu. It's a long way from here, in northern Brittany, on the Aber Benoît. The road barely exists. I'm not really sure who will remember us. Our loved ones, maybe?"

Lieutenant Grelier lets out a hoot of laughter. "Then we're fucked!"

Nicolas waves to him as they walk away, the gesture swallowed up by the darkness. Adrien goes in front, shuffling, desperate for sleep. He hasn't said anything for a while, and his swaying gait could be mistaken for drunkenness, or sleepwalking. Red's big form keeps pace with Nicolas; he is somber, nodding and shaking his head and murmuring as if having a distressing conversation with himself. They reach the corner of the Rue du Commerce and stop near a large overturned hay cart behind which are two cannons placed top-to-tail and several crates of ammunition. Two men are seated there in armchairs, smoking pipes, their rifles on their laps. They are silent, unmoving, their gazes unfocused, lost in thought, maybe dozing. They look up and recognize Adrien, wave to him, muttering, and subside into gloomy silence again.

Farther on they hear laughter, muffled protests, a fit of coughing. The 105th is billeted nearby, behind the town hall, in a disused warehouse where two misers, wealthy traders at Les Halles, hid tons of flour during the siege, banking on a rise in prices. One night in late March, as they were loading a wagon, they'd been surprised by a patrol that shot them on the spot to the cheers of the jeering, spitting crowd drawn by the commotion. Adrien bids his companions good night and walks off without looking back. Red and Nicolas watch him vanish into the darkness and then reappear in the glow of a lit streetlamp, the only one on the street, like a large, solitary star flickering in the shadows. They stand there for a moment, near the two useless cannons and the two men slumped in their chairs.

"It's sad, anyway," says Red.

Nicolas tries to make out his features but can only see the mass of hair and beard poking out of his cap. He didn't think this colossus capable of sadness or low spirits, or even that he knew the meaning of the words. But Red sighs, murmurs, "How will all of this end?"

Nicolas racks his brain for something to say, a lie, one of those grandiose phrases that sound so intoxicating in meeting houses and workers' clubs, but he can't think of anything because he's short of breath, and also because he knows now that no words can chase away the misery.

"What do you want me to say?"

The other man places his big, heavy hand on Nicolas's shoulder.

"Nothing, don't worry about it. Let's get some shut-eye . . . Tomorrow's another day, and we'll try to make it to one more sunset."

"You're a poet, my friend."

"Sometimes. But it never lasts long. Shall we? We'll come up with more pretty words tomorrow."

"I'm going to have a look around."

Red stifles a yawn behind his hands and stretches. "You don't think we've walked enough for today?" He thumps Nicolas on the back and moves off with long, slow, almost noiseless strides. He disappears at the corner by a stall reading "Wood and Coal," and Nicolas turns and goes back in the other direction, finding enough strength left in his exhausted legs to walk a little faster. He could navigate this labyrinth of streets with his eyes closed. He hears a train puffing in the distance ahead of him, then the squeal of its brakes. He wonders what train is still running at this hour, and where it's going. Then he remembers the armored train people have been talking about for days, the one nobody dares believe in anymore. Soon he reaches the foot of the viaduct and continues, heart thumping, beneath the iron bridge.

The night suddenly seems less black. A pale mist, particles of light float among the façades. 10 Rue de Constantine. This is it.

Last January, when the windows were rimed with ice, he'd gotten up to restoke the fire in the stove, woken by the passage of the first train from Montparnasse, and then climbed back in bed with Caroline, who had curled her warm body around his chilled one with a sleepy murmur, bundled up in two night-gowns, her small feet clad in thick socks. Yes, in January, in the depths of that winter of hunger and death, in their shabby gar-ret, they had lived hours stolen from fatigue and despair, secret nights spent whispering to each other and laughing like chil-dren, nights when they warmed each other with bodies burn-ing from a sweet fever.

They'd embraced the good times when they came, holding them close for fear they would escape and creep away to die in a corner, like a starving cat spared by the blade of a cook in a cheap canteen.

He catches sight of the window on the top floor of the nar-row building, and his heart clenches with memories of happier days, their castle in the clouds, their tower of miracles.

One evening in late March, returning from Montmartre in an insurgent Paris, they'd drunk their fill in cafés crammed with people spilling out onto the pavement, a joyous crowd singing of a new day and toasting wildly with beer mugs full of promises and dancing on the grave of the old world along with the broken glass under their feet. They had both gone home totally inebriated, falling into doorways to kiss and giggle.

Happy times. Caroline. Tomorrow night he'll be on leave, and they will try to believe in them again, for a few moments.

He gazes up at the dark window. He would love to see a candle flicker to life in the window, for Caroline to appear and beckon him to come up. But, of course, there is no light in the blackness, and he is angry with himself for expecting the impossible, like in the old stories when rubbing an oil lamp causes a genie to appear. So he turns back toward the billet, lowering his chin and turning up the collar of his jacket, clenching his fist around the shoulder strap of his rifle to give himself courage. He quickens his pace in the shadows, the occasional gaslight or lantern hung above a door gleaming in the darkness. Here and there he trips on a protruding cobblestone or a rut in the pavement. Cats dart past and are swallowed up by the night; rats scurry in the gutters, uttering their sharp little cries, sinister in the gloom.

Two storm lanterns mark the entrance of the building in which the 105th is billeted. The watchman is asleep, slumped in the corner of the doorway, his rifle across his lap. Nicolas enters the dormitory, lit by a few quivering flames, the atmosphere thick with fatigue and grime. He shrugs off his gear, and exhaustion pushes him onto his pallet; sleep knocks him unconscious before he can even turn over.

FRIDAY, MAY 19TH

2

The man pulls her to him, and she doesn't know how he still has the strength to grab her this way, by the shoulder of her blouse, and hold her close to his pale face that burns with fever, with his stinking breath and his body almost nude beneath his rags. Caroline doesn't resist or try to free herself, because she can hear his rapid, shallow breathing, and feel the wild pounding of his heart beneath her palm, braced flat against his chest. Men have seized her like this before, drawn her to them to strike her or lift up her skirts, sometimes both at the same time. Their hands, always brutal and hard and dirty.

"You'll tell my kiddies . . . you'll tell them I was brave, won't you? And tell my Léonce that her man was a real one, yeah? You'll tell them?"

She whispers in his ear, *Yes, of course, rest easy, I'll tell them.*

"Cos I did it all for them, defended the Commune, by God . . ."

She promises again. All she knows about him is his first name, Jules, and that his battalion, the 72nd, was devastated in the streets of Issy last week for lack of ammunition and reinforcements, and that the poor devil has hung on for eight days, his knee destroyed by a bullet, delaying again and again the visit from a surgeon for fear his leg would be cut off. She wishes he would let her go, now. She knows there's no hope for him; what remains of his thigh is swollen with gangrene. Doctor Fontaine has told her he doesn't know how the man has enough blood left in his body to keep his heart beating. She wishes he would release his grip, because she is suddenly afraid he will pull her down with him into the abyss on the verge of which he is teetering.

His fingers tighten on her shoulder, and he moans, his face contorting, moving the stump of his leg beneath the rough gray sackcloth blanket covering him; she can see it rising and quivering like a pet animal startled from sleep. His arm lowers slowly to rest on his chest, his fist clenched. His head sinks deeper into the pillow as if something were suddenly pressing on it. He lifts his gaze to her and stares. Tears brim in his eyes, but they don't fall.

"I need to look at you, before . . ."

A smile stretches his lips, and his fist unclenches, the lined palm he turns toward the ceiling like a beggar's, waiting for alms.

Caroline doesn't notice that he has stopped breathing because she is holding her own breath, listening for the rest of what he had to say. Then, suddenly, she realizes that the wet eyes are no longer focused on her, unless it's from so far away that surely they can see nothing at all.

She closes his lids because she doesn't want to know where his eyes are looking now, and because she's afraid that the pupils are like dark tunnels to nothingness, capable of drawing her in. She stands up and pulls the sheet over the gray face with its eight days' growth of beard, and suddenly the smell hits her like a wave of heat from a fire. She backs away and bumps into a man passing behind her in a navy-blue smock, his thatch of white hair tucked beneath a black skullcap.

"What's this?" He growls the words more than he speaks them, his head hunched low between his shoulders. He is sturdy and solidly built, his hands large and work-worn below his rolled-up sleeves. Caroline looks at him in horror and then apologizes, murmuring "Doctor Fontaine" and wiping her damp forehead with the back of her hand.

"What are you sorry for? That this man has died?"

"No, it's because . . ."

"What? Gangrene, is it? I never smell anything anymore, myself. Perfume, of course, or a branch of lilacs ten meters away, well, that's different. But bodily fluids, excrement, rotting flesh . . . I've seen bodies in every possible state, from puffed-up with gas to mostly liquified . . . some I've opened up have been so swollen with the stench they let out an almighty huff from beyond the grave. And then there are the ones they bring me that are only skin and bones, as dry as mummies. Learned pretty quickly how I'd end up eventually, like the rest; a putrid soup and then stripped completely bare; everyone looks the same after that, once the trappings we call our human appearance have gone. Appearances, you see; it's all just appearances . . ."

He gazes for a moment at the corpse stretched out in front of them, then bends and pulls back the blanket.

"The dead, ah! the poor dead suffer great pains."[4]

"He suffered terribly, it's true . . ."

Doctor Fontaine smiles indulgently at her. "I don't doubt it. But I was quoting a poem by Baudelaire. It was a sort of motto for me when I was still working as coroner. The poets are always right, don't you think?"

She shrugs. Around them, the large room is full of groans and gasps. It seems to her as if the atmosphere of suffering has taken on a life of its own, thicker now, and is filling her head with dull throbbing.

"I'm not familiar with poetry at all, Doctor."

"That will come . . . when all this violence has calmed down."

"It'll never calm down for anyone but the dead."

---

[4] [Translator's note] Charles Baudelaire, "The Kind-Hearted Servant of Whom You Were Jealous," tr. William Aggeler, 1954.

The doctor chuckles softly. He rummages in his pockets, pulls out the stub of a cigar, lights it.

"I'm afraid we've proclaimed a republic of words that will soon be a republic of the dead, now that you mention it, and that's what frightens me, you see. It's a bit like we doctors tried to heal injuries simply by shouting obscenities, or to cure disease using magic spells. They talk and talk at the Hôtel de Ville; they gossip on the barricades; they hem and haw about what reinforcements to send against Versailles, and in the meantime Monsieur Thiers is planning his onslaught. Thus poetry as a refuge, as an indestructible place where we can soothe ourselves with words, because they are themselves a means of exchange that doesn't cost anyone anything. At my age I've heard too much, read proclamations promising victory and then had to settle for mourning defeat. Perhaps that's why I've taken more care of the dead than the living, because at least I don't have to lie to them about what's coming and my inability to stop it."

He has spoken without looking at her, his face turned toward the wounded and dying. Then a scream makes them both jump, and the doctor hurries toward a man who is trying to struggle out of his pallet at the far end of the room, dragging the stumps of his legs.

Caroline thinks about what he has just said. It seems to her, though, that the Commune has matched its actions to its words. And—in her opinion—there are some words that bring warmth to the heart when you have nothing else to share but the hope for a bit of happiness. They felt that the other day, she and Nicolas, when they strolled in the Place du Trône among the children and their games, and the passionate discussions on street corners, and the street peddlers and barkers exchanging insults. Passing squads of national guardsmen called out to bystanders on the pavement, blowing kisses to the girls at large and proposing impossible dates with them. Here and there an artillery cart or ammunition wagon had clattered noisily past on the cobblestones. There was a war passing, rumbling and swaggering, and they'd stopped to watch it go by, knowing they would have to fight it soon enough. They had crunched barley-sugar sweets and drunk a few glasses of beer in front of cafés and taverns buzzing with rage and laughter and hope. They read the posted decrees, decisions, and call-ups of the Commune, and there could be no doubt that every bit of it would be implemented, because it was for the good of all, and no one could be against it unless they were bad or vicious. A new world was being printed every day; their dreams were right there to be read in black and white, in the bright light of day, freed finally from the nights, from their fogs and their terrors. It was the springtime of life, all of this, and the rosebushes that climbed the walls and spilled out onto the sidewalks, showering them with perfume, seemed to confirm it.

They had walked for hours in the quiet city that trembled with the glorious anxiety of time suspended. They had taken advantage of these moments the way you spend a salary advance without regret, knowing that payday is coming soon.

Doctor Fontaine has lifted up the man with the amputated legs and is holding him beneath the arms as if he were a baby, speaking quietly to him, their foreheads almost touching, while the man cries and groans and moves what remains of his legs the way toddlers walk in the air when you hold them that way, his face wet with tears. Caroline comes over and straightens the mattress and blanket, which are soiled with brown stains. The acrid, heavy odors of urine, shit, and vomit fill her nose and mouth and seep slowly down the back of her throat, where they will lodge in her stomach like rancid oil. Behind her she can hear the injured man moaning, his voice reedy and breathless; then he clears his throat and says, *Kill me, kill me, I can't, I'll never*, and Fontaine murmuring calmly that no, he will live because he is brave and because he can't turn his back to this gift from God, to which the man replies that no one has ever given him anything, *not your God, not anyone*.

"You need to rest now," says the doctor. "Please. You must recover your strength."

He carries the man back to his bed and places him on it gently, his arms straining with the effort. Caroline kneels on the edge of the mattress and takes the man's hand, which is cold and dry, thick and hard as a vine, and holds it as he lets his head fall back on the sack stuffed with rags serving as his pillow and looks at her pleadingly.

"You, tell him, I can't live like this. I'm a carpenter . . . I'll be worthless! I won't even be able to go out walking with my Génie, or run after my kids!"

"Don't say that," she murmurs. "Don't say that."

"And my feet hurt, and my knee where I knocked it last year . . . can you believe that? They've thrown 'em in the glue factory, but I'm in as much agony as if I still had the bullets in me!"

Doctor Fontaine takes a small brown glass vial out of his pocket.

"Give him this. Just one swallow. We can't let him become dependent on it, but it will soothe him. He'll see things differently when he's gotten a bit of his strength back."

Caroline raises the man's head and slips the slender flask between his lips. He grimaces at the bitter taste of the laudanum but swallows the liquid in a gulp. She stands and goes to fill a tin mug from the pail beneath a stone sink. The man drinks greedily, then lets out a sigh.

"What's your name?"

"Noël . . . Noël Malardier. 87th battalion. We were at Bourg-la-Reine, lending a hand to a volunteer corps, when they retook the village."

Noël raises himself on one elbow and looks at her steadily.

"We fought well, you know."

He gulps back snot and tears, his eyelids heavy.

"Of course I know. My sweetheart is in the 105th. What's your wife's name?"

"Nicolette. But I call her Génie. It's quicker, and besides, she's so smart, and so fine. Not like me! She's always reading, you know. I have a hard time sometimes, but she helps me. She's a milliner. You'd look nice in a hat . . . And my little ones are Clotilde and Gaston and the youngest, who's six months old; we named her Louise, for Louise Michel, because Génie belonged to the same club as her, and the older Louise seemed to have such a big heart."

He falls silent, out of breath, and lies back, his eyes half-closed. Caroline pats the back of his hand with her fingertips.

"It's going to be all right. Rest now."

When she stands up, she sees that Doctor Fontaine has disappeared. Slightly dizzy, she sees the other aid-station nurses who have arrived to begin the next shift, already leaning over the wounded, comforting them or changing dressings. Distributing a bit of bread and broth to those able to feed themselves. There are Germaine, Lucie, and tall Lorette, who is bent double above a man lifting his bandaged head. Caroline moves toward them, massaging the small of her back. These all-nighters always leave her in knots. The window shows a square of blue sky. She forgets, sometimes, that the sun can still rise.

The man is sitting, waving his arms as if chasing away flies. He is Captain Mercandier, of the 45th. He arrived ten days ago, skull broken, brain exposed. Doctor Fontaine had summoned a surgeon called Lefeuvre from the Hôtel-Dieu, a man he knew at Sebastopol, who worked miracles there with gentle trepanation to relieve brain swelling, suturing meninges with gold thread. One out of five of his patients survived with few aftereffects. He is said to be able to repair skulls as if they were porcelain teapots. Before the siege he used to come to the morgue often, to practice on bodies after Fontaine had finished examining them, working as meticulously as if the patient might wake up complaining of a headache. He was forever irritated by not being able to gauge the results of these operations, and complained that he would never be able to understand why death had to be final when any other machine, if correctly repaired, could start back up again. He and Fontaine had endless philosophical debates, sometimes at night in the autopsy room over a slack-jawed corpse washed down with bleach beneath a white lampshade slowly blackening from oil-lamp smoke, sometimes over a glass of beer in the bright gaslight of a city café. Lefeuvre firmly believed that, by the dawn of the twentieth century, humans would be able to conquer death by preventing its onset or reanimating organs and bodies via the combined effects of chemistry and electricity. Fontaine, on the other hand, saw nothing attractive in the idea of a very lengthy life, much less an eternal one, which he viewed as an ordeal he would never willingly undertake.

"I'm telling you, they came again tonight! There were three of them, and they finished off the wounded with their bayonets!"

Lorette shakes her head, her hair bound under a sky-blue scarf, and her thin chest and shoulders twitch in a forced laugh.

"You were dreaming, Citizen Captain. The Versaillais are nowhere near coming to slit our throats that way!"

Her eyes meet Caroline's as she speaks, seeking affirmation, but Caroline avoids her gaze and bends over the captain's bed.

"I've been on duty all night, and I've not seen or heard anything. And anyway, the Versaillais are in Versailles, not Paris."

She wants to believe her own words. She forces herself to meet the man's eyes and pastes on a smile to be more convincing.

"Right, treat me like an idiot . . . I saw the drubbing they gave us at Issy. And Vanves? They whipped our arses as if we were just a bunch of kids. Courage isn't worth much against them. I'm sure they're in Paris already, hiding away in every nook and cellar, ready to spring as soon as the word is given. You'll see!"

He sinks back on the pillow, hands on his chest, unmoving, like a recumbent effigy.

"But I've already seen them. Three nights now, they've come."

"They haven't killed anyone tonight," says Lorette.

"I know what I see when they carry them away in the morning, all these dead. And there are always others who've been stabbed by MacMahon's[5] scum."

He speaks with his eyes closed, his lips barely moving. Then, suddenly, his face relaxes, and his mouth falls open slightly. He begins snoring softly.

"Dreaming of throat-slitters, poor man. As long as they're only bad dreams . . ."

Two old men in flat caps and dark smocks come into the room, each carrying one end of a stretcher. They nod to Caroline, and she points at the body of Jules, barely discernible beneath the sheet.

"How many today?" asks one of the men.

"Two," she says.

"Only two?"

"Why? That not enough for you?"

The two men set down the stretcher and take off their caps, wiping their foreheads. White hair is plastered to their bare heads.

"The fewer there are, the less heavy they are to carry, Citizeness."

---

[5] MacMahon: Head of the regular army under the government installed at Versailles and led by Adolphe Thiers.

"Let's say it's the weight of sorrow," the second man says. "We've just come from the cavalry barracks on the Rue Dupleix; they had eleven there. Half of them civilians. A house got hit by two artillery shells, one after the other. They're having a right good time, the gunners at Mont Valérien. You know, one a shift would still be too many for us; we feel the same as you. I didn't get involved in the Commune to do this, but at my age they said I'd be more useful this way. Imagine, seventy years old and people think you're not good for anything anymore! But if it comes time to pick up a rifle and defend the barricade, I'll leave the dead where they're lying and give those bastards what for!"

His companion nods, his expression pensive, then adds, low, as if talking to himself:

"We've got guns . . . cannons, too. It won't be like '48."

All four of them fall silent. They look at their feet, and for a moment one might have thought them in prayer. Then Lorette turns back toward the room where fifty poor devils are just waking up.

"We've just drawn some water from the well," she says. "Nice and cool. If you'd like . . ."

"Wouldn't say no!"

They fill their mugs and drink thirstily, then sigh gustily, breathless, water dripping from their chins onto their shirtfronts, then pick up their stretcher without a word and get to work.

Caroline watches them. They make their way carefully between the pallets, nodding to the mass of wounded humanity around them as they pass. Most often, Commune members assigned to this grim work behave like baggage porters or movers tasked with shifting a cumbersome piece of furniture. They talk loudly, lumbering among the mattresses, sometimes stepping over patients to move faster, moving the corpses roughly, telling jokes with the most inappropriate punchlines, promising the patients they'll be back tomorrow to pick them up. But these two, whom she has never seen before, have come to fetch sorrow and carry it in their arms, as they've just said. Some of the injured men watch them with that combination of curiosity and apprehension that pedestrians always show when a hearse passes by.

She watches now as they slowly lift the body of Jules, who died only a little while ago while looking at her face, and it seems to her that his moist eyes are still fixed on her. His head lolls on the canvas of the stretcher, and she wishes she knew where he was now. What this body is already becoming. If something of this man remains, still vibrating in the air, secretly. A soul, maybe. And if that soul is still capable of seeing, of feeling sadness or regret. She's thought about all this before, when her mother died with her hand in hers, carried off by a fever there'd been no way of fighting. She had waited, sitting on the edge of the bed, unmoving, as if under some sort of spell, for something to happen. An aunt had shocked her out of her grief-stricken stupor some two hours later by dissolving in tears over the deathbed. She'd been thirteen years old at the time and had never wondered these things since then, undoubtedly because life, so often suddenly brutal and cruel, had demanded more urgent reactions.

The two undertakers pass her again on their way out, muttering, and she is left alone near the shelves where they keep bandages and a few surgical instruments. She would love to get out of here. Her duties are finished for now; she'll be back this evening for the night shift. She wants to breathe a bit of fresh air, drink a bowl of warm milk, and sleep. Sleep.

In the big room, murmured conversations can be heard among the groans of pain. Low voices, weighted down with fatigue. Requests for news from the patient in the next bed; anxious questions about a friend who wasn't doing well. The nurses respond, reassure, crouch down to wipe a forehead with a cool cloth or clasp an outstretched hand.

Émilie, a girl of barely sixteen, is joking in her high, girlish voice with a huge bearded man who gestures animatedly with his sole remaining arm, sitting up on his mattress. Both of them burst into peals of laughter, and the clear, joyous ripple of the young girl's laugh makes the murmurs fall silent briefly, as if to better enjoy this cool breeze wafting through the room.

Caroline takes advantage of the moment to grab her shawl and her canvas bag and leave. In front of the dispensary, Doctor Fontaine is helping some guards lift a blood-covered man onto a stretcher. The man's features are impossible to make out. His jaw sags to his chest, quivering in a mess of bone and flesh. Caroline meets the doctor's eye and sees in his expression horror and exhaustion so powerful that she wants to tie him down and make him sleep for three days. With a motion of his hand he orders her to leave, then bends over the wounded man to murmur reassurances in his ear.

She walks with long strides to the corner of the street and turns, stopping in front of a haberdashery, Madame Ophélie's Ribbons and Buttons, to catch her breath, close her eyes, and soak in the noises of the street. Children's laughter. The calls of a window fitter. Through an open window on the top floor of a building across the street, she can hear a woman singing. It's hard to believe that life can be so simple sometimes. She starts walking again in the direction of the Rue Vavin, the street crowded with horse carts and wheelbarrows. Two drays full of cobblestones wait outside a wine merchant's shop, their four big horses unmoving, heads low, their huge, muscular backs and shoulders and rumps gleaming in the morning light. A large crowd is busily constructing a barricade on the corner of the Boulevard du Montparnasse. Women dig in the road and fill sacks with large shovelfuls of earth that men in shirtsleeves, both national guardsmen and civilians, heave up to a low wall of hastily mortared cobblestones. An officer standing on the deck of an artillery wagon directs the operation. Screeching children climb on the three cannons surrounding him, clinging to their wheel spokes and cavorting around the gun carriage. One of them sticks his head into the barrel of a twelve-pounder, and Caroline feels a chill of fear run down her spine at the idea that a stray shell might go off. The child emits a long scream, muffled and mournful, a terrifying, bloodthirsty, animalistic cry that makes her jump, her eyes filling with tears. He pulls his head out of the cannon, his hair disheveled and black with soot, grotesque and crowing with laughter.

She crosses the worksite, responding with a shrug of her shoulders to the greenhorns who call out to her to lend a hand. Hansom cabs trundle past on the boulevard, sleepy drivers huddled into their cloaks, compact masses crowned with top hats. It's all so calm, the air so sweet. Images from the communal room last night, in the dingy lamplight, crowd back into her mind, and the smells, and the groans and cries of terror from those who sensed Death dragging its invisible carcass toward them among the pallets, and she can't understand how, from one street to the next, on the two sides of a single door, so much light and such darkness can exist in the same world. She hurries up the Rue Delambre, skirting a levee of cobblestones with more howling children on top, and crosses the deserted Boulevard de Vanves, as full of birdsong as a village lane.

Loose cobblestones glint in the sun on the Rue de Constantine, doubtless pried out and tossed there by a bunch of drunkards trying to play ninepins. Horses sometimes get a hoof stuck in the gaps, and children twist their ankles and skin their knees on the edges. It's like the mouth of some prehistoric monster, full of sharp little teeth capable of scraping through even the thickest leather and grinding the hardest bones to dust.

Caroline hops from one foot to the other. Two men sitting at a table outside a wine shop whistle admiringly and make remarks about dancing and the opera. She curtsies to them awkwardly and keeps going, weaving between the ruts, and hurriedly opens the door of the tiny workshop owned by Mademoiselle Bastide, the seamstress who lives on the ground floor of the building and rents them their room. The old lady barely looks up from her work to return her greeting hoarsely, her ever-present little pipe stuck in the corner of her mouth. Lalie, the apprentice, leaps up and hurries toward Caroline, pushing her back outside and closing the door carefully behind her. Strands of hair escape messily from her sun-yellow cap. Her smile and her dark eyes are bright with happiness. She is seventeen. She laughs and hops up and down on the cobblestones, cheeks pink.

"It happened!" she says, taking Caroline by the shoulders. "I . . ."

She twirls once, making the folds of her skirt swirl around her.

"Yes? Tell me!"

"We went dancing last night near the Bastille, and then we went out for a bit of air, and . . . well, we kissed, and then we danced some more, and he told me he loved me, and he said as soon as this is all over we'll get a house together!"

Caroline flings her arms around Lalie, and they cling to each other, giggling and dancing a few steps of the polka. They pull apart and look at each other, and Caroline's expression turns serious.

"And your parents? What will they say?"

Lalie sighs and rolls her eyes.

"Évreux is so far away. They still have my sisters and brothers to keep them busy, and Calvados to make them forget about me. And anyway, soon girls won't have to ask their parents' permission for everything, right? You told me that once! That the Commune and all that would change women's lives."

She glances toward the workshop and moves toward the door.

"In the meantime there are still bosses, though I suppose this one could be worse." She turns to go inside, then whirls back to Caroline. "Hey . . . I'm supposed to meet him tonight at around five. He told me he could get away from the shop; it's on the Rue Saint-Nicolas, in the twelfth. We can spend a few minutes together. Will you come with me? I'd like you to meet him, tell me what you think of him . . . if he's a good fellow, if I can trust him . . ."

Caroline laughs. "What do you expect me to say? I don't know anything about that sort of thing!"

"But—you and Nicolas! And—what you told me once, about when you were younger. You do know something about men. The bastards and the good ones!"

Nicolas. She summons up his image, but it falls away, and again she can see nothing but the pallets full of wounded men she's just left behind, and the grave face of Doctor Fontaine.

"So? Will you come?"

The girl's face has moved closer to hers, suddenly serious. "Are you all right?"

"Yes, of course I'll come. Stop by and fetch me; I'll be upstairs."

Lalie plants a kiss on her cheek and disappears with a bound back into the dim shop.

Caroline stands pensive for a moment, a bit dazzled by the sun. The other day she attended a gathering of the Women's Union for the Defense of Paris. It had been full of laughter, clamoring voices, protests. A few men had stood in the back, sniggering sometimes at the daring words swirling around them, but they hadn't been overly bold about it because the unhappiness thrumming in that crowded room wasn't just about what the bourgeois imposed on them anymore, but also their daily oppression by their own domestic lords and masters. From the men they worked for to their fathers and husbands, women were abused in all directions, beaten, screwed against their will, girls on the streets selling themselves for a few sous or shut up in brothels. "Some of them should have their cocks cut off; then they'd have something to howl about!" one young woman cried, brandishing a pair of scissors. "Yes, seeing as it's their excuse for everything," shouted a fat woman wearing a man's cap.

Caroline had been intoxicated by the passion in the room, the gleeful exclamations and the distraught ones, too, and she could feel the hope in that hot, overcrowded room like the beating of an immense heart, and it seemed to her that when they spilled out into the street, all these women, happy at long last, could flick their shawls and sweep away all the ancient limitations that had held them down since the dawn of mankind.

A woman had shouted from the platform then, calling for a bit of quiet, because Citizeness Elisabeth Dmitrieff was about to speak. The hum of conversation grew softer as a woman with blonde hair and eyes so bright that the gaslight paled in comparison took the stage. Her voice was clear and firm as she relayed the fraternal greetings of the International Workingmen's Association to the Commune of Paris and its revolutionary efforts. The whole of Europe was watching Paris and its people. Citizen Karl Marx was following the situation closely from London. It was the first time Caroline had heard the name. Behind her, a woman cried out: "Tell him not to worry; we're following it even closer!" There were guffaws all around her. "No one's following it closer than us. We've got our noses right in it, and it doesn't always smell good!"

The speaker waited for the laughter to die down, waved away the buzz of talk with the slow, deliberate gesture of a pianist about to rest masterful fingertips on the keys. In the renewed silence, her forehead gleaming beneath the golden hair wound around her head, she continued speaking, giving a report of what had been accomplished—and saying almost nothing about what still remained to be done. It was an enormous task, one that would take more than a generation to complete. She spoke of the emancipation of all workers, of the whole human race—which included women, who were more than just the wives of mobilized national guardsmen who'd been given jobs to do, and who should become full-fledged citizens in their own right. "The right to vote!" shouted a voice in the room. "Equality!" responded another. "Of course," Elisabeth Dmitrieff said. Of course. Around her, the women on the platform smiled and nodded in agreement, their faces determined.

The room rumbled loudly with approval. Then Citizeness Dmitrieff announced that the common women of Paris must show not only men but the whole world that they were worth as much in combat as the finest soldiers. They would have to hold the barricades, the true fortifications of Paris, erected by the proletariat and forged from the cobblestones of the streets and boulevards. The hour of battle was approaching; Versailles had decided to punish Paris and its people for their impudence. To invade the city as if it were a foreign country to be brought in line by the sword. To shell, to stab, to pillage.

The buzz of the crowd had grown louder, punctuated with shouts and threats, and then someone began to sing "La Marseillaise," faintly and shakily at first, but the song was taken up by a thousand throats by the third line. The women on the platform sang along, arm in arm. Caroline edged closer to the dais to get a better look at their faces, filled with grave joy, their eyes heavy with fatigue, maybe, or the worry of doubt. For two weeks now Versailles had been advancing, attacking, maneuvering. And the Commune had been talking, equivocating, debating, struggling. Nicolas had told her that in some National Guard battalions they lacked respect for the officers, arguing with their orders and talking about arresting the generals or marching on the Hôtel de Ville. There were rumors of an army of 50,000 men ready to besiege Paris, and the idea was beginning to sink in . . .

She is startled from her thoughts now by two muffled explosions in the distance that seem to come from the north, toward Auteuil or La Muette. The sparrows in the trees continue twittering. A blackbird warbles contentedly somewhere, unseen. It's as if the sky is singing. But the fatigue catches up with her now, rising up her legs and pressing down on her shoulders. She enters the house, weary and sun-dazzled. The darkness is tinted red, and it takes her a moment to make out the narrow staircase with its irregular steps, which she climbs holding on to the banister that wobbles beneath her hand.

The room is bright, overlooking the street. The odor of furniture polish can't quite disguise the faint smell of dampness. The grayish ceiling is stained with brown rings that give it the look of a poorly drawn *mappa mundi* with the outlines of continents and islands shakily sketched. A cast-iron stove obtained from a rag-and-bone man at the Porte de Bagnolet stands in one corner. Caroline still wonders how Nicolas and his workmates managed to haul it up that breakneck staircase.

She tosses her clothes on a chair. Naked, she slips on a worn man's shirt with holes in the sleeves. The bed is almost deep enough to drown in. The mattress, almost too soft, seems like it could swallow her up like a warm, soft swamp. She seeks out Nicolas's scent on the sheets and the pillow and drops off to sleep with a deep, contented sigh.

3

The man is sweating beneath the black cloth, perspiration beading on his temples and rolling down his cheeks. He wishes he could wipe this irritation from his skin, but his right hand is occupied with slowly turning the ring that controls sharpness, his left swiveling the optical chamber to adjust the frame.

Composing. Filling the rectangular space with what people don't usually see, what they observe too little, what they want to possess without understanding its disturbing beauty, without having admired the richness of these decadent jewels that were so well described and displayed in the last century. Rediscovering, thanks to the precision of photography, sensual power, mesmerizing sweetness. Perhaps near-brutal crudeness, too.

The sweating man thinks the customers will like this. He tries to be innovative, surprising, in his composition, his daring. He plays a great deal with light. Natural or artificial. Today's bright sun makes any fantasy possible. A reflector or mirror cleverly placed offers an infinity of solutions. Suddenly the perspective deepens, the subject coming into sharp relief.

Of course, most of his customers fled Paris in the first days of the insurrection, terrified by the shouts, the bursts of gunfire, following the example of the whole public sector— elected officials, magistrates, police—in an immense tactical withdrawal, the better to plan their counteroffensive. The move had also been a bid to spirit their heirs and some of their possessions to safety, certain that surely this carnival of destruction, this collective epilepsy, couldn't last long. But alas, things had dragged on, and they'd been forced to negotiate with the Prussians, to regroup and regain their strength, and for nine weeks now the city has been nothing more than a farmyard with its animals running free, pigs and steers and cows, each species a different sort of blowhard, with their women in the streets waving guns, claiming to enforce justice and equality for the people. The sidewalks are full of arrogant, puffed-up hens and cocks crowing commands at their sloppy battalions from atop their dung heaps. Barnyard clucking. Idiocy, brutishness. Base instincts, mindless outbursts, sheeplike enthusiasm. Drunkenness elevated to a lifestyle. The common people's true selves, heedless of the laws that normally keep them in check, half-witted, oafish, and pleasure-seeking. Raucous and erratic. This is what comes from a war led by cowards, and from months of terrible siege. Weakness in the face of the mob they call a republic, or a democracy. A France abandoned by its army, governed by good-for-nothings, now handed over to the infuriated dregs of society. And retribution waiting to happen.

But soon the call for revenge would sound, and when the bloodletting was over and the city purged of its evil humors, the customers would return, greedier than ever, more demanding, eager to make up for the dreadful weeks during which they'd been unable to indulge their singular vice. Enthralled by the unvarnished honesty of the images, by the obscenity of the poses, stunned by the rawness of certain close-ups, these respectable bourgeois men who preach virtue to their daughters, deploring the moral decline of the populace, screwing their housemaids in storage rooms and narrow corridors, all used to lewd prints of imaginary scenes, restaged and embellished—they're thunderstruck by these lifelike scenes, their trembling fingers often hovering over the proofs as if they think they'll be able to feel the texture of the skin, slide inside the womanly parts on display, arouse the flesh gleaming under the photographer's lights.

The man straightens up. He is wide-shouldered, heavyset. His burgeoning paunch isn't yet straining the buttons of his vest. Drooping mustache, graying sideburns. Close-cropped blond hair. Black eyes. He wipes his forehead with his handkerchief and checks his watch, then emits a grunt difficult to interpret. Frustration, maybe.

Everyone around here calls him Monsieur Charles. Charles Gantier.

The young girl he now approaches, who is lying on a bed, says her name is Émilienne. She also says she's fourteen years old. She's naked, reclining on her side, one leg lifted in a way that shows off everything Charles Gantier wants to be shown. Silently, he adjusts her pose a little so that the cleft between her legs opens a bit wider. She lets him do it. Her face shows nothing but tired indifference, as if she's a long way outside her own body. Detached. A few meters from the bed, a man in shirtsleeves is seated on a small sofa, one arm lying along its back. He wears a worker's cap with the brim pulled low on his face, which is sunken as if someone smashed it in with a mallet. His black beard swallows up the rest of his features. He doesn't move, one hand resting on the revolver lying next to him on a red cushion.

Monsieur Charles goes back to his camera and slides the glass plate into position.

"Look at me and smile."

Supporting herself on one elbow, the girl tips her head back so her mass of red hair tumbles down behind her and gazes sidelong into the dark room, a half smile on her lips.

"Yes, I like that. Don't move."

The photographer releases the lens cap, his watch in his hand. His lips move, counting off the seconds. He closes the shutter and glances at the girl.

"Done."

She doesn't move at first, face frozen though the smile has dropped from her lips, blinking, suddenly blinded by the flood of light now streaming through the window. Her face is pale against her flame-red hair. She looks around, frowning as if she has just woken from sleep, stares at each of the two men in turn, then pulls a sheet over her nakedness, hides her face, and begins to cry.

Monsieur Charles motions to the man sitting on the sofa.

"Deal with her before she gets the whole neighborhood sniffing around here, like the day before yesterday."

The man gets up and shrugs on a jacket of thick gray canvas, stowing his gun in an inner pocket. He retrieves a bundle of clothing from a chair and tosses it at the girl.

"Get dressed."

When she doesn't react, he yanks off the sheet she has covered herself with and throws a petticoat and chemise in her face. She reaches up slowly, trying to slip her arms into the sleeves. For a moment she struggles feebly in the sack-like mass of cloth, then her head and hands reappear and she stops moving again, her mouth half-open, seeming stupefied, or astonished, maybe, and then she looks down at herself, runs her hands over her body through the cloth, and looks up at the man standing over the bed, scrutinizing his face, and then at the photographer, who is busily fiddling with his equipment. The man puts his hands under her arms and lifts her to a standing position. She lets him do it, and once she is on her feet, swaying slightly, she considers the ground and her feet and then wiggles her toes, still with the same air of stupid astonishment.

"What's wrong with her?" Monsieur Charles demands.

"You pushed her too far, that's what's wrong. You'll have to help me."

The photographer sighs and approaches. While his assistant

grips the girl by her shoulders, he holds her pantalets near her feet and takes hold of one of her ankles to guide it, but she doesn't move, doesn't even tremble, her legs stiff, like a wooden effigy planted in the ground. He stands back up and tries to push her into a sitting position on the bed, but the girl seems to regain her wits somewhat, straightening and back-handing the man in the face. He falls backward in surprise. She bursts out laughing at the sight of him as he goes head over heels and then sits up, rubbing his cheek, outraged. She laughs and giggles and hiccups and mocks this gentleman who has been knocked over; she's like a mischievous, cruel child, and at this instant maybe she thinks she's in the courtyard of her building playing. She's having so much fun, in fact, that she doesn't see the blow that crashes down on the back of her skull and makes her crumple without a sound. The man quickly puts the pantalets on her and adjusts the petticoat around her waist, then hauls her easily over his shoulder like a big floppy doll, her arms dangling down his back.

"What are you doing? Open the door for me."

Monsieur Charles, still on the floor, seems to gather his wits and hurries to a door. It opens into a tiny room with closed shutters that serves as a storeroom. The man dumps the girl onto a mattress and gags her with a handkerchief he pulls from his pocket, then binds her wrists and ankles. He stands up, muttering a few words in a language that sings and rasps in his throat; a prayer, or a curse, in the Gascon spoken on the Plateau de Lannemezan.

When he steps back into the studio, Monsieur Charles has vanished, undoubtedly into his darkroom, to fiddle with his chemical baths and glass plates. The man from Lannemezan sits down and flips through the album of recent shots and feels the excitement he always feels at the sight of these indecent poses, these widespread legs, and, especially, these terrified or vacant faces. They stir fantasies that would never occur to him when he's in a brothel laboring on top of a girl or taking her from behind like a dog; he's always too busy thrusting, holding back the supreme moment when he will be swept away by a flood of pleasure no dike could hold. Nor is he ever the least bit interested in taking advantage of what's on offer when the photos are taken, except when Monsieur Charles suggests it during special sessions, and then his member is called on to perform extraordinary things, because there are customers for that, too. "The day will come when people sell death directly to greedy crowds at sordid shows. Remember the Boulevard du Crime? People couldn't get enough of the plays there, full of all kinds of murders and abuse. I bet a lot of those spectators would've paid a small fortune for all of it to be real, to happen right under their noses. We won't see it ourselves, to be sure, but one day photographs will come to life like a magic lantern, and every dirty little indulgence, and the big horrors, too, will be within people's reach for a price. Believe me, Pujols. You don't have to be a psychic to predict which swamps of muck we can make them wallow in. Just look at their taste for vice and violence. If we give ourselves the means—which is just a matter of technique, electricity, and the proper sequence of events—then a whole new type of trade will open up. Fortunes will be made in the mechanical display of base desires and gruesome impulses."

So Pujols, for now we know that is his name, Henri Pujols, consents with good grace to these acts of coitus frozen forever in time, to the muttered instructions not to move and the outlandish positions demanded by the photographer, which he refers to using a strange word pronounced with his index finger held skyward, his eyes wide, as if invoking a divine commandment or uttering a magic spell, something like *camrafoutra*, and which require the man from the Pyrenees to engage in extravagant contortions he must then hold, unmoving, for interminable seconds. Of course, sometimes, when the desire in his loins burns too high, he quenches it in two or three jerks of his pelvis while the smut artist is busy with his black box, pretending not to feel anything, pleased to find that his cock remains in place, the woman still impaled as she should be.

But he has also discovered with these photographic images, whose existence he hardly imagined before coming to Paris, the refinement of a more secret pleasure, intimate and wholly private, buried as it is in the depths of his soul.

Before, before the war, the siege, and this Commune that claims to rob the rich, combat vice, and promote virtue—that is, to turn upside down the natural order of things since the world began—Monsieur Charles used to take his photos in whorehouses where he was well acquainted with the madams, and where some of the girls would, for a price, submit to the coarsest acts in front of the lens. But that had required him to make appointments, transport the heavy camera, and be certain that his players would be game for the activities he wanted. A customer who was a bit "special," as the girls termed it, could always be found who was willing to copulate in front of a third party, often for free, as long as his face didn't appear in the photo. Like Pujols today, hiding his mutilated face beneath a leather mask of his own devising, and repellent in its own way, those faces—sometimes well-known and often respectable— were rendered anonymous beneath a mask of velvet or red or black silk, depending on each man's taste.

That was before. Before their first meeting, in a brothel on the Rue Saint-Lazare, where Charles had set up the tripod of his black box in the half-light of an alcove to capture the servicing of some pleasure-seekers aroused by the display, or Sapphic contortions directed by the madam, who often participated in these herself with unfeigned emotion.

Pujols, a regular at this particular well-kept brothel, had been drawn into the room by the commotion caused by the

visit of Monsieur Charles Gantier, "My grrrrrrreat friend
Charles Gantier," as Madame Claveau had said, rolling her
Burgundian r's in her throat and setting her necklace of paste
jewels atremble. He had been immediately fascinated by the
artifice required to obtain the photographs, finding it somehow
obscener than the unstudied voyeurism in which he indulged
when ordering the girls into strange positions before ramming
himself into them. But freezing these moments through photography (Monsieur Charles had brought along several pictures
that the madam had purchased to put into an album for important clients), making these moments of voluptuous stupor last
forever, deliberately prolonging the lascivious strain, was to
offer oneself freely the time to climax in silence, elevating desire
to an idea, even an ideal, a bit like being at prayer . . . it was
much more powerful than imagination, and less fleeting . . .

After the session, Pujols had insisted on helping the photographer lug his equipment home, and in the course of conversation they had discovered their mutual opinion that the
whores who agreed to be photographed, even the most beautiful, even the youngest ones, the ones who were still virtually
children and posed in front of the camera for a particular type
of client, all had something in their eyes, on their lips—an
indifference to what was happening, or a blasé or falsely sala-
cious attitude, depending on the position or the act required of
them. "What you need is a little bit of innocence, or fear,"
Pujols had remarked. "That would be even more exciting than
the debauchery you expect on these girls' faces, or the cold
apathy you sometimes see." Gantier had seemed repelled by
this suggestion from the stranger with the battered face, falling
silent for long minutes while their hansom cab was stopped on
the Boulevard des Italiens by the passage of a military convoy:
swaying carts, limping or balky horses, somber-faced soldiers
with backs bowed beneath the weight of their rifles and haversacks. "What do you have in mind?" he had murmured, finally,

and Pujols had seen mingled curiosity and desire glittering in his eyes.

"You'd need women who don't do this sort of thing as a profession."

"You mean models who would be paid expressly for that? You can't be serious! What I ask them to do far exceeds the simple nudity they're used to."

The cab had begun jolting over the cobblestones again, and Pujols had remained silent for a long time, looking out the window at the hungry urchins sitting on the curbs in the cold December air, their thin legs trembling beneath their tattered clothing, and the very young girls leaning with feigned nonchalance against the doorjambs, their faces gaunt with starvation, gazes insistently following the men that passed them. At the elderly couple staggering along, arms around each other, holding one another up, bodies pressed together, wobbling toward imminent collapse. The man asleep—dead, perhaps—on the doorstep of an elegant townhouse. The lines of people waiting in front of the shops that still sold a few meager food items at exorbitant prices. He had let the spectacle pass before his eyes of this city tormented by famine and misery, forever astonished by humans' capacity to endure suffering.

"No," he had said, finally. "You need women who have never done it. Who don't enjoy it. Force them. That will get you the fear I mentioned. There are plenty of ways to compel them, to lessen their reluctance. I know a few myself."

"But where would you find them?"

"Look around. You see what the Parisians have been reduced to. Who among these people wouldn't sell their soul for a crust of bread, a bit of bacon, a potato? The promise of a cup of hot soup?"

Monsieur Charles had glanced out the window. His eyes met the imploring gaze of a woman dragging two small children by the hand. He saw a couple of municipal workers struggling not to drop a stretcher on which a corpse jostled, only partly covered by a filthy sheet.

"It's abominable. It's wholly despicable. I—"

"Of course. You know what's abominable and what isn't. Your filthy photographs, with those wide-apart thighs, those arses offered up, those open cunts. Because they belong to whores, and because you sell the photos to good, solid middle-class men who touch themselves discreetly, with so much tact, through their fine woolen trousers, it's clearly respectable. Even artistic, perhaps? And that, undoubtedly, is what gives you the authority to judge what's despicable and what isn't. So know, at least, what you're looking for. See your desire, your vice, all the way through to the end. You're looking to corrupt innocence; admit it. Do violence. And then capture the surprise, the fear, with your cameras."

Pujols had fallen silent again then, as the cab turned down the Rue de Varenne, silent and deserted. The horse's hoofbeats echoed off the façades, sounding almost funereal. Charles Gantier had looked down thoughtfully, his hands clasping the pommel of his cane.

"I have often kept company with evil," Pujols had continued, his voice deep and low. "I liked it. Maybe I'll tell you about it one day, if we see each other again. I fully believe it was an art form, in its own way. I had an unintentional mentor. A brilliant idiot, who, like you, stopped at the very edge of the abyss. He showed me the way, and I leaped . . . and was lost, perhaps, I don't know . . ."

"I don't understand anything you're saying."

"Of course you do. We're cut from the same cloth, you and me."

They had carried the equipment up to Monsieur Charles's apartment without saying anything more. When they parted, Henri Pujols had scribbled his address on a scrap of paper. 15 Rue des Missions.

Two days later, the photographer sent him a message. *I've thought a great deal about our conversation. I believe I understand what we have in common. Come to me; I have things to show you that will shape the future.*

Pujols remembers their meeting the next day in a tiny, cluttered studio, a former water closet that Gantier had made over on the second floor of his building, filled with miniature tools—pliers, files, saws, vises, magnifying glasses—that had made him think of a clockmaker's workshop. Acrid chemical odors had hung thick in the air, mingling with the smells of metal and wood. Lenses of all sizes were neatly arranged above a workbench, shining like jewels in their padded boxes.

Charles Gantier had put into his hands a wooden case the size of a large book, which had been fitted with a copper lens. The sliding back of the case could be opened and a glass plate inserted, and the photographer had pressed a small lever next to the lens with a trembling finger, producing a sharp click, the tiny shock of which Pujols felt reverberate beneath his fingertips.

"A fraction of a second!" Monsieur Charles had cried. "As soon as I've perfected an emulsion capable of securing an image that quickly, I'll be able to take candid photographs, unposed, capturing movement—life itself! Great events are about to take place! The war will soon be in the streets of Paris, beneath our very windows, and I want to record every last convulsion! My colleagues are photographing these imbeciles posing on their barricades in front of their cannons, swaggering and triumphant—but I'll capture them under fire, facing real soldiers, in the furor of combat, and then we'll see who is braver: this national disaster, this street rabble in their military caps, or the line regiments commanded by our best officers. The truth will be laid bare to the eyes of History!"

"You will photograph Death right under the Grim Reaper's nose!"

"Of course . . . I saw the remains of a battle once, at the end of April, when the Communeux attempted to occupy Bougival. It was . . ."

"Disturbing, I'm sure. Just like your pictures of whorish girls."

Monsieur Charles had flushed, his breath seeming to catch in his throat. He had loosened his detachable collar and smiled awkwardly.

"I've thought of gelatin . . ."

Pujols didn't understand. He'd wondered what Gantier could possibly have seen to call that material to mind, in what state some bodies might have been. But not even his diseased imagination could manage, despite his twisted, macabre fantasies, to conceive of such a thing.

"Yes—gelatin, for the photosensitive layer. It's twenty or thirty times more sensitive to light than collodion. I'm almost there. Tomorrow, or the day after, perhaps. I'm about to turn photography on its ear, you understand? Capturing natural movement, without affectation or artifice. It will be the final stage before the recording of moving images . . . and at a mere hair's breadth from the action! Do you see? Photos taken under fire, amidst the smoke of the fires, on both sides of the barricades! And it will earn me far more than the snapshots I sell to these gentlemen. Félix Tournachon[6] and his romantically posed photos of poets will be a thing of the past! Bet on it! Soon, photographs will replace the inept illustrations in newspapers, which only seem there to entertain children!"

He had paced the room, unable to contain his excitement, hands sketching arabesques in the air, outlining a future whose shape only he could see, like a clairvoyant, or a madman.

---

[6] Félix Tournachon: Real name of the famous photographer Nadar.

Henri Pujols flips through the *Album of Masks,* in which obliging clients of the whorehouse on the Rue Saint-Lazare screw girls in a wide variety of positions. All the participants, male and female, wear simple domino masks or more elaborate ones, depending on the fantasy of the moment. Some of them, their faces hidden beneath molded constructions of paste-board with impassive features, turn toward the camera a mere blot of dark nothingness, like a dead man returned from his otherworldly wandering to couple with living flesh.

He contemplates these pictures and the bizarre ideas they bring to mind for long moments, images of black masses and witches' Sabbaths and sacrificial ceremonies forming and com-ing to life, led by priests in wax masks and deep scarlet hoods, intoning sacrilegious prayers and blasphemies. His head whirls with chaotic imprecations and visions of bloody, obscene monks, and the din it creates in his mind is so loud and so strong that it almost seems as if, in some of the photos, the fig-ures begin to move, groaning. He wrenches himself out of his own morbid thoughts, stunned by what he thinks he just saw in the waking dream state he had slipped into for an instant. He shakes his head, trying to clear the torpor, takes a few steps across the room, and heads for the closet into which he locked the girl just a short time ago. She is asleep, her back to the door, curled in the fetal position. With the dose of drugs Monsieur Charles made her swallow, no more will be needed tonight, when he takes her to join the others.

He knocks three times on the door of the laboratory where the photographer develops his photos and calls that he's going out for a walk. Gantier's voice dismisses him with a grunt, so he pulls down his wide-brimmed hat, being careful to hide his battered face, and then goes down the back stairs and out into the courtyard, which is echoing just then with the laughter of a woman and the sound of squabbling in the gutters, sounds to which he pays no attention at all.

4

They put the sash on him before he left the police station, assuring him that this way, his authority, conferred by the people, would be clear to all, demonstrating even to its enemies that the Commune cares about order and public safety, unlike the old cops, who had ensured the bourgeoisie's peace of mind by harassing the poor. It was Loubet, his deputy, the only *flicard* who hadn't fled to Versailles after the proclamation of the Commune, who insisted that he wear the sash, and then handed him a revolver that he tucked deep into a pocket.

Antoine Roques. Elected police delegate to the Sûreté only a month ago. A bookbinder by trade. He hadn't wanted the job, given his longstanding, deep-seated loathing of anything to do with the police. But the assembly had judged him the most sensible, the most astute. And the Commune needed a reliable man like him here, as at a combat outpost. And then Rose had squeezed his hand and looked up at him with her large, deep blue eyes. Rose, who used to adore reading the crime stories in *Le Petit Journal*, before it was outlawed for pouring so much filth on Paris and its people.

The sash is too tight. It digs into his middle, making it hard to take a deep breath. He slides a hand beneath it and tugs on the fabric, but it doesn't seem to have any give, so he tries to loosen the knot Loubet just tied with such ridiculous solemnity. Antoine Roques detests all outward signs of authority. He wants to toss this piece of cloth in the gutter.

But since it's the red of revolt, the red of blood, this strip of flag, he keeps it on.

It's seven o'clock in the morning. He is walking up the Boulevard Saint-Martin, flanked by a captain from the 138th battalion, a big, bearded man named Colin, a taciturn but pleasant fellow, who darts anxious glances over his shoulder every now and then to make sure none of the thirty-five men he rousted from their camp beds just a few minutes ago are dragging their feet.

The streets are empty and peaceful beneath the pale sky. Antoine Roques can't help but listen carefully for the rumbling sound of cannon fire in the distance. A messenger rode up a little while ago, breathless, to announce that the Versaillais were bombarding the fortifications between Le Point and the Porte d'Auteuil, dozens of large guns installed during the night, naval cannons. The whole west of Paris is nothing but explosions, collapsing walls, panic.

The beginning of the end, he'd thought as the messenger spoke, while around him a flurry of preparations for retaliation and the recapture of lost territory began. The air filled with loud voices, men swearing revenge, each confident in his own strategy. All they needed was ten thousand Federates to march on Versailles. They should attack the troops massed ahead of Paris from the rear. They should concentrate all of their cannon fire on a specific point, to break the Versaillais lines. It all seemed so easy in the calm of dawn, the sky paling above the rooftops. For a moment, he had wanted to believe it. It seemed impossible that the people who had taken up arms, their dream slung across their shoulders, and had spent two months constructing bastions of hope, could be defeated by so little, swept away like sawdust from the wooden floor of a seedy bistro. Then a sad lucidity had taken hold, and he had begun to see the citizens milling agitatedly around him like so many pathetic marionettes thronging at the gate of a rickety castle.

Going out to meet the patrol sent to accompany him had seemed preferable to remaining there, and the cigarette he'd rolled with trembling fingers had done him good as he stood there listening to the soft noises of the neighborhood gently waking up.

The soldiers' footsteps echo off the façades. They grumble, cough, mutter, rifles shouldered, bayonets thrust through their leather belts, military caps tilted over one eye. Their steps are heavy, lagging. Two or three of them seem to be asleep on their feet. They pass an oncoming cart pulled by an old nag that snorts and flattens back its ears, shaking its big head as if to express its exhaustion. The driver lets the end of his whip dangle above the animal's bony spine. His grayish top hat is dented, his face dark with stubble, and his thick eyebrows droop so much that they almost cover his eyes. He salutes the patrol with a hairy hand and then breaks into a fit of coughing, or perhaps laughter, it's hard to tell, then spits, wheezing, his whole body convulsing so that the horse shies. A few of the men look back at this curious horse and driver and chuckle, joking among themselves in low voices: "That devil Clovis! Still a grimy old bastard!"

A hundred meters farther along, the barricade on the corner of the Rue Saint-Martin has the look of a garbage dump where have people have come to get rid of worm-eaten furniture, piss-soaked and bug-infested mattresses, and hand carts with broken wheels.

Captain Colin stops walking, his thumbs stuck into his belt. "Look how the Commune is defended while they're cannonading us to death. Bunch of useless idiots. I don't even see any sentries."

"Who's responsible for it?" Antoine Roques asks.

"No idea. Some club or other; they'll have asked the commander of the 11th legion to send a few guards who come when they don't have anything better to do."

A ginger cat has just appeared atop the motley heap, perched on a wheel that juts out of the barricade as if a carriage has buried itself deliberately in the rubbish. Antoine Roques nudges it away with his elbow.

"There's a sentinel for you. What more could you want?"

The captain shakes his head, sighing, then raises his eyes to the building in front of which they've stopped.

"This where your suspect is hiding?"

"Far end of the courtyard, on the left, second floor. Ferdinand Courbin."

Colin turns to his men. "Three of you boys stay here; make sure no one leaves."

Antoine Roques pushes open the door, and the soldiers crowd into the entryway and spill out into the courtyard, their rifles pointed at the windows. Unseen pigeons coo from the rooftops. The captain posts a guard at each exit. The men seem to have woken up now; they obey quickly, checking to make sure their guns are loaded. Roques leads four soldiers into a stairwell dimly illuminated by a skylight. Their heavy shoes and boots thump loudly in the half-light, and Antoine feels carried along by the noise, fully invested in his mission. This Courbin is reputed to be a civil engineer for the Council of Bridges and Roads, and he was seen by a foreman who worked under him lurking around the ammunition storehouse on the Avenue Rapp a few days before it exploded.[7] The man's specialized knowledge must give him a thorough understanding of explosives, and he would probably know where to procure them in large quantities. His brother-in-law

[7] On May 17th, an explosion destroyed an ammunition depot on the Avenue Rapp, causing the deaths of some forty people and the collapse of several surrounding buildings. Without the intervention of the firefighters who saved large amounts of ammunition and powder from the flames, the disaster would have been much worse. Sabotage was the likely cause of the blast, but no serious investigation was ever undertaken.

is a captain in the 3rd artillery regiment of the Versaillais army.

Reaching the landing, they pause for a silent moment in front of the tall, varnished wooden door. Then the soldiers take hold of their weapons, and he pounds on the door, shouting "Open up! Sûreté Générale!" Hearing himself talk this way, he isn't sure anymore what sort of act he's part of, or what role he's supposed to be playing. He remembers hearing the same words barked in '51 during the coup, when they came to arrest his father. And a mere three weeks ago, Rigault's[8] men were behaving like common Ancien Régime police thugs, hated and feared everywhere in the city.

Two bolts click, and the door opens to reveal a woman with her hair down, dressed in a chiffon peignoir.

"Gentlemen?" She smiles timidly, gazing sweetly at the armed men at her door as if they might have come begging for a crust of bread or some spare rags for the poor.

"Is Monsieur Corbin here?"

"Well—" Her eyes dart to the right, down a hallway. Antoine shoves her aside and enters the apartment, two guards on his heels. Deep carpeting. The scent of coffee. He has just enough time to see, through a half-open doorway, the blurred silhouette of a man, his arm outstretched toward them. The detonation is ear splitting, lifting him off his feet, and he hears the soldier who was standing behind him cry out. He flings himself to the floor and sees the soldier lying on his back, body convulsing in a death spasm. He has been shot in the head. Antoine Roques fumbles for his revolver, seizes it clumsily and

---

[8] Raoul Rigault: Chief of police of the Commune. Forced to resign on April 23rd due to his brutal methods and the random arrests he ordered, in addition to being totally ineffective against the Versaillais and extremely unpopular with the people. During the Bloody Week, he fought at the head of a National Guard battalion. Shot by Versaillais troops on May 24th on the Rue Gay-Lussac.

cocks the hammer, but another gunshot screams past above his head. The door at the far end of the corridor bursts open. Flat on his belly, he fires back, twice, three times, blindly, because his eyes are suddenly filled with tears, and he manages only to blast chunks of plaster and puffs of dust from the walls and ceiling. He can't hear anything. Someone grasps the collar of his jacket and yanks him to his feet, almost bellowing "This way! Quickly!" into his ear. It's the young guard who returned fire at their attacker. He is already running through a dining room, overturning chairs in his path, knocking into a china cabinet.

Roques tries to follow but finds his shoulders weighed down by the hands of a screaming woman while a little girl clutches his knees. He struggles, holding on to a sideboard to keep his balance. The woman is scrabbling for his neck, digging her fingernails into his skin, so he delivers a sharp elbow-thrust to her face that knocks her to the floor, her frilly nightgown up around her thighs. He tries to disentangle himself from the grasp of the little girl, who is still clinging to his legs, but he can't manage it, so he slaps her away with the back of his free hand and seizes her by the hair. She lets go soundlessly and rolls beneath the table. He starts running again, dodging the dark furniture, navy-blue velvet armchairs, and pedestal stands laden with porcelain.

He doesn't know how he finds his way to a dimly lit service staircase, guided by the shouts of the young guard. He doesn't know how he manages not to tumble down the stairs, leaving his ankles twisted and back broken. He staggers out into a narrow street still only dimly touched by the rising sun and sees the soldier disappearing around the corner of a shop into a stinking alleyway, tripping on the filth-smeared cobblestones. He emerges suddenly onto the boulevard behind the barricade, out of breath, his leg muscles tight and stiff like meat gone bad. Two little boys stand staring at him, astonished. One of them is holding a rifle taller than he is, its bayonet pressed to his dirty cheek. The soldier reappears, dragging his feet, pulling off his flat-topped cap to wipe his forehead.

"He's gone! Evaporated, pfft! He killed Albert, a friend—almost a brother! We worked together for Dugrand, the saddler on the Rue des Cendriers. I'll kill that son of a bitch. Traitor—*saboteur*—assassin! I won't even stand him up against a wall, just *bang!* Right in his murdering face!"

He doubles over, spitting and coughing. Vomiting, maybe. He is panting, leaning on his rifle. When he straightens up, his sweaty face is pale, his eyes shining with tears.

Antoine Roques realizes he is still gripping his revolver in his hand. He looks at it as if the thing sprouted from the end of his arm in his sleep, then lets it drop into his pocket. He unties the red sash so he can breathe a bit better, rolls it up and clutches it in his fist. Relief. The air seems fresher.

Captain Colin hurries toward them, five men on his heels. "Well?"

The chief of police shrugs. The answer is obvious. "Well nothing, as you can see. We lost him. We'll see if his wife has anything to tell us."

They go back to the apartment, where the body of the guard who was killed has been covered with an embroidered cloth. The woman, clutching a bloody handkerchief to her nose, and the little girl are sitting on a sofa, pressed against one another, watched over by a soldier leaning against a dark wooden sideboard. The men have spread out into all of the apartment's rooms; they can be heard opening and slamming the doors of armoires and closets, shouting to each other and hooting whenever they find something valuable or startling. A finely wrought candlestick, a fragile ornament, a gilded angel hung on a wall, wings spread. Roques comes across two men in one bedroom, the bed still unmade, in the process of rummaging through a dresser drawer overflowing with lingerie. They sniff the feminine undergarments, joking, scattering corsets and petticoats and pantalets.

"Get out of here."

The men gape at him, surprised.

"You're soldiers of the Commune, not Prussian or Versaillais thugs. Get out."

"We're conducting a search," retorts one of them, a petti-coat slung over one shoulder. "We have our orders. And any-way, there's no risk of that Madam's arse getting cold!"

The other laughs silently.

"Important things have been found in places like this before."

"I'm the one in charge of this operation. I expect you to behave decently."

Antoine Roques remains in the doorway, holding out an arm, inviting the men to leave the room. They sigh. The petti-coat is tossed onto the bed.

"Have it your way . . ."

They brush past him contemptuously as they leave, their chins raised defiantly. Someone calls out from the other end of the corridor. He hears the men exclaiming. Something falls to the floor and breaks. They have found a desk overflowing with papers in a dim nook, lit only by a transom window. The cap-tain is bent over a plan sketched hastily on a large sheet of paper.

"Look at this. The placement of the barricades from La Butte-aux-Cailles all the way to the Pantheon. And here, the area where the munitions storehouse and the military school are."

Roques examines the maps. Crosses and arrows drawn in blue ink. The barricades are represented by a red line traced across the streets.

"We'll take the woman with us. That might draw the hus-band out."

"And the girl?"

Antoine Roques levels his gaze at Colin, who has asked the question as if the answer can be read in his face. He tries to think, feels as if a wave of heat is pressing down on him. He thinks of Bertrand, his little boy. Wonders what the Versaillais would do with children if . . . and what will *we* do with them? Will the Commune throw children in prison, the better to fight against spies and traitors? His own questions bounce back at him like a ball thrown against a wall. The men around him are waiting for him to say something. In the next room, the wife weeps and struggles. The little girl is whimpering.

"Give her to the neighbors. Confiscate any documents that might prove espionage, treason, and homicidal attack."

The woman is slumped on her sofa, her face buried in her hands, sobbing loudly, her daughter huddled against her. The ostentatious display of sorrow makes Roques want to throw a bucket of cold water over both of them. The guards in the room hover uncomfortably around this makeshift *pietà*, staring at their own feet and twiddling their thumbs in their leather belts. One of them offers the woman a handkerchief. Roques stops him.

"They're fine as they are. We'll separate them at the station; easier to do it there than here. We'll let them know then. Bring them along now."

Two guards take hold of the woman and her daughter amid a fresh eruption of screams. Roques turns his back on the scene and hears the dry cracking sound of a slap, muttered insults. He leaves the apartment and stops for a brief moment on the landing, leaning on the banister. Behind him, the woman's sobs intensify, and now she is the one hurling insults at the men, threatening them with the punishment soon to be inflicted on such Communard trash. The soldiers laugh at her. "You're the one who should be concerned about punishment at the moment," says Captain Colin. "And you'll soon see." Roques considers going back inside and calming the men down, then decides that this shrew deserves to be afraid after the forty deaths and dozens of amputated limbs caused by the explosion at the Avenue Rapp warehouse. He starts down the stairs, and the sobs and cries fade away. Doors close with muted creaks on the lower floors as he passes, people who are curious but unwilling to be seen.

When he reaches the courtyard, the clear, cool morning air tempts him to look up at the blue sky with its light scattering of clouds. On the corner of the boulevard, people are busy at the barricade. Three artillery carts have stopped in front of it, and he can see men hacking cobblestones out of the street with picks and chisels. Others are attempting to transform the rubbish heap into a small fort, balanced precariously on top of a crooked table, a door, an old bed base. He heads back down the boulevard toward the Place du Château-d'Eau, breathing deeply, suddenly full of self-confidence. He would love to go for a walk along the Seine. Feel the breeze off the water against his skin. He remembers the family strolls on the quays—When was it? Before the war? It seems like so long ago—with Rose and the children, fried food and Chinon wine and the still-hot fritters drowning in cream that Bertrand and Mariette devoured. He doesn't know what the future holds, but he knows the flavor of those bygone moments, the Sunday afternoons when bodies seemed to forget the fatigue of the working week. He felt the same thing for a few days at the end of April, a lightness, a peaceful gaiety in the soft, cool air. He'd looked around him then, at a Paris rising to its feet like a prisoner kept too long in chains in a dungeon cell: stretching its arms, straightening its back, dazzled eyes blinking at the simple light of day. "If only it could last," his friends had said over mugs of beer. "Best take advantage of it before the sticks come out again. It'll have been something, at least, anyway," the more pessimistic ones had responded.

In the square, a bugle is sounding an off-key call for the battalion to fall in. The Federates line up at an unhurried pace, grumbling, jostling each other, bayonets clanking. Sergeants bellow at them. Two companies manage to organize themselves and proceed in disorderly ranks toward the Boulevard du Temple. Antoine Roques can't help but think these troops are far too easygoing to be able to measure up, as they undoubtedly must do one of these days, to Monsieur Thiers's army, which has been training and preparing for weeks. A few curious onlookers linger, but most of the passersby quicken their steps, darting furtive glances at these accidental soldiers. Only a few little boys mimic the men, marching alongside them, laughing, with sticks over their shoulders in the guise of rifles.

He decides he'd rather avoid this motley squad, with their erratic drumrolls and orders bawled by a captain standing in his stirrups facing a cohort of national guardsmen who continue to chat amongst themselves, guffawing and occasionally glancing in disbelief at the red-faced man on horseback.

In front of the police station, the duty officer with his cap brim pulled low over his eyes is sweet-talking a woman who sashays past with a laundry basket balanced on her hip. He greets Roques with a lift of his chin and a smile at the corner of his mouth. Loubet hurries forward to meet him as soon as he enters the foyer, a look of embarrassment on his face, followed by a couple and three children.

"You have to see this. They've just arrived, and . . ."

The man detaches himself from his little family and shoves Loubet aside with a sweep of his powerful arm. He is dressed in a faded, threadbare blue smock covered in dark spots and blackish smears. He smells of iron and axle grease. He plants himself in front of Roques, his eyes gleaming with fatigue, or perhaps sorrow. Behind him, his wife keeps her head down, the children clinging to her skirts.

"We have to talk to you. It's about our daughter, Virginie."

"See Inspector Loubet about it. I have work to do."

The fist that grasps him by the collar of his jacket, nearly lifting him off the ground, is hard and powerful. Urgent. It isn't a fist to be trifled with.

"You're the one I want to speak to. You, the new police chief. It's about my daughter, Virginie. Understand?"

The man's face is very close to his. His voice is low, hoarse. This is the kind of man who doesn't shout; who hardly ever repeats himself. He clearly believes that the very fact of his saying something makes it worthy of being listened to, and woe to anyone who doubts that he is capable of matching his actions to his words.

Antoine Roques places a hand over the iron fist.

"Let's step into my office."

He ushers the man and his family into a room lit only by a narrow, barred window and two candlesticks smoking on a desk piled with papers. He offers them three chairs and waits as they seat themselves self-consciously. The children squabble silently over their mother's lap, and in the end it's the smallest one who cuddles against her chest, while the other two, a girl and a boy of perhaps nine or ten, share the remaining seat. Then silence falls like a stone, and Roques is nailed to his chair by five pairs of eyes that shine gravely in the half-light. The only sound is the father's breathing, wheezy and full of sighs.

"It's about our oldest daughter, Virginie. Moreau is our name. My wife is Léontine and I'm Ferdinand. We live at 15 Rue des Petites Écuries. And these are my children: Marie, Élodie, and the boy is Denis."

The children gaze wide-eyed at their father, faces filled with surprise and perhaps some anxiety at hearing him list their names, as if they suspect they might have been brought here, to the police station, to be punished. The man looks over at his wife, who takes off the lace scarf she's wearing on her head and drapes it around her shoulders. She sits very straight in her

chair, holding tightly to her little girl, who has closed her eyes
and seems to have fallen asleep.

"Go on; you tell him. You were there," he says.

"We were on the Rue Oberkampf, coming back from the
market. We were in a rush because I'd left the little ones alone
at home. We passed a wine merchant who was pricing some
wine from Bourgueil; that's where Ferdinand . . . that's my husband, Ferdinand . . . grew up, so I said to Virginie, 'Stay there
with the baskets; I'm going to buy a bottle for your father,'
and . . ."

A deep sob cuts off her words. She tries to catch her breath
as the children watch her, silent and attentive, and she smiles
at them with her eyes full of tears, and continues:

"When I came out of the shop she was gone, my baskets
had been dumped out on the pavement, and an old woman
shouted out her window that they'd forced Virginie to get into
a hansom cab, that two men had taken her, and she pointed
down to the far end of the street where the cab was just turning the corner, and I didn't know what to do, you see, whether
to leave my baskets there for someone to steal, so I screamed,
but there was no one—or there were people passing by, but
they didn't even turn around. My God, there was nothing I
could do!"

Antoine Roques searches around on his desk for a piece of
paper and a pencil to take notes, anything to put up a front,
to make it look to these people as if he's in a position to do
something. But he knows that in Paris, right now, there is no
chance of finding this girl, who must already be imprisoned in
one of the secret brothels opened by pimps and procurers
since the Commune outlawed prostitution and soliciting and
began arresting streetwalkers and pressing them to go and
find honest labor in the workshops. He also knows that all the
usual police informers vanished after the old beat cops and
almost all the officers departed for Versailles, and that most of

the underworld's denizens, who are usually so ready to snitch, are awaiting the return to order promised by Monsieur Thiers so they can reorganize and resume spreading their filth.

"So we've come to you, to file a complaint," he hears the father say in a low voice, in that resolute tone that makes his voice almost a rumble.

Roques doesn't know what to say. He scribbles a few words, pastes a thoughtful expression on his face. A question finally occurs to him, and he asks it, even though he knows it's pointless:

"Where did the hansom cab turn?"

The woman points to the right, as if she is still in the street, indicating the direction.

"Down the Rue Saint-Maur. My God . . . I should have chased it . . ."

He writes. He wishes they would leave, these poor people. There's nothing he can do for them.

"And these men; did anyone see their faces?"

"The old lady my wife mentioned, she said they were masked, that they wore scarves pulled up over their faces, the way people talk about. She said the driver was wearing a top hat and had a hairy face, like those big monkeys you see at the zoo. That's all she saw. And she said that Virginie was struggling but couldn't cry out because they held a handkerchief over her mouth."

Antoine Roques pictures the dark, hirsute man they passed this morning on the boulevard. He remembers the jokes of the men, who seemed to be familiar with him. While he is thinking about this, the room is utterly silent. The woman presses a handkerchief to her face, weeping soundlessly. The man rests a hand on the desk and leans toward him, gazing at him intensely.

"I'll do everything I can. We'll try to find this cabman, to start with. He should be able to lead us to his accomplices."

They nod. The children look at him with their mouths half-open. No one moves. Even the smallest one, in her mother's arms, stares up at a dark corner of the ceiling. The police officer stands. They make no move to get out of their chairs, so he tells them he needs to get to work right away, because this is a serious business and must be addressed as quickly as possible. He'll keep them informed, of course, they mustn't worry. The father stands and extends a hand over the desk and Antoine Roques shakes it, feeling the short, hard fingers, the callused laborer's palm. The woman and her children stand in their turn, feet tangling a bit in the chair legs, and they all leave without another word.

When the door has closed behind them, he is angry with himself for letting them hope their daughter will be found. He can't imagine what reason there might be to hope. He sits back down and lets his gaze roam over the clutter of papers and files surrounding him and wonders if he should begin—and end, maybe—by getting the hell out of this shambles. He doesn't know anymore. He hears the Courbin woman screaming for her daughter out in the corridor, and the sound jolts him out of the morass of dark thoughts into which he was sinking.

The cabman, damn it all. He has to find the cabman. In two days, nothing more will be possible.

5

I n the street, in front of the wine merchant's shop, three men speak in low voices, gesticulating wildly. One of them wears a national guardsman's jacket, a bayonet hung from his leather belt. The other two are haggard, hairy, and covered in sweat. They fall silent as Pujols passes near them and stare at him warily, then begin murmuring again. He walks with the long, quick strides of a mountain-dweller toward the Rue du Bac, which is teeming with carts and carriages. A dray is blocking the road, and its horses are being beaten to make them move. The two beasts balk, neigh, snort. Two men brandish sticks and bark commands in the Picardy dialect. Pujols sees the bloody back of a Percheron with a blond mane. The animal's legs tremble, and it shakes its head and stamps its shoes on cobblestones dirty with urine and dung. Curious onlookers gather on the pavements, cabmen shouting from their box seats, cracking their whips. Children romp among the bystanders' legs like idiotic dwarves in a forest. Pujols shoulders his way through the crowd, inwardly cursing all of these gaping imbeciles. He fingers the grip of his revolver in his pocket and wonders why he doesn't simply finish off the wounded horse with a bullet, and then deposit a second one in the skull of the man beating the animal, splattering the cobbles with his moronic brains. A child barrels into him, and he shoves it away discreetly with his knee, sending it stumbling between the ankles of a woman who cries out with surprise, thrown off balance, and then gives the brat a solid slap. The boy, rubbing his cheek, stares up at the tall, dark figure, which begins to walk away and then suddenly turns and stares, smiling, and the boy hides behind the skirts of the woman who smacked him because the smile on that battered face is the grin of a sly dog baring its teeth without growling, capable of ripping out your throat with a single snap of its jaws. The stranger's black eyes are dull and flat, two deep holes like the wells in which desperate people drown themselves.

Pujols thinks about what would have been possible if he'd encountered the kid after dark, in one of those narrow streets always laden at night with brats left to run free by the adults who spawned them, who are off pickling their livers in some seedy cabaret. Knife or revolver? He pushes away the barbarous thoughts, which creep uninvited into his mind sometimes and which he has had to resist for the past few months after having given into them for so long—for the sake, he believes, of elevating his crimes to fine art. Madness, all of it. Shadowy raptures, dark poetry composed in crypts. Macabre reveries. Forbidden loves.[9]

He has tried to fight it all. He'd abandoned himself to excess this past year the way others drown their sorrows, or joys, in alcohol. He'd loved that sort of intoxication, in fact. The morbid strangeness, the fascinated disgust at what can spill out of a mutilated body. The acts of carnage he'd perpetrated during the siege, battling the Prussians, left him sated to his very core with meat and guts and blood, like a butcher devouring the merchandise at the abattoir door, a meat cleaver in one hand and a knife in the other, full to bursting with raw flesh, in a stupor of killing. He spent two months wiping out patrols, slaughtering guards, dismembering tipsy privates, castrating officers as they emerged from cathouses. He led a small

---

[9] See *L'Homme aux lèvres de saphir*, published by Rivages Noir.

troop of a dozen peasants, the Bloodletters of the Night, who were obsessed with vengeance after the pillaging or burning of their farms and unspeakable abuse of their families by the Boches.

Then, one day, bored with these killings, he had abandoned the group, though not without informing on them to a Bavarian colonel with whom he'd emptied a few beer steins at an inn in Saint-Ouen.

He missed Paris. Its noise, its crowds, its women . . . Fresh from his kingdom of blood, he'd forgotten that Paris had been under siege for three months in the dead of winter and was in the grip of famine, its streets overflowing with misery all along the waiting lines in front of the shops. Hollow eyes, gaunt faces, rickety frames could be seen in every alleyway. And the bodies lying in the dark corners where they had fallen to be found in the morning, stiff and openmouthed, faces twisted hideously with pain and despair. Even the light spilling out of the big cafés on the boulevards seemed harsher than before, and the bourgeois, still oh-so-proud in their fur-collared frock coats, their women ensconced in thick dark coats, darted anxious glances around them because in the shadows, all around the bright island where they tried to maintain their social status, bands of hungry children might be waiting with knives to deprive them of a few gold coins.

Pujols had quickly found lodgings on the Rue des Missions, in a hovel left vacant by a young man who'd starved to death a few days earlier, a philosophy student who'd fancied himself a bit of a poet, as the nearly deserted building's landlady, Viviane Arnault, had scornfully put it. Pujols had impressed her, captivated her, softened her, and charmed her with war stories, heroic and bloody, explaining away the terrible injuries to his face as the result of a blow from the saber of an enormous Turk. In the end he'd climbed into her big bed from time to time to satisfy her naïve widow's lust as payment for the food she kept hidden in the cellar. The arrangement was mutually beneficial; the widow said she adored his soldierly ways, and Pujols received bed and board for the price of a fuck every now and then.

Now, he makes his way through the curious crowds as if they are just so many waves breaking against his stern. He knows he is of a different species than them, perhaps a different time. He sometimes feels like he belongs in a future he senses will be opulent and untamed, full of modern brutality and inhuman progress. Everything will change except mankind: spineless, uncouth, submissive, hateful, quick to hunt in packs or flee in herds. Deserving of nothing but scorn and punishment. Blood and tears. And he, Pujols, already feels in perfect alignment with what he knows is coming. In harmony. A one-man band. He sees preparations going on every day in Paris for a monstrous slaughter, a massacre like no city has seen since the barbarian pillagings of antiquity or sackings of the Middle Ages, and he doesn't want to miss it. A foretaste of the century to come.

Madame Viviane, the landlady, has a brother who is a captain in the army at Versailles, who has recommended that she not set foot outside her home once the troops have entered Paris, because Monsieur Thiers and his generals are going to wage true war on this army of bandits. No quarter is the only command. To take prisoners only when there is no way to avoid it. To destroy the National Guard and annihilate the rabble that has been terrorizing the good people of the city for two months. Order must be reestablished in a way that will last fifty years. All means are justified and will be used to punish the Commune and ensure that these wretches pay for their crimes. The soldiers will be operating wholly without restriction. Madame Viviane is impatient for the feeding frenzy to begin. Sometimes when Pujols is riding her, she gets carried away and grunts at him to treat her like a filthy Communard, and the man behind her, pressed against her arse, has to fight to keep from laughing at such stupidity in order to keep pounding her without going soft.

For several days, it has sometimes been at the sound of cannon fire that she has moaned, calling him "my gunner" as explosions cause the windows to shake and a few flakes of plaster to fall on her frantic rump or her fat white belly, like powdered sugar on a cream puff.

The stupidity of the middle classes and their minions against the vulgar hopes of an insane mob. Soon, war at the street corner. The battlefield on your very doorstep. Madame's bloodbath is ready!

Pujols stops, nose high as if he can smell the odors of what is to come. There has been an occasional whiff of burning in the air since this morning. He and Monsieur Charles went last week to see the bombed-out Champs-Élysées and take some photographs. The destroyed houses, the smoking ruins. He would have liked to get closer, for a better look at the gutted buildings, the luxurious interiors of the private homes with their remnants of a happy, peaceful life exposed to the wind and the rain, that privacy revealed to every eye. He'd wanted to toy with these secrets laid bare by the violence and shock of an explosion, displayed like the insides of a gaping cadaver, like the indecent crevice of a twelve-year-old girl with her thighs spread. He'd wanted to relish the sight of the devastation the same way he does with the private parts exhibited in Gantier's photos, but the National Guard wouldn't let anyone through, and he had had to content himself with imagining the obscenity of the spectacle as Monsieur Charles muttered angrily about respectable people's homes being destroyed while the hovels of the proletariat scum remained standing.

Reaching the Rue de Rennes, he stops at the Croix Rouge crossroads, which has been transformed into a stronghold, its streets blocked by enormous barricades. Children caper among stacks of rifles beneath the amused eyes of national guardsmen who aim playful kicks at them as they pass, bellowing with laughter. Other brats, perched atop the redoubt barring the Rue de Sèvres, armed with large sticks and wooden swords, yell and pretend to attack each other. One tiny boy sits astride the barrel of a cannon, bouncing and kicking his heels as if spurring it to a gallop. Three women pass near Pujols, shopping baskets on their arms, chattering in low voices. He is startled by this vision of armed peace, this attitude of blithe unconcern while surrounded by fortifications and bayonets and the faint rumble of artillery fire. He tries to picture the violence that will soon descend on this scene of tranquility. Then, the dull thudding of a bass drum sounds from the direction of the Rue de Rennes, toward the Boulevard Saint-Germain. In the distance he can make out a line of Federates advancing at a good clip to the heavy rhythm of drumbeats, behind a red flag. Curious crowds begin to gather on the sidewalks; the soldiers seize their rifles and shoo away the children, who scatter like a flock of chattering sparrows, and resume their posts at the gun battery and wait, leaning nonchalantly on their guns. Someone starts singing "La Marseillaise," which is quickly taken up by the men in the entrenchment. The onlookers applaud. *Vive la Commune!* Two men shrug and turn on their heels, casting hostile glances over their shoulders.

Pujols looks up at the sky, then takes his watch from his vest pocket. It's late. He hurries toward the Rue de Sèvres and around the barricade unnoticed, voices rising behind him as people call out in welcome to the National Guard. He flees from the shouts of these unwashed masses. Running almost. When he turns onto the Rue des Missions, silence falls abruptly upon him, and he can hear nothing but the permanent buzzing that fills his ears and his skull. The streets are calm here, almost empty. People walk quickly, with somber faces and bowed heads. Street corners conjure them out of sight, and slamming doors swallow them up. Most of the shutters are closed, the streets deaf and blind.

He turns the heavy key and pushes open the doors of the carriage entrance. The caretaker's lodge is shut, its shutter closed. Viviane must have gone out to run a few errands or visit that friend of hers who runs a haberdashery on the Rue Notre-Dame-des-Champs. He steps into the courtyard, his feet crunching on the cobblestones, and looks up toward the windows with their drawn curtains. The last remaining renters departed last Monday for fear of the bombardments, to take refuge with their family in Normandy. Thanks to his landlady's keys, he has been able to collect a few costly ornaments from the deserted apartments, sometimes a bit of well-hidden money people didn't bother to take with them, convinced that in a few days, order reestablished, they would be able to return home to their peaceful everyday lives.

In the closed-off courtyard, the distant rumble of the cannons slips languidly away like a silk scarf, and the spring-mad birds launch their song into the clear air.

Pujols crosses the cobbled yard diagonally and enters a foyer, ignoring the stairs on his right and stopping in front of a door secured with a huge bolt. A lantern hangs above it, which he lights and adjusts its flame so that it is thin and bright, watching it dance for a moment in its iron cage.

Roughly hewn steps lead down into a narrow tunnel with walls of damp stone, greenish and covered in dark blotches. At the bottom of the staircase are two doors, one leading to the cellar where Madame Viviane stores her provisions, and the other solid-framed and studded, its heavy lock rattling when Pujols unbolts it. He stops abruptly on the threshold, struck by the odor, close and dense like a cloth suddenly draped over his face. The stink of excrement and urine, thick and acrid, fills his mouth and squeezes his throat. It's to be expected, of course, and it gets more and more unbearable every day. He hears them before he can see them. The clinking of chains. Their moans. A burst of demented laughter followed by choking sobs. When he can breathe a bit more easily, he steps forward, lantern held high, and can see nothing at first but the beaten-earth floor of this passage cut into the rock, narrow and deep, ribbed and vaulted like a miniature cathedral, and then naked legs in a jumble of underclothing and petticoats. His heart throbs with panic then, because he can see only five feet, and his mind immediately begins to cobble together a macabre fantasy: one of them has been attacked by the other two, who have begun to devour her. He wants to get a better look, so he moves closer and realizes that it's nothing of the sort. Only his imagination, again, overwhelming and intoxicating him as it sometimes does.

They are huddled together, shivering beneath the dark gown they've ripped open to cover themselves with it like a cloak. Their faces are invisible beneath the grotesque mask of their manes of hair, which blur into a single viscous mass; they look like three faces on the single head of some telluric monster disturbed in its shadowy cave by an unwelcome visitor. When they move, all that can be seen is a single gleaming eye, like a frightened Cyclops, as their tangled legs shift weakly.

Pujols, surprised and disturbed, doesn't move. He takes one step forward, lowers and then raises his lantern again, and regrets that he can't take better advantage of what's on offer here—but he knows this creature is an unexpected and bizarre offshoot created by darkness and terror, brought to life by the flickering lantern flame.

They are surrounded by puddles and brown heaps. The straw he spread on the ground to serve as bedding for them is scattered in dark clumps. The pail of bread-and-water gruel he left them has been overturned. He'd added a mixture of alcohol and drugs to it, to make them sleep while he figured out what to do with them. He can't tell them apart anymore, can hardly remember their first names. Blanche, Angèle . . . and the third one, what was it? Noémie? Marie-Jeanne? No matter. They've been reduced now to a strange, nameless shape, something that might interest Gantier, always so partial to new curiosities.

Then something leaps on him with a cry, and suddenly his coattails are gripped by three hands and he falls heavily on his side on the slimy floor, his lamp going out and rolling God knows where, and he kicks to free himself from these hands grasping and tearing at him, pulling him deeper into the shadows. He can feel fingernails digging into his neck, fingers scrabbling at his face, trying to find his eyes. He strikes out as best he can with his heels and the toe of his boot, yanking the clawing fingers away from his face and throat, and the vision he had a few minutes ago of women capable of eating each other springs back into his mind, and he is sure in that moment that they will attack him with their teeth and rip him apart alive, so he punches with his fists, hitting the wall and screaming with rage and pain, twisting and thrashing and trying to stand, but now stench-filled damp hair sweeps across his face as something hard and compact slams into the small of his back. He howls again and is answered by low moaning laughter. He feels a rasping breath against his cheek and then teeth sink into his neck and bite his earlobe with an animal whine. He screams with pain, strikes out blindly, a face, a temple, and manages to shove the girl aside, then rolls onto his back and gets to his feet. He doesn't know if the wetness beneath his fingernails is the girl's slobber or his own blood. The pain in his ear dazes him and tinges the darkness around him with red, and he realizes suddenly that he is leaning against a door.

He can hear them groaning and muttering to one another. Sometimes a small, sharp laugh rises from the dull murmuring.

He feels around for his lantern and relights a flickering flame with great difficulty. A faint gleam touches the bodies of the three girls, who hunch together, shaking, their naked legs clamped tightly together in a reflexive, vain attempt at modesty. His eyes linger on one of them, nude to the waist, with long blonde hair and skin so pale that he can see the tracery of blue veins on her arms and thighs . . . fifteen at most, and already so womanly. He remembers the brutal pleasure he took from her and the sobs and cries of pain as he fucked her, the way she pleaded for mercy from the depths of a soul limp from opium. All of this surges back into his mind and seizes him anew, even here in this cesspit, in the blackness of this tomb, and he wonders what it would be like to possess her mere inches from the others, and then he recoils from the filthy ideas that rush into his head, and he hates this slovenly, shameless creature for tempting him again. The desire to make her bleed is overpowering, and he is already moving toward her with his hand on his knife, but he stops himself and flees, distraught and furious, breathless, suffocating under these foreign desires that are trying yet again to possess him.

He bursts wildly out into the street, narrowly avoiding knocking over a woman who is passing by on a man's arm. She utters a cry of surprise and turns, her face indignant, and then shock and horror twist her plump features and threaten to make her smart little hat slide down onto her forehead. She elbows her companion, who also turns and gives Pujols a look of abject horror, then hurries away, dragging the woman with him.

Pujols watches them go, cursing them inwardly; then, running a hand over his face, he realizes that their fear was due to more than just his battered face; he is covered with muck, like a pig wallowing in its sty. His clothes, his hands, his face. There is a sweetish, almost sugary taste on his lips and at the back of his throat. He worries for an instant that those two imbeciles are going to alert the police, but then the reassuring thought comes to him: what police, in this shambles Paris has become?

La Rousse made himself scarce, along with every other man assigned to ensure law and order, in the first days of the insurrection. That's the kind of courage displayed by the city police and their commanding officers; at five against one, armed with clubs and revolvers, they're self-satisfied and smug, quick to celebrate their easy wins as noisily as possible. But faced with this fanatical mob with its countless injuries to resent, in this city where the advent of liberty, equality, and justice is being proclaimed everywhere, the *flicards'* bravery has melted away like rancid butter in a hot oven.

He returns to the courtyard of his building and washes himself off at the pump, but he can't manage to get rid of the stink, like a human cowshed, that clings to him stubbornly, so he goes up to his room. Inside, a dreadful silence falls upon him, and he tiptoes around like a thief, wary of every squeaking door. He feels like a stranger in this place; nothing seems familiar. He undresses in front of the tarnish-spotted mirror, fills the basin with the rest of the water in his jug, and soaps and scrubs his face and arms. Then he drenches himself in cologne, puts fresh clothes on, and bundles together the soiled garments. He is on the point of leaving again when he reconsiders and takes from a drawer in his worm-eaten dresser a handful of cartridges, making sure his revolver is tucked safely away in the inner pocket of his frock coat. He takes the stairs down four at a time; the clock shows that the hour is getting late, and his obliging landlady, the indolent Viviane, will be home soon.

He heads back up the Rue des Missions almost at a run, making for Saint-Germain. He passes barricades being added to by national guardsmen and local residents. The streets are down to bare earth now, their cobblestones heaped in front of the Pantheon, on the corner near the School of Medicine. Clusters of men, shouting to encourage one another, heave on ropes attached to cannons that jolt over the rugged ground. Women fill sacks with dirt that are then passed along human chains to further fortify the Place de la Sorbonne. People drink wine and beer on the terraces, toasting loudly. *Vive la Commune! Up yours, Versailles!* Paris seems quite content. Children play and shriek; pigeons peck at crumbs on the sidewalks. Pujols doesn't understand how people can wait with such joy for the imminent bloodbath. He crosses the Seine via the Pont Saint-Michel, squeezing through the narrow passage left between the barricades and the buildings on the Boulevard Sébastopol. They stop him to check his papers, so he takes off his hat and shows them his battered face, his twisted mouth. "War injuries, Comrade." The fellow recoils instinctively for an instant but collects himself quickly, straightening his military cap. Always the same. That horror, and then a kind of respect. In these moments, Pujols always ends up believing that his past really was spent fighting snarling enemy soldiers in some far-off campaign. The sentry looks away, then gives him a little shove to keep moving. "It's all right, go on." So he keeps going, appalled and excited by these preparations for a new kind of war, in which every square will be a battlefield, every street a position to be conquered or defended. No more heroic heavy-cavalry charges, no more strategies calculated like a game of chess. Now people will sneak and infiltrate and creep along walls and watch from windows for the danger; they will attack the enemy from the rear, spray them with bullets at point-blank range, slit throats in back alleys, finish off the wounded in narrow lanes. He is almost dizzy at the thought of the coming carnage, and muses that Monsieur Charles will have a great deal indeed to do with his black boxes, to capture the unrelenting savagery coming for the insurgent rabble crouching on the ground behind their piles of cobblestones, defending to the death their pathetic heaps, their cardboard fortresses, their sandcastle walls studded with flags as red as if they were already gorged with the blood that will soon flow. National guardsmen are seated on ammunition crates around a mitrailleuse on the corner of the Rue Rambuteau. Farther along, near the Rue Réamur, the noses of two cannons are pointed at the embrasures that have been made in the mass of rocks and cobblestones. Everywhere there are hundreds of armed men camping behind the redoubts, smoking their pipes or cleaning their rifles.

He walks for nearly an hour that way, through the evening crowds in the warm air. Sweat on his forehead. He is short of breath. Images of those girls hurling themselves on him assail his mind, and the idiotic, mindless fear he felt. He can't rid his memory of their cries, their grunts. They didn't say a single actual word. They might as well have been nothing but captive, starving animals.

On the corner where the Rue Béranger meets the Place du Château-d'Eau, a girl is selling branches of lilacs, and Pujols catches a whiff of their perfume as he passes her. He remembers a springtime back home, the Pyrenees still snowcapped, his mother gathering handfuls of the pale violet clusters to breathe them in, burying her face in the blossoms. It was so long ago that he has forgotten almost everything; he has shed that life like a snake its skin.

Troubled, he crosses the vast square, which has been transformed into a fortress guarded by barricades rising as high as the second floor of the buildings. The cafés are full. In front of a little dive on the Rue de l'Entrepôt, national guardsmen stand and drink mugs of beer and smoke, their rifles over their shoulders. There are women toasting with them, military caps askew atop their chignons, cartridge belts around their waists.

Pujols quickens his pace to reach the Quai de Jemmapes. A scarlet barrel hangs above green shutters: Chez Miron, wineseller.

The bar is dark and low-ceilinged. The windows flanking the entrance let in a dim light that the sooty beaten-earth floor, dark wood tables, and assemblage of tarred planks that serve as a counter seem to absorb without reflecting even the faintest gleam. A man at the far end of the room is sprawled back on his chair, propped up against the wall, his mouth open. In front of him are a glass of absinthe and a carafe of water. Near the window, three men play cards silently. None of them looks up, but Pujols knows that every move he makes is being watched. Behind the counter, the boss, Miron, a small, chubby man whose cheeks are hidden beneath blond muttonchops, acts like he doesn't see Pujols resting his elbows on the bar. Pujols asks for a drink, and the man sighs and comes over.

"A glass of white. A good one."

"Shouldn't be a problem." The man takes a full bottle out of a cupboard and uncorks it carefully. "Brand new, this one. Nice little '69 Anjou. Got it in April."

Pujols inhales the wine's perfume, then sips. Not bad. The owner pours himself a glass.

"We've met, haven't we? You've been in here before."

"Yeah. With Clovis."

Pujols hears movement from the three men behind him near the window. The boss darts a quick glance over his shoulder, then lets his gaze drift out the open door, toward the canal.

"What do you want with Clovis?"

A chair scrapes the floor behind him. Pujols turns and sees one of the men standing, cap pulled low over his eyes, hands in his trouser pockets. Knife. Pujols thinks he can make out the long shape of the Eustache knife the man's fist is already gripping. The man's two companions have also turned toward him. He isn't afraid. Not of them. The revolver is heavy in his pocket. He has felt it bumping against his thigh all afternoon as he walked, and it didn't reassure him them, pursued as he was by a shadow, perhaps his own, in this city teetering on the edge of madness. But here, facing these yokels from the Porte de Saint-Ouen, he has nothing to fear.

"I need to see him. He's a friend; I know he comes here often."

"Haven't seen him today. Go and look somewhere else."

"We're friends, he and I. We met through Bébert from Saint-Ouen, if that means anything to you."

"You know the Pointe?"

Pujols nods, takes off his hat. The man tries to hide his surprise, but his forehead creases in spite of himself. "What's wrong with your face?"

Pujols shakes his head and purses his lips, trying to look embarrassed.

"It's not a very nice memory . . . happened when I was younger, on the farm, back home. We were attacked by Spanish bandits. A hammer blow did what you see here. I wanted to help my father, but . . ."

The two henchmen still sitting at the table nod. Approvingly, even sympathetically. The man standing in front of him pulls himself together, straightens his back, puffs out his chest, seems to grow bigger somehow.

"I can find him for you—Clovis—but it'll cost you. For the time it takes me; for the bother. He's not an easy fellow to pin down."

Miron, the bar owner, comes out from behind his counter and approaches the man.

"Come on, Cristo, no trouble. Leave it be."

The man named Cristo shuts him up with a wave of his hand. "How much have you got on you?"

The two other men have stood up behind him. They exchange a glance, decide not to move.

Pujols feels his jacket, puts his hands in his pockets and pretends to rummage around. He finds the grip of his revolver and wraps his fist firmly around it. When he takes it out, slowly, carefully, no one seems to understand what he's doing.

Cristo is hit in the neck by a bullet and knocked backwards, surprise on his face, then collapses on the table at which his two cronies were sitting. One of them crashes backward along with his chair, and, while he is struggling to right himself, Pujols walks over and shoots him in the heart. The other is in the process of drawing his knife when he takes a bullet in the head and smashes into the wall behind him before slumping over the table. Cristo twists and writhes, clutching his throat as if his hands have been bewitched by some evil wizard and are trying to strangle him, and he's trying to fight the spell. He rolls off the table and falls heavily to the ground across the body of one of his companions and lies unmoving on his back, breathing heavily, coughing and choking, his mouth full of blood. Then he convulses and dies, and Pujols searches his pockets and comes up with a sort of short-bladed penknife, razor-sharp, which he flings across the room.

When he stands, he sees the man who was sleeping at the far end of the room standing now behind his chair. He is twisting his cap in his hands, shamefaced, as if about to beg a boss or a master for forgiveness.

"I didn't see anything," he says. "I was asleep. Can I go?"

Pujols beckons him closer. The man takes three steps. The soles of his shoes scrape and drag as if unwilling to move any farther.

"Go on. Nothing you can do for them now."

The man comes closer, hesitating. He is limping, his body crooked, twisting with each step. He glances at the three bodies, scratches his beard.

"I don't know 'em, these chaps, myself. Who are they? They from around here?"

He leans over for a better look, gripping a table edge so as not to fall, his body lopsided.

"We're closing, Gustin," says the owner from behind his counter. "You can pay tomorrow."

"Oh—yeah," says the man. "'Course. Sorry. Don't mean to interrupt your conversation."

He puts on his hat and limps like a broken puppet to the door. As soon as he's gone, Pujols stows his weapon. There are shouts in the distance, and the rolling of drums. Miron raises a finger in the air as if trying to figure out the direction of the wind.

"That's the call to arms of the 123rd. They say they're striking hard near Passy."

"Tell me where I can find Clovis. I'm in a bit of a hurry."

The bar owner rakes his gaze over Pujols's disfigured face. He pours another glass of wine and holds it out, his hand wavering slightly.

"He's seen on the Rue des Écluses Saint-Martin a lot; I think he might even live around there. He's a strange fellow, you know, and—"

Pujols turns his back and leaves, heading alongside the canal almost at a run. A skinny dog starts to follow him, and he chases it away with a kick to the face. The dog yelps. A fisherman standing at the water's edge turns, calls the dog, swears at Pujols. When he crosses the lock, the dazzle of sun off the water is blinding and he shakes his head to clear it of the painful light. At last he spots the hansom cab on the street, Clovis's top-hatted figure sitting atop it, unmoving. He raps on the coach's door, and the man jumps and turns to him, his eyes dull slits in his hairy face.

"I need you. Go on, drive. We're going to my place."

He climbs into the cab, and the whip cracks and the coach sways into motion. The driver shouts unintelligibly at his horse. They have to slow down and stop at each barricade, sometimes showing the national guardsmen the pass Pujols always keeps on him, a paper filled with stamps and false signatures given to him by a pencil-pusher at the Prefecture who declared allegiance to the Commune simply for the sake of some peace and quiet. Clovis weaves deftly through the city's streets. He has driven his cab, drawn by a series of nags who've died between its shafts, around Paris for five years now, and he knows the place like the back of his hand.

Sunk deep into his seat, Pujols can hear Paris simmering around him, elated and singing. Bursts of shouting, children's laughter, the song a woman is softly humming when the carriage brushes past her, bugle calls, drums beating, orders and curses, advice and warnings, the heavy clattering of carts and ammunition wagons on the cobblestones—the city is a hive of noise, the common people thronging the streets where twilight is already falling. He surprises himself by feeling an unaccustomed surge of goodwill toward these multitudes, thinking that the blind, unaware of the world's ugliness, must love their discordant music, their wild harmonies.

When they arrive in front of the building, Pujols gets out to unlock the double doors of the carriage entrance, and the cab clatters into the courtyard. Madame Viviane hasn't returned. Clovis doesn't climb down from his coach box, so Pujols has to drag him toward the cellar by his sleeve.

"What are we doing here?" the man grumbles.

"There isn't much time. We're headed for a major dust-up, and I don't want them found here. We've got to get them out and take them to Gros-Tonton."

Pujols lights a lantern, turns the key. He hesitates before opening the door. He can hear Clovis's hoarse breathing behind him, smell his putrid odor. He pushes the door open, keeping his back foot at the ready. He's afraid they will attack him again like before, and regrets not having brought a club or even a simple switch to keep them in line.

The cold air inside hits him, stinking like a cesspit. He makes out the three huddled bodies, their pale legs entangled, the ghostly white of their chemises. Their pallid nakedness. They are whimpering, barely moving. "Mercy," pleads one. "Let us go," begs another.

"What's wrong with them?" asks Clovis.

"Nothing. Help me."

They take the girls out to the hansom cab, forced to hold them up because they're so weak. Unsteady on their feet, weighing almost nothing. Their fragile arms seem about to break in the men's big fists. They install them on the coach's seats and tie them firmly down. Clovis pulls two plaid blankets from a trunk and tosses them over the girls' shoulders.

"There you go. Looks more chic," Clovis says, holding up a lantern inside the cab.

Pujols looks up at the sky, which is still pale, dotted with swallows. The courtyard is a vast, shadowy well. It seems as if the night is trying to fall early. The coach rattles slowly toward the entryway; the lantern flame quivers but doesn't seem to cast any light. The shadows in the street lie low to the ground, giving a bluish cast to the façades of the buildings. He begins to climb up next to Clovis on the coach box, but the other man stops him with a brusque gesture.

"No. You need to stay with them in there. In case we get stopped."

Pujols is about to protest, but Clovis, once again enveloped in the folds of his greatcoat, clicks his tongue at the horse, so he climbs into the coach and settles himself in a corner, where he can keep an eye on all three of them. Two are sitting across from him, the third beside him. He can't tell them apart anymore. He remembers choosing them for their fresh complexions, their slim waists, the shapeliness of their bodies. Monsieur Charles declared himself enchanted and charmed with each delivery. And he wasn't the last to derive a bit of quick, brutal pleasure from their exhausted, opium-laden bodies.

At first, they close their eyes as the coach lurches and sways, as if they are being rocked to sleep, their heads nodding gently, their pale little faces framed by dark hair. He can see nothing of the one next to him but a straight-nosed profile and a long neck, her head held high and unmoving. She closes her eyes, too, but doesn't give herself up to the bouncing of the hansom cab. Her hands rest on her thighs, flat, immobile. A small ring on her hand sparkles occasionally in the gloom. He wonders if she's the one who led the attack on him in the cellar earlier. She was the most rebellious, resisting the poses the photographer commanded her to assume for as long as she could, requiring the largest doses of drugs to render her compliant. A new shudder runs down his spine, and he watches her out of the corner of his eye even as he looks out the window at the hustle and bustle in the streets.

They make their way past the obstacles placed in the roads, maneuver around a barricade, slow down in the middle of a crowd gathered at a crossroads around a speaker whose voice is lost in the buzz of his audience's conversation. A fresh breeze fills the coach as they cross the Seine. A brightness, too, which causes the suddenly wide eyes of the girls sitting across from him to gleam as they look at him. They blink with fatigue, or astonishment, perhaps, but they don't stop staring at him, their faces blank and empty. He stares back for long moments, but their gazes don't drop. He raises a hand sharply, growling low in his throat, but they don't move, don't flinch, don't betray any sign of fear. Nor do they react to the noisy passage of ten artillery wagons and two large carts, or the shouts of the horsemen escorting them. Their large, wide eyes are riveted to his face, insensible to anything else. He feels the tiniest of movements next to him, turns to look at the girl, and freezes.

She is looking at him now, too. She sits very straight, her hands folded in her lap, and she is smiling at him widely in a way that shows all her teeth, her eyes the dull black of muddy pools. Pujols shrinks back against the carriage partition, trying to get as far away as he can from those white, white teeth grinning in the dimness.

Outside, the Boulevard des Italiens creeps past slowly, and to distract himself from the anxiety that has seized him, Pujols looks out at the café windows, their lamps being lighted in the dusk, and the crowds bustling past in their dark coats. The strains of an accordion rise and fade away. The sound of a ballad being played on a squeaky barrel organ comes closer to the cab, and he finally sees the woman singing, a Phrygian cap[10] on her head, a wide red scarf draped over her shoulder, standing in the midst of a half circle of onlookers. The song is about victory, gunners, the future, and happy children. Love. Pujols shrugs his shoulders and laughs at this incredible naivete, this fourpenny aria. The cab, which has stopped for a moment, starts moving again. The horse begins trotting when they reach the Boulevard Poissonnière, and now the city outside the window is nothing but a fleeting series of shadows and voices accompanied by the jolting noise of the cab.

Relax, Pujols tells himself. In less than an hour they'll be there, among the shanties with their sagging roofs patched with sheet metal and tarred boards, surrounded by rickety fences and gardens filled with garbage and motley debris, in which a gnarled tree grows here and there, daring to produce only a few leaves that quickly fall. In the middle of the whole miserable mess they'll find Gros-Tonton—Uncle Fatty—in his castle, a sturdy house built by those who owed him favors using materials stolen from work sites. And there amid the bizarre clutter of his parlor, reclining on a red sofa, will be his wife Esmerelda, tall, pale, and plaintive, nicknamed thus because they say she is a gypsy, even though her man first pulled her from the streets dead drunk, having been thrown out of a whorehouse by a pimp near the Gare Saint-Lazare.

In less than an hour, Gros-Tonton will accept the delivery

---

[10] Phrygian cap: A brimless, conical cap symbolizing liberty and worn during the French Revolution.

and pay cash like he always does, certain of being able to sell the girls at exorbitant prices to those Prussian bastards holding siege on the other side of the fortifications. And then Pujols can plan his escape from the death-trap Paris has become, before hellfire is unleashed there. He smiles beneath his wide-brimmed cap.

He turns to the girl sitting next to him, who is still smiling at him. And her white teeth, nearly phosphorescent in the fading light of day, and her blue lips, which are so thin as to look sharp, are a bite she is sending him from a distance, like a macabre kiss, and he feels a nasty shiver run down his spine.

6

T he night had passed in fitful sleep, broken by startled
awakenings, eyes straining into the darkness among the
snores and smells of the men.

"Eh! Up!"

In his dream, an enormous fellow had seized his shoulder
and was about to hit him, so Nicolas had shoved the arm away,
one fist flailing at the form hovering above him. Red dodged
the blow and straightened up, laughing. Behind him and all
around the room, men are busying themselves near their camp
beds, strapping on their gear and shouting to one another.

"What the hell's going on? What time is it?"

"Almost seven. Can't you hear?"

Nicolas sat up. At first he couldn't hear anything over the
hubbub of the men getting ready, then a faint thrumming noise
began to infiltrate his skull, like distant endless thunder, off to
the west. He looked up at Red.

"They've been bombarding the ramparts for an hour. Passy,
La Muette. A real disaster; there's panic. We might as well have
spent last night pissing into the wind. They must have received
two or three hundred guns overnight. It's hell out there."

Nicolas got to his feet. His head whirled, the dizziness making him want to fall back on his pallet.

"How do you know all of this?" he asked.

"I got up early to have a chat with the mess girl, you know,
the little blonde . . . anyway, we were sitting there with a few
others, and a captain from the 60th rode up on horseback with

two or three men. Said it was just like Gravelotte all over again. That the Versaillais had brought in their cannons at the crack of dawn and everyone was starting to fall back. That's why we've got to assemble now."

There were roughly two hundred of them in the street, forming straggling lines, still buckling their belts or munching a bit of bread and sausage taken from their haversacks. Others rinsed away their morning breath with a mouthful of red wine or metallic-tasting water from a flask. They muttered, snorted, shook themselves in the chilly air. Many were vacant-eyed, still groggy from poor sleep and the abrupt awakening. Nicolas and Red scanned the throng for Adrien, having shared a can of lukewarm coffee passed to them stealthily by the blonde mess girl. The boy arrived limping slightly, one of his boots under his arm, his shirt still undone, his jacket tossed over one shoulder, his bayonet in one hand and his rifle in the other. His lips twitched in a nervous smile when he saw them, and he came to join them, swearing under his breath. Red asked him what had happened to him, and he didn't answer at first, setting his sack on the ground, handing Red his rifle while he finished dressing. There was a wine stain on the front of his shirt. He smelled of alcohol; his breath was terrible. There was dried blood on the knuckles of his hands.

Red gave him back his things.

"Where did you spend the night? Our little stroll in the Bois de Boulogne wasn't enough for you? I thought you were down for the count."

The young man snickered and asked Nicolas what he was drinking from the can. "Water, right? To rinse out your mouth? Must be water." Nicolas handed him a flask, which he emptied in long swallows.

"I was in the Latin Quarter. Is that surprising, coming from a hog-slaughtering pork butcher? After a few hours of sleep I get bored, so I have to stretch my legs, take my mind off things. And there's more than just students in the cafés!"

An officer strode along the lines of soldiers, shouting for silence in the ranks, encumbered by the saber clanking against his leg. The buzz of conversation died away gradually, the men raising their heads and closing ranks a bit. From the west came the rumbling, cracking sounds of the guns. Swallows called overhead, feathers glinting in the first rays of the rising sun. Forced march to Auteuil to provide reinforcements for the defenders. Bayonets to cannons.

All around them, Paris was stirring. Windows opened, people leaning out and applauding. *Vive la Garde nationale! To Versailles!* The shouts resonated in the silence of the nearly empty streets. The men's footsteps, the thumping of their boots, their murmured voices spread out along the cobblestones in a long, somber cortege.

Adrien rubbed his hands together, wiggling his fingers as if to wake them up.

"Been hitting yourself again?" enquired Nicolas.

"No. I had to settle a score . . . some fop who was saying the people would never be able to liberate themselves because they're too lazy, too stupid, and they settle for so little in life that they can't dream any farther than the end of their street. That the Commune is already too good for the lower classes, who don't deserve the great ambitions some have for them. So things got a bit heated, and there were a couple of other fellows who joined in, and some men from the barricade came into it on my side. We chased them to the Pont Saint-Michel, and one of them almost ended up in the Seine, but a patrol went by just then, so we had to get out of there quick. We could have told that sergeant we were chasing Versaillais spies, and he wouldn't have wanted to know anything about it, the half-wit."

Nicolas and Red smiled but didn't speak. A faint whiff of

smoke reached the men's noses, then dissipated. A few of them sniffed, looked up at the sky, glancing at their comrades, reading the same fear in their faces.

"Anyway, your fop seems to have been a strange fellow. Thinks the Commune is casting pearls before swine, does he?" said Red.

"They're called dandies. I've read about them," said Nicolas.

The boy hooted with laughter. "Bet he wasn't feeling so dandy after we finished with him, the bastard."

Nicolas was about to respond when he suddenly realized that the ranks of Federates had slowed down. They had run up against a long line of horse-drawn carriages, carts overloaded with passengers and baggage, and pedestrians laden with large sacks and suitcases, children trailing behind them. Someone asked where they were going. *It's hell back there*, they said, gesturing behind them toward the west and its still-blue sky. One well-dressed gentleman holding two children by the hands described houses on fire, bombs falling randomly, dead bodies in the streets. His wife, her hair tumbling from beneath her little black hat, burst into sobs and wheeled on the soldiers, jabbing her shredded parasol at them.

"This is because of all of you, you thieves! Drunkards! You and your Commune, this—this government of beggars, led by nobodies! This paradise for lowlifes and prostitutes! It's your fault they're shelling honest people and throwing respectable families out onto the streets, you thugs, you, you—worthless creatures! But soon order will be restored, and they'll shoot you all, and hang the whores you lie with!"

The men had stopped in their tracks and gathered around her. They listened in silence, unable to take their eyes off of her. Some of them snickered into their beards, but most simply gaped at her, astonished, their faces grave, the way people sometimes listen to madmen who prophesy disasters that everyone senses are imminent.

Her husband took her by the arm and murmured into her ear in an attempt to calm her, but she wrenched herself away and continued ranting.

"Yes, you pitiful wretches! The true France will soon bring you and your orgies to justice! And you'll be—"

A man made his way through the crowd of his comrades. He pushed them aside with his broad shoulders, his rifle strapped across his chest, the men parting to let him pass. The woman abruptly stopped speaking, and there was silence, broken only by the sounds of heavy breathing, throats being cleared. He came to a stop in front of her, his head barely rising above hers, his back very straight, his gaze locked on hers. The moment stretched on, every eye focused on the bayonet gleaming mere centimeters from the little black hat, the disheveled hair. The woman opened her mouth to say something, but it was as if she couldn't find enough air, or her tongue had become unwilling. She simply stared around, wide-eyed, at the ranks of men that seemed now to be closing in on her.

"I feel very sorry for you, Madame," the soldier said. "And I pity you."

He took a step backwards, looked the woman up and down, smiling sadly, then spat at her feet. He turned to the others, his features suddenly drawn with exhaustion.

"Let's go. We have better things to do."

Just then a captain rode up hurriedly, reining to a halt when he saw the column of Federates beginning to walk again, murmuring quietly.

"What in God's name is going on here?"

"Nothing," someone answered. "Just a lady asking for directions."

The men laughed. The officer shrugged his shoulders and spurred his horse onward to retake the head of the line.

"Did you see that?" asked Adrien. "That bourgeoise should be shot for saying that."

Nicolas didn't answer. He spotted the soldier who had faced down the woman a few meters ahead of them and wondered what a man like that was made of, from where he summoned such uncommon strength and dignity, and he thought to himself that, whatever else they were, these men marching so ponderously toward danger, they all bore in their hearts the same courage, the same mad hope.

"Do you know him?" he asked Red.

"Him, over there? A bit. Everyone calls him Jacquelin. He sells flowers at Les Halles."

"That's why he knows how to talk to women," put in Adrien.

"Sure it is. And not everyone has that skill, right?"

They passed the town hall of the 15th arrondissement, where a small crowd had gathered, carrying pickaxes and spades, shouting encouragements to one another. "Everyone to the barricades!" A red flag was hoisted atop the pole in front of the building, accompanied by the strains of "La Marseillaise."

They quickened their steps. The sound of singing died away as they turned down the Rue Lemaire as if smothered by the smoke-tinged wind blowing off the Seine. On the quay opposite the Pont de Grenelle, the men slowed down to look up at the dark smoke rising above the rooftops against the blue sky. They could hear the explosions distinctly now, great heavy thuds dulled by distance but making the air seem to quiver around them.

"We're in for it this time," Nicolas said.

As they crossed the river, Nicolas tried to make out the barricade rising below the bridge, remembering the glum lieutenant from last night. Grelier, he was called. Augustin Grelier. Some twenty or so national guardsmen stood atop the cobble-and-earth structure, raising their weapons in salute as the company passed. Nicolas wasn't sure he would recognize him again; it had been so dark that he remembered the man mostly as a sad-faced shadow, but he thought the man standing on the redoubt just above the embrasure through which the nose of the cannon could be seen, waving with a raised fist, his other hand on his heart, bore a strong resemblance to the lieutenant. He called out at the top of his lungs:

"Lieutenant Grelier! *Salut et fraternité!*"

The men around him looked at him in surprise, then repeated after him in chorus, "Lieutenant Grelier! *Salut et fraternité!*" The clamor of voices was loud enough to overpower even the thundering noise of the cannons, and almost seemed capable of smothering it for good. The lieutenant didn't move, but Nicolas thought he saw his chest expand slightly—then he lost sight of him abruptly, as all of them were thrown to the ground in a tangled heap, dazed, deafened by the massive explosion and eruption of flame that suddenly licked along the Rue de Boulainvilliers in front of them like the tongue of some fantastical dragon, shearing the roofs off the surrounding buildings and sending fragments of slate and burning rafters, shards of glass and bits of pulverized stone and chunks of posts as thick as tree trunks raining down on their heads.

"They've blown up the gasworks!"

Nicolas lifted his head, trying to catch his breath, his mouth full of dust and hot air, his tongue dry and rough as a strip of leather. Red pulled himself onto all fours and shook Adrien, who was flat on his belly beneath a heavy piece of timber. The boy sat up, his hair white with plaster, a bloody cut gleaming scarlet on his blackened face. He looked blankly for a moment at the friend gripping him by the shoulders as if manipulating a puppet, then pulled himself together and rubbed his forehead, swearing. He turned to Nicolas and asked if he was all right, then tried to get up but fell back on his rump, still dazed. They all shuddered again as another blast hurled into the air an enormous glowing ball that then exploded, releasing a cloud of black, incandescence-streaked smoke, metal shrieking and grinding horrifically. The ground shook, and the surrounding buildings collapsed further, rumbling dully.

Eventually the men began to move again, struggling to free themselves from beneath the debris, stamping out fires and heaving fragments of masonry and wood off of one another, helping haggard comrades to stand, some of them with bloody faces or crushed shoulders, wincing in pain, stooping to search amid the chaos for their rifles or military caps, finding them beneath a table that had been flung all that distance, a hat stand next to it with a top hat still perched atop one hook. They combed the rubble for long moments, bending over some men just barely moving, some groaning, some stilled forever, their skulls split, brains oozing out.

Nicolas and Red lifted a very young soldier with two broken legs onto a stretcher improvised from a door. He trembled wordlessly with pain, eyes rolling in his head. They transported him to the quay, where female aid station attendants had rushed and now stood waiting beside a wagon. The women bent over the injured boy, giving him something to drink and wiping his forehead with a damp cloth. "You'll be all right, my lad, the doctor will fix you right up; you'll see." He looked from one to the other in terror and closed his eyes, fat tears spilling down his cheeks.

"You can't say anything to my mother," he murmured. "She doesn't know I'm here."

They assured him that his mother would be proud of her boy, and one of the women stroked his cheek with the back of her dirty hand, gently, urging him softly not to worry.

Returning to the street, they paused for a moment in front of the smoking shambles in which the men of the company were now rummaging—the wounded and the dead now evacuated—in the hope, perhaps, that the explosion had brought down on their heads a rain of silver or gold pieces from a woolen stocking stashed in the back of a shattered armoire. They didn't speak, hunched over, as focused as if hunting mushrooms, and the only sound was the crunching of broken glass beneath their shoes and the muffled thumps of the Versaillais cannons, which no one seemed to notice anymore.

Nicolas was reminded of a time in the aftermath of a storm when an English two-master had been wrecked on the beach, the small crowd of villagers picking through the debris while others climbed into the ruined hull and tossed out anything that looked even slightly valuable to their famished eyes. There had been two corpses lying in the seaweed-strewn wreckage, and people maneuvered around them without even glancing down. The local curate had arrived, preceded by an altar boy holding a cross, his rosary in his hand, face in deep shadow under his enormous hat, and he had crossed himself as he surveyed the disaster, watching from the rocks benevolently, hands folded across his middle, as his flock rummaged unrestrainedly in this dilapidated offering that seemed to have fallen from the sky. Then, suddenly, he had rushed toward the beach, shouting at these ungodly plunderers, threatening them with the wrath of the Almighty for such disgraceful pilfering. The women had turned to him first, bowing beneath the scarves covering their hair, and then the men had paused, too, full sacks at their feet, and finally the whole bunch had returned to the village in procession behind the cross, passing small objects to one another discreetly, to be closely examined whenever the sun shone through a gap in the clouds and gleamed on the ocean.

Nicolas struggled to make sense of what he was seeing. Not poverty-stricken Breton villagers subdued by the superstitions declaimed from the Sunday pulpit and by the fireside at nightfall, when they dreaded hearing Death pass by in his chariot or the knock at the door of some undead sailor cast out by the sea, but members of the National Guard. Soldiers of the Commune. The people in arms. Rooting with the points of their bayonets through the debris of war, hoping to unearth some paltry trinket. He ordered them in a firm voice to fall in, calling on their courage, their dignity, but no one listened to him. Some distance away the captain drew his revolver and fired into the air; the noise was nothing compared to the blast that had just rattled the area, but the men looked up at him and straightened, adjusting their jackets and caps. Others, farther away, rose from their hunched positions, shaking off the dust that covered them and shouldering their rifles again.

Nicolas joined the other three sergeants, and they reassembled their squads, trying their best to encourage the men, but their words fell flat in this silence broken only by the rumbling of the guns. They began marching again slowly, picking their way through the debris clogging the street, the obstacles that had to be stepped over or maneuvered around.

"Where are we going, anyway?" Adrien asked.

A shell whistled past them to the left, toward Auteuil, exploding with a dull bang. Red hunched his shoulders, then jerked his chin at the plume of gray smoke rising into the sky. "You can't tell?"

The youth didn't reply. He crouched suddenly and straightened up with a medallion in his hand. Gold, maybe. He inspected the object, turning it over in his hand.

"'To my daughter Jenny.' You hear that, Red? Jenny!"

Red didn't seem to have heard him. They had reached the intersection of two streets where a house had toppled into the middle of the road like an immense torn sack, spilling out its contents. There were officers there, standing in front of a wine shop with closed shutters. One of them held the bridle of a horse that trembled and shook its head at each detonation. The men were arguing, gesturing emphatically.

"Two columns!"

The captain climbed onto the platform of a cart and ordered the men to patrol from the Point du Jour to the Porte d'Auteuil. The cannonading was particularly heavy in those areas, he said.

"But we aren't gunners," one man objected, stepping forward. "What good will we do?"

Nicolas came closer. He recognized General Dombrowski, his face drawn, uniform gray with dust, and a colonel from his general staff. The colonel climbed onto the cart in his turn.

"The ramparts are virtually undefended. We must hold them from behind the lines until reinforcements come. We're expecting three thousand Federates the Central Committee has promised us. And artillery."

The colonel turned to Dombrowski and gave him a questioning glance. The general nodded.

"You should know that many of your comrades are fleeing, fearful of the sudden increase in violence. You must hold them back, reassure them with your presence. Versailles has to know that Paris is being defended, not given over to invasion."

"And if they leave anyway? These citizens? What do we do then?"

The colonel hesitated.

"Let them go and hold the line."

A hum of murmured voices rose from the crowd of men.

At a signal from the captain, the sergeants reassembled their men and formed their squads.

"This is the time to show them!" shouted the colonel.

"Show them what?" a voice called.

"Just your face! That should scare them!"

Laughter. Other suggestions were bellowed. An artillery shell struck one hundred meters straight ahead of them and destroyed the top two floors of a building. The men fell silent and began to march.

The time to stock up on water and ammunition was early in

the afternoon, in the warm air, beneath a blue sky that hadn't yet been entirely blackened by the smoke of the fires.

Nicolas feels as if he's been caught up in a whirlwind. Time passes strangely, seeming either infinite or instantaneous. The morning is like a staircase without a banister, whose steps occasionally give way, and which he is climbing in the dark.

There are thirty of them in the Rue Boileau, trees drooping gracefully over the high walls of private homes, their leaves quivering with each cannon blast. Behind their yawning metal gates, the houses are burning. The fires roar and moan, tongues of flame licking through the blown-out windows, triumphant, like a rioter on the balcony of a princely palace. Nicolas has barely turned his head toward the fires when, behind him, the men cheer and clap at the collapse of a roof or the explosion of a window. Pride and dignity are aflame here, not the old world. In every member of the bourgeoisie there slumbers a bookkeeper capable of allowing losses when he is sure of future gains, to be savagely recouped in a working man's sweat.

Red catches up to him and walks beside him for a moment without speaking. The ground trembles beneath their feet. Roiling black smoke pours into the street every few minutes.

"What the hell are we going to do—really?"

"Have a look; see what's what. We're going to garrison house 67, and then we're clearing off."

"And what are you hoping to see when you have this look?"

Nicolas shrugs.

"So you don't get it?"

An artillery shell whines past above their heads, and they all flatten themselves to the cobblestones. It bursts fifty meters away in a garden, felling an enormous chestnut tree in a mighty crash of leaves and broken branches. When they get to their feet, they realize they are covered in dirt, grass, and flowers.

They brush themselves off, shaking their heads in astonishment and chagrin at this scattered burial.

Nicolas spurs them onward with loud shouts, surely needing to hear an echo of his own courage, and runs ahead of them with agile grace. They follow him smartly, rifles held high across their chests, breaking into two lines on either side of the street, in the shelter of the high walls concealing the villas and gardens of the rich. They cross the railway line, where the Point du Jour signal box is nothing but a blackened, smoking ruin. Their path is dotted with cottages and huts in the middle of tiny gardens, and they pick their way between craters as wide as houses, hopping over piles of rubble crawling with rats. They pass two abandoned barricades, untidy heaps of cobblestones topped with boards and overturned carts. Up ahead, nothing remains of the Porte de Saint-Cloud but a trench lying between two jumbled masses of dirt and broken masonry. In the space of a single instant, silence falls again, heavier and more terrifying than a bomb. Walking on, they look around anxiously. One of the men scans the sky, his rifle raised and ready to fire as if he is hunting, hoping, perhaps, to destroy a shell before it hits the ground. Nicolas clambers up the remains of a staircase to the top of the rampart. Thick coils of smoke rise from the fortifications; the air smells of gunpowder and disturbed earth. Flames leap from the toll station at bastion 64. A twelve-pound cannon sits nearby, its shells neatly arranged in two crates. A military cap has been placed atop the cannon, a bayonet thrust into the ground next to it.

In the distance, in the streets of Billancourt, Nicolas can make out wagons trundling and horsemen galloping. There are soldiers everywhere. Even the smallest spaces seem to be swarming with people, as if the place is being overrun by vermin carrying a plague ready to spread. Two cannon blasts flash silently on the Île Seguin, among the trees; the sound of the explosions follows an instant later, and a shell detonates on the

Bayonne road, obliterating the street and sending a clump of trees into the air like a tossed bridal bouquet. Only naval cannons have such range, such power. He decides to go down and rejoin his men and is just turning when a monstrous buzzing noise rattles his eardrums and he feels himself being lifted off his feet and flung to the ground in searing, suffocating darkness.

He finds himself crumpled at the foot of a section of wall, folded over on himself, his mouth full of dirt, which he spits out, wheezing. He tastes blood. Dirty water. Iron. He tries to stand but falls back to his knees because, around him, the trees and houses and sky hover and whirl like a carousel. He spits again, coughs, trying to expel from the back of his throat and his bronchial tubes all the filth he inhaled when he gulped in what could have been his final breath. Fifty meters to his right another shell hits, the explosion reaching his ears only as a muffled roar, and he flattens himself to the ground again behind the piece of wall, arms covering his head, as bricks and splintered wood rain down on him. He crawls on his belly to what remains of the staircase and lets himself roll to the bottom of the slope. It feels as if most of his bones have been cracked and disconnected from one another and are now moving and grinding together painfully inside his body, held together by nothing, seeking only to pierce his skin and tear his muscles. He lies on his back for a moment, trying to catch his breath, waiting for the excruciating chaos in his body to subside. He tries to think of Caroline, summoning her image into his mind, forcing himself to remember the softness of her skin, the curve of the small of her back, all the tender, intimate things he knows about her, but a stinging sensation in his chest pushes him to sit up, his breath coming in gasps, and spit out the blood filling his mouth. With a burst of strength he didn't know he possessed he pulls himself to a standing position, dazed and swaying, chest tight, every rib feeling as if it's about to puncture his heart or his lungs. He even manages to take a few steps toward the faint snatches of voices that reach his ears: cries and moans in the smoke, thick as pea soup. He makes his way toward a figure leaning over a man on the ground. Then the air brightens suddenly, the sun insolently cutting through the haze, outlining shapes and making colors flare in bright relief, and he recognizes Adrien, his face covered in blood, talking to the comrade lying at his feet.

The youth turns to Nicolas and watches him approach for a moment, openmouthed, his arms dangling loosely at his sides, and then he runs to him and flings his arms around him and hugs him fiercely, thumping him on the back with his fists the way children do when they're happy, or overcome with grief.

"My God, I thought you'd been killed up there on the rampart!"

"Where's Red?"

"Just over there. He's all right. Bleeding a bit from that thick skull of his, but it's nothing much."

Nicolas approaches the man on the ground. The right sleeve of his jacket is nothing but a blood-soaked tatter. His arm lies some distance away, naked and white, palm spread skyward. His face, soot blackened and scorched red, seems peaceful, his eyes shut. He just looks like he's sleeping. Nicolas bends over, his ribcage a corset of pain, and feels the wounded man's neck for a pulse. It's there, but weak and rapid, more of a quivering. The man is barely breathing, his lips moving slightly, trying to say something, maybe. His eyes open and dart around and up at the blue sky, as if looking for something. Nicolas leans closer to the man's ear and grimaces; the pain in his torso is so excruciating, like an iron band encircling him and making it hard to breathe, that he's afraid he might collapse on the prostrate form.

"What is it you're saying?"

"*Mio padre. Angelo Ricciardi.*"

"Italiano?"

The man answers with a groan. His breathing cuts off, resumes.

"*Sì. Dillo a mio padre. Che sono morto per la libertà. Suo figlio Ettore . . .*"

He doesn't finish. His head falls to the side, mouth open. Two artillery shells explode at almost the same instant, two hundred meters away, and the ground shakes. Two enormous black trees of smoke sprout suddenly, shot through with glowing red veins.

Nicolas and Adrien flatten themselves to the ground. The sun pales and vanishes. They lift their heads in the dimness.

"What did he say?"

"He was talking about his father. Said to tell him he was dead. I think that's what he said, anyway. Did you know him?"

"A bit. Ettore, he's called. He was born near Venice. Talked about it all the time. He kept a red shirt[11] in his sack; said it belonged to his father."

Nicolas retrieved the Italian's cap and replaced it on his head.

"We'll have to bury him."

"Not here."

"There's a cemetery, not far away. We just passed it. We can leave him there."

Nicolas goes through the dead man's pocket, finds tobacco and a few pieces of hardtack. Next to his heart, folded in a piece of waxed cloth, is a leather wallet containing photos of a woman and a little boy in their Sunday best, a letter whose envelope he doesn't dare open, a newspaper clipping, and a fragment of a gold chain. He holds them in his palm for a

[11] Red shirt: Part of the "uniform" worn by followers of Garibaldi, some of whom came to France to fight alongside the Communards.

moment, these snippets of a life, and wonders what to do with them. He looks at the soot-blackened face of the dead man with its white beard stubble, and wishes he knew why he came here to die, so far from his loved ones. It strikes him that he doesn't really understand at all, deep down, what is driving these men and women to keep fighting, to hold the line when everything is starting to come apart, when they can't truly hope for anything but to stay alive. Is the dream that knits the proletariats of Europe together so strong as to bring these valiant hearts across rivers and mountains, leaving behind those dearest to them? Is the hope so wildly powerful that they're ready to die so that others, one day, can realize it?

Nicolas tucks the wallet into his pocket with his own relics: a medallion that belonged to his mother; a tiny bag of beach sand whose phantom aromas he breathes in sometimes with his eyes closed; a lock of Caroline's hair. He looks at the dead Italian again, remembers his name—ah yes, Ettore—searches his brain for a few words to say, to pay tribute to his sacrifice, but can think of nothing; nothing that anyone can hear, anyway. Then he rejoins the rest of the patrol, a somber group of silhouettes clustered on the side of the road. The artillery shells have destroyed a wall and split a tree in half the way lightning does, sometimes. The men are sitting beneath the tender green leaves of another tree, washing their cuts with water from their flasks and bandaging them with strips torn from their shirts. Red, leaning against a closed garden gate, has a bandage wound around his head. There is dried blood in his red hair.

"I'm fine," he says, before Nicolas can open his mouth. "It's nothing. Everything's all right, God damn it all. What do we do now, Sergeant?"

"One of our men has been killed. Ettore, the Italian. We can't leave him here."

"We'll have to carry him. We're already having trouble hauling ourselves around."

Red passes him some water. He rinses out his mouth, spits, swallows a couple of brackish mouthfuls.

A few men have gathered around the corpse, talking in low voices. One of them unrolls the blanket tied to his haversack, and they lift the dead man onto it.

"Look," says Nicolas.

Red stands up, straps on his rifle, and walks toward the others. He picks up a corner of the blanket, and they all lift it, breathing heavily. The sun has reappeared and shines down on the cortege, dazzlingly bright, obliging them to look down. Silently, stooping, they hobble along, their feet dragging. The bombardment has shifted toward the Porte d'Auteuil. A few shells overshoot the mark and explode farther away, but they don't even raise their heads any longer to see what might well be heading straight for them.

The small cemetery lying along the Rue Boileau has sustained heavy damage from the shelling. They wander for a moment among the uprooted tombstones, the shattered wooden crosses, the holes with their crushed caskets revealing contents no one wants to see. Nicolas remembers the stories his grandmother used to tell about the dead roaming near cemeteries or climbing church towers in the night to ring the bells at odd hours, waking you in the middle of a bad dream. He doesn't dare look down into the open graves at the grotesque faces revealed to the light. For a moment, he's reassured that the war hasn't awakened these terrifying sleepers, but, watching his comrades move silently among the tombs, somber and covered in filth, he wonders if perhaps they aren't dead already, all of them, and unaware of their fate, and suddenly terror floods through him, strangling and suffocating him, so he cries out to break the spell that could be possessing them all. "Let's go!" he cries, "Nothing for us here," and the men seem to come back to life, and he can hear their voices again, ringing and familiar, and then they're all back out in the street again, bearing their dead away from this place where they might have lost him and forgotten him.

It takes them an hour to reach La Muette via the deserted streets with their smell of fire, where they relinquish the Italian to an aid station set up in a school.

They are forced to shoulder their way through the crowd of stretcher-bearers, their rifles held in front of them. Women, their uncovered hair disheveled and tumbling, driven mad by the bombardments, walk alongside the moaning wounded, holding the hands of recently unconscious bodies, of bleeding, prostrate children with pale faces and staring eyes who suddenly begin screaming the moment they are set down on dirty mattresses covered in brown stains. Families search for their loved ones, shouting for new lists of the dead and injured to be posted, demanding to speak to some doctor who is nowhere to be found, lashing out at the harassed aid station attendants whose sleeves are rolled up to reveal forearms covered in blood, or falling to their knees in the street, blocking the way for others and praying to a God who will not answer them.

A hunchbacked old man and a very young girl lay Ettore's body out across two student desks in a room serving as a morgue and begin to wash him. The other men file out and only Adrien and Nicolas remain for a moment. "There's this, too," says the boy, lifting a corner of the blanket whose folds conceal the detached arm of their dead comrade. He hesitates, then takes the bare arm and offers it. The girl, already very pale beneath the mass of her dark hair, turns even whiter and looks away. "Now, now, my girl," says the old man, without looking up from what he's doing, "It's just part of him, that's all. You've seen others, haven't you?" The girl sighs and holds out her hands to Adrien. She takes the Italian's arm, trembling, and rests it against his side.

"His name is Ettore Ricciardi," says Nicolas. "105th federated battalion."

The old man makes a note in a wrinkled notebook with stained pages.

"Leave him with us now," he says. "We'll take good care of him. And, anyway, I think there's probably plenty for you to do out there."

They rejoin the others in the teeming courtyard filled with cries and sobs. The cannon fire, which had seemed to quiet down a bit, has started up again relentlessly. The sky occasionally darkens with enormous plumes of smoke pushed eastward by the breeze.

When they arrive on the Avenue de l'Empereur, they find hundreds of national guardsmen gathered before the town hall of the 16th arrondissement. Heavy artillery hastily brought down from the ramparts lines the sidewalks. There are some twenty guns, surrounded by chaotic heaps of ammunition crates. An officer is shouting for carriages to be brought so the cannons can be transported somewhere they will be useful, but no one listens to him. He calls for horses and gunners. He bellows at a colonel who screams back at him, "Horses? Horses? Mine died right under me at the Porte d'Auteil this morning at around ten o'clock. It's still there, if you're interested. Reassemble your men and put together an expedition yourself! Don't you see what's going on here?"

Nicolas spots Boisseau, one of his lieutenants from the 105th, a former blacksmith who won his stripes in battle during the first siege. He runs toward him, and the man turns and looks at him, astonished.

"I thought you'd all been killed, by God! What's happening at Point du Jour?"

"Not a soul left on the ramparts or the barricades. The Porte de Saint-Cloud is undefended. I had a look toward Billancourt; the place is crawling with Versaillais. We were under fire for two hours, lost a man. What about here?"

"Dombrowski wants to try something. I've just spoken with

him. He's looking for volunteers while we wait for the reinforcements he's requested from the Hôtel de Ville. Come with
me."

Nicolas trails after the lieutenant through the crowd of men
sitting in groups with their rifles as if they're planning to set up
lodgings right here. Two soldiers are standing guard in front of
the registry office, and Boisseau has to give his name and rank
before they let him pass. "This citizen is with me," he tells
them.

The room is hot as an oven. Nicolas is reminded of the
baker's where he used to take refuge sometimes when his
father came home drunk and nasty as a violent storm at sea.
Except that back then it was winter, when sometimes the rain
didn't stop for days and felt like it might soak your bones soft
and then dissolve you altogether like a handful of salt. His first
glimpse of the general is from behind, leaning over a table with
a map spread out on it. His uniform is covered with dust.
There is no saber at his belt, but a revolver in a black holster
instead. There are officers standing with him, listening and
nodding their heads. One of them asks when the ammunition
and rockets will arrive. Another assures him that they're
already on the way. "The servants, too?" Dombrowski asks,
not looking up from the map, which he seems to be searching
for some secret outcome, a hidden key. "Yes, of course," someone says. The Central Committee has taken the full measure of
the situation. Booby-trap the gates. Erect well-fortified barricades. Here and here. We still have five thousand men, and the
reinforcements will be here soon. We need civilians for the
earth-moving work. The men scratch their beards and think
aloud. The west of the city has emptied out even more over the
past three days. Paris is a ghost town.

"They'll never breach the city walls," declares one colonel,
the commander of the 9th legion. "We're strong enough to
stop them. All we need to do is reorganize, devil take it!"

He has spoken loudly, and the rest of the men fall silent and look at him. Dombrowski straightens up, massages the small of his back. He looks around blankly. His pale eyes seem drained of all color.

"If that's all we need to do, then we're saved."

Some of the men smile and start congratulating one another. Others look closely at the general, reading the irony in his expression. The colonel who spoke pastes a cheerful expression on his face with visible effort. Someone clears his throat; somebody else straightens his jacket. A few sabers clank softly. And in the depths of this silence, like a blood-thirsty lunatic breaking down a door, the endless thudding of the shells, and the faint tinkling of the glass chandelier over-head.

"Gentlemen . . . Citizens . . . we know what we have to do now."

The room empties out. Dombrowski doesn't move, still bent over the map, but his expression is vague and his gaze unfocused, lost, perhaps, in the examination of his own dark thoughts. The only ones still in the room are an aide-de-camp and two disheveled officers from his general staff, who slump heavily in their chairs, exhausted, exchanging doleful glances. Dombrowski walks to an armchair and sits down, head in his hands. He stays unmoving for long moments, dozing, perhaps, then looks up and notices Nicolas and his lieutenant.

"Ah, yes. Boisseau. Tonight, eight o'clock in the Auteuil market hall. We've managed to round up some free corpsmen taken from poorly commanded battalions."

He looks at Nicolas.

"I recognize you; it was you last night, the munitions cart and the battery in the Bois de Boulogne, wasn't it? You were at the Fort de Vanves the other day, with the 105th, I think?"

Nicolas nods.

"It's thanks to men like you that we might still win this

fight. But can we mobilize enough of them? About the action last night—I want to thank you again for your courage. It might not have done much good, as you can see, but at least we will have done all we could, no?"

The general tries to smile but can only manage a grimace. Nicolas draws in a deep breath and speaks.

"May I ask for your thoughts on the situation?"

Dombrowski scrutinizes his face. The other officers look up and straighten a bit in their seats, shaken out of their torpor.

"Right now, we should be hearing the drums of the five battalions I asked for, the wheels of the ammunition wagons. The whole arrondissement should be busy constructing barricades and installing the guns we still have on them. If that were the case, we might—might, I say—have a hope of regaining control of the situation, even if only temporarily. But do you hear any drums? During your reconnaissance this morning, did you see well-fortified, well-manned barricades?"

He shakes his head in irritation, slowly rubbing his hands together.

"Does that answer your question, Citizen?"

"Yes, sir. I—"

Dombrowski looks at him, his eyes shining with fatigue.

"If I may speak freely, I've had the same feeling as you for the past few days. Soon we'll have to fight street by street."

The general sighs. He settles himself more firmly in his chair, hands on the armrests.

"Then fight we shall. What else can we do?"

A tremendous explosion makes them all jump. Flakes of plaster drift down from the ceiling. A window quivers and then breaks. Dombrowski stands and scans the room, then puts on his cap and picks up his saber. He goes back to the table with the map, sweeping the plaster dust off of it with the back of his hand.

"Dust," he mutters. "Dust . . ."

"Come on," says Lieutenant Boisseau. "Let's go see what we can do."

Outside, the national guardsmen have leapt out of their neat little clusters. An artillery shell has fallen a hundred meters away. Black smoke billows out the windows of a low building. Nicolas looks for his men and spots them in the middle of the avenue, rifles shouldered, standing around a field mess kitchen, holding out their tin cups. The woman, assisted by a young boy, distributes brimming ladles of soup and fills mugs with coffee. She even has sugar, she announces, and the guardsmen rush to get a piece or two.

Nicolas manages to get a heel of bread and some bitter but hot coffee that he gulps down a few yards away from the crowd, standing in the sun beneath a crystalline blue sky, and in this moment of tranquility he lets himself be lulled by the quiet, closes his eyes, thinks of Caroline. But his heart beats faster and clenches painfully as he imagines her alone in a Paris on the edge of ruin. *Caroline*, he murmurs. But it's the bugle that answers him, a harsh sound like a scream. The order to fall in.

7

L alie had to deliver a finished item to an old lady customer on the Rue de Sèvres, so the mistress gave her the money to take a hansom cab. She had knocked on Caroline's door at around five o'clock, and Caroline opened it almost immediately, stretching, still sleepy, her hair tousled and her bodice undone. She'd tried to sleep, had managed an hour or two, was awakened again and again with a start by the terrible thudding explosions that inspired a horrific dream in which a wounded, mutilated man she was nursing turned suddenly toward her and was none other than Nicolas, disfigured and nearly dying. She'd dressed hastily, throwing a sky-blue shawl over her shoulders, and they left arm in arm, walking fast, Lalie chattering happily.

They'd found a hansom cab cruising for custom on the Boulevard du Montparnasse. The street was crowded with people dragging baggage and children, pushing wheelbarrows loaded with bags and the few possessions they had managed to take with them, all going in the same direction, fleeing the bombardments. Lalie finally fell silent, her face suddenly serious, watching the crowds come and go, and Caroline listened to the distant thunder of the cannons. Her nightmare returned unbidden, the ravaged face of her lover turning to her, groaning. Thirty minutes later, they climbed the stairs to the third-floor apartment of the customer, the widow of a cloth merchant, who opened the door with a heavy chair leg in her hand, but not before asking who was knocking, demanding specific details to be sure the insurgent rabble hadn't come to slit her throat. While Lalie unpacked the dress Mademoiselle Bastide had completely made over, the old lady watched the street from behind her curtains. *They will come, won't they? Don't you think they'll come?* Caroline asked who she was talking about, and the widow explained that she was awaiting the arrival of "our good soldiers," who would cleanse the streets of the common filth that had overrun them. That brave General MacMahon was already firing on the ramparts, and they'd soon remove these suppurating tumors infesting Paris with the point of a bayonet.

She had talked on and on, her wrinkled hand clutching the velvet curtain which she occasionally hid behind, panicked, as if someone down in the street might take umbrage at her surveillance. *I'll be the first one to spot them, and I'll go down to serve them my best wine, the one my husband kept for special occasions.* She favored the gown Lalie presented to her with a cursory glance and then slipped a hundred-sou coin into her hand before resuming her sentry duty. *Thank you, young lady. I'll pray for you, and for this detestable business to be over at last.*

Now they hurry into the busy streets, full of shouts and laughter and music. As they pass the barricades—more checkpoints, really, consisting of heaps of cobblestones and an overturned cart—they are catcalled here and there by idling national guardsmen and are even forced to send packing an oaf or two who claim to offer "safe conduct" with an arm around the waist. They cross the Seine via the Pont des Arts, and in the fresher air on the river they pause for a moment to gaze upon Paris, which looks so tranquil beneath the vast sky. They chat about little nothings before this vision, speaking of comfort, of beauty, of freedom. "When all this is over," Lalie says, "we'll be able to enjoy it." Caroline doesn't reply. When all this is over. For whom? When? How? A bullet in the head to erase the grand dream we've been pursuing for two months? She doesn't dare answer the girl, who is smiling romantically down at the river. She just takes her by the arm and steers her toward the opposite bank.

"Come now, enjoy your sweetheart's company. While . . ."

She doesn't finish. Lalie turns to her.

"While what?"

"While it's still light out, for heaven's sake!"

They shrug and smile at each other, then walk toward the Quai du Louvre and along the Seine, passing strolling couples and carriages keeping pace beside them. A brass band plays a polka, the horns clamoring joyfully. They buy two barley sugars from a white-bearded old man who has set up his stall on a cart; he smiles at them from beneath his derby hat, explaining that it's his wife who makes them. "For you it's free," he says to Lalie, "because you're in love. It's written all over your face." They walk on, laughing, crossing the path to reach the Rue du Louvre, where they are forced to stop at the barricade defending the street. A national guardsman perched atop the wall of cobblestones shouts at them to be on their way, holding his rifle in his hand and accompanying the words with a rude gesture. They walk away protesting indignantly, the man swearing at them. The neighborhood has been transformed into a trench camp teeming with patrols, the sidewalks of the Rue de Rivoli crowded with men, some of them seated in armchairs that have been tossed there or playing cards using ammunition crates as tables. They are often forced to retrace their steps and make unexpected detours, finally ending up on the Rue des Petit-Champs. Lalie starts to complain that her leg hurts; she twisted an ankle yesterday and has been limping ever since. She talks about hiring a hansom cab, saying that she has the money to pay for it. They walk on, the girl limping and sighing and muttering the name of her beloved to give herself courage. They walk up the nearly deserted Rue Notre-Dame-des-Victoires, forbidding in the shadows of the tall buildings. At the corner of the Boulevard Poissonnière, they spot another barricade and avoid it by taking the Rue Saint-Fiacre.

"That's it, now, really," says Lalie, reading the street sign. "I can't keep going like this, not all the way to Saint-Antoine."

Caroline takes her arm encouragingly, murmuring that they'll find a solution.

They emerge onto a boulevard swarming with people. Two carriages are going down toward the Opera, and one in the direction of the Place du Château-d'Eau. The latter is stopped, its path blocked by a crowd. They can see the dark form of the driver beneath a shapeless hat.

"Come on," Lalie says.

She takes off almost at a run. Caroline tries to hold her back for a moment, then decides to follow. Sitting down a bit and letting herself be carried after almost two hours of walking doesn't seem like a bad idea to her at all. The coach has started moving again; Lalie shouts to the driver to stop and open the door.

Caroline doesn't understand where the screams are coming from that make passersby turn and freeze in terror, screams that seem unending. Then she realizes that their source is inside the coach, which is picking up speed, Lalie clinging to the door and in danger of losing a foot, as a man's arm pushes her away, trying to close the door again. Running now, Caroline comes up alongside the carriage and seizes the door handle in her turn and sees the girls in chemises, screaming, pulling against the ropes and straps binding them.

Then everything turns upside down. She sees Lalie stumble and fall, rolling on the cobbles, and feels someone inside the coach grab the collar of her blouse. An awful blow strikes her in the temple, and she falls to her knees, catching hold of arms and cold hands flailing at the air in every direction, striking her, grasping at her clothes in their turn. Their cries have turned into moans and grunts, and she is on all fours, trying to protect herself from the kicking feet and scratching nails, and she can't see anything, can only feel the vibrations of the coach in her legs as it goes faster and faster, unable to speak or even cry out, conscious of nothing but the sensation of bouncing down the rocky slope of a bottomless abyss.

She's falling. She's rolling down a staircase without end. Her whole body hurts. Her head thuds against a wooden bar, her shoulders hitting a jerking, jolting floor. It's completely dark. Is she locked in a trunk?

A casket.

She tries to cry out, but a piece of cloth has been stuffed into her mouth, stopping her. She wants to take deep breaths, fill her lungs with air, try to calm the crazy pounding of her heart, but she chokes and splutters, suffocating, nostrils flaring wide. Then it all comes back to her: Lalie, the hansom cab, the horrifying sight of the girls, the man she didn't see. *He's taken me.*

Slowly, gradually, she manages to think. She's still in the hansom cab, which is jouncing roughly along a street or a road. She can feel rope around her wrists and ankles, cutting into her skin. A road. She pictures those parts of Paris where the roads have been picked apart, near the fortifications. The clusters of foul, shabby huts thick with misery as black as the faces of the boys clad in rags you see playing in puddles or pretending to be swordsmen on the boulevard. *He's taking me there to kill me and throw me in a ditch.*

She struggles, kicks at the wooden panel, moans from deep in her throat. *I'm going to die.* If she can only scream, she might wake herself up from this nightmare. She tries to free her hands from the cords binding them, but she can't do it, so she lies still, trying to calm her breathing and gather her thoughts. She imagines the minutes to come. They'll take her out of this trunk, this recess, and that will be the time to act, to call for help, to run. But it's nighttime. But her ankles are tied together. A wave of panic washes over her. She pictures a man with a knife in his hand. She can already feel the blade slicing into her throat, so sharp that she won't feel any pain at first, her life gushing in torrents from her gaping neck. She will watch herself die.

Maman. Come back. Maman will come back and chase them away and take me in her arms. I'm her little girl. Sometimes she used to hold me when someone had been nasty to me, and she soothed me and cradled me and whispered soft, sweet things into my ear.

The coach stops. She hears movement above her. She realizes that she's beneath a seat, in a trunk. They're talking. Muffled voices. The shifting gleam of a fire. The creak of a door opening. They're not coming for her. The fear ebbs. They aren't going to kill her. She tries to imagine what they're going to do with her. Maybe she isn't capable of imagining what they could do with her. Maybe it's better to be killed right away than to endure that.

No. Life. I will fight them.

A commotion in the carriage. She hears the girls moaning, the sound of them being struck. Their pleas. Then a deep silence in which she can hear the crackling of a fire.

Then, a sudden racket. A board is pulled away, and hands grip her by the arms and lift her. Come here. She can't see the man's face at all. She smells his acrid, animal odor. The smell of a stable. He makes her sit down on a seat in the coach, ties her by the wrist to a door. Don't move. Don't make a sound. Or he'll kill you. Believe me. He'll kill you. He takes a little vial out of his pocket. Drink this. It'll help you.

She is astonished by his soft, almost gentle voice. By his actions, too. Stripped of all brutality. A gloved hand supporting her neck as she drinks the bitter potion. And even his fingers, brushing the hair away from her face as if to see her better.

Don't move.

She doesn't move. She lets herself slip into a light doze, in a sort of cocoon that lulls her to sleep. A spider web, maybe.

8

The man behind the dividing wall insists loudly that he wants to see the police chief because there's been a horrific massacre and they have to come right away. His speech is slurred, his voice heavy with drink. Antoine Roques is in the midst of rereading the deposition of the Courbin woman, who continues to deny that her husband is a spy for Versailles, despite the maps, plans, and notes found in his desk during the search, which they've been thrusting in her face for hours. No, he's nothing but an honest citizen whose success isn't due to anything but hard work, never expected to be handed anything on a plate the way too many naïve and lazy people do these days, never broken even a minor law. Always on the side of law and order, of course, not like all these thieves being let out of prison so that decent people and even priests can be locked up instead.

She'd quickly regained control of her emotions. Éliette Andrieu, married name Courbin. She'd dried her tears and quieted her sobs to confront these two ad hoc policemen, appointed by the Reds or gone over to the enemy side, not bothering to conceal the hatred she felt for them, these awkward oafs veering between intimidation and restraint, these idiots trying to make her tell where her husband might be hiding now.

Antoine Roques listens to the guards trying to calm their drunken visitor, explaining that massacres are far from a rare occurrence right now, what with these Versaillais pigs trouncing the National Guard and bombarding Paris, and that he'd do better to go somewhere else and sleep it off if he doesn't want to get a good thrashing. The Quai de Jemmapes, he insists. He saw everything, three local grunts slaughtered like rabbits, bam! Bam! Bam! *And that other one, he was looking for somebody . . . can't remember the name . . . Clovis, or somethin' like that . . .*

Clovis. Not exactly a common name, and yet this is the second time he's heard it today. Luck comes when you least expect it, hand in hand with random chance. Better grab it before it gets away. When he steps into the hallway the man is being bundled toward the exit by a couple of guards. Roques orders them to stop and bring the man to him; he has to shout to make himself heard because the lobby of the police station is swarming with people who have come to file a complaint about the theft of a flower pot or the disappearance of a cat— the price of which, per kilo, has dropped sharply since the siege ended. The man shakes off the hands grasping him and hurries toward Roques.

"Ah! Here now!"

Roques ushers him into his office. The man sits down with a sigh, shaking his head as if to rid himself of his indignation at such treatment. He shifts his weight from one side of his rump to the other in his chair like a timid boy. He smells of cheap wine and old cheese. He's dressed in a worn smock that must have been blue once but is grayish now, stained and patched at the elbows. A sailor's cap is perched atop his gray hair. A thick mustache gives his face a surly look, and his shadowed, bleary eyes and sallow, deeply lined skin speak of immense fatigue. Antoine Roques asks his name, and he looks around warily from beneath his bushy eyebrows before answering:

"Colignon. Augustin Colignon. Born April 9, 1821, in Silly-en-Gouffern."

"Where?"

"Silly-en-Gouffern. It's in Orne, in Normandy. Even I forget where it is exactly, sometimes, you know. It's . . ."

"Why were you shouting like that? What's this massacre?"

Augustin Colignon shrinks back in his chair, which creaks shrilly. He looks down.

"Can't tell you. That fellow . . ."

"What fellow? Talk!"

Colignon stands up.

"Can't. Let me out of here."

"If you try to leave this office, I'll have you locked up for obstructing justice."

The man sits back down. He takes off his cap and sets it in his lap.

"Now, you were talking about a fellow . . ."

"I was at Miron's. Little dive on the Quai de Jemmapes. I think I must have fallen asleep. Miron don't care; he leaves me alone, long as I don't bother anyone, and at least it's quiet there, better than my place. Anyway, I about fell out of my chair when I heard it! Bam! Bam! Bam! Three gunshots, and that barbarian with his pistol, and the three others on the ground—well, one of them was on the table first, but then he fell, too. Lot of smoke, there was, too, room was full of it, you could hardly see, and it smelled like powder. Reminded me of the army. Sebastopol."

"You were at Sebastopol?"

"Damned right I was! Almost died there, too, like so many others!"

"So, your barbarian, as you call him . . ."

"Wore a big hat. I only saw him from the back, and when he saw me, he gave me one of those looks . . ."

The man trails off and covers his eyes with his hand, as if to protect himself from the killer's gaze, even now.

"It's a look you don't forget. Like his eyes were shooting fire, but black, you know?"

Antoine Roques can't quite picture it, but he can see that Colignon is trembling as he tells his story.

"Had you had much to drink?"

"No more'n usual. Two, three glasses, and just a bit of the hooch. Miron makes it special for good customers like me. But what I'm telling you, that's for sure—I saw and heard it all perfectly!"

"Go on."

"So I asked if I could leave, and I got out of there without even finishing my drink! He was a bizarre one, anyway, that fellow; his face was all smashed in under his hat, like he'd taken a shovel to the face. Nose flattened, and his . . . you know, above his eyes . . ."

"The brow bone."

"That's it! All crushed; you could hardly see his eyes! I saw men like that in the war, faces taken right off by a gunshot or an exploding shell. Not pretty to look at, the poor fellows, I can tell you that! Not many of 'em lived to tell the tale."

"But he spoke to them before he killed them, right? I heard you saying that in the corridor just now."

"He was looking for someone called Clovis. A cabman, I think. Looked like it meant a lot to him. I pretended to be asleep because I could tell the whole business was going to go sour. One of them asked him for money to tell where he was, the legendary Clovis. That's when he went after him and shot him. Must not've been in the mood to go to the bank; I understand that."

"Do you know him?"

"Who's that?"

"Clovis. The cabman."

"No. I know lots of people, not him, though. Name means nothing to me, I swear."

Roques levels a keen gaze at the man, hoping to look intimidating, as if he can see into the deepest reaches of Colignon's mind, to sow a bit of doubt and fear. But the other man stares back guilelessly, picking a clump of sleep out of the corner of one eye with a dirty fingernail.

"Where were the bodies? Did he kill them all in the same place?"

"Near the door, in front of the window. Practically in a heap, all three of them, stone dead."

Roques stands, opens the office door, and calls a guard.

"Put him in the staff room. Don't let him out of your sight. I've got to go out."

He calls for Loubet, who appears immediately.

"Come on; we're going out."

"Alone?"

"Yes, alone. You have your gun?"

"Always, these days. We'd be the only ones in Paris without one!"

On the way, Antoine explains the reason for their errand. A triple murder. A man with a battered face, a mysterious cab-man named Clovis, probably mixed up in the kidnapping of a young girl. Loubet, happy to be doing real police work again at last, like before, doesn't question it.

"Do you miss the Empire? The siege?"

The inspector gestures emphatically in denial. "God, no! But you must admit, since the Commune came into being, we haven't had much to do! Fewer thefts, fewer crimes. But what I love about police work is chasing down thieves and criminals and arresting them, you see?"

Roques understands. This morning, during the failed arrest of Courbin, the Versaillais spy, he felt that instinctive impulse, that sort of inner thrill, in spite of the shootout. He nods.

They arrive on the quay as twilight is falling. The water in the canal is the color of lead. A very small boy dressed in rags fishes with a line tied to a long stick. He clicks his tongue to attract the fish as if they were chickens.

"They biting?" Loubet asks.

The boy looks up and eyes him from beneath the brim of his cap, then spits in the water.

"Watch it, smells like pigs around here," he mutters.

"So young, and yet he's already got a keen nose," Roques says.

"It's instinct. Some family lines, it's in the blood. Condition of survival for them. Like animals who have to learn very early to detect predators."

"You can't say that. They're human beings. I can't believe you'd even make the comparison. Society isn't a jungle where the stronger ones always control and feed off the weaker ones."

"And yet that's what's happening, isn't it? That's how things work, seems to me. Don't they?"

"They do, but it's not written anywhere that it always has to be like that. That's the world the people have risen up against; it's why the Commune was formed, why it's fighting, to build something new. Don't you think? Dignity, equality, liberty— they're still to be won."

Loubet shrugs. "If you say so . . . sure, you're right," he says, without conviction.

Roques is about to ask him why exactly he joined the insurrection in its first days, but just then he spies the bar a bit farther along the quay.

Miron Wines and Liquors

The name of the place is clumsily written in green on a yellow board hung over the door. A crude representation of a barrel fashioned of sheet-iron and painted bright red serves as a sign.

They enter the tavern, which is dark and completely empty, lit only by two lanterns hanging from posts. The owner is sitting at one of the tables. Playing cards are scattered across its surface, and he is holding one in his hand, considering his next move. Finally he decides, and only then does he deign to turn to Roques and Loubet, gathering up his cards as he does.

"Well, well, here's a couple of smart gentlemen. And yet I managed to win anyway. It wasn't easy. What can I get you? On the house."

He walks around behind the bar, feet shuffling, and lights an oil lamp, which he sets on a shelf in front of a mirror. Then, hands flat on the zinc counter, he looks from one to the other, awaiting their orders.

"Sûreté Genérale," says Loubet.

"I didn't doubt it for a moment."

"Are you Hector Miron, the proprietor of this . . . establishment?"

"Yes, that's me, in the flesh. Will you have a drink?"

They don't answer and begin surveying the room. Antoine Roques starts off in one direction, Loubet in the other. The air smells of soft-soap and cheap wine. There is a vast dark spot on the beaten-earth floor near the window. Roques stoops down and scratches a fingernail across the dampness. Loubet disappears into the shadows at the back of the room. They can hear him opening and then closing a door.

"There's an exit out the back."

The owner rolls himself a cigarette behind his counter, lights it, blows the smoke toward the two policemen.

"May I ask what you're looking for?"

Antoine Roques approaches him, smiling widely.

"Of course. I think you might even be able to tell us. Three men were shot dead here with a revolver early this afternoon. Did you happen to see or hear anything, by any chance?"

Miron twists his mouth, knits his eyebrows. Acts like he's searching his memory. Roques wants to backhand him across the face, teach him a few things about being a mocking little prat.

"No, can't say I recall anything. Not a lot of people have

been through here today. Folks' minds are on other things at the moment."

Roques sighs. Reaches deep within himself for the strength not to leap over the counter or break a chair over the man's head.

"They fell here, in front of the window. Does that still not help your memory at all? Perhaps you were out at the time, and nobody told you anything? In that case, the bodies could have been removed without your knowledge. We aren't always in control of everything, even in our own homes, you know. And I'd understand if you didn't want to admit to such a minor weakness, in front of us."

Miron's face has lost some of its arrogance. He looks at this *flicard*, so calm and courteous, talking the way people do in books, and he seems caught between a rock and a hard place. He is undoubtedly used to rougher manners from the city sergeants and the middle class. Roques can sense him questioning his own assumptions, his frame of reference wavering. He takes a bottle down from the shelf behind him and pours himself a stiff drink.

Roques catches the scent of plums from his glass.

"Who told you these ridiculous things? That idiot Gustin, I'll bet. He was deep in his cups, I can tell you. I had to throw him out because at a certain point, he turns into a total crackpot. Last week he saw a three-master sailing on the canal, even saw sailors on the bridge. Does that sound like a man with all his marbles to you? I threw him out because after a few glasses he can't remember how much he's drunk and refuses to pay. Not that I don't give him credit; I even let him drink for free sometimes, have for as long as he's been coming here. But, you understand, characters like that aren't good for the reputation of an honest establishment . . ."

Roques nods, smiling, waiting for the flow of hogwash to dry up. "Especially one managed by a respectable and law-abiding individual such as yourself," he says. "That's exactly why we've come to talk to you."

Miron senses the irony in his voice. He's about to respond but catches himself, hesitates, drains his glass, slurping at the last traces of alcohol.

"We're wasting time," Loubet murmurs. "I'll deal with him."

Antoine Roques stops him with a gesture.

"So nothing happened. Duly noted. By the way, do you happen to know a man named Clovis? A cabman by trade. They say he's often seen around this neighborhood."

The man nods immediately, seeming relieved to be able to give them something. "Yes, I know him. He comes in for a drink or two sometimes. Lives over by the locks, on the Chemin de Pantin. He's even got a little patch of grass for his coach and nag."

"What about the man who was looking for him?"

The bar owner steps back, flapping a hand in front of him. "No . . . I . . . I've got nothing more to say to you. I don't know anything."

"Are you afraid? Of him? Why, if you don't know him?"

"Leave me be. You can arrest me if you want. Throw me in the clink. I'll never talk."

"Three deaths is no small matter," observes Loubet. "You might have killed them yourself, after all. That would explain why you made them disappear, no? Three isn't as many as Troppmann,[12] but that won't matter on the scaffold."

Miron shrugs his shoulders and lets out a chuckle.

---

[12] Jean-Baptiste Troppmann: Convicted of killing, for financial gain, a whole family (four children and their mother) in a field in Pantin in September 1870, after previously killing the father and oldest brother. This "Pantin massacre," to use the term coined by police investigators and obligingly repeated in *Le Petit Journal*, had an enormous public impact at the time. Troppmann was guillotined on January 19, 1870; his execution at Roquette prison drew a large crowd.

"Look around you. Who's had time to worry about three stiffs in the past few weeks? This whole godforsaken Commune is about to turn into a giant slaughterhouse, a massive free-for-all, you'll see, when the bourgeois come back with their army of fusiliers. I knew this whole mess would end badly. There are rich people and poor people, it's always going to be that way, and the rich will always be stronger than the poor because they know how to stick together to protect their piece of the pie. The plebs are too stupid to do the same thing. We'll be forcing them to eat their own shit in the end, and there won't be enough for everyone, and people will fight each other to get a bite."

He falls silent and pours himself another shot of plum brandy. "Who'm I kidding," he mutters, as if talking to himself. "We're already eating shit."

He leans toward Loubet, points a trembling finger at him. "And let me tell you something, copper. I couldn't care less about Madame la Guillotine. You can bed down on top of her if that makes you happy. When the time comes, I'm going to a barricade in Belleville, where I've got some pals who really believe—strong as iron—and I'll let myself be blown full of holes to show Thiers and his dogs how we die with panache around here. But not before killing a few of those bastards myself, by God! So do whatever you want. But figure it out fast because it's closing time. I'm not getting any more customers in here today; the two of you are bad for business."

Loubet looks questioningly at Antoine Roques. The Federate police chief doesn't know what to think anymore; he tries to compose his thoughts a bit before speaking. He knows where to find the cabman; he has learned of a disfigured killer's existence, and he's starting to believe the two might be linked to the kidnapping in the Rue Oberkampf. He turns to Miron.

"Close your pigsty for the day then, if you want. But I'll come back tomorrow with an official order for administrative closure. I can't prove anything for now, and I don't have any more time to waste with you. But tomorrow I'll have my men with me, we're going to find our evidence, and then we'll help you shut down for good."

The man doesn't answer, and they leave. Night is already falling, the sky darkened by black clouds moving in slowly from the west.

"I don't get it," Loubet says. "That pathetic wretch deserves to spend the night in prison. You saw him laughing at us."

"Possibly. But we won't get anything else out of him today, and I think we should keep him on the griddle for a few more days, with this threat of closure. He'll crack eventually; I'm certain of it. One thing's for sure; he's terrified of this killer Colignon told me about, the man with the messed-up face . . . and I don't think it's his face that's scaring people, I think it's something else. As if this man gives off a sensation, something like an odor—you can't see it, but you feel its effects. A whiff of evil, of malevolence. I don't know how to describe it. Remember that he shot these three men without flinching, from what the witness said. And if he's mixed up in this kidnapping, as I'm beginning to think he is—and maybe in others, too—it's possible we're dealing with someone particularly dangerous, someone whose soul is completely corrupt."

Loubet laughs softly. "You're beginning to develop a taste for it, aren't you?"

"For what?"

"Police work. You're even convincing me."

They take a few more steps. Roques looks for the boy who was fishing earlier but sees only a young couple holding hands, walking swiftly, laughing unreservedly.

"Can I buy you a beer?" asks Loubet. "This is worth toasting!"

They reach the Rue des Récollets and turn on the Rue du Faubourg Saint-Martin. Arriving on the boulevard, they see a café whose windows are full of light, twenty meters behind a barricade. People are singing and shouting. Women's laughter ripples like a stream in the shadows.

"Here," says Roques. "This looks like a good place."

9

The 105th has been assigned to the Place du Roi de Rome, where three barricades were hastily constructed the previous week when the Versaillais threat became clear. They've spent the rest of the afternoon digging holes in front of the redoubts, bringing cobblestones and sacks of earth to reinforce the crude heaps piled there like at the stake where Joan of Arc was burned. It has to be able to hold for at least an hour under fire, enough time to retreat in an orderly fashion.

Cannons have been brought, mostly eight-pounders, and immediately arranged in a battery. On the butte of Trocadéro, two twelve-pound cannons are meant to hold the barrier that the square now constitutes.

Earlier, Nicolas and Red climbed the small hill via the massive granite staircase and saw immediately that despite all these measures they would be overwhelmed within fifteen minutes. Enemy troops would infiltrate the adjacent streets and attack the defenders from the rear. The gunners showed them their ammunition: forty shells, no more.

"We'll have to be sparing with what we've got and be sharp with the backsight adjuster," said a sailor, spitting on the ground. "We'd need ten cannons and five hundred shells to hold the position and have a chance of slowing them down a bit. Look there; look at that firepower. When all that enters Paris, nothing'll be able to stop it."

He indicated the curtain of black smoke lit from within by explosions destroying fortifications and blasting monstrous cavities in the streets. There were fires everywhere; people weren't even trying to put them out any longer. The wind carried the odors of burning and gunpowder to their noses, and they felt cinders sticking to their skin and brushed them away with hands already soot-blackened.

"We can't hold this. We'll leg it as soon as things start heating up. What good would it do for us to die slumped over our guns? We'll be more useful somewhere else, where there are people to protect. All those bourgeois pigs have left here already; what's the point? Let them bomb their own pretty houses. What the hell does it matter?"

The coppery light of the sinking sun glared blindingly through a gap in the wall, and they pulled down the brims of their military caps. Nicolas and Red went back down toward the square, where the men were lining up at the mess wagons. They ate a decent hash prepared by two grim-faced women dressed in black, one of them short and round, the other slender, almost skinny, reminding Nicolas of the February evening when Caroline had taken him to listen to Louise Michel speak at a club in the 18th arrondissement. The woman's tall, dark figure had appeared on the platform, and the room had exploded with joyous applause the speaker had had difficulty quietening, a shy smile on her lips and a laughing look in her eyes which, as soon as the room was silent again, had regained their grave expression, their piercing intensity. Then her voice had risen, warm and powerful, the full force of her breath driving each word, and Nicolas had had the feeling, during these long moments when thought and deed were one and the same, that the crowd—mostly women—didn't dare catch its breath before she did. The flow of her words was interrupted here and there by applause, and everyone took advantage of these pauses to shout, to cough, to exchange a snatch of conversation with a neighbor. They had emerged into the cold night with brains buzzing and hearts thumping, and they had gone with some others to drink a beer on the boulevard, happy and dreamy-eyed.

Thinking back to that night fills his chest with a dull pain he's never felt before. He has never missed Caroline so fiercely. He'd always been impatient to see her, of course, knowing once they were together that these were the happiest moments of his life, so much so that he'd wondered sometimes if such fulfillment, such peaceful joy, weren't simply an illusion that could vanish at any moment like the popping of a soap bubble or a childish dream. But this is something else, and he can think of only one word to describe it: fear. The fear of knowing she is far away from him, and thus alone, because he's certain he could protect her better than anyone else. The fear of losing her. It gnaws at his insides, aching like a punch to the gut, leaving a painful, carved-out place in its wake. It turns his stomach, makes it hard for him to breathe.

In the twilight, lit by the glow of burning buildings, red-gold flames rising above the rooftops, he can hear the incessant rumble of the cannonade, like the belching of a monster devouring everything in its path. He looks around him at the men chatting, laughing, smoking their pipes, lounging on the ground near stacks of rifles. Some of them look pensive, but most affect the very air of resolute calm he lacks. He doesn't know if they're resigned to defeat or merely bound by the furious desire not to be vanquished without a fight. For the first time in his life perhaps, since he's been old enough to think and to have memories, he feels truly alone, and the thought of shortly being even more so is terrifying.

He looks around for his friends and spots Adrien near the mess wagons, talking to the tall woman in black. She still had a coffee pot on the fire, its sides burnt black, and hands the youth a cup of dark, steaming brew. As he nears them, Nicolas realizes they are talking of Le Bourget.

"We were practically neighbors, and we didn't even know

each other!" the boy says, with a wide smile. "Let me introduce you to Madame Lucienne, from Le Bourget. She must
have left after the battle with the Prusscos, just like I did!"

"I lost everything. My husband, my little shop, everything!
My sister and I ran through the ruins—bullets whistling past
our heads, so close we could hear them—and we managed to
make it here, to Paris. And now, wouldn't you know it, there's
a war on here, too, except this time it's the people who are
being attacked by 'respectable' French citizens, those bastards! Well . . ."

She stops for breath and puts a hand on Adrien's shoulder.

"Yes, we're both locals! I knew his mother before she was
married," the woman said. "A wonderful girl; everyone loved
her! If she could talk, my sister would say the same. Right,
Rita?"

Rita nods and presses a hand to her heart.

Madame Lucienne ruffles Adrien's hair, and he closes his
eyes like a cat being scratched behind the ears.

"You knew her better than I did. I was only five when
she . . ."

"And so smart, so industrious! She always regretted not having gone to school. Would have liked to be a teacher. She'd
started working with Rita, teaching her to speak, but she didn't
get to finish, poor thing."

Adrien looks about ten years old, and he suddenly seems
very small to Nicolas in his National Guard uniform, with the
wide leather belt hung with cartridges and the long Prussian
dagger the boy has never wanted to talk about. He listens to
them listing their common acquaintances with pleased exclamations and bursts of laughter, the anecdotes and memories
they evoke distracting him for a moment from his own melancholy thoughts.

Two shells explode at almost the same instant on the
Avenue de l'Empereur. The ground trembles under their feet.

The cart serving as a mess wagon creaks and shakes, its pots and pans clanking. The mess woman darts a glance at the plumes of smoke blossoming in the middle of the road, accompanied by the sharp cracking sound of windows breaking. Rita rolls terrified eyes and sets about putting out their cooking fire, then begins stowing away the dishes.

"We're getting out of here now, and fast. We're going to head toward Saint-Michel and the Pantheon; I need more supplies, and there are people needing to be fed there, too. Can't be of any more use here. I've been told the National Guard supply office will look after you now, lucky dogs!"

A small man with a mustache passing by overhears her and lets out a guffaw. "The supply office! If you don't need anything, they say, feel free to ask them for it! For two days now we haven't seen so much as a crust of bread, not even a sip of broth! We'll end up eating cats, like during the siege!"

He staggers off, waving his arms, shouting about the wait making him thirsty.

"I'd come with you if I didn't have anything else to do," says Adrien. "I think I'd quite enjoy cooking up some grub. I'm pretty good at it, actually."

The woman puts her hands on his shoulders.

"When this is all over, I'm going to open a little restaurant near Aubervilliers. I know a place that's to rent, perfectly situated, and I'll hire you as a cook! You're a butcher in civilian life, too, and you know charcuterie; we should do business! We'll feed the laborers and the poor."

She puts her arms around Adrien and hugs him tightly. He nestles against her thin chest, closes his eyes, smiling softly.

"Go on now, my boy. You look out for yourself. You know where to find me in Le Bourget; you can come any time you like. I'll be waiting for you."

The boy thanks her. Madame Lucienne. He murmurs her name several times, low, for his own ears alone, like a good-luck mantra. Nicolas takes his arm. The woman is packing up the last of their things, her sister hitching up the donkey that pulls their cart.

"Come on," says Nicolas, quietly. "We can't stay here. Let them go."

They move away slowly. Federates have gathered at the barricade defending the Rue de Passy. A hundred of them, standing immobile around an officer perched on the tongue of a wagon. Red catches up to them.

"Wroblewski has withdrawn from La Butte-aux-Cailles, apparently. Things aren't looking good," he says.

They approach the improvised assembly. The man speaking is a colonel. The situation is difficult, he says, but Paris is preparing to resist heroically. All of the troops manning the strongholds outside the ramparts have been forced to withdraw into the city. Now another battle is brewing, one in which the National Guard, fighting in its own territory, would have the advantage. Barricades are being erected everywhere.

Murmurs. Mocking laughter among the men.

"Where are the reinforcements? We have to get out before we're trapped!"

"And the ammunition?"

"What point is there in defending the wealthy areas? They're already destroying their own palaces!"

A clamor of voices arises, every man calling out his own solution. One group crouches around a captain who is tracing strategic diagrams in the dirt.

"Everyone to your positions!" shouts the colonel.

Some national guardsmen approach him.

"We should organize patrols and do reconnaissance all the way to the gates! Saint-Cloud, Auteuil, La Muette! Leave no room to be surprised! We're not going to stay here and wait for them!"

"Shut your damned mouth, Colonel!"

Sergeants are already moving off, calling their men to decide what they should do. Soldiers come running from all over the square to hear the news. Small groups form. What to do? Good questions are asked, impossible answers given. It seems that Dombrowski is going to attempt a sortie. La Cécilia is planning something. They want to be part of it. But no. The Polish general knows what he's doing. Don't disturb him in his maneuvering. How many men? Two thousand? Not even. Free corps.

No one knows anymore.

The colonel starts speaking again, calling on the courage and discipline of the National Guard, but no one is listening to him now. He leaps down from his perch and pulls out his revolver, which he waves in the faces of the men surrounding him.

"I'll make you fall in line! I'll shoot any man guilty of insubordination!"

He belches and wipes the slobber from his mouth with the back of his hand. They laugh in his face, meeting his gaze scornfully. Soon he is speaking only to men's backs.

"That would be quite something, for us to kill each other," Red remarks to the colonel.

His powerful voice carries over the rest of the conversations.

"Do you think there are too many of us, so many you want to weed a few out with your gun? If you're looking for someone to start with, here I am! Because I'm sick of you, you and your pretty speeches! Go on! Maybe your bullets will hurt less than the line infantry's! And then at least I won't be here to see the catastrophe you're leading us straight into!"

He sticks out his chest, offering it to the colonel. Silence falls and stretches on and on. Soldiers approach him, but make no further move. The colonel stares at Red, biting on his mustache, his fist hanging by his side. Every eye is fixed on him.

Men come and position themselves around Red. Nicolas puts a hand on his shoulder; Adrien takes him by the arm.

"Six bullets won't be enough. See how many of us there are," says a voice.

Night falls slowly on them all in a silence broken only by the pounding of the bombardment. Between the thundering impacts, which come closer and closer together, they can hear the sound of buildings collapsing. Their faces turn pale, almost white, and it is a strange, wan crowd that waits now for the officer to make some decision.

He looks at the revolver in his hand and shrugs, stowing it in his holster.

"Imbeciles," he mutters between his teeth, looking around at all of them. "You really don't understand . . ."

The men part to let him pass. He walks with his head down, then pauses. Slowly, he turns back to Red.

"How could you . . ."

His voice breaks. He clears his throat and resumes.

"How could you expect an officer of the Commune to fire on a soldier of the Commune? Have we gone crazy—you and me, but me especially—that it's come to this, that we'd even think about it? After these weeks of mad hope, of dreams finally made possible? I'd like to believe we haven't lost that— humanity that all this violence against us can never destroy. I don't know how people will speak of us when we're gone, but at least they won't be able to reproach us with having killed our own."

He tries to smile, but his face twists into a bitter grimace. He turns quickly and walks with long strides toward the ammunition wagons in the center of the square. The men disperse, murmuring. Red asks Nicolas if it was the Commune that produced this kind of men, upright and wise.

"Or is it these men that produced the Commune, instead . . . ?"

"Look at us," jokes Adrien, "philosophers now, are we? I could use a drink to get the taste of this out of my mouth! What do you think—one last glass before the battle?"

He isn't laughing anymore. He rummages in his pockets, where a few coins clink. He glances over at Madame Lucienne and her sister, who are just finishing hitching their donkey to the mess wagon.

"Well, shit," he says. "Guess I'm going to see how these guns work, first. At least then I can be sure of understanding something."

Nicolas and Red watch him set off for the barricade on the Avenue de l'Empereur, dragging his feet, his rifle on his shoulder.

"What are we waiting for?" asks Red.

"Beats me. It's a funny question, isn't it? In theory, we know what we're waiting for, right? Or at least we're hoping for something vague."

"Bread for the kids and schools so they'll be less stupid than us?"

"That's one example."

"But waiting's not enough. It's not like a train—it won't come unless you go looking for it. That's the Commune, I think. We've gone to look for it instead of waiting a few more centuries for it to fall into our laps."

Close by, on the Rue Franklin, an artillery shell explodes on a rooftop, decapitating the building. Pieces of the roof fly into the air and crash to the ground around them. Loose stones roll at their feet. They smell gunpowder and burning wood. Red looks up at the cloud of smoke drifting over their heads.

"Will they ever stop?"

"You have a gift for asking impossible questions."

Red sighs.

"I'm tired. I'm going to try and get some sleep. They'll know where to find me if things heat up. What about you?"

"I'll stay here for a bit."

They go their separate ways. When he looks back, Nicolas can see nothing of his friend but a dark silhouette walking quickly toward a group of guards sitting or lying down alongside crates of ammunition. The night begins to blur shapes, to drain colors. He walks back to the empty quay and climbs over a barrier intended to defend the Pont d'Iéna, where a dozen guards doze, leaning against the parapet. In front of him, on the Champ de Mars, campfires burn in a village of huts where battalions from the 14th and 15th legions are billeted. He can make out the comings and goings of sentries, a few storm lanterns hung from posts casting their quivering gleam. His steps reverberate off the dark façades of the buildings lining the deserted streets. The gas lamps have been extinguished, and the night seems to spread outward like mist from the corners, the cellar windows, the alleys where rats scurry. Here and there he spots the flame of a brazier, hears the distant echo of the conversations around a barricade.

A pair of lamps mark the entrance to the clinic on the Rue Lecourbe where Caroline spends her days and some of her nights. It's a school that's been abandoned for ten days, evacuated as the bombardments grew nearer, its classrooms transformed into dormitories, and as soon as he steps inside, a fetid odor mingled with the smell of chloroform hits the back of his throat and makes his stomach flip over. Pushing open the door of the first room, he can see nothing in the gleam of the night lamps suspended from the ceiling but the row of pallets on which the wounded are lying. A sliver of light shows from another room at the far end of the chamber, and he picks his way on tiptoe through the darkness where he can sense, rather than see, the men moving restlessly in their sleep, mumbling and snoring, here and there a faint complaint or the whine of a sick child. Nicolas hardly dares to breathe for fear of signaling his presence to these exhausted bodies, the stench of gangrene and filth so thick in the air that it seems to cling to him, and he's afraid that he stinks now, too, that he's as grimy as they are, his skin crusted with dirt and permeated with smoke, soaked with sweat for two days straight. He feels suddenly ashamed of showing himself to Caroline in this state; he examines the hands he can't see, knows they're dirty, greasy, the fingernails black. He rubs them against his jacket, vowing not to touch her until he's washed them.

In the next room, lit by two candelabra and an oil lamp, he finds a woman sitting asleep at a table, her head resting on her folded arms. All around her are piles of neatly folded cloths, vials of brown or transparent liquids, earthenware pots lined up on a shelf like at an apothecary's shop. He knocks softly on the door, and she wakes with a start and a little cry, turning toward him openmouthed, eyes wide with fear. She is young and redheaded, her green eyes round with surprise and terror. She asks, stammering, what he's doing there, who he is, darting dismayed glances around the room.

"Are you Émilie?"

She nods, her red hair gleaming in the flickering light.

"I'm looking for Caroline."

She stands up, stretching, hands at the small of her back. He sees her fatigue then, her drooping eyelids.

"I was asleep," she says, as if in apology. "It's quiet tonight."

The bombs are silent for a moment, and they look at each other, in astonishment, perhaps. Nicolas counts the seconds in his mind as if, by continuing to count, he could make the respite last. String time out like a rosary, to make the prayer go on longer. The parish priest did it in his ice-cold church, his eyes closed, lips moving, on his knees before a granite Christ. The silence seems to oppress the young girl, and she sits down again heavily, her face sorrowful.

"Who are you?"

Nicolas turns toward the new voice, a man's. He is short

and stocky, broad-shouldered, dressed in an overlarge smock of roughly woven cotton and an apron stained with blood. His sleeves are rolled up, showing powerful forearms. He looks like a butcher. He has the fierce air of a slaughterman, but he wears the fine gold-rimmed glasses of a philosopher.

"I'm looking for Caroline. Are you Doctor Fontaine? She told me—"

"She didn't come in today. We were expecting her at six o'clock this evening. Nobody's seen her since yesterday morning. Who's asking for her?"

"Nicolas Bellec. Sergeant, 105th."

The doctor scrutinizes his face. "She's mentioned you. What are you doing out in this state, at this hour?"

"I've come from the Place du Roi de Rome. We're holding three barricades there. My watch doesn't start until five o'clock, so I thought I'd . . ."

The man listens, nodding. He takes off his glasses and wipes them with a handkerchief he pulls from his pocket.

"Do you think she'll be in later? I could wait for her . . ."

"She's never been late. She even has a habit of coming in earlier than she's supposed to and leaving in the morning well after the day shift nurses have already arrived. You should go and rest, get a bit of sleep before your watch. I'll tell Caroline you were here as soon as I see her. Isn't that right, Émilie?"

They both turn to the young girl, who has fallen asleep at the table again.

"You see," says Doctor Fontaine. "Everyone's exhausted. A young girl like that, she should have been dancing at a ball tonight. Her friends came looking for her, but she preferred to stay here, to keep watch in this storage room amid the blood and the moaning, and look, the fatigue has caught up with her."

In the common room, a man screams, then begins weeping and moaning. Émilie wakes up again, stands, but the doctor gestures for her to sit back down.

"Don't stay here," he says to Nicolas. "This is no place for you."

"Not tonight, no. But who knows what tomorrow will bring? And besides, if you're here, at least you're not dead."

Fontaine smiles sadly.

"Sometimes that would be better. Some lives are unlivable. Did you know some people here beg us to kill them? Twenty years old, blind and deaf, or with both legs amputated. Sometimes I don't know what keeps me from . . ."

He turns away abruptly, takes a lamp from a desk, lights it. The man in the dimly lit room next door is still groaning. They can hear others stirring on their pallets and complaining. Fontaine walks off, the light in his hand casting its swaying yellowish glow on the men on the floor, on their bandaged faces.

Nicolas flees, pursued by the plaintive noises of the room, brushing and shaking at his clothing to rid it of the smell. He is almost running in the shadows beneath a lowering ceiling of clouds lit by explosions, tripping and stumbling, and he jumps with sudden fear when he sees a lantern bobbing at the end of a street. The Boulevard du Montparnasse is a dark trench dotted with a few quivering lights. He couldn't exist there; there's nothing beyond the fiery night but a hellish nothingness. He stops in the middle of the road, turns southward, and it seems that a horde of silent disembowelers, clawed demons, will come surging out of the blackness at any moment. He had the same terrors when he was a little boy in bed on his creaking mattress, on stormy nights when some elderly relative or other had woven horrible tales of ghosts and revenants in front of the fireplace. He imagined creatures emerging from the sea, hurled ashore by gigantic waves, crawling through the streets of the village, scratching at the doors and tapping at shutters, crying like children, and he thought that someone in his house—his mother, maybe, or one of his sisters—might take pity on them, moved by their groans, and would open the door and let them in, and he imagined the carnage that would follow. He lets these childhood obsessions wash over him now, and the memory of his sisters and his mother suddenly fills his mind, and once again he feels alone and lost in the depths of an endless night where all roads fade to nothingness.

From behind him comes a burst of booming laughter. Women's shouts. A song. An out-of-tune bugle and cascading laughter echoing in the dim light of a lantern. The din is coming from the barricade on the Rue Vavin. An accordion whines and then begins its melody. A polka. They must be dancing. Nicolas smiles. The monsters withdraw back into the shadows.

Caroline.

On the Rue de Constantine, the sky is a shifting, red-tinged, glowing ceiling. The cannon fire is less intense here, but the closer explosions make the air vibrate, and occasionally they hear the leaves of an acacia tree whispering as it leans over the barrier from behind a garden gate. He goes into the building and up to the third floor; he wants to shout, to call out, but he stops on the landing because his legs suddenly refuse to climb the stairs. He stays there for a moment, leaning against the wall, and his eyes gradually grow accustomed to the darkness and he makes out a sort of ocher vapor cloud hovering in the stairwell like the breath of a dragon. He looks up at the chamber door and hopes, fleetingly, that it will open and that Caroline will appear, a lamp in her hand, smiling at him. But then he tells himself that she must be sleeping. He climbs the last few steps and feels for the key in the hole in the wall where they always hide it. When he opens the door, a faint scent of soap and lavender reaches his nostrils, and he goes toward the empty bed and lifts the blanket and sheet—in vain, he knows, because sometimes hope is so strong that it believes in magic. He lights a candle, and the golden flicker soothes him and he gives himself up, in the perfumed clutter of the room, to the deep, heavy sleep of brutes and lovers.

SATURDAY, MAY 20TH

10

They had to calm them down, because what happened on the Boulevard Saint-Martin had whipped them into a frenzy, and he and Clovis had to punch and kick them until they quieted down a bit, forcing them to drink large glass-fuls of the potion so they'd go to sleep right away and allow themselves to be transported without alerting all of Paris, a city ready to gather into mobs on the slightest pretext at the moment, anyway. Now they've also had to deal with this other one, who all but got into the cab while it was moving, whom they knocked out and tied up, then hid in a trunk built beneath a seat. Pujols wanted to kill her and dump her body in the remote area where they stopped to bind her, but Clovis refused to do it, arguing that it was too dangerous so close to inhabited buildings.

Pujols has made sure the girls don't have too many visible signs of the beating they gave them; Clovis managed not to get carried away this time. The shapeless, inarticulate ape in his carapace of cloaks, leather boots, and battered hat, face hidden by the hairy non-beard clearly linking him to his tree-climbing cousins at the zoo—Clovis, savage and placid, can sometimes become a dangerous machine, quick and violent and difficult to stop. Fortunately, in the cramped confines of the cab, his punches lacked force and momentum, and they were enough to quiet the girls down without marking them too much.

Quickly they slipped into the inky blackness of a moonless night in a part of the city tapering quickly into a straggling bunch of ramshackle huts and tiny stone houses, sometimes former farm outbuildings, set on either side of streets that were still country roads and led to villages outside the fortifications. Clovis had to light the carriage lamps because the horse kept stopping and shying, frightened, maybe, by the shadows that swallowed everything up, the ground shifting beneath its shoes and the coach's wheels in muddy puddles or skidding on the disjointed cobblestones.

On the Rue d'Aubervilliers, they passed the workshops of the Eastern railway, where lanterns were glowing here and there like stars fallen into the nothingness. Occasionally there was the whine of metal, a tearing, grinding sound, even though there were no trains coming or going from here anymore. Pujols had strained his eyes into the night, trying to pick out the slow movement of a maneuver, any hint of motion in one of the dark blocky shapes he saw on the rails, but nothing moved, and he shivered in the dark, hardly able to see his own hands in front of his face, and he cursed himself for such over-sensitivity while the girls, forced to sleep by the drug, breathed invisibly near him, sometimes groaning softly or moving abruptly when their arms or legs stretched out involuntarily, striking him and making him afraid they would launch them-selves at him again, like furies galvanized by a nightmare, sud-denly transformed into ghouls determined to rip him to pieces with their little white teeth.

He'd felt better when he sensed the cab passing beneath the viaduct and then clattering along the rutted surface of the Rue de l'Évangile, alongside the gas storage tanks whose contents he sometimes caught a whiff of.

There's a large bonfire burning in front of Gros-Tonton's house. Pujols sees by his watch that it's after midnight. A man is throwing the pieces of a chair into the fire; they can see a sideboard, some packing boxes, the corpse of a dog in the flames. Children run and yell and dance around the fire, their silhouettes sometimes seeming to dissolve in the light and then reappearing in a shower of sparks, laughing shrilly. A garish saraband. A gremlins' Sabbath. One of them tosses a handful of black powder into the flames; a tongue of flame leaps, hissing, and the children shriek in fear and delight.

Pujols approaches and feels the welcome heat of the fire, the comforting light, and he watches the flames creeping over the surface of what they're devouring, the skin of the dog gleaming with fat and then covered with light-blue sparks like a chiffon veil. Men stand on the edges of the bright clearing, sometimes visible in the flickering light only by the moist sparkle of their eyes or the glow of the pipes or cigarettes they're smoking. There are six of them, and Pujols knows they've been observing him since he got out of the cab. Despite the crackling of the flames, he can hear the sound of someone breathing behind him, and then he feels the blade of a knife pressing against the back of his neck, at the base of his skull.

"What the fuck are you doing here?"

He slowly lifts his right hand toward the pocket of his coat, but the pressure of the knife blade increases, breaking the skin.

"Don't move, or I'll cut your head off."

"I'm here to see Gros-Tonton. I have something for him."

Another man has come up on his right. He holds an old single-shot pistol in his hand. The brim of his cap is pulled so low it hides the entire upper half of his face. Huge, light mutton-chops frizz out from his cheeks. His lips are clamped tightly together, marked by a bitter twist. The children fall silent and then disperse into the night. The only sound now is the fire crackling. The body of the dog whistles and sizzles, dripping teardrops of fat into the fire.

"You know Cristo?"

It's the man with the pistol who has spoken, almost without moving his lips.

"Why? Should I know him?"

The man lifts the brim of his cap and looks at Pujols, squinting as if to see him better, then he glances at his associate, who still has his knife pressed to Pujols's neck.

"You sure you've never met him?"

Pujols understands. Then remembers. The three bums from the Quai de Jemmapes. The bar owner called one of them Cristo.

"Oh, yes. I remember. The last time I saw him, he was dead. And the two idiots with him, too. But that was the first time I'd ever seen him, I swear!"

Another exchange of glances behind his back. The man with the pistol is sweating. His skin shines in the firelight. The pressure of the knife blade eases off. The man standing behind him shuffles his feet, or shifts his weight. Pujols thrusts out an arm blindly and seizes the man's wrist, twists it, then spins round and grabs the knife—a sort of bayonet, actually. He buries it in the man's neck, twists it sharply, feels things snap and split in the man's throat, like cartilage. As the man reels away, trying to pull out the blade, Pujols is reminded of killing pigs on the farm when he was younger. He felt the same thing once when slaughtering a hundred-and-fifty-pound porker, and his father scolded him for making the animal suffer too much. He is already aiming his revolver at the other man, who lowers his own gun. No one is left around the fire.

"Get rid of that!" shouts a falsetto voice behind him. "And don't ever let me see you around here again!"

The man with the pistol goes to the one writhing in his death throes on the ground, his hands gripping the long dagger. He raises him up, and the man vomits a gush of blood on him and then falls into his arms, dead, maybe. He whistles, and two men emerge from the shadows and help him carry the body away.

"Now this is going to be complicated. You should have waited for me to come out."

Gros-Tonton extends to Pujols a hand chubby as a giant baby's, and they shake vigorously. He wears a crimson top hat and a vest of mauve silk. His riding boots reach almost all the way up his short legs. Pujols, at the sight of him, so short and fat, always wonders how he has managed to assert his authority over the whole quarter. Gros-Tonton admitted once that he had at his service a band of particularly devoted and vicious professional assassins who would kill their own mothers and fathers if he ordered them to. At least one of them actually did it, they say, without a qualm. Right now, though, the little man is smiling at him sardonically.

"You should have come out earlier," says Pujols.

Gros-Tonton smiles with all his missing teeth.

"Actually, I wanted to see how you'd get yourself out of it. I know the two gentlemen who were toying with you; they'd have taken their time, had a bit of fun. No hurry."

He gestures at the hansom cab, from which Clovis hasn't budged, pretending to be asleep, one finger on the trigger of a hunting rifle whose barrel he has sawn off, and which he always carries with him when he and his coach venture into certain areas.

"What have you brought me?"

"There are three of them. Youngest one's twelve or thirteen at most. They're asleep at the moment; they have a tendency to get a bit upset, so we had to calm them down."

Gros-Tonton calls out behind him in almost a singsong voice. There is the sound of a door creaking and hurried steps behind a fence of tarred wood, and then two young men, puny teenagers, emerge at a run and stop in front of their master.

"Go get the girls from the cab and take them inside."

Clovis climbs down from his seat to help them, and they carry out the somnolent girls, who react with slow movements, their limp legs twitching weakly. The chemise of one of the girls is soiled, her legs mottled with brownish spots.

"They'll need a wash," observes Gros-Tonton. "They stink like sows."

He goes over to the girls, sniffs them, feels their bodies. He lifts their chemises to look at their bellies and shoves his fingers between their thighs, then smells them with disgust.

"Go clean them up for me. And no touching, got it? Ask old Marcelle to deal with them, dress them back up a bit."

The two boys exchange a knowing glance their boss doesn't see.

"Be careful if they wake up," adds Pujols. "They bite."

Gros-Tonton bursts out laughing.

"My clients will like that! The Boches love to bleed a little. Now, we'll have a toast."

He ushers Pujols toward a studded wooden door that looks like something from a medieval castle. A sort of vestibule, narrow as a closet, leads to a second door equipped with a peephole. Gros-Tonton knocks on this door a dozen times at different rhythms, like an access code, and it opens for them. The man standing before them is young, tall, well built. His skin is brown, his black hair curling gracefully around his clean-shaven face. Pujols thinks he might be Spanish. Men like that used to come around the village when he was a boy, often smugglers, swarthy, a bit wild, willing to exchange some of their merchandise for a night's lodging. They'd seduce the daughters of the house sometimes, girls who were engaged already and would show evidence of pregnancy several weeks later, still denying any sinful behavior. Few people bought their stories of immaculate conception, however, and matters were occasionally settled with a rifle shot or two up in the mountains, or the little burden would be bundled off to an old village lady, a witch, or maybe just crazy, who talked to bears and told fortunes in exchange for a ham or a few chickens.

"This is Louison," Gros-Tonton says. "My right-hand man.

The best. He's blood, a member of my family. A distant cousin. Right, Louison?"

The man nods, blinking. In the low light cast by the wall sconces, his long eyelashes make his eyes look like a woman's, and his fine-featured face is as expressionless as a wax mask, but the ticking of a muscle beneath the skin of his jaw betrays his strained nerves. He is in his shirtsleeves and a blue vest; the chain of a watch hangs from the fob pocket.

Pujols can't figure out where he's hiding his knife—because he must be carrying one—and he stares at the man's hands; the suppleness of his gestures, the silence, the appearance of seeing nothing, seeming never to rest his gaze on anything at all, mark him out as a knifeman so swift that he'll cut your throat without anyone seeing him move a muscle.

Gros-Tonton sits down in his thronelike armchair, and Louison comes to stand to his right and slightly behind him, one hand resting on the throne's back. Pujols takes a seat on a green velvet sofa whose cushions sink softly beneath him. On a low table with legs sculpted like lion heads that seem to guard access to its inlaid surface sits a bottle of liquor, the pear eau-de-vie adored by the master of the place.

"Come now, pour us a drink," he says to Pujols. "I'm beginning to work up a thirst."

There are only two glasses. Pujols darts a glance at the knifeman, who stands unmoving, his gaze somewhere in the distance.

Gros-Tonton shrugs. "Don't worry about it. He never touches the stuff."

Pujols fills the two glasses. Gros-Tonton reaches immediately for his and raises it toward Pujols before draining it in one swallow. He shakes himself and exhales noisily. Pujols takes a drink, feels the fire descending into his belly, tears springing to his eyes. At the back of his throat is a hint of dead leaves, decaying plant matter, as if someone has distilled the undergrowth from a forest.

"How much did we say? A hundred for each?"

Gros-Tonton snaps his fingers and gestures to Louison.

"Go get me three hundred francs."

The man doesn't move at first. He looks at his master, clenching his teeth. His hand digs into the high seat back, his slender fingers sinking into the padding. Pujols meets his flat, almost glassy eyes. The revolver in his pocket, against his thigh, is unreachable. Gros-Tonton's throat could be slit before he had time to react at all, and if it isn't this evening it will happen later tonight, or tomorrow, or sometime soon. As suddenly as an undetectable breeze causes a door to slam. Eventually, Louison moves off with his silent, graceful steps. Pujols notices that he's wearing slippers, canvas sandals like the Basques love to wear, but embroidered, delicately worked. He disappears through a door he opens noiselessly at the far end of the room.

The little king of the neighborhood smiles, a satisfied expression on his face. He holds his glass out to Pujols, who refills it.

"He's the best, that one. Knife, pistol, garotte. He can do it all. Without him I'd never have been able to rid myself of Raymond's band at La Chapelle. Him and his bastard son and all the trash he surrounded himself with. They tried to pull one over on us with the Prusscos. Bunch of louses! It was all over in a week; the survivors ran off to Drancy as fast as their legs could carry them. Won't see them round here again anytime soon!"

Pujols watches him fidgeting in his chair, pulling at his collar, then leaning back, self-satisfied, his hands on the armrests. He could tell him that Louison, that *artiste* with a knife, would send him to an early grave one of these days and take his place—which he was already occupying, no doubt, between Esmerelda's thighs. He could tell him that he'd know that blank-eyed assassin's gaze anywhere, like an emptiness where everything seemed to disappear into an abyss: he recognizes the lightless blankness of his own depths in it. He knows it all. He's learned it from the men he's spent time with over the past few months, experts with the garotte, the bag over the head, and from his own readings. Isidore,[13] without knowing it, had plunged into this chasm and had found at the bottom, drowsing like a venom-eyed serpent with poison skin and barbed teeth, the vile creature that possesses some men's souls, showing them that ordinary people's diversions are bestial spasms next to the exquisite pleasure of murder. He knows it all, too, because he has learned to recognize it in himself.

But what would be the point of telling him? This dim-witted monarch prospering and reveling and indulging himself, this stupid, lecherous tyrant, sitting among his miserable subjects in his kingdom of flimsy shacks, of wretched shelters, of bumpy roads trailing off into nothingness, studded with ruts and swamped with sticky mud—he reigns, Pujols believes, over the rabble of the city without ever suspecting that one day someone else, someone more vicious and a bit less stupid, will kill him and plant their filthy arse in his armchair. Pujols realizes that he is smiling at the idea. Gros-Tonton leans toward him, looking surprised.

"You look quite pleased with yourself. Is it the cash making you so happy?"

Pujols agrees and raises his glass.

"To your health!"

The little king drains his glass again, and his eyes shine more brightly, his eyelids blinking more heavily. They hear a door open, and Louison appears, catfooted and silent as always, with a small canvas bag he hands to his boss.

"There. You can count it for yourself." Gros-Tonton puts

---

[13] Isidore Ducasse, Comte de Lautréamont, author of *Les Chants de Maldoror*, with whom Pujols has spent time in the past. See *L'Homme aux lèvres de saphir*, Rivages Noir.

the bag down on the low table, but Pujols doesn't take it right away. He nods his thanks, forcing a smile.

"This will help me get out of Paris. I have no desire to end up caught between the bullet of a mitrailleuse and the point of a bayonet. They'll give no quarter."

"Those bastard Reds are bad for business. They poke their noses into everything, watching all that happens, patrolling . . . They've come here more than once, claiming to be monitoring the Prussians. A likely story! It's not easy to make a transaction right now with their barricades and their National Guard. The girls can't go out in the streets anymore, or they'll be arrested! A man can't even play dice anymore! It was easier with the city sergeants and the bourgeois cops who'd close their eyes and shut their gobs for a little dough every now and then. Can't even talk things over with the ones we've got now!"

"This whole thing shouldn't last much longer now. The army'll regain control of the situation, but in the meantime, best to hole up somewhere because it'll be bloody. Those gentlemen up at Versailles aren't playing around, from what I hear. They want to punish what they call 'the dregs of society.'"

"I'm going to clear out, too. All those idiots will come hide out around here, and we'll end up right in the middle of a manhunt. Thanks, but no thanks! I'll have to cross Prussian lines, but I know an officer who'll give me a safe conduct pass. The girls you've brought me will grease his palm a bit, too; one of them looks nice and young, and that son of a bitch loves fresh meat. Helps himself to anything over ten years old whenever the opportunity presents itself. He told me that himself one evening when I had some drinks with him and one of his lieutenants; you could have knocked me over with a feather when he started undressing a little thing who must still have been playing with dolls! She was drunk herself, sniveling, flopping around in those big hands of his. I stayed to watch; first time

I'd ever seen anything like that. So young . . . there are broth-els that offer that sort of thing for connoisseurs, but I've never dared myself. Costs a pretty penny, too. Anyway, he's always scouring the area for a fresh supply; it seems that, between Le Bourget and Aubervilliers, the peasants hide their daughters the same way they do their chickens when there's a fox about."

He gets visibly warmer as he speaks, flushing red and sweat-ing. Next to him, slightly in the background as always, Louison looks down at him with an enigmatic smile, unmoving, barely seeming to breathe. He doesn't even blink when Clovis enters, his hat shoved far back on his head, rebuttoning his coat. Amid the wrinkled folds of his face, between his bushy beard and his hair, the meager light cast by the lamps and candles illuminates his strange blue eyes with a pale gleam.

"It's done."

Arms crossed, he waits near the door. Pujols stands, slips the bag of money into his pocket.

Gros-Tonton remains seated, his eyes squeezed half-shut by the smile rounding his fat cheeks. He extends a hand languidly to Pujols, who shakes it firmly.

Outside, the bonfire is still burning. The children are shout-ing and capering round it again; a bit farther off, men stand talking in low voices around a brazier.

"Well?" demands Pujols.

"Well what?"

"The girls."

"Too dirty. And then afterward I didn't want to anymore."

As they pass near the fire, the yelling children, Pujols looks up at the twisting plume of sparks that rises from the flames before dying in the blackness. Inside the carriage, the girl is slumped over, asleep. He checks to see that she's still securely bound, then settles himself on a seat. Even then, he can't keep himself from making sure, in the firelight, that the others are really gone, that none of them are waiting for him, crouching between the seats, ready to rip out his throat with their teeth. As the coach starts to jounce along the road again, he can't understand why he is still so afraid, as if he'd been attacked by creatures risen from a tomb, undead abominations determined to punish him for what he'd subjected them to. He's heard stories like this, legends born in countries he didn't even know existed, far to the east in mountains haunted by ancient curses and roamed in the night by ghouls and vampires.

He feels the bag in his pocket, filled with thirty ten-franc gold coins stamped with the face of Badinguet,[14] and his fears dissipate, and he lets himself relax against the back of the seat, chiding himself for his own foolishness. A breath of cool night air tickles his face. In two more days he'll be far away from this chaos. These shadows. He wants sunshine, warmth. He would like to see the sea. He's seen it in watercolors, paintings, flat and so stupidly blue, and found it strange, he who has never known anything but the slopes and inclines of the Pyrenees, with their unreachable horizons and unattainable peaks. The sea. Not the ocean and its storm-filled endlessness. He's been told that the Mediterranean soothes every torment, cures the diseases brought on by the fetid city air. It seems you can even swim in it. Peace. Rejuvenation.

In the darkness of the coach, jolting with each rut in the road, he gives himself up to extravagant fantasies, imagines himself living there for the rest of his life, serene, purified. Living simply. As a child, he wanted to be a shepherd and live as a hermit in the mountains with his flock and just his dogs for company. Seeing no one, tucked away snugly in his cabin in front of the fire, even in winter. He'd dreamed of it at night, huddled beneath his blankets as, outside, the sky silently crumbled, smothering every living thing in deep snow. And now he

---

[14] Badinguet: Mocking nickname given to Napoleon III by the opposition.

imagines himself in front of that shimmering azure infinity, lost in meditative wonderment, the heat his only clothing.

They pass through several barricades manned by exhausted or negligent sentries and avoid others. Pujols realizes that most of these barriers, when one can't simply cross them with a leap like a hill of gravel, can simply be taken from behind, and he chuckles to himself at the idea.

It's nearly three o'clock in the morning when they reach the Rue des Missions. The sky rumbles and glows, filled with flickering light from the fires. Clovis drives the carriage into the courtyard and stays for a moment on his box seat, watching the night burn. When Pujols offers to let him sleep that night in a nook at the back of Madame Viviane's porter's lodge he refuses, says he'll be fine as he is, that he's leaving early in the morning. He climbs slowly down from his perch and takes a full pail of grain out of the trunk at the back of the coach.

"Horse needs to eat first, then me. You got something?"

Pujols says he'll see. He tiptoes silently into the dark lodge, but the door creaks and the floor squeaks.

"Is that you?" asks Madame Viviane.

"No, it's the National Guard, here to pay their respects."

She laughs. *You big idiot. Come on, hurry.*

In the dim light of a lamp he finds a heel of bread and some bacon along with a half-full bottle of wine. He takes these out to Clovis, who is murmuring to his horse, the animal's muzzle buried in the pail. The man pays no attention to him, so he sets the food down on the footboard.

In the bedroom, the warmth reaches him at the same time as the woman's heady perfume. A candle is burning on the dresser, covering Madame Viviane's nude body with a dancing amber veil.

"Where have you been, you scoundrel?" she asks in a throaty voice.

He pulls off his jacket and vest and undoes his belt buckle.

His trousers fall to the floor, and she groans and shudders las-
civiously at the sight of his underpants.

"You seem to have some scandalous ideas in your head, my
dear sir."

He finishes unlacing his shoes, steps out of his trousers,
and climbs into bed. Madame Viviane Arnault, the honest
widow of a respected—if not respectable—shopkeeper, lets
out a long cry when Pujols buries his mouth between her
thighs and sets to work pleasuring her. He is seized by the
desire to bite, to tear at what he feels beneath his tongue and
lips, damp and hot, and then to plunge himself into what is
left and spit the flesh between his teeth into this woman's
face. But the desire burning low in his belly quashes the
impulse. He turns the woman over onto her belly and rams
into her so hard that she freezes at first, with a sharp little
cry—of surprise, no doubt—and then her rump begins to
gyrate beneath his battering thrusts. He growls unintelligible
things in a low, strange voice, as if something else inside him
is speaking through him, the language foreign, sometimes
husky, sometimes shrill. *Yes, you're right, don't stop*, she
gasps, and he shouts, the way you would to dogs, or a flock
of sheep, pounding again and again into the arse pressing
upward against him.

He grips her hips and can see nothing of Madame Viviane
but her hair spread out on the pillow and the hollow curve
of her back shining with sweat and the fat white globes he is
clutching in his hands. She is nothing in this moment but a
receptacle, a moist sheath into which he is pouring his fury.
If he could, he would break her in two and finish in her
mouth, but when he feels her orgasm shaking her, her body
clenching hard around his member, he climaxes, howling
with rage, and pulls himself out of her, flinging himself down
beside her.

She whimpers, almost crying, crushed into the sheets.

"Oh, you great bastard! You're going to kill me! You'll rip through my pussy into my belly one of these days—and I'll beg for more!"

She says crude things like this when she's just enjoyed herself immensely. Sometimes beforehand, when she comes looking for him. Pujols discovered this to his delight early in their relationship. It was so surprising to hear such obscenities from a woman's mouth.

She tries tentatively to caress him, but he pushes her away, disgusted by her sprawling body, this limp mass of flesh that no longer stirs any desire in him. He listens to the incessant sound of the bombardment outside. Sometimes a door thumps, a window vibrates. It's so close. The city's about to crumble around them. He'll leave tomorrow night. He still needs to pay one last visit to Gantier. He'll have to get out via the Porte de Clignancourt and go back to Saint-Ouen, where he struck up a friendship with that Bavarian officer last year.

He gets out of bed and puts his clothes back on. The floor creaks beneath his shoes. Viviane asks him in a muffled voice, her face in the pillow, where he's going. When he doesn't answer, she turns over and sits up, her naked breasts bared, hair in disarray.

"Where are you going now? What is this business of yours, all these comings and goings? Some days I don't even know where you are anymore, and you come back at all hours of the night! And that cellar you have the key to—what are you hiding in there? I don't want any trouble when all this anarchy's over and the police are back in operation. I hope you aren't mixed up with anyone from the Commune, because that would put us right in front of a firing squad! They're going to suspect everyone; we'll need to be irreproachable, show them we've always been on the right side!"

He has let her talk and looks at her now, naked, her hair unkempt, her plump shoulders and breasts gilded by the candlelight, and he tries to remember what he's doing there, why he came into this room. He even wonders who this woman is, because everything suddenly seems strange, far away, almost unreal. He could go to her and shove all of her grating recriminations back down her throat with a single stroke of a blade, but right now he's got better things to do. And besides, it's not like she's going to run out into the empty streets, practically beneath the bombs, to rat him out. And to whom? He has time yet. If he has to, he'll deal with her later, before he leaves. It's probably not a good idea to leave too many traces of himself behind anyway, even if, in the terrible upheaval that's on its way, every possible trail will be awash in blood.

"Go to sleep and get the hell off my back."

She murmurs plaintively that he's nothing but a scoundrel and lies back down, jerking the sheets and blankets over herself angrily.

In the courtyard, the horse trembles and flicks its ears at each detonation. The bombing is less intense now, but the sky is still unnaturally light from the fires. In the coach, Clovis, stretched out on a bench seat, is a shapeless mass vibrating with cavernous snores.

Pujols shakes him awake.

"Help me."

Clovis sits up and looks around, surprised.

"What?" he says.

"Her. You don't want to take her home with you, do you?"

They untie the girl and carry her to the rear of the courtyard, where the cellars are. She can barely keep on her feet, murmuring and complaining. Pujols takes the key from his pocket, pulls the heavy door open with an effort, and pushes the girl inside.

He tells Clovis he can go home now, or sleep here, if he wants. The other man climbs back onto his bench seat in the coach and disappears beneath his cloak.

At the pump, Pujols fills a pail with water and drops in the piece of stale bread he's taken from the back of a cabinet. He lights a storm lamp and goes back to the cellar. Anyone seeing him with his pail in the middle of the night like that would think he was going to feed a sick animal.

In front of the cellar door, rummaging in his pocket for the key, he realizes that he doesn't know what she looks like. It's important, the face. It's what gives the rest of the photo the feeling it must have of tarnished innocence, of alarm, of abandon or lasciviousness the customers like so much. This girl has literally fallen into his lap, and he will have to do something with her, tomorrow, probably, now that time is so short. He'll have to go to Gantier's first thing in the morning and offer her to him.

Unexpectedly, he finds her standing up. She recoils, her chest heaving with fear, but she meets his gaze. A few strands of hair fall about her face, giving her a wild look.

"What do you want with me? What am I doing here?"

He's almost surprised to hear her speak. Her voice trembles, choking slightly at the end of her question. He lifts the lamp higher, to get a better look at her. She is breathing rapidly, her mouth open. She holds her arms stiffly at her sides, fists clenched. Suddenly he is the one who doesn't know what to say. He puts the pail down on the ground in front of him, because he's afraid she'll throw it in his face and then take his revolver.

"You have to eat."

He doesn't know why he said that. He doesn't give a damn whether she eats or not. He feels ridiculous before this girl who is facing him down.

She glances at the pail and spits on the ground.

"Let me go."

"Tomorrow."

"What difference does that make to you?"

She lifts a hand to shield her eyes from the lamplight and looks at his face. She leans forward slightly, then recoils again.

"What's your name?"

"What's yours?"

He chuckles ironically. "They call me Maldoror. I'll come and get you tomorrow, you'll see. And I don't give a fuck what your name is, in light of what I'm going to do with you. With everything happening at the moment, nobody will pay any attention."

He sees two tears roll down the girl's cheeks. She tries to say something but can't get the words out. There it is. She's starting to weaken. This is his favorite moment, when the fear hollows out an emptiness inside them that makes them crumple in on themselves like an item of clothing deprived of its hanger. He stows his gun in his pocket and backs toward the door, reaching for the handle. The moment he opens it she leaps forward with a cry and seizes his collar and pulls on his arm, but he smashes a fist into her temple and kicks her away, stunned. Once he has closed the door behind him, he presses his ear to the flap but hears nothing. Nothing but the thunderclaps of the artillery shells still falling on the city. That heady sound of war approaching, that thudding of barely contained violence.

Out in the courtyard, his eyes on the sky lit here and there by plumes of fiery smoke, he thinks for a moment and feels pleased with himself. Maldoror. The name came to him in a flash, obvious and rather farcical, deep down. His secret pseudonym. The ghost name of he who exists and yet has no reality.

"I'm the only one who knows you."

11

A ntoine Roques has to shoulder his way through the crowd to get into the police station. There are around thirty people huffing and shouting, and the two guards in front of the door have to hold them off with their rifles crossed like a barrier. The early-morning chill is doing nothing to cool their fervor. "I have to speak to the chief of police! It's serious!" The two soldiers, military caps askew, explain that there is no real police chief anymore; only a delegate to the Sûreté elected by the men of the 65th.

Roques is barely inside the lobby when he is accosted by the sound of other cries. A man is standing there, his front drenched with vomit. He staggers, brandishing a chair over his head, which he brings crashing down on another man who bellows curses at him and grabs the chair and breaks it across his back. The two drunkards roll on the floor, furious and grunting, bumping into the furniture. Limbs entangled, they struggle, flailing pointlessly without doing any great harm to one another. A cloud of dust rises from their bodies; they reek of filth and alcohol. Three guards hurry over and hover around the furiously scuffling duo, trying to avoid being pulled into the fray the way one keeps warily clear of the churning gears of an immense machine. Eventually they manage to grab one of the men and shove him against a wall, subduing him with a smart rap from a nightstick. The other man, still on the floor, continues to yell and thrash around, lashing out with his fists, grunting with effort. Drunk out of his mind, he punches empty

188 - HERVÉ LE CORRE

air, strangles nothingness. The guards let him flap for a moment, laughing at him, and then decide to act. One of them kneels on his chest while the other two grab his arms and legs. Two or three slaps restore his wits a bit, and they are able to haul him to his feet, unresisting. He leans against a wall, face very pale, eyes half-closed, breathless.

"Put them in the cells to cool down a bit, and let them go around midday," says Roques. "We've got better things to do."

One of the guards shrugs and approaches the first man, who is sitting on the floor, groggy.

"Won't make any difference. This is the third time this week. Day before yesterday it was right out in the middle of the street, in front of a school. One of them had his naked arse out when we got there."

The man against the wall sways and snickers. "Yeah, I did that—popped his fat arse out so I could give it a good kicking, the son of a bitch!"

Antoine Roques watches as the guards take the two winos away. One of them mutters something that makes all of them burst out laughing. The commotion in front of the entrance hasn't calmed down. Loubet, by the door, beckons him over.

"Another woman's been kidnapped," he says. "There are two witnesses in your office. Two women who saw everything."

"And those men? What's their story?"

"They say their landlord is sending heavies after them, to collect the rent they owe him. They want us to do something before it turns nasty."

"The kidnapping. Where did it happen, and when?"

"Last night on the Boulevard Poissonnière. We'll have to speak to the Sûreté Générale about it. We can't deal with this on our own."

"The Prefecture isn't sticking its nose in around here. No chance."

Outside, the shouts grow louder. The two guards brace

themselves on their rifles as if holding the door shut against the force of a battering ram. Roques hesitates. There are the two women waiting for him and the two bastards trawling the streets in search of their next target. So many people who have to be helped. This is the job he's been elected to do.

"I'll speak to them."

He advances toward the little crowd. The people fall silent. He explains who he is and what he's going to do. He will listen to everyone. But first he has a serious case to attend to. Lives are in danger. He asks them to be patient. They mutter a bit, sigh heavily, agree to wait—but they aren't leaving, not until they get some answers.

"Come in, but keep it civilized. Otherwise I'll have you thrown out."

A small man in a blue shirt with a red badge pinned over his heart comes toward him, pushing his hat back on his head.

"You talk like an old-time *flicard*, Citizen. All that's finished now. They're all at Versailles, those pig policemen. This is Paris, and the Commune! Respect the people! The landlords don't make the law anymore—we're the law now!"

There are murmurs of approval: It's true, otherwise it wouldn't be worth fighting so hard for! My brother's a lieutenant with the 113th, and my sister works in an aid station at Montparnasse! And my sons are on the barricade, where they should be! Each member of the group declares his contribution in a loud, firm voice, adding it to the great pool of hope as something clear, something proud.

As the crowd enters the station, pushing and shoving a bit, Antoine Roques heads for his office, followed by Loubet. He sees a young redheaded woman from the back, a gray shawl thrown over her shoulders. She doesn't turn; she is too busy blowing her nose and stifling the sobs that make her upper body shake. Next to her, a plump young blonde woman turns her pretty face with its bright eyes to him and smiles shyly, the smart little black hat atop her curls secured with red-tipped hairpins.

Roques pulls over a chair and sits down next to the women. The young girl keeps her head down. Her breathing is quick and shallow. Strands of hair fall over her face from her messy chignon.

"My name is Jacqueline Floche," the blonde woman says, "28 Rue de la Fontaine au Roi. I was on the Boulevard Poissonnière last night, and I saw everything. I was on the way to my night shift in the mess, 77th battalion."

Sitting very straight in her chair, she puts a palm flat on the desk, and Roques can't keep himself from smiling. She's not the type to be taken in, and he imagines that the squaddies to whom she serves soup would do well to remember it.

The redheaded girl has calmed down a bit. She straightens up, and her green-eyed gaze settles on the policeman.

"Tell me, mademoiselle . . . what is your name?"

She gulps in a breath as if she's about to plunge into deep water.

"Poirier. Lalie Poirier. I live on the Rue de Constantine in the 16th arrondissement. I'm a seamstress. Well, I . . . I was with a friend, Caroline. We were going to meet my sweetheart on the Rue Saint-Nicolas—he's a carpenter. And my leg hurt, we'd been walking for a long time, and I'd twisted my ankle the other day . . . And then I see a hansom cab. There aren't many of them around right now, so I tell Caroline, come on, I can pay, and I go up to it and call out to the cabman, but he doesn't answer, so I open the door, and the driver whips his horse and I get dragged along and fall, and just then Caroline came to help me, and I fell and I couldn't see what happened after that . . ."

She bursts into tears. Loubet rolls his eyes, glances at his watch.

"I saw the whole thing," says Jacqueline Floche. "The little one fell, and the tall, pretty girl, Caroline, she was holding on to the door, and I saw a hand grab her and pull her inside the cab. The horse was almost galloping, everyone was screaming, and people were so shocked that nobody reacted. The coach took off like that toward the Place du Château-d'Eau and those idiot national guardsmen just watched it go without doing anything, too busy flirting with girls and monitoring the street corners as if that accomplished anything."

"What was in the cab? Did you see anything?"

Lalie Poirier clutches her sodden handkerchief and shakes her head as if trying to put her memories in some kind of order.

"A man, there was. I didn't get a very good look at his face, but it was sort of . . . disfigured. Not nice to look at. But it was getting dark, you know. And . . . I think I saw some girls. About my age, maybe, I don't know. In their nightclothes. But I'm not sure. It all happened so fast . . ."

She trails off, sniffling. Roques pulls out the handkerchief Rose gave him this morning, still perfumed with lavender, and hands it to her. She wipes her eyes, her cheeks, her nose, grief overflowing from every part of her face.

"You will find Caroline, won't you, Monsieur l'Inspecteur? You'll find her?"

Antoine Roques is certain of it but doesn't want to make any promises. There's no telling what tomorrow might bring, and it seems to him that any promise made from now on is nothing but a cynical lie. But he has learned enough now to end this interview, to hurry straight to Miron's and find out more about the killer with the broken face.

"And the cabman?"

Jacqueline Floche's mouth twists in thought.

"An overcoat, a dented top hat on his head. Very hairy, and bearded, like an animal. You couldn't see his face at all."

"Had you seen him in the area before?"

Both women shake their heads. Jacqueline Floche takes Lalie's hand in hers and squeezes it.

"The poor little one stayed with us last night; she couldn't go home in the state she was in, it's too dangerous. We came here first thing this morning. There have been other women taken like that, right off the street, I hear. People are talking about it; they're afraid, you know. And things are already difficult, with what's going on . . ."

Roques takes down their names and addresses and stands. He asks the young girl if she feels strong enough to return to her home on the other side of Paris, offers to send two guards to escort her, or even a carriage if he can find one, but she refuses.

"I'll walk her as far as the Louvre," Jacqueline Floche says.

They rise in their turn, their thank yous mingling. The buzz of conversation in the entrance hall dies away as they emerge from Roques's office.

"Now," he says, "what's this business with rents?"

An old man steps forward.

"We live in the Passage Saint-Louis, behind the hospital. With all this mess, the workshops closing and men enlisting in the National Guard, there are a lot of people who can't pay their weekly rents anymore. We decided as a group to write to the Commune and tell them; we hoped they'd send someone to us, but those gentlemen must have other things to attend to right now . . ."

"Other than arguing about what the hell they're doing up there, for God's sake?" cries a woman.

"Well," the old man continues, "for the last ten days, there have been men coming at all hours of the day or night, demanding to be paid. There are always four or five of them, burly fellows with dirty faces, carrying axes and knives and meat hooks, and they're forcing their way into people's houses, grabbing women and children, threatening to come back; they say they'll hurt them next time, they don't care how many people are outside! They say they're only good enough to sleep outside with dogs! Only yesterday they very nearly threw Marie Suchod out the window! Her little ones screamed and held on to her and hit the men with their fists! Other times they pound on the doors, shouting, and when people let them in, they ransack the place looking for money!"

"They're the landlord's boys," says a young woman.

Her dark eyes burn in her thin, pale face. A strand of brown hair falls into her face, and she brushes it angrily back.

"Monsieur Carmon, he's called. A young greenhorn who's taken over from his father, who ran a factory in Normandy. He wants us to leave so he can rent to others at even higher prices!"

"Where does he live, this Carmon?"

"Of course he left Paris with the other bourgeois pigs; he's probably living it up near Versailles! If he's still here, he'll be at 64 Rue du Château-d'Eau. My mother used to clean house for him before the war."

"That isn't far. We'll go and have a look," says Roques.

"We could come with you, if you like. We'll surely find at least one of those worms in the area."

The crowd rumbles in agreement. The black-eyed girl lights up the gloomy place and the solemn group with a wide smile. He would happily go with her to this Monsieur Carmon's house, if only to try and make her smile again.

"I have men for that. Two companies from the 188th, as you may already know. I'll fill out a mission order for my colleague, and they'll head straight there. If any of you want to go along, you're free to do so. But the National Guard and the vigilance committee who appointed me are here for that."

Loubet, behind him, puts a hand on his shoulder and murmurs quietly that he should consider wrapping things up. People begin to leave, slowly, pensively. To his great regret, Roques sees the dark eyes walking toward the exit with everyone else. He hurries after her.

"What's your name?"

The woman turns, warily, and weighs him up from behind the strands of hair that have fallen across her face.

"Just to know whom I should follow up with, I . . . why not you?"

"Maria. Maria Belmont. You have my address. There's a committee meeting tonight at nine o'clock on the Rue Saint-Maur, at the religious school there. I'll be there, along with a lot of others."

She looks him straight in the eye, her chin raised, lips pressed together. Then she turns with a quick, light movement, and Roques watches her go until he loses sight of her behind the swinging door before turning to Loubet, who is waiting impatiently behind him.

"So, what next? Where can we find this Clovis?"

"We'll do what I've just said. You go now with a description and arrest warrant to Colonel Dupuis of the 10th legion. I know him well; he'll take this seriously. All of the battalions should be informed as of tonight. We'll put it in writing; it will be more official that way. Go and see what's happening with this landlord and his goons. Do the questioning yourself or leave two men there."

They go back into Roques's office, and he busies himself writing his instructions down on a scrap of paper. He rereads it out loud, and they agree on the terminology. Two stamps, one signature. Loubet leaves immediately, accompanied by five guards.

Antoine Roques decides to act alone. He takes a revolver from his desk drawer and goes out. The sky is clear. Swallows emit their shrill cries. He walks quickly, enjoying the beauty of the moment, briefly picturing the lovely, passionate face of Maria Belmont. He murmurs her first name to himself and then feels irritated by his own giddiness, despite the new spring it has put in his step.

At the top of the streets leading to the Boulevard Magenta, women and children are reinforcing the barricades. Piles of cobblestones. Sacks of earth. Rails made of trees thrown on their sides. On the Rue des Vinaigriers, two wagon beds are being hauled upright against the cobblestone wall by a dozen guards and laughing women who shout encouragement. In the center of the barricade, the muzzle of a cannon peeks through a brick-built embrasure. Two or three companies of the 110th are encamped on the sidewalks. Tents have been set up along the street; yawning men in shirtsleeves emerge from them with backs bowed to piss against the palisades. Others are still asleep beneath wagons, rolled in blankets. Some of them crowd around a smoking stove where a mess woman serves coffee and a very young girl hands out pieces of bread. They laugh and joke; the woman smiles. Someone whistles a simple tune. Three little boys with National Guard caps pulled down around their ears carry pails of oats and water to the horses.

Roques has slowed down to better observe this peaceful state of war, this sort of board game in which the Parisian working class, the Commune, and the Central Committee of the National Guard argue over each turn without winning any of them, all of them still certain they'll win the game. Everyone knows the news isn't good, that the Versaillais are nearing the city in the south and west. Everyone knows the beginning of the end is almost here. And yet everyone seems to be depending on luck, chance, and courage to ensure that this waking dream in which the people have been living for two months now doesn't turn to a nightmare. The old world, which everyone thought had been abolished forever, the former order of things demolished, its middle class fled, is preparing to return in a roar of fire and steel, and it will be brutal and unforgiving. All one has to do is read the Versailles newspapers, with their calls for murder, for atonement by blood, and for the barbaric commoners' death for their sins.

He passes these stacks of rifles, these batteries of cannons, these crates of ammunition, and he wonders if he's the only one who knows that they aren't fakes, that they're there because soon they'll be pressed into service in the clamor and butchery of war. He walks away quickly, forcing himself to think only of the man for whom he's searching, that criminal loose in the streets even before the unleashing of the assassins authorized and sworn in by the wealthy. And he realizes that he, too, is trying to take his mind off his anxiety by cutting down the tree that hides the forest.

When he enters Miron's bar on the Quai de Jemmapes, there are two pairs of drinkers seated at the tables, empty glasses in front of them, playing dominoes and dice. The only sound is the clicking of the dice in the cup and the tick-tock of an unseen wall clock, but Roques is certain that just before he pushed open the door, the room was full of friendly chatter beneath its low ceiling that dampens sound by pressing it to the floor. The two men playing dice look to be somewhere in their twenties. They affect not to see or hear the new arrival, in case he might be someone sent by the National Guard, or one of those new cops from the Prefecture who might be able to identify them as recusants or deserters and have them arrested on the spot. As if the simple act of looking up at him and meeting his eyes might give them away and cause a squadron of bloodthirsty puppets to descend on them then and there. Roques wonders if he really looks that much like a cop, which isn't his profession, and which he only became five weeks ago. He's starting to think that he's giving off a particular odor, the scent of grubby offices and old paper and sweaty guardrooms and cells and latrines, that unique smell that wafts from every object, every room, every wall in the police station. Sort of like the way fishermen carry the smell of the sea and the catch with them everywhere they go. And he theorizes, as he leans his elbows on the bar, that some special sense of smell must develop in people who have done something serious enough to make them fear the police, an almost animal instinct that enables them to spot anyone who might be looking for them. Miron, who has had his nose buried in a newspaper, clears up any misunderstanding:

"Hello, Monsieur l'Inspecteur. What can I get you? I've just made some coffee."

The dice have stopped rolling. The players are frozen, looking at one another uneasily. Roques turns and watches them, smiling.

"Make it a coffee, then," he says.

Miron pushes a large, steaming cup toward him along with two lumps of sugar. Roques can hear him rummaging beneath the counter.

"So, barkeep, have you thought of anything new to tell me since yesterday?"

The dice players stand. One of them drops a coin on the table. They put on their hats, nod in farewell, touching a finger to their brims, and leave. The two remaining customers, behind their dominoes, observe the scene, and then they, too, rise and leave without a word.

"You must have a special talent," says Miron.

"Why do you say that?"

"A talent for scaring customers away. For causing me problems."

"Everyone's got problems at the moment. But you haven't seen anything yet, as far as you're concerned. Tomorrow I'm shutting down your racket. I'll ask the colonel of the 10th legion to requisition these premises as a mess hall. All I have to do is sign one piece of paper."

Silence. Two women pass by on the quay outside, laughing.

"Talk to me about the man who killed three of your customers yesterday afternoon."

Miron sighs and shakes his head, then takes a bottle of

hooch from the shelf behind him and pours himself a glass, which he empties in one swallow.

"What do you want me to tell you? You already know what he looks like; Gustin told you."

"Come on. You know this man. You're afraid of him. Talk. If I can arrest him, you'll never have to hear his name again, except on the day he keeps his date with Madame la Guillotine. And he'll never know you gave us any information about him. Tell me what you know, and I'll keep out of your hair."

"You can't possibly understand. He's like . . . he's like the Devil. When he looks at you with those black eyes, sunk deep beneath his forehead . . . it's like he's playing with your brain from a distance, and you don't know where you are anymore, or what to say . . ."

"Ah, so we're all the way into witchcraft now, are we? It must be devilry, then, that explains the disappearance of those dead men yesterday? What you need is a priest. Or a good psychiatrist, maybe."

"You shouldn't joke like that. When you end up face-to-face with him, you'll be singing another tune."

Miron pours himself another shot of liquor. He is obviously in need of comfort, his eyes wide, forehead gleaming with sweat, jaw quivering.

"You're the one joking right now. Does he come here often?"

"Sometimes. He'd come to meet Clovis. They always sat over there, at that table in the back, and if it was occupied, all he had to do was go over and ask the people sitting there to move and they'd get up immediately, almost as if they were relieved! People would whisper when he was here, like they were afraid of him. Even the really hard ones, sailors with arms like oak posts, knifemen from La Chapelle, the worst lowlifes— even they kept their distance from him. They'd eye him up; they knew he wasn't from around here, or they found him bizarre, like a different species. I don't know . . . They were like a bunch of dogs around a wolf."

"But Cristo, he insisted, didn't he? He wasn't afraid of either the wolf or the devil, you might say."

"Cristo was crazy. And he'd been drinking yesterday."

"Your establishment should be called 'The Drunken Dog.' It would explain a lot of things."

Hector Miron doesn't understand the allusion. An uncertain smile twists his mouth.

"Did he speak to you?"

"Just hello and goodbye, if he bothered to say anything at all. Never a goddamned thank you, that's for sure. All I know is that his first name is Henri, and he's got a southern accent, rolls his r's, I think. I'd hear him do that from behind the bar, or when I went over to serve them. They'd always stop talking, but I could hear the last few words before the pause."

He falls silent, his well run dry. Antoine Roques lets the silence stretch out a bit, in case he lets a last, seemingly insignificant, detail or two trickle out, anything that might lead somewhere, but Miron has retreated into a gloomy silence, his gaze fixed blankly on a dark corner of the tavern. He has clearly told all he knows, but Roques wants to test him just a little more.

"Now you can tell me—what happened to the bodies? What did you do with them?"

The man shrugs his shoulders.

"What difference does it make to you where they are?"

"Simple curiosity. I'd like to know how someone can hide three corpses so completely in two hours, the way you did."

"Some people I know. Just grunts from the Porte de Bagnolet. I sent word to them, and they came and took the bodies somewhere on the Rue des Carrières d'Amérique, or maybe tossed them over the ramparts near the Pré-Saint-

Gervais. What would you have done, with three carcasses in your dining room?"

Miron has regained a bit of energy, and he stands very erect behind his counter, almost arrogant. Antoine Roques would love to shut him up, knock him down a few pegs.

"We're talking about three men, not dead dogs you happened to find on your doorstep. I thought you were ready to ascend the barricades with your friends to defend the Commune, that you had a few human scruples left . . ."

"Dogs or not, those three weren't worth much. What, are you going to recover them so you can give them a funeral ceremony? And as for the Commune and its principles . . . I have a feeling those gentlemen up at the Hôtel de Ville are only out for themselves. Other than the Versaillais army, we the people ain't seeing nothin' headed our way so far."

Roques doesn't know how to answer. The entrance of three patrons talking loudly and elbowing one another keeps him from pondering the point. The men wear National Guard uniforms but are bareheaded and have neither guns nor leather cartridge belts. As soon as they see Roques, they fall silent and sit down at the table farthest from the bar.

"Three beers for three defenders of La Villette!" cries one of them.

Roques decides he'd rather not know where these dubious servicemen have come from and leaves without a word. Outside in the sunshine, all is peaceful. Children throw stones into the canal, shouting loudly, trying to hit a board floating in the brownish water. He watches them for a moment, his mind in turmoil, incapable of summoning a single sensible thought. He's chasing a bloodthirsty shadow, a terrifying phantom, in an insurgent city that is devastated, perhaps just as he himself feels, by the difficulty of finding itself in this labyrinth of hopes and promises that seems, at the moment, to only lead to dead ends. And the minotaur he's pursuing will be nothing but an insignificant calf once the army reaches Paris; of that, he is sure.

Right now all he wants to do is go home, pack a few bags with Rose, and leave the city to join their children in the safety of Uncle Charles's home. To hug them to him, to play with them. To find simple work and spend peaceful evenings at home. And to rediscover Rose's body in private pleasure. He lets his mind drift in the fairy tale for a moment and realizes he's smiling stupidly at nothing.

He quickens his step as he approaches the lock. No. He would miss Paris too much. He knows the insurrection will be crushed, that this undreamt-of moment will soon come to an end. Still . . . This city has a unique genius for revolt and revolution. It has been starved, bombarded, humiliated, and when the powerful ones thought it was dead, it rose up, rebellious and generous, defying the old world and calling, beyond the besieged ramparts, for public well-being and a universal republic. Roques lets these grand words, the expression of grand ideas, whirl around and around in his mind, and the little mental carousel soothes him, refreshes him. There's no question of leaving this city of infinite tomorrows, especially now. That would be to act as shamefully as those louts who abandon their wives when they're pregnant or about to give birth. He doesn't know what the Commune will beget, or what legacy it will leave to History after it is brought down. But he must be here. With Paris. Perhaps because such a miracle could only happen here—this showing the laboring world, the humble and the oppressed, the path to be followed. The leaving behind, perhaps, of Red children who will make sure their heritage bears fruit.

And he would miss the hustle and bustle too much, the everyday chaos, the crowds on the boulevards, the clatter of the omnibuses, the cry of a knife grinder in the street early in the morning, the voice of a newspaper seller shouting out the headlines, the narrow streets of the faubourgs and their village-like tranquility. The ill-behaved little boys that jostle you in the market, the great brouhaha of the market halls, coarse smells mingling with the perfume of flowers. And the train taken on Sunday mornings out into the countryside near Montrouge, the dozing children who wake up just as you pull into the station. Paris, the city-world where anything will always be possible.

The low houses along the Rue des Écluses are separated by lawns; the sun and a faint breeze ruffle the soft emerald grass. The scent of lilacs, mauve clusters drooping over a wooden fence. A wine and liquor shop stands on the corner of the Rue de la Grange aux Belles; he hears men talking loudly in the dark space within. Glancing inside, he can just make out their faces, reddened by flickering lamplight. The eyes of a cat lying on a shelf glow as the animal watches him. He thinks about going in but decides against it. He knows there is a hansom cab company depot on the Boulevard de la Villette. He looks at his watch and is astonished to see that it's past eleven o'clock. Time seems to be passing very strangely, either agonizingly slow, drop by drop, or in flooding rushes. He crosses the barricade on the corner of the Boulevard de la Villette, where a dozen men are sitting or lying on the ground, using sacks of earth as pillows. Others, farther along, sit in front of a haberdashery with closed shutters, playing a noisy game of cards, laughing and swearing.

On the boulevard, some poor devils push wheelbarrows, and a pair of oxen pull a wagon overflowing with manure. Three women carrying shopping baskets walk together, talking seriously. A tall barricade of earth and cobblestones bars the boulevard, its cannon pointed toward Belleville. Roques doesn't see any ammunition crates. A bit farther, the Rue de Mexico is cut off by a veritable wall three meters high pierced by an embrasure.

In front of the depot warehouse, some national guardsmen have set up an encampment. He wades through the smoke from their fires and the scents of cooked meat and tobacco. No one questions him. It's quiet. The men converse in low, calm voices.

He enters via an enormous, wide-open coach gate. The building is almost empty. Fifty or so hansom cabs and open-top carriages are lined up by the far wall. He takes a few steps forward, hoping to see someone.

"Are you looking for something?"

He turns to see a large fellow walking toward him with a firm stride, the pompon of his strange hat swaying in front of his face. The man has already reached his side and bows at the waist.

"Can I help?"

"Antoine Roques. Sûreté Committee, 10th arrondissement."

The man wrinkles his nose. Knits his brow. Looks at him sideways, suspicious, hostile.

"Sure. And I'm Auguste Blanqui's brother."

Roques takes out his letter of accreditation from the Prefecture, unfolds it, points out the stamps and even Raoul Rigault's signature.

"Okay, okay. So? You looking for a hansom?"

"Yes, actually. One driven by a man called Clovis."

"Dunno him. A name like that, I'd remember."

The man shakes his head and turns his back on Roques.

"I've been told he lives around here. He stables his horse and carriage on a little patch of grass somewhere near the Rue des Écluses. But I'd like to know his exact address. Might he be listed in your books?"

"I have no idea, I'm telling you. And I've got work to do, so if you don't mind . . ."

"If you prefer, I can come back this afternoon with ten men

and search your premises. Turn them completely upside down. Maybe then you'll have a bit more time for me."

Roques has spoken coolly, evenly, but there is a firmness in his voice that echoes off the iron beams. The man, about to retreat into a glass-windowed office, hesitates and holds the door open.

"Come in," he says. "No need to get upset over something so minor."

The office smells like the police station, the same aroma of old paper, mildew, and dust, but it's lacking the odor of men, of sweat and dirty water. The furniture is drab, its varnish chipped. There are several gray metal filing cabinets. A map of Paris is tacked to the wall, peppered with dots of color, winding routes in red and green along the tracery of streets and boulevards. The man goes behind his desk and takes a large green folder out of a drawer.

"I know him, your man. He hasn't been here since last year, just before the war. But everyone knows him. Quite a strange fellow, not chatty, always dressed in rags like a scarecrow. Dirty, too. I remember the manager said something to him about it two or three times, but he didn't give a damn. I don't even think he was paying his license fee anymore."

The man is leafing through his register as he speaks. He puts his finger on a line of text at the bottom of a page.

"Here it is. Clovis Landier, he's called. Last we knew, he was living in the Passage Feuillet. That's between the Rue des Écluses and the Rue du Canal."

Thanks, and goodbye. The man, suddenly talkative, launches into a diatribe about the poor wretches who live in this area, but Antoine Roques is already closing the door behind him, cutting him off.

He retraces his steps all the way to the canal, paying no attention to anything around him. The Passage Feuillet is a narrow alley that probably gets no more than a few hours of sunlight a year. Puddles of stagnant green and black water pock the cracked pavement. The air stinks of cabbage, urine, and cold ashes. Voices float out of the windows; a baby squalls. A bird in a cage hung from a shutter hurls itself against the bars with tiny, sorrowful cries. Roques crosses paths with an old woman coming from the opposite direction, her face swallowed up by the folds of a black scarf. When he approaches to speak to her, she starts and groans, looking up at him with her toothless, gray, corpse-like face, blinking.

"I'm looking for Clovis. Clovis Landier, the cabman."

The old woman's face contorts in what might be a smile, her lips parting and her eyes all but vanishing between the folds of her virtually closed eyelids.

"It's that one, with the blue door," says a croaky voice from overhead.

A woman is leaning out her window, a basket of laundry on her hip.

"The old lady don't have all her marbles anymore; she won't answer you. It's on the second floor, on the side of the courtyard. I don't think 'e's there, but if you arrest 'im, keep 'im locked up tight. 'E frightens children."

Roques thanks her with a wave and walks toward the building. Water gurgles in a gutter as if it has suddenly begun raining, and he looks up at the blue sky, which is powerless to lighten the shadows in the alley.

"What's 'e done, for a cop to be looking for 'im? I thought the Commune rid us of all o' them sorts."

Roques doesn't want to know what sorts she's referring to. What does it matter? He simply acknowledges her with another wave of his hand, without turning around again. Behind him the old woman mumbles indistinctly, groaning, begging, perhaps. He turns and can't see anything of her except her bony hand outstretched toward him, trembling. He fumbles in his pocket for some money, finds a couple of coins that he places in the deep hollow of her palm. Her fingers snap closed instantly, like a living trap, a kind of enormous, skeletal spider, and he feels the long fingernails snag his skin for an instant and shudders before turning away from her moaning thanks.

The stairwell is dark, the banister wobbly. A tiny, filthy window lets in a grayish light that shows the stained, blotchy walls. He rams the door with his shoulder, and it opens, hitting a chest of drawers. A bed, two chairs, a table covered with a blue checked cloth. A wood stove with a rusty flue pipe has been installed in front of the bricked-up fireplace. A small table built into a corner holds a pitcher, an enameled basin, and a piece of soap. A towel hangs from a hook next to a small mirror. The basin is full of black, brackish water with a deposit of gray sludge around the edges.

Roques completes an entire circuit of the room in a mere twenty steps. There is a wooden trunk with black metal hinges under the bed. When he opens it, a soft, sweet-smelling cloud rises into his face. Rice powder, faded perfume, lavender. He doesn't dare touch what he is seeing: women's clothing, neatly folded, stacked and ironed. A pale blue blouse, a chestnut brown skirt, a pair of ladies' boots. A leather belt, a lace cap. He lifts out a cookie tin whose lid is decorated with a pastoral scene: a pair of shepherds, a few sheep in the distance, tall trees. He takes it to the window and opens it, and a photograph of a young woman smiles up at him, a pretty blonde with laughing eyes. On the back, an inscription written in a slanted, angular hand. *Aline, Compiègne, June 12, 1863.*

For an instant, Antoine Roques's mind is transported to a country hillside where this girl, wearing a blue blouse, her skirt spread out on the grass around her, sits beneath an immense tree. The sun is shining, and the air is full of simple, peaceful happiness. He tries to recall the simian figure he saw the day before yesterday on the boulevard, perched on the box seat of his cab, and try as he might, he can't manage to insert that character into this bucolic vision. He puts down the photo and picks up an envelope: *Monsieur et Madame Clovis Landier, Rue Basse, 26, Compiègne, Départment de l'Oise.* He is debating whether or not to read the folded letter inside when he spies another photograph sticking out of a small notebook: *September 25, 1865.* Here is the pretty blonde woman again, holding the arm of a tall brown-haired man with a closely trimmed beard and thick eyebrows. They are both young, twenty-five or so, and you can tell, from the half smiles that crinkle their eyes slightly, that they are trying not to laugh.

In front of them, two little boys of perhaps three and four years are holding hands, dressed alike in white shirts and impeccably pleated grey trousers. Their blue eyes gaze shyly at the camera. The taller one looks strangely like his mother. Two fingers of her right hand rest on his shoulder.

Antoine Roques examines the man's face. Clovis Landier bears—*could* bear—a resemblance to this man. This young, ordinary, happy man. He sets the photos down on the windowsill and looks from one face to the other, hoping that one of them, through the smile, the look in the eyes, the tilt of the head, might tell him something, reveal to him a fragment of truth, but he sees nothing in them but the serenity of commonplace, unremarkable people, of a happy family. He turns and looks around the room again, hoping to see something, anything, that will tell him more. He feels beneath the mattress, finds nothing, returns the coarse canvas blankets to their previous positions. Heavy footsteps sound in the street. He hurries to the window in case it's Clovis Landier, but it's only a man limping crookedly, nearly falling with each step he takes.

Antoine Roques looks back down at the box and the photos he has replaced on top of it, and he feels like scum, a bit ashamed of having found out this man's other life, a life from before, lived with people he loved, perhaps lived by a different man than the one he is now. This man with the frank, open face has become a kind of bogeyman, a violator of women, undoubtedly guilty of the worst things. He must be found, arrested, interrogated, and tried. He must answer for his actions. Does he remember what he used to be? The life he used to have? Does he remember loving this woman, cherishing these children? Playing with them on the shady banks of a river? What remains to him of all that?

Unmoving in front of the window, one hand resting on the fragments of this life, he is struck once again by the realization that he knows nothing, or almost nothing, of people and their suffering. The ones who rise up against injustice, but also the ones who sink into shadow. He never thought the job of policing he was assigned would lead him to such reflections, such serious doubts. The distant sound of a bugle brings him back to the insurgent city, the streets barricaded with courage, defended by a disarming army of volunteers who drag their gaiters, when they wear them at all, behind their officers while complaining like a band of indecisive mutineers.

He replaces the contents of the box and returns it to its nest of clothes in the trunk of memories and closes it as if it were an old grimoire full of secrets and magic. The faint perfume dissipates, and voices he didn't hear until now rise and fade away in some distant past.

Antoine Roques slips back down the street like a thief. He almost regrets having cracked the secrets of the man he is hunting and come across someone he wasn't looking for. He hurries through Paris, indifferent to the commotion. Are we ever sure of what we're looking for? Of what we want? He walks even faster, his mind beset by questions he has never asked himself before.

At the police station, Loubet informs him that the landlord Carmon's thugs have been found and that a trap is being set for them. La Cécilia has been forced to retreat and is preparing to withdraw into Paris. He feels a terrible weight settling on his shoulders and closes his eyes for an instant, trying to put his whirling thoughts into some kind of order.

"It's really the end this time," says Loubet with a sigh.

Roques thinks he can hear a bit of relief, even satisfaction, in the other man's voice.

"Every man will have to be at his post when the time comes," he says.

Loubet shrugs.

"I've never left mine. It's the only thing I have to be proud of."

Roques looks into his eyes, trying to guess his intent. The other man stares back unblinkingly, a faint smile on his lips.

He must be careful not to turn his back to Loubet from now on.

SUNDAY, MAY 21ST

12

Caroline wakes up shivering, opening her eyes to impenetrable darkness, and for a few seconds she stops breathing as if this tomblike darkness has absorbed all the available air. Then she fills her lungs with a gasp, panting and sobbing in terror. The odor of excrement and urine clings to her skin from sleeping in a dry sewer bed. Yet the pit of her stomach is now growling savagely, her guts twisting, so she climbs to her hands and knees and feels around for the crust of bread she took out of the pail of water. Beneath her hand, the soft, cold thing is like touching dead, rotting flesh, and she shudders. Fighting the urge to gag, she tears off a piece and puts it into her mouth, holding it there for a moment to warm it up before she swallows it. She manages to eat two more scraps of the soaked bread this way without vomiting, and the ravening beast in her belly quiets down. She listens and can hear only the sounds of her own body, the throbbing of her own blood in her temples, and, very far away and high above, the muffled thuds of the bombardment. Once she notices that sound, she can hear nothing else, as if the reality of what's happening outside has come to make itself known even in this lightless hole.

She decides to stand up and sways for a moment on her feet as the darkness swirls around her like an invisible carousel of which she can sense nothing but the vertigo. She takes a few steps with her hands stretched in front of her and runs into a wall, twisting a finger and breaking a nail, putting the painful digit in her mouth with a tiny wail like a little girl's. Moving again, she feels her way along the wall, which is cold and damp, rough and flaky, until she finds the door and flattens her ear against the flap, straining to hear something, anything—a voice, or footsteps—but no sound penetrates the thick wood.

She retraces her steps and, sitting down, feels the fetid dampness underneath her. She squeezes her thighs together because she is suddenly seized with the desire to urinate and doesn't want to do that here like a caged animal. She curls in on herself, tensing all her muscles, trying to control her breathing and quiet the pounding of her heart. She isn't injured, she tells herself, or weakened, for now, and this body is her fortress, into which she has withdrawn and which she will defend to the death. Above her, Paris trembles beneath the cannon fire. She thinks of Nicolas, and each rumble she hears is killing him; every shell that falls is cutting him down. She starts shivering again, her knees knocking together, and she can't hold it any longer and rises and walks to a wall and squats, whimpering.

When the door opens, she is huddled against the wall, trying to control the trembling of her body. The bright rectangle lit by the storm lantern dazzles her, and she sees the man coming toward her only as an enormous silhouette. She tries to resist his grasping hands but finds herself lifted and draped across his shoulders. What few shapes she can discern turn upside down and slip away, and then she's surprised to see cobblestones going past below her—a courtyard, it looks like, gleaming in the daylight. She is tossed onto the bench seat of a hansom cab, cries out, and sits up across from the man, whose face is half-hidden beneath a large hat, his dilated pupils fixed on her. A revolver, straight and hard as an iron bar, is pointed at her forehead by the arm emerging from his greatcoat-like garment.

"Don't scream. Don't move."

The carriage begins to clatter across the cobblestones, picking up speed once they're out in the street. Caroline closes her eyes. The curtains at the windows are drawn, and the city outside them is nothing beyond the metallic rattle of the wheels but a confusion of sounds that reach her in bursts, vanishing almost before they reach her ears. Explosions, somewhere in the distance. Voices that brush past the cab, both male and female. She wonders for a moment if this isn't just one of those dreams from which you can't wake up, the kind that starts up again as soon as you fall back to sleep. She tries to think of Nicolas again, but nothing comes to her except memories from childhood, her mother bent over the ground with a hoe, her father leading an ox by its halter. Snow, and playing with her brothers, sliding in the big meadow behind the house.

The carriage stops suddenly, and the door opens. Another man appears, this one dressed in rags, his face covered by a thick beard. He glances up and down the street and gestures to the other to hurry up. She is pulled out of the cab by the collar of her blouse; the fabric tears, and she feels the cold air on her bare shoulder. She is desperate to look around, to scream for help to anyone who might be nearby, but she is shoved into the foyer of a building and bundled up a staircase lit by a skylight. Fourth floor. She forces herself to notice points of reference, to apply her reason to a tangible reality. The honey-colored stone staircase, the polished wooden banister she runs her palm along. The dark blue door that opens to reveal yet another man. He is in his shirtsleeves, his collar open. He looks startled, backs into the vestibule, shouldering open another door that opens into a room flooded with light.

"What the—"

Caroline is put down on a sofa, and she waits for the room to stop spinning before she looks around, trying to understand even a fraction of what is happening to her.

The man in shirtsleeves stands unmoving in the center of the room, observing her, his hands on his hips.

"What is this?" he asks.

The man who brought her here takes off his hat to reveal his battered face. Caroline has seen these kinds of wounds when they were still open, raw flesh and the white of bone. He goes to a pedestal table holding a carafe and some glasses and pours himself some wine.

"I took quite a risk. You can't tell, but she's a really beautiful one."

"She's a slattern. Look at her. What sewer did you pull her from? My God, you must have found her in some hovel on the Aubervilliers road! Anyway, I wouldn't want her even if she were a veritable Aphrodite. I've decided to wait and see what happens. In a few days, people will be fighting in the streets, buildings occupied and ransacked, not to mention the pillaging we can expect from the army rabble. I need to put my albums, my equipment, somewhere safe until things get back to normal. I've already started doing it. And, as I told you, I've perfected a new camera that should allow me to take some images on the spot of what's about to happen. I know General Clinchant well; I'm going to send him a message to allow me to accompany the troops and photograph their reconquest of Paris. I'll be the first in the world to capture military operations live! Do you realize? With my invention, people won't just see soldiers posing with their guns beside them or leaning on their cannons—they'll be able to admire them in motion, in combat! This is the future of photography! Movement! Action! A bit out of focus sometimes, perhaps, but oh, how expressive!"

The disfigured man looks around, spies a basin, and seizes a cloth, which he dampens in the water and uses to scrub Caroline's face, parting her hair so the photographer can see her better. She struggles feebly at first, but then her arms fall weakly back to her sides and she lets him do it, her skin burning, scraped by the rough material, with that mutilated face above her, the man gritting his teeth as he works.

"Look," he says at last, stepping back a few paces to better appreciate the result of his handiwork.

The photographer approaches. He nods.

"Yes. But she stinks like a goat. Did you . . . ?"

"No. Didn't have time. I just kept her in storage for a bit, like the other ones."

"She doesn't look very accommodating. Look how she's looking at us. I like it."

The photographer glances at his watch.

"Fine. This should only take an hour or so. We'll doll her up a bit."

Caroline stands up and closes her eyes. She staggers as if she's drunk, and the two men stare at her in astonishment, perhaps waiting for her to fall back down. As soon as her legs feel a bit steadier, she launches herself at the shorter of the two, seizing the photographer's ear and twisting it and hammering at him with her fist before knocking him to the ground. The man lets out a sharp cry and curls into the fetal position to shield himself from her bare, kicking feet. Then a pair of powerful arms lifts her up, her arms held clamped to her sides, her breasts crushed flat, and she struggles, screams, tries to bite, butting her head backward against an iron-hard chest, but she isn't getting enough air, and in a dazzle of light from somewhere inside her own skull she sees the photographer getting to his feet, dusting himself off.

At first, she doesn't dare open her eyes. The hand between her legs, rubbing softly, the smell of soap, the barely lukewarm water being poured over her from a pitcher—these things pull her out of the torpor in which she's floating, unsure if she's asleep or not. Then, suddenly, she sees the broken face very near her own, smells his fetid breath, tastes something bitter on her tongue and recognizes it as laudanum, which they some-times give to the wounded men when they have to amputate a limb.

The two men busy over her don't speak. They work. They touch her body, wash it, wipe it, handle it neither roughly nor gently, but carefully, and she feels as if they've stolen it from her and are playing with it the way little girls play with their rag dolls. Images and sounds occasionally pierce the fog in her mind and then vanish. The hansom cab and its clattering wheels. Nicolas walking beside her on an empty street. Her sis-ter Marianne falling in the mud one Sunday, crying and waving her arms while the other children laughed. Dogs devouring something and fighting. Caroline withdraws into herself, barri-cading herself away amidst the chaos that threatens to overtake her, and she concentrates on what is being done to her, on this place where she is, on her chances of escaping. She can't always keep the visions from coming, but she manages to push them away, the way you'd wave away a cloud of gnats.

Then they are carrying her, laying her down, turning her over. She can feel their methodical hands on her. The photog-rapher gives instructions. There. Like that. No. Lift the leg higher. She hears clicking, then a faint grinding sound. The molded ceiling above her. A blue-and-black hanging tacked to the wall behind her. She doesn't dare move. Sometimes the ruined face of the man who brought her surges into her field of vision. She thought she had retreated far enough into the impregnable recesses of her own mind, but now she can feel all her defenses giving way beneath rising fear. She doesn't know what chasm she's suspended above at this moment. These men might throw her into the Seine or into some deep hole some-where, or leave her to die in the cellar from which they took her this morning. The world narrows until it is only these two men, handling her the way you would a stunned animal before it's gutted. She tries to summon back the images of Paris, of the

Commune rejoicing in the streets, of the mad few weeks the city has just experienced, the aid clinic and the pain and the blood, the cries of the wounded and their grateful smiles and grimaces of suffering, of Doctor Fontaine and Nicolas, Nicolas. She repeats his name over and over in her head, but nothing comes to her, not the sleepless nights, nor the crazy hope that drove them to roam the city late into the night, drunk on the spring air.

They toss her clothes on top of her, and she clutches them to her despite the stink of the cesspit clinging to them. She puts on her blouse and pulls on her skirt, contorting herself on the bed because the intense dizziness that has come over her strips her of the tiny bit of strength she would have needed to stand up. She is relieved to have her filthy garments back on, to hide her body again from the eyes of the men on the other side of the room, who aren't looking at her right now but are speaking in low voices, face to face, gesturing broadly. She sits up, leaning against the wall, and tries to make the room stop whirling around her. The men's voices reach her more distinctly now, their tone angry.

"Take it or leave it, Pujols. Everyone needs money."

The photographer walks away and takes a few coins from a desk, slipping them into an envelope and holding it out to the other man. For a moment, neither of them moves. The photographer stands there with his hand outstretched, while Pujols considers it, his wolf-like jaw working in his smashed face as if he's chewing his words before he says them. Suddenly he strikes the hand holding the envelope, causing the coins to scatter and clink on the floor, and then he slaps the photographer, who falls into an armchair behind him.

"Give me some money, damn you! Not bloody alms! You're rolling in it; I know you are!"

The photographer is all but swallowed up by the armchair, the hulking carcass of the other man looming over him. He flaps his hands in front of him, repeating "No!" several times in a falsetto voice, and then suddenly he leaps on the giant, clinging to his neck, managing to extricate himself and even push the man away. The two roll on the floor, grunting and cursing. They strike at each other, but their punches lack momentum and have almost no impact—though Pujols's huge fists do more damage, naturally, and the photographer scratches and bites and forces the other to protect his battered face and eyes with his hands.

Caroline inches to the edge of the bed. The floor is still rocking a bit, but she can feel the warmth and firmness of the parquet beneath her feet, and she is waiting now for the right moment to stand and make a run for the door, only a few meters away. To give herself courage, she estimates how many steps it will take for her to reach it. There's a vestibule, she remembers. She can't recall whether the front door is locked or not. Scanning the room, she spots an ivory-handled cane leaning against a chair. She'll have to grab it on her way out.

She stands up. Her heart hammers in her chest, and she takes three deep breaths, then turns and tenses, ready to run.

She starts at the sound of a gunshot that lifts the photographer off his feet and sends him sprawling on his back, both hands clutching at his chest. He gasps and thrashes, kicking at death, which is already lying heavily upon him, as Pujols gets to his feet and finishes him off with a bullet in the face. Caroline lets out a scream and launches herself forward, seizing the cane, but Pujols grabs her by the arm and spins her around, aiming an unsteady blow at her face that just misses her. She takes advantage of the moment to hit him with the cane, but the heavy pommel is in her hand, and she only manages to strike his ear.

He howls with pain, clutching the side of his head, waving the revolver: *Bitch! I'll kill you, you dirty whore!* She backs up, holding the cane at the ready, but she bumps into a piece of furniture that stops her from going any farther. She whips the cane in circles in front of her with the pommel forward, like a mace, but Pujols disarms her with a backhanded blow and hits her in the forehead with a right cross and then again on the back of the neck, and she crumples, her face covered in blood, and suddenly she can't feel her body anymore, she can't feel anything, no pain, no weight; she is nothing now but a mind, watching and listening to everything happening around her, trapped in a lifeless envelope. She expects to rise up out of herself any moment, like in the stories priests tell, to see her corpse slumped against the wall beneath her.

She never thought death would pause, would allow a brief moment of respite before the nothingness. She's never asked herself that question before, but none of the dead people she has seen ever seemed—even slightly, even for a moment—to be still of this world. She watched her father sink into the mattress, swallowed up by his last breath, the final words she said to him—flung desperately at him—clinging to his still-feverish face, seeming to be without echo in the void where he had gone. And now she can hear Pujols moving around the room, muttering, emptying drawers and rummaging through the furniture, ripping the doors off of wardrobes and desks, scattering papers and equipment and trinkets. And now, unable to move, in the depths of her spirit, fading like a smothered fire, she feels the final terror that belongs to the world of the living. There is some solace in the thought that her father could hear the tender, sorrowful words she murmured to him, that he was able to depart with that happiness, at least.

13

They are bent beneath a rain of fire. A horse pulling an artillery wagon is thrown into the air, its entrails spilling out, and falls, kicking, into the hole blasted beneath it. The muzzle of the twelve-pound cannon is buried in the ground as if poised to fire on Hell itself. Ten men fling themselves at the wheels to haul it upright again; they hang on the spokes, but the cannon doesn't budge, and then they're obliged to flatten themselves to the ground to let the shrapnel from a shell that's exploded twenty meters away slice through the air without taking their heads off.

Nicolas gets up, looks for his rifle, recovers his cap, readjusts the sack on his back. Red is already standing, his face distressed, looking around at the men rising only to crouch again almost immediately under a hail of bullets. There are almost a hundred of them huddled along what remains of this road, a track pockmarked with craters leading straight through the Bois de Boulogne. Behind them, the fortifications and the Porte d'Auteuil have disappeared in the smoke of the Parisian fires, blown back on themselves by the wind.

"We're going!"

Someone has given the order in a moment of quiet; nobody knows who. The column begins to move. Nicolas shouts "Space!" and the men create some distance between themselves so as not to die in groups. They walk fifty meters and then stop as two explosions cause the ground to heave and lift in front of them, then start again. A bugle sounds. They freeze and fall silent so they can hear better.

Retreat.

They've spent this whole morning trying to penetrate the Versaillais lines. To break the solid belt of artillery fire. A wall of iron and fire has risen in front of them. They've attacked, fallen back, attacked again. Now they're withdrawing before they're all killed.

They run. "To Paris!" one man shouts. They all take up the cry in a chorus, running fast. Adrien catches up to Nicolas. He's covered in blood and guts. He stinks; you can smell it even over the odors of gunpowder and smoke. Nicolas asks him what happened, and the boy wipes his mouth, spits out something soft, coughs and spits again.

"I was almost right under the fucking horse!"

A man cries out behind them and falls forward. They hurry to him and take off his cap, and half of his skull comes away with it, the mess of his brains slopping over their fingers. A mitrailleuse's bullet has taken off the back of his head.

"Get down!"

The shell hisses past above them without hitting them. The men scatter into the ditch, hurling themselves into holes.

"Where are they?"

They turn and look down the road, and they see the mitrailleuse in battery formation under a dead tree. Adrien cocks his rifle, uses the dead man as a support, takes aim.

"Don't bother. They're too far away. We've got to get out of here."

They let themselves slide down into the ditch and creep out of the line of fire.

"What about him?" says Adrien, gesturing to the corpse in the road.

Nicolas tries to think of what to say.

"We'll come back for him . . . tonight."

They dodge among the little hillocks of earth churned up by the bombardment, splashing through water-filled holes along with the other men, who pant with effort and swear every time a fresh salvo pins them down. The ground heaves around them again and again, showering them with dirt, and they dig themselves out and run a bit farther and jump into the next hole—knowing that each one might turn out to be their final resting place. Straightening up, they see their comrades rising around them too, and in this way their filthy army of exhausted hunchbacks finally limps its way to the ramparts, where two eight-pound cannons are firing blindly at the Versaillais lines in an attempt to cover them. Adrien seizes Nicolas's arm.

"Hear that?"

No. He can't hear much of anything at the moment, his ears full of whistling and murmuring.

"The drum! The drum! They're advancing! They're calling up the march battalions!"

They pass the Porte d'Auteuil in a throng, artillery shells whistling past above their heads, pursued by explosions seemingly coming from everywhere, and hasten through deserted streets strewn with rubble and blocked in places by the tumbled ruins of collapsed buildings. Flames burst out of windows here and there. The men walk as fast as they can. A few stretchers found God knows where are carried by four at a time, they are so heavy, and the staggering men so exhausted. The wounded men on the stretchers, their skin black with dirt, move feebly, raising an arm or lifting their heads to speak to someone, something. The stretcher-bearers talk to them. *It's going to be all right, Comrade.* And they lie back down, pretending to believe the words.

An aid station has been set up in a church. The pews and prie-dieus have been piled to one side, and twenty women bustle around, carrying pails and clean cloths, bloody as butchers, amid the dead and wounded. There are easily a hundred patients in rows on the floor, some of them without blankets or even lying directly on the tiles. Behind the altar, a moribund Christ closes his eyes.

Nicolas has come in to help an injured comrade limp to a pallet; the man's leg has been mangled by shrapnel from an artillery shell. He approaches a sergeant who is desperate to go home to the 12th arrondissement. The man's hand has been half torn off. He seems confused and as if he isn't feeling any pain, appearing to view his wound, bandaged in a blood-soaked scrap of shirt, as nothing more serious than a mosquito bite. He waves a pocketknife in the face of the aid-station nurse who has installed him on a straw mattress, speaking in a low growl, muttering curses at the woman, who has seen and heard it all before and simply smiles while keeping safely out of reach of the short blade tracing shaky circles in the air. Nicolas confiscates the knife and attempts reason when the man abruptly collapses and begins weeping. He's a clock-maker. He starts talking about his children, his wife, about the ruined future. "We're fucked," he says. "Fucked." The nurse promises him that they will treat his wounded hand at the hospital, that he'll be able to work again. And as for the future, it belongs to the people. She declares this in a firm, clear voice that rises above the groans and the cries, squeezing the patient's shoulder. The man laughs silently and coughs. "You're a funny one, you are," he says.

Nicolas straightens and looks around, overwhelmed, at all this bravery laid low, these good intentions brought to nothing. He longs for Caroline, wishing she were here lending a hand, as he watches the women work, ask questions, straighten up from a wounded man, hands on hips, breathless, discouraged, perhaps, by the patient's condition. He remembers the day he went to see her at her aid station; it was calm then, nothing like this, only about thirty patients, and he had found her pale and sweaty, her apron covered with brownish stains, the scarf covering her hair nearly unknotted. She had watched him approach as if she had no idea who he was; it had taken a moment before she smiled, as if she had to make an effort to shift into a different reality, to remember that something existed other than this chamber of horrors, this army of mutilated men, some driven mad by what they had seen or suffered. He looks for her again now, desperate for the small miracle of her appearance to occur, but then he realizes, yet again, that miracles have no place in this world, or in his beliefs.

He turns and spots Red on the other side of the nave near the vestry, which has been turned into an operating room, wandering beneath the vaulted ceiling with a dazed expression on his face. He is dragging his rifle loosely behind him and doesn't seem to recognize Nicolas at first. He is looking for someone. He stops in front of Nicolas, shakes his head.

"All right, my friend?"

"Yes, yes," says Red. "It's just . . ."

"Are you hurt? Do you have pain anywhere?"

Red shakes his head absentmindedly, his gaze unfocused.

"We could get out of here," suggests Nicolas. "I'd love a drink."

He takes his friend by the arm and steers him toward the main door, its panel open to reveal smoke-tinged fog reddened by the glow of the sunset. Coaches are lined up in the forecourt, waiting to transport cargoes of wounded to the hospital. Stretcher-bearers come and go, turning in circles, uncertain of where to set down their tossing occupants, the canvas of the stretchers brown with blood, the air ringing with curses and shouts—sometimes the bearers', sometimes the patients' themselves, if they are still capable of any kind of speech. No one knows who is giving the orders, who is organizing the transfers, which hospital is the destination.

Nicolas and Red stand for a moment in the middle of the milling throng, unsure of how to help, afraid of causing further problems. Two artillery shells explode near the Seine. A third seems to lift a house completely off its foundation; they see it rise into the air, off toward the ramparts. Red, still in a daze, follows the bloody, prostrate men with his gaze, some screaming and clutching at a leg they no longer possess, trying to staunch the blood that wells between their fingers. Then Nicolas tugs at his sleeve, and they walk away, crossing the Rue de Passy, picking their way through the rubble until they reach a nearly intact bar on a narrow lane, directly across from a house that has collapsed in on itself, charred beams poking out of the debris.

The bar is empty. Two candles burn on the counter, and two more on a pair of tables. The place feels like a chapel in the middle of nowhere. The flame of an oil lamp hanging from a beam dances and smokes. The air smells of wine, stone and saltpeter, burnt fat. They can hear cooking noises coming from the back, fat sizzling, the clatter of something being stirred in a pot. Nicolas calls out. He's losing his voice, so he clears his throat and asks again if there's anyone there. Red sits down at a table, his face like that of an exhausted devil in the reddish candlelight. He props his rifle against the wall and runs his finger along the cutting edge of his bayonet. Someone is still stirring something in the back, at the end of a corridor, in a room whose cracked door shows a sliver of golden light. Then a shadow moves, blotting out the glow, and a silhouette emerges, limping. It's a tall man with a large mustache and sideburns, a worker's cap on his head. He's wiping his hands on a rag, which he tosses onto the bar.

"Well, well," he says. "Ghosts."

Nicolas steps over to the counter and warms his hands over the candle flame.

"Why would you say that? We're not dead."

"You look like it. Pale, defeated, stinking. Just like dead people."

"Well, these dead people are thirsty. Give us some wine and a bit of something stronger for my friend."

The bar owner glances over at Red, whose eyes are closed—asleep, perhaps—and takes down some glasses and a bottle of red wine and another bottle, this one of some clear alcohol, that he uncorks with his teeth and sniffs warily.

"This stuff should wake him up. A cousin of mine makes it, near Lamballe, from apples and honey. He puts something else in it, too, some kind of kelp; who knows why they do what they do out there in the sticks. That's what gives it the funny smell, but one sip and you won't mind anymore."

The man speaks without looking at him, his voice even, as if he's talking to himself. Nicolas is tempted to tell him that he's from Brittany, too, but he doesn't want to start a conversation about that. Only to sit down and stay there for a while, to hold his fatigue in his lap and rock it a bit.

"Go on, sit yourself down, I'll bring it to you. Don't want you passing out on me; I wouldn't be able to get you back on your feet. You hungry at all, by chance?"

Nicolas feels tears spring to his eyes. He nods, and then goes to sit across from Red.

"If you've got anything."

The man serves them. His gestures are precise, considerate. You might think him a waiter in an elegant boulevard café. He disappears into the back room, still limping. They hear him murmur something, and then a youthful voice answers. Red doesn't speak. He simply shakes his head, eyes downcast.

"Joseph. Are you all right?"

Nicolas never calls him that, never uses his first name. He's always Red to everyone, because of his hair, and the flag. It seems to pull him out of his torpor a bit, and he stares at

Nicolas for a moment without saying anything, blinking as if he's just waking up.

"I was afraid."

"We're all afraid."

"Not like that. Not like I was earlier."

His eyes shine with tears.

"I couldn't remember whether I'd died or not. I was looking for myself on those cots in that church. I thought I saw my dead body, but it wasn't me."

Nicolas is confused. Red looks at him without really seeing him, that dazed expression still on his face. It's like he's in another world, and is stunned by what he's discovering. Nicolas shakes himself to get rid of the large, cold hand that has just come to rest between his shoulder blades. He thinks about the bar owner's welcome, his remark about ghosts. For a moment, in this dim room, across from a friend lost and alone in some distant, unreachable realm, he gives way to doubt, his mind disturbed by a slow-moving whirlwind.

Then an enormous explosion shakes all the dust from the ceiling and lifts the floor beneath their feet, jostling them in their chairs as if they weighed nothing at all. They look at each other, dumbfounded, clinging to the table. They can hear stone crashing in the street, glass breaking. There is a terrific thundering clatter whose vibrations Nicolas can feel in his legs, then the sharp dry crack of a building collapsing close by.

They are both paralyzed by the sudden silence that follows. Strangely, they both drop their gazes at the same time to the candle on their table, whose flame doesn't tremble, rising and stretching in the dimness without a flicker.

"You see?" says Nicolas. "You aren't dead, because you can still die. They're still trying to kill us. That's a good sign."

Red smiles. Punches him gently on the shoulder.

"We won't let them do it," he says, hitching up his belt dramatically.

They go to the threshold and look out. The night outside is choked with dust, pocked with hissing fires. Nicolas takes a few steps into the rubble-strewn street.

"They'd rather raze Paris to the ground then leave it to the people. There's no limit to how far they'll go."

They go back inside to their drinks. Red tosses back a large gulp of hooch and flushes red as it burns its way down his gullet.

"Holy shit! What's this medicine?"

"Some Breton firewater. A sort of Calvados seasoned with seaweed, or so I've been told. You needed it just now, to put a bit of life back into you."

As they sit down, the bar patron returns with two steaming plates, which he sets down in front of them. It's some kind of stew, and their mouths water at the scent. They swallow noisily and blow on the first spoonfuls to cool it down.

"What's the meat?"

"Horse. It died on the corner of the Rue Vital. My cousin's a butcher, so we went and took a few cuts. Hadn't been dead more than two hours, don't worry. I give my little ones the same food as you; I wouldn't poison them with a rotten carcass."

They eat. No one speaks. They're starving, delighted. They burn their tongues a bit on the first few bites and then shovel it down, mouths full of the tender, flavorful meat. The limping barman is a hell of a cook. They lick their plates clean, wash the stew down with a swig of wine, lean back, stretching their legs. Red folds his arms behind his head as if readying himself for a nap.

"If it turns out that we're really dead, this just might be our own little corner of heaven. Too bad I don't believe in all that claptrap."

The barman, behind his counter, grunts and smiles. They're all quiet for a few minutes.

"There aren't many people left around here; they've all run

off for fear the rabble will slit their throats, and it's their own army who's blowing up their nice apartments and mansions. You're my first customers of the day. Though the street's not exactly inviting at the moment, it's got to be said. Where have you come from in that state?"

"Versailles," Nicolas says. "A round trip in one day, to drown Thiers in Louis XIV's bathtub. Just a healthful little stroll."

"As bad as that?"

"No words for it," says Red. "We didn't make it a kilometer into the Bois de Boulogne before they tore us to shreds. They've been in better form against us than they were with the Prussians, the bastards. And we ain't seen nothing yet. As soon as they enter Paris, it'll be a massacre. And all this time, milords in the Central Committee have been talking and talking instead of sending reinforcements."

The man shakes his head in chagrin.

"I could tell as soon as you walked in. You looked like you'd come from Hades itself. That's why I talked about ghosts—didn't mean to offend. Can I offer you a little after-dinner sweet, to make up for it? Walnut liqueur. You can tell me the latest news."

Red and Nicolas decline. They have already eaten and drunk their fill, and they thank him. It's also time for them to get back; their company is preparing to withdraw to the other side of the Seine.

"If it weren't for my bum leg, I'd have enlisted in the National Guard myself. Opened this place last year, with a little inheritance. It's all I've got—well, that and my debts, and my little ones to feed, so I cling to my bar like an idiot . . ."

There haven't been any explosions for a few minutes now. The lame barman holds up a finger and cocks his ear.

"Seems like it might be calming down."

The three of them listen to the strange silence the way you

await the imminent arrival of something dangerous. Suddenly, there is the sound of footsteps overhead. The scraping of a piece of furniture against the floor. Nicolas flinches involuntarily.

"It's Lucienne, my daughter. She's putting away the laundry."

"We'd better be off," says Nicolas. "How much do we owe you?"

The man waves his words away. "Nothing at all. I'd be ashamed to take any money from you."

"What's your name?" asks Red. "Mine's Joseph. Joseph Favereau. My friends call me Red. And this is Nicolas Bellec. We're from the 105th."

"I'm Ferdinand Magnier."

He extends his hand. They shoulder their rifles and put their dented, filthy caps back on. Handshakes. Smiles. All three of them have tears in their eyes.

"It's an honor to have met you, Citizens. You're not the first to come through here, but I've never seen men so . . . I don't even know the word . . . shattered. That's it. Shattered. When I first saw you earlier, you hadn't been physically wounded, but it almost seemed worse than that. Especially you, Joseph. Your eyes were totally empty. It was dreadful."

"You seem to understand people well," says Nicolas. "No one's ever spoken to me like that. As if I were important, or unique. I needed it."

They pause on the threshold, in the night, their outlines only just visible in the dim light filtering through the door. They wish each other courage and luck. They promise to see each other again, after this is all over. Then the two soldiers step out onto the cracked pavement, which crunches beneath their feet.

"There are other good days to come," says the man from behind them.

They salute him, but the gesture is lost in the darkness. Soon enough, voices and firelight rise up ahead of them. Snatches of conversation and song. Nicolas longs to retrace his steps and chat with Ferdinand in the half-light about the secret human things the man seems to understand, and then go, full of real courage, and turn Paris upside down in search of Caroline.

14

Pujols has spent the last hour ransacking the apartment, overturning the furniture, pulling up the rugs, tearing out the poorly nailed-down floorboards in case they might conceal a hidden cache, smashing holes in any parts of the walls that seem hollow. No treasure. No hoard. Five hundred francs sensibly stashed in an envelope at the back of a desk drawer; a stopped watch on a gold chain whose key broke off in his fingers. He kept the chain and hurled the watch against a wall so that it broke apart. He has flipped through the photograph albums, found a few surprising or disturbing photos, piled everything into a suitcase in case he might be able to resell them, even at a ridiculously low price, to some twisted individual. The days to come promise to be uncertain and dangerous, and he'll need every available resource to make it through them—and, after all, why not make the most of the situation?

He has repeatedly stepped over the photographer's corpse, sometimes tripping over its legs in his haste, cursing at this dead man who had the temerity to fall right in his way and sometimes seems to be coming alive for the express malicious purpose of obstructing his comings and goings, bumping one last time into the looting assassin. He has walked through the pool of blood spreading outward from the shattered head and turned with curiosity to look at his own footprints gleaming scarlet against the dark floorboards.

Now he is sitting on a sofa for a moment, scrutinizing the

pillaged room, exhausted and furious, incapable of thought, drained of all willpower. He touches the envelope full of money in his pocket, feels the links of the gold chain beneath his fingertips, and savors this simple pleasure the way an infant delights in stroking a favorite toy.

An explosion rattles the windows, and he looks out and sees black smoke mushrooming above the rooftops. Then another shell bursts even closer by, and a window flies open, letting in a gust of smoke- and gunpowder-scented wind, so Pujols wrenches himself out of his torpor and makes one last round of the apartment in case he's missed anything. Just as he is picking up the suitcase, he hears a groan from the girl, who he thought was dead, and he sees her, on the other side of the room, moving her legs and opening her eyes and starting to cry. He can feel the revolver in his coat pocket against his hip, and he squeezes its grip in his hand, decides to finish her. Not to leave any witnesses, not a single one, because soon the city's going to be crawling with soldiers and police who will be working doubly hard to restore order and purify Paris of the crime that will have thrived during these weeks of anarchy. And those louts—and the good citizens who will surely be putting up the flags and bunting to welcome them back and encourage their redemptive labor—will make no distinction between him, Pujols, who never questioned anything about the old bourgeois world and was content to walk its fringes alone, to traverse its hells and take what advantage and enjoyment he could from them, instinctively applying the law of the jungle—no, they won't distinguish between the murders and vicious acts he has committed and the barbarism of the hated rabble, these armed animals, drunks, gluttons, thieves, and assassins, the descendants of '93 and '48, who will have nearly succeeded in overturning the old order and the laws they found so unjust, turning on their own guardians and protectors, and—the ultimate crime—

who are guilty of having shown the world that such a thing was possible.

He approaches Caroline—suddenly he remembers her first name—and is cocking his revolver, already preparing to watch her face cave in beneath the impact of the bullet, when she opens her eyes and stares directly into his own, her expression astonished, questioning, exhausted, clear and blue in the shadowy corner where she lies sprawled, and Pujols can't accept that anyone would look at him like that, as if expecting an explanation from him, as if his actions aren't justified, and he hesitates, thinking that if he slices out the light in those eyes he will erase the questions they're asking him. He unfolds his knife and feels, creeping along his spine like a nefarious insect, the deep shiver he always feels when anticipating bladework, his mastery over the movement and effort it requires, the quick, sharp penetration, the faint hissing sound, and then the dampness and then the blood, that feeling of omnipotence at the idea that he is the giver of death, yes, that he is giving it the way you slip a gold coin into a beggar's palm for the simple pleasure of bestowing such an extravagant favor.

"What are you doing?"

She is blinking as if fighting sleep, but she doesn't take her eyes off him. In response to her question, he brandishes his knife threateningly at her, but she doesn't react, only gazes at him wearily, resignedly, then closes her eyes.

He doesn't understand. Usually it is terror that pleads or weeps or radiates out of eyes already seeing nothing but the abyss opening up in front of them. He doesn't understand the way this girl is holding her own against him, questioning him while looking him straight in the eye with that strange detachment. Then an idea comes to him. He'll keep her alive. Tomorrow he will leave Paris via the Porte de Clignancourt and try to find that Prussian colonel stationed at Saint-Ouen, the Bavarian who was so polite but also so utterly vicious that even he, Pujols, was almost disturbed by it. Herbert, he was called. The one with whom he's spent a few memorable evenings. Safe-conduct passes might be very expensive these days, and this girl could be a valuable form of currency after all.

"Right, then. I've got something better in mind for you. You can stare death in the face, you've got bravado, but let's see if you'll still want to keep those eyes wide open when you see the life I'm planning for you."

He hoists her over his shoulder and is astonished at how light she is. He feels her limp, soft body against him, her belly, her breasts, and he can't keep from sliding his hands beneath her skirt for a better grip, his fingers between her thighs. If he weren't in such a rush he'd be tempted to take her right here on these stairs he's hurrying down at the moment, pound her against the banister, and—why not—once that was done, to toss her over it, just to hear the crunch of her body hitting the ground three floors below. But he dismisses these urges that have seized him low in his belly without too much difficulty because an artillery shell explodes a few streets away, and a cloud of plaster dust fills the stairwell.

Out in the street, he finds Clovis standing near his horse, murmuring in its ear and stroking its neck. The man turns and watches him toss the girl into the coach, unmoving.

"What the hell are you doing?"

The horse's legs tremble. Its spine quivers with an enormous shudder. A drumroll sounds in the distance.

"He's afraid. He's going to die."

Two figures emerge from the smoke at the end of the street. National guardsmen. They pause, look, approach. One of them has seized his rifle, and they can hear the breech clicking as he arms it.

"Ho there, Citizens!" he cries. "We need this carriage!"

Clovis turns his back on them and climbs up onto his box

seat. The guard aims his rifle at him and plants himself in the middle of the street.

"Not another move, friend."

Clovis lets go of the reins. He rummages beneath his seat and pulls out a bottle, from which he takes a healthy swallow.

"Got enough there for me, too?"

The other soldier has stopped three meters from Pujols, bayonet pointed at him.

"Where are you going like that? Who's in the coach?"

"What the fuck business is it of yours?"

Clovis tosses the bottle at the guard who was asking for it, forcing him to twist awkwardly to catch it. The shot from the hunting rifle doubles him over, and he cries out and drops to his knees, his hands clamped over his gut already coated with blood. He looks around, astonished, and falls on his face in the dirt.

The soldier who was brandishing the bayonet at Pujols probably doesn't even hear the shot that kills him cleanly with a bullet through the head. He staggers backward and falls, his rifle across his chest. Pujols hurries over, grabs his feet, pulls him toward the building entrance. He calls to Clovis to help him, so the cabman climbs down from his perch slowly, walks around the horse, stroking its muzzle, and picks up the other guard's wrists, but his hands slip in the blood so he seizes him by the collar of his jacket and drags him across the cobblestones, muttering things to the dying man, who cries and moans. They leave the bodies and weapons beneath a staircase, covering them hastily with a tarpaulin they find there.

Then they flee without another word to each other. The horse is spurred to a trot through streets where people are knocking down the remains of walls, carrying shopping baskets, pulling children along by the hand. Raising their eyes skyward every time a new artillery shell explodes. It takes them less than ten minutes to reach the Rue des Missions. In the

courtyard, Madame Viviane is scrubbing a doorstep with a
stiff-bristled brush. She pretends not to see them, working
busily, wringing out a mop over a bucket. The horse blows out
a breath. It tosses its big, lathered head with a groan, showing
its yellow teeth. Clovis gets down and presses his forehead
against the horse's, talking softly to it. Farther away they can
hear the beat of a drum, the call of a bugle, the clamor of
voices. Dark clouds of smoke scud across the blue sky, driven
by a southern wind. Pujols gazes at them, worried, and glances
at the roof, because it seems to him that the flames will come
at any moment, leaping between the chimneys like an agile,
hungry monster. He lifts Caroline off the seat and sets her on
the ground, swaying, and supports her as they walk to the cellar entrance. Madame Viviane rises, leaning on her mop.

"Who is that girl? Where did she come from? And where
are you taking her?"

He doesn't answer. Caroline stumbles on the large cobblestones, forcing him to brace her so she doesn't fall. The woman
seizes his arm, tugging so that he turns toward her.

"Hey! Answer me when I'm talking to you!"

"Shut up."

Without looking at her, he shoves her away with a sweep of
his arm, and she falls on her rump. He can hear her howling
and swearing at him as he descends the few steps leading to the
cellar door. Opening it, he is struck once again by the fetid air
of this crypt and pushes the girl inside, but she clings to him,
nearly dragging him with her, and he kicks her away from him.
He locks the door hastily, clutching the key in his fist because
his hand is shaking, and when he emerges into the courtyard,
Madame Viviane, her hair undone, screaming, flings herself at
him and hits him with her mop, and he cowers beneath the
blows, takes a step and strikes her beneath the chin with the
fist holding the key. He hears her teeth cracking and breaking,
sees her cheek tearing, ripped open by the blade of the key,

and he straightens as the woman spins around, staggering three or four steps like one of those dancing bears kept on a chain at a fair and forced to turn in circles, and then crumples on a doorstep, her face streaming with blood, her dislocated jaw gaping in a grotesque grin.

Clovis is giving water to his horse, who plunges its muzzle into the pail and then is still, as if observing its own reflection in the water.

"We've got to go," says Pujols. "Tonight."

Clovis doesn't answer, his face bent near the animal's.

"Damned idiot," mutters Pujols, going up to his apartment. He pushes open the door with his shoulder and goes directly to the large dresser, opening a drawer, taking out money and jewelry and stuffing it all deep into his pockets. In a wardrobe he finds his big canvas sack and crams a few articles of clothing into it along with a matchbox full of revolver cartridges. From the kitchen he takes a knife, the one for meat that he sharpened himself three days ago, wrapping it in a sheet of newspaper. He stops in the middle of the room, trying to reflect, and can't think of anything but the horse out there dying in the middle of the courtyard, and he wonders where on earth they will manage to find another one right now, at a time when the streets are filled with the sounds of running and shouting and with armed men straggling in defeated groups or following the drums. Maybe they can blend in with them. He thinks about the two national guardsmen they killed just a little while ago, of their uniforms, their guns, and a plan begins to form in his head.

Just as he is preparing to step out onto the landing, he is thrown against the banister by an explosion, and the staircase is split in half by a jagged crack that spreads step by step down to the ground floor and widens with a deafening snap. He creeps down, too, his back against the wall, as chunks of plaster fall around him and the whole building seems on the verge of tumbling down.

The courtyard is nothing but a dark well full of fog that burns his eyes, so thick that he can't see where he's putting his feet. The horse whinnies somewhere in front of him. He feels his way, step by step, collides with an overturned bucket, bumps into the animal lying between the shafts. It kicks its legs and looks up at him with maddened eyes. Pujols calls out to Clovis and strains his eyes through the pea-soup haze, waiting to see his voluminous silhouette emerge, disheveled from the explosion, but nothing moves except for the smoky fog whirling and billowing around him. He moves forward again, blind and disoriented, and trips over the broken frame of a window in the middle of a jumble of stones and slate. The fog is less thick here and lets through a dull shaft of light, and he sees that part of the building at the rear of the courtyard has collapsed, its roof and façade torn away, rubble piled as high as the second floor. And on top of this heap, dark and hunched, rummaging through the gravel and stone blocks with his bare hands is Clovis, who turns toward him, eyes wide, hair white with plaster dust.

"The girl," he says. "She's under there, in the cellar!"

"She's dead by now. Come on, we've got to find a horse. Yours is about to meet its maker. We're leaving tonight. We have to get to the Porte de Clignancourt, toward Saint-Ouen."

"They're all Prussian, out there."

"Exactly. We'll be safe with them while we wait for things to calm down."

Clovis is perched on a beam. He wipes his forehead with the back of his hand and stares at Pujols without moving.

"I'm not going anywhere, least of all to the Prusscos. That girl's down there somewhere. We can't leave her to die like this."

Pujols laughs. The cabman's expression is serious, almost dignified, in spite of his tattered clothes and the dust whitening his face and hair. He looks like a homeless philosopher ready to give the day's lesson from atop this heap of ruins to which he bears such a resemblance.

"You weren't so scrupulous when it came to the others. Did you maybe think that by handing them over to Gros-Tonton we were putting them in some sort of boarding school for girls, to protect them from vice and depravity? You helped me take them, keep them quiet, transport them, didn't you? And who was it that got an eyeful at the photographer's, and was quite happy to take a little taste, free of charge? That was you, not somebody else, who fucked them, right? And just a couple hours ago, I didn't exactly have to encourage you to kill that national guardsman, did I? So what's gotten into you? Afraid of the Last Judgment or something? The return of the police? You think your regrets will be enough to save you? You're complicit and you're guilty, and Madame la Guillotine is waiting for you just as much as she is for me."

"No one and nothing is waiting for me anymore, not even the guillotine."

Clovis turns his back on Pujols and continues searching through the debris, tossing it aside. *No witnesses*, Pujols says to himself, and he takes out his revolver and cocks it. Clovis turns back to him when he hears the click.

"Aim well. I'm already dead anyway."

Pujols raises the weapon, extends his arm, draws a bead under Clovis's neck to take recoil into account, to be sure of taking off his head with a single bullet. Suddenly he is shocked by a violent blow that strikes him full in the face, and he finds himself on his back, groping around for his revolver, and sees Clovis standing over him, a stone in his hand.

"I told you I wasn't going anywhere. One move and I'll bash your face in; you won't even dare look at yourself in a mirror anymore—and that's if I don't gouge your eyes out. I'll leave you with your whore of a landlady, Madame Viviane Arnault, as it says over her door. I found her over there, her face a lopsided nightmare; I'm not even sure she's still alive. You'll have to finish her off with your bare hands because I need this."

Clovis picks up the revolver, examines it, spins the cylinder.

The dust has settled now, but something is burning in one of the gutted apartments, and smoke billows from time to time over the two men, engulfing them in the same suffocating veil.

Pujols squints at him through the haze and his own tears, spits out the blood filling his mouth, brings a hand to his forehead, feeling the enormous lump there. He doesn't dare touch the rest of his face, because it feels like every bone in it has been broken. He doesn't know if he'll be able to stand up; his legs feel weak as water, barely answering his brain's commands, incapable of carrying him anywhere.

"That little girl down there—I'm going to get some people to help me look for her. I won't let her die this way."

Clovis vanishes into the smoke, hunchbacked and shuffling like an old man. Pujols hears him murmur a few words, and then the shot makes him jump, and the dragging steps cross the courtyard, echo beneath the entry arch, fade away in the street.

Pujols listens to the fire crackling in the silence. He calls out to Madame Viviane, who doesn't respond. He looks up at the dirty sky with its tattered shreds of dark cloud. He manages to roll onto his side and raise himself up on an elbow, then begins crawling through the debris. Blood flows unchecked from his nose and mouth and drips onto the cobbles, and the pain and the effort wrench groans from him that he can't hold back. His strength gives way again, and he slumps onto his stomach, laying his head on his folded arms carefully because he's afraid even this slight pressure will cause his skull to burst, and he lets himself go, numb, closing his eyes.

I just need to sleep. He feels the mass of his body weighing him down as if he could sink into the granite cobbles, into a hole where there would be no more pain.

15

C aroline makes out a broken sliver of light overhead, like a tiny bit of daylight frozen in a night sky. She sits up, not sure what she's seeing. She's afraid it might be the effect of what they made her take—when was it? Yesterday?—laudanum, probably, which clouds your mind until you can't tell dreams from reality, the present from the past. She's seen its effects on wounded men to whom Doctor Fontaine prescribed a few doses to soothe the pain of an amputated limb or a piece of shrapnel continuing to burrow into the flesh like a white-hot blade. Some of them spoke of imaginary visitors they were convinced they could see at their bedsides; others sank into a blissful half sleep and then demanded more of the drug as soon as they woke up, trembling and anxious, some ready to do anything for another swallow.

She tries to pull together her thoughts, her memories, but they're like a disordered flock of sheep that run and leap in every direction, pursued by wild dogs. Snatches of a dream, impossible to link together. The noise of a gunshot, hands on her body, touching it without shame or gentleness, sunlight filtering into an apartment. Blows. She feels her face, and pain blooms beneath her skin. She recalls the man with the disfigured face and the smell he carried on his body, of sweat and smoke; it's still clinging to the back of her throat. The horse's hoofbeats, the clattering of the coach through the streets.

She suddenly remembers the explosion, the muffled

cracking above, the crushing sensation that made her ears ring and flattened her to the ground as if the air around her had been compressed—and then the silence, more crushing still, and the cry she let out because she knew she was buried beneath the ruins of a destroyed building, buried alive, her jailer probably dead or gone.

She has remained lying on the ground in this tomb with its cesspit-like odor that will soon mingle with the stink of her own corpse, straining her eyes into these impenetrable shadows, this death before death, this nothingness where, still alive, she has tried to imagine her own end, her mind fogged by the drug they made her take and the terror that made it impossible to move or even really think. For hours. Time stopped passing for her, a prisoner in a present eternity, an infinite forever.

She raises her eyes now toward the thread of light, and for an instant she can't see it anymore, horrifyingly—but eventually she spots it again, clear and fine like a strand of angel hair caught in the blackness, and she hopes this tiny crack will widen, that the ceiling of this cellar or vault she imagines she's in will cave in and open a way out for her. The building has clearly been blown to pieces, she tells herself, and might crumble further still; she remembers, during the first bombardments early this month, seeing houses that were almost intact, their façades barely cracked, collapse a day or two later because a shutter slammed in a breeze—so she stares at the bright filament and strains her ears for even the tiniest cracking sound that might signal the final destruction of this cellar.

After a while, she stretches out on the cold, slimy surface beneath her because her stiff back has turned her into a wooden statue, and she thinks—yes—that something is moving up there, almost imperceptibly, but her eyes blur and burn, so she closes them, and when she opens them again nothing has changed, nothing has obeyed the willpower she's been directing, for hours, perhaps, at the inert matter around her.

She could pray, of course, the way she saw her mother do so often when grief and misfortune visited them, when hunger gnawed at them, when death loomed over a baby's cradle, over her father's bed, murmuring pleas to that blind and deaf god who invariably ignored her cries for him to lay a merciful hand on a forehead burning with fever and take away the sickness. Nothing ever answered those prayers in the silence broken only by the ticking of an ancient clock, counting down the time that remained. When once, in church, on a gray cold morning when the stained-glass windows were dim and colorless, the priest explained that God had called a soul to his side, where it would know eternal rest and joy, Caroline had stared at the vaulted ceiling above her head and seen nothing but stone and the wispy smoke of the altar candles and, behind the altar, a skeletal torture victim doubtless sick and tired of hearing all the lies offered up in his name.

Shivering, she sits up and turns to look at the opaque walls, and the luminous strand reddens at the back of her eye and is gone. She feels her way around the whole of the space, grop-ing the walls, and she bumps against the bucket and hears water sloshing inside it, so she kneels down and drinks and recovers a few bits of soaked bread with her fingertips, which she swallows, gagging. Reaching the door, she runs her hands over its frame in the hope that it might be cracked or broken, and down near the floor she feels a faint current of air blowing softly on her hands and feels better; she stands up and pounds with her fists on the frame, which doesn't vibrate. She cries out for help, telling herself that surely someone passing by will hear her; she screams until her throat is raw and then listens but can hear only her own blood thrumming in her skull.

She will have to dig. She has nothing on her except for the skirt and blouse she doesn't remember putting on. Not even a hairpin. She gropes her way along the walls again, feels noth-ing beneath her bare feet but the sickening dampness. She must dig. She returns to the door, stoops down again, feels the air flowing over her skin. She scratches the beaten earth with a fingernail, but it is so packed and hard that she hardly scrapes it. Then she thinks of the bucket. Of its iron handle. She finds it, locates the points where it's attached, the hooks, and pulls hard on them, straining, and her finger twists and a nail bends backward, and the bucket slips and tips slightly, a bit of water splashing on her ankles. She lets out a cry of pain and puts her finger in her mouth, pulling at the bloody nail with her teeth, and she shudders at the thought that she could have spilled all the water, remembering what Doctor Fontaine had said to her once: you can go a week or two without eating, but you can't live more than two or three days without water. She thinks about how he used to instruct the nurses to force patients to drink if they wouldn't eat. "At least if they die, you won't be responsible," he often said, after they'd struggled to keep a stubborn patient hydrated.

She plunges her arm into the bucket as far as it will go. There are maybe five liters of water remaining, and she sobs over the pail without producing any tears to add to the store. She rolls onto her side, exhausted. Far off in the distance she can hear the sound of explosions that sometimes seem to come from the very bowels of the earth.

I'm here, buried alive, soon to be dead. And you?

She wants to sleep, to stop thinking. But she's afraid of the dreams that might come, so she simply allows tattered memories of happy days to drift through her exhausted mind.

16

They sleep now, stretched out beneath the only tree still standing on the Rue de Passy, because last night neither of them caught a single wink. Because last night the Versaillais cannons tightened their fiery embrace of Paris. Two hundred, three hundred cannons, maybe. Showers of stones, bursts of glass exploding from blown-out windows. It snowed ash, rains of sparks pouring from the black sky, the shells moaning before they fell.

For protection, they had flattened themselves against the bottoms of building façades that trembled against their backs, slate falling from the roofs like hatchet blades and smashing at their feet. Men with cracked skulls ran screaming through the streets before tumbling into a ditch.

Red had gone into an intact building, kicked open a door, and led the others into a ground-floor apartment. They'd shut themselves into an enormous living room opening onto a garden. Adrien had opened the French doors and settled himself in a wicker armchair on the terrace, his rifle across his knees, and abandoned himself to the perfume of the lilacs. They could see the bushes' leaves quivering with the impact of the bombardment.

"A person could get used to this!" the boy kept saying. "Even with the bombs!"

They'd looked for something to eat, finding only a box of cookies they shared and two bottles of liqueur they emptied by the light of three large candlesticks, toasting the health of the fine ladies whose maids must have served the drink to them in the elegant little glasses that sat atop a dessert trolley on a silver tray. Then they'd stretched their legs out on the armchairs and closed their eyes, but every new explosion shook them awake, plaster dust sometimes powdering their hair, and they could hear objects falling on the upper floors, and they'd glanced at the ceiling, trying to estimate how long it would take for it to cave in on their heads.

Just before dawn, a captain and three of his men had burst in yelling and slamming doors, pointing their rifles at them, ordering them to stand up with their hands in the air. They were swaying on their feet, visibly drunk. Nicolas had been obliged to give their names and the number of their battalion, and the four imbeciles had held him and his companions at gunpoint, and the group of them had stayed like that, unmoving, shouting over one another. Nicolas found it all too easy to imagine the moment a nervous finger would squeeze a trigger a bit too hard; the captain was shaking as he brandished his revolver, and in the flickering candlelight his grimacing face looked truly idiotic. The bombs fell thicker and faster around them, the garden lighting up with sudden flashes and subsiding back into blackness. A shell fell nearby, and two of the room's windows shattered. The drunken men all turned their heads in a single motion, looking stupidly astonished, as if they'd only just realized there were cannons firing. Red had thrown a chair at their heads and then hurled himself on them. Nicolas disarmed the captain, who slid down a wall into a sitting position and began laughing or crying, difficult to tell, and slapped the man two or three times to snap him out of his intoxicated stupor. The officer had looked up at Nicolas, his eyes full of tears, grinning like a child. He stank of alcohol and tooth decay. His men lay flat on their bellies, Red stalking among them with bayonet at the ready, muttering inaudible curses, while Adrian gathered their weapons and emptied their ammunition pouches of bullets and the tobacco he found there.

They had thrown the men out into the street with kicks to the rump for good measure and watched them stagger away, silent and swaying, their rifles shouldered, three cartridges in their pouch—just enough to scare off a few sparrows—threatening to report them to the colonel of the 74th battalion. Hearing this, one of them guffawed and made a rude noise with his mouth.

A bugle had sounded the call to muster at around six o'clock, and they'd joined about four hundred other men in front of the 16th arrondissement town hall. All around them the city was exploding, blown to smithereens. A colonel had addressed the troops on behalf of General Dombrowski. Reinforcements of both men and artillery were on the way. For now, there was nothing they could do. Pointless to try and mount the ramparts, which were under constant, unending fire. A new assessment of the situation would be made at around midday. He spoke loudly and clearly, this colonel without a military cap or regimental sword, the collar of his jacket undone, his voice firm, and the men listened to him quietly. Dozens of them had left in the night, frightened and discouraged, declaring that they would go defend the barricades in their own neighborhoods. Those that remained didn't dare think too much about it, for fear they would do the same thing.

Then the men had gathered in groups around the mess wagons. There was even coffee, a treat that brought exclamations of pleasure. The soldiers of the Commune kept their eyes fixed on their steaming cups, sipping and speaking in low voices. The soldiers of the Commune were nothing in that moment but a squadron of murmurs, a battalion of exhaustion, somehow still standing.

At around eleven o'clock, the cannons fell silent. They

could still hear rumbling now and then from the direction of Mont Valérien, but the battery guns had stopped firing.

"They're coming," said Adrien. "They'll be here before nightfall." Nicolas and Red hadn't replied, because there was nothing much to say after that. All three of them had stood listening to the silence. An occasional bird—mad, no doubt—trilled sharply. But they were listening farther, over the permanent ringing of their ears, as if they might be able to perceive the footsteps of the line regiments entering Paris.

Then they'd slept a bit, because there was nothing else to do, and because they didn't have the strength to do anything else.

"To arms!" Now a man runs past them in the street, grasping his rifle in both hands in front of him, bareheaded. "There's a line at the Porte de Saint-Cloud!"

In the surrounding streets, voices take up the cry. Men emerge from the buildings at a run, rushing down from upper floors where they have been quartered, pulling on their clothes, tripping and stumbling in their untied shoes or hurriedly donned boots. Gun belts, holsters, pouches, rifles tucked beneath arms, slung over shoulders, or hung from belts. They finish dressing and adjust their gear in the middle of the street. Officers ask for orders; sergeants try to assemble men in groups. Nicolas counts about fifty guards from the 105th around him.

"Is that all?"

"That's all," answers Langlois, a seasoned old warhorse, his forehead bound in a bloody bandage. "There are three companies at Belleville, remember?"

The men await orders. They wonder where the Versaillais are. Stationed at the Point du Jour? They're regrouping. Bringing in more artillery. Who said that? Some boys who were loitering nearby. So what do we do?

A captain called Mouchet is concerned, all the same, with

the distribution of ammunition. He sends ten Federates to get some from the town hall. Two artillery wagons have been sitting some distance away for three days now. Where are the gunners, they wonder. Who knows how to use these machines? Two men step forward. Nicolas recognizes two of the drunkards they disciplined last night. They explain that they held a bastion at the Porte de la Chapelle during the siege against the Prussians.

"Yes, but what about horses?" one of them asks. "Are we supposed to haul the thing ourselves?"

The colonel who spoke earlier now appears, adjusting his uniform.

"We're trying to find some," someone tells him. "To pull the cannons."

The colonel snorts with laughter. "Horses? Here? Now? It'll take ten men to pull each cannon; that's the only option left to us now. And do you even know what you'll do with your fucking cannons then? What position? How much firepower?"

The men hesitate, murmuring. Some of them think they should beat a retreat from here, where all seems already lost. They're already picking up their sacks and rifles, waiting, arguing with comrades who try to persuade them to stay.

"A colonel should know all these things," says a big man with a drooping mustache, his cheeks darkened with three days' growth of beard.

The officer scans the crowd of military caps clustered around him, looking for the man who spoke to him, then heads turn toward the corner of the street.

Six cavalrymen arrive at a trot. Dombrowski and his general staff. They dismount and vanish into the town hall along with all the officers present. Keep ready to move, someone instructs the men.

Nicolas oversees the distribution of ammunition. Thirty cartridges per man. Canteens are filled and the mess wagons emptied, the provisioners announcing their withdrawal to

Montparnasse. For an hour, men run in every direction. Platoons form, companies assemble. The two cannons are pushed and pulled in opposite ways across the cobblestones, their wheels rolling heavily like a mortuary wagon's. One patrol is sent on reconnaissance along the Seine, another toward the Porte d'Auteuil.

Red comes up to Nicolas, who is cleaning his rifle.

"So?"

"So, what?"

"What do you think of all this?"

Nicolas snaps the breech back into place, slides it back and forth, adds a bit of grease. He doesn't think anything. He is floating in a cold bath of exhaustion and sadness.

"We're fucked, right?"

His friend squats down next to him and puts his hand on Nicolas's arm to stop him tinkering with his weapon and looks him straight in the eye, waiting for an answer.

"We are fucked, aren't we?" Red repeats.

"Not as long as we're alive," Nicolas says.

Red stands up.

"So, not for much longer, then."

A tussle has broken out a short distance away. The crowd parts. Two men are rolling on the ground, punching and throttling one another. They're pulled apart, set on their feet, and then two lines of men face each other, bayonets at the ready, shouting insults. There are accusations of desertion, of treason. Then the rifles drop, and a group of about fifty national guardsmen runs off, crying, "To the barricades! We'll take them street by street!"

Two captains emerge from the town hall at a run in pursuit of the deserters. They order them to return, threaten to have them shot. One of them draws his revolver and fires over their heads. A man in the running crowd turns and shoulders his rifle. The others stop, too, and turn, ready to fire in their turn.

"What do you say now, Capitaine?"

"There are no more officers, no more orders! Just the people now, the people in arms!"

The captain holsters his gun, turns, walks back toward the town hall with his head down. The squadron starts running again toward the Place du Roi de Rome. A red flag is hoisted at its head amid a clamor of shouts.

"We should do the same thing," remarks Red, watching the group recede into the distance. "We won't win here. You must have seen that yesterday, in the Bois."

Nicolas doesn't answer. He finishes reassembling his rifle and stands up. His friend doesn't drop his gaze.

"What do you want me to say? We're going to fight. We're going to try to get out of this alive. I just want to live for a little while when all this is over. With my Caroline, somewhere peaceful. And some children playing and squabbling. That's a pretty simple bit of happiness, and I deserve it. And so do you, and everyone else. And one day, maybe in twenty years, who knows—we'll have our revenge on the bourgeois, the killers. That's another reason we have to stay alive, by God! Because whatever happens, they won't be able to kill all of us. We'll have to forget the terror, find reasons to live, regain our strength and our will. All of us—the poor ones—there are more of us than there are of them. There's no way they can keep us under their thumb for much longer. What we've tried to do here will serve as an example, and our mistakes—what we've done wrong—that will be a lesson."

Red spits on the ground and then laughs silently.

"If I understand you, we'll be magnificent losers. Is that the word on the streets?"

Nicolas nods, then stands up abruptly. A young girl is speaking to a group of soldiers, and he can hear their laughter from here, see their hands brushing the girl, their arms trapping her in a kind of moving net. His heart leaps when he recognizes her, and he dashes toward her.

"Lalie?"

She turns quickly, her cheeks red, her hair tumbling loose beneath her cap. As he nears her, a man steps between them, bayonet in hand.

"Where are you going, Comrade?"

"I know her. She's come to speak to me. Let her be."

"Yes, it's true!" Lalie says. "He's the one I was looking for! Sergeant Bellec, of the 105th!"

"We're from the 112th; what does it matter? And there are no more sergeants! Militarism is dead! *Vive l'armée du peuple!*"

The soldiers around her laugh. One of them, his face flushed, cap askew, puts his arms around her and pulls her against him, one hand already lifting her skirts. The others push and shove. Her shawl is torn off to reveal a bare shoulder. Lalie huddles in on herself, her arms crossed over her chest. The man clutching her wraps an arm around her waist and yanks her backward against him, undulating his pelvis and laughing.

"Let her go!"

Nicolas tries to evade the soldier who is keeping him away from Lalie, but the man grabs his shirt collar and drags him backward. The bayonet point comes to rest against his throat.

"Go look somewhere else for your whore. You want her all for yourself, and we've decided to share her, right, boys?"

"*Vive la Commune!*" the boys shout.

The flat side of a rifle butt strikes the man on the side of his head, and he falls to his hands and knees, only to be lifted off the ground again by the kick Red gives him. He flops onto his belly, the barrel of the rifle pressing against his neck.

"He told you to leave this girl alone," Red says.

Silence in the ranks. The men watch, suddenly sober. A few hands are still grasping Lalie, who disengages herself slowly, twitching her shoulders as if freeing herself from a thicket of brambles. Nicolas takes her by the arm and leads her away from the dispersing group of men. Red aims a final kick at the ribs of the man on the ground.

"And *vive la Commune*, Citizen! I'm giving these out for free today. If you want more, just ask!"

Nicolas urges Lalie to sit down in the Louis XV armchair he was napping in earlier. She pulls her shawl more closely around her shoulders, her whole body shaking.

"I had to see you."

"Caroline?"

She nods.

"Where is she?"

She tells him the whole story. Their journey across Paris to introduce Caroline to her sweetheart, apprenticed to a cabinetmaker in the Faubourg Saint-Antoine, the fatigue and limp that had overtaken Lalie and the hansom cab passing at that exact moment on the boulevard, and the good luck they thought they'd had for a second time that day, because there were probably only fifty hansom cabs left in all of Paris and they'd found two of them along their route on the same day, except that it wasn't luck but misfortune that had come to grin horribly at them, and it had taken Caroline off at a gallop in the middle of all those people who hadn't seen anything, they were too busy strolling along the sidewalks and joking with the national guardsmen, who were guarding the street corners as if someone might steal them . . .

Nicolas listens, his eyes on the ground. He stares at the ants collecting breadcrumbs, but what he's actually seeing is the coach bearing Caroline away into a night of terror.

Lalie stops, sniffles, catches her breath.

"Someone brought me to the police. A station in the 10th, behind the Porte Saint-Martin, on the Rue du Château-d'Eau. Roques, he's called, the cop who questioned me. He's not really a cop, I mean, but from the Commune . . . anyway, he said he would look into it. That other girls had been taken by the same coach, with the same cabman, a dark fellow covered in hair, like an animal . . . that's what they told me. And this policeman seemed to know where to look, I thought. Because that cabman had been seen in the area before."

She buries her face in her hands.

"It's all my fault. I'm the one who dragged her into that part of town; I'm the one who opened the door of that coach even though it didn't stop . . ."

She sobs. Nicolas doesn't know whether to comfort her or slap her. Without her girlish whim none of this would have happened, and he would have been able to hold on to the slender thread of hope that a real life could still happen after the agony of this immense dream they'd all shared. And yet he finds himself picturing them walking together through Paris, Caroline and Lalie, happy and free, both peaceful and in love, for a brief moment in this conflicted city, slightly intoxicated by the bright days with which the working class of Paris had been blessed for a few weeks, despite the approaching war, the threat of a bloody return to the old world. And for that, for the few blissful hours the two of them had shared on that afternoon, he feels the urge to thank this girl.

She rises. She must go. She sniffles again and wipes her nose on her sleeve.

"You needed to know," she says.

Of course. Knowing that, he knows nothing. Caroline in the hands of criminals somewhere in Paris, in the middle of a civil war as of tonight. And now? If she were dead, he would know she was at peace. What a stupid idea. The empty words of a priest. Death is nothingness. And to live in peace is all he wants right now. With her. She's alive, and they will find each other again. And he will find her. He will have to go and see this Communeux *flicard*, since there's at least one of them. He takes Lalie by the shoulders, and she sags limply against his chest.

"Where will you go now?"

"To my mother, in La Butte-aux-Cailles. I want to be with her and my little brothers. We'll be better off together, with what's about to happen. And I can't do any good here."

"I don't know if anyone can do any good. What about your sweetheart?"

She gazes at the soldiers sitting in the street, talking in low voices. She wipes her eyes with the back of her hand.

"That was before. Now it's too late."

She lifts a hand and rests it briefly on Nicolas's cheek. It's cold, and he presses it to his face, to warm it up.

"Look out for yourself. And find Caroline. You can both come to see me at Mademoiselle Bastide's, or my mother's. Madame Claveau is her name. Léontine Claveau."

The young girl walks away. She takes off her bonnet and tosses it on the ground, and her red tresses spill over her shoulders. He can see that she's limping slightly, but she strides forward courageously, her head held high, her hair glowing softly in the sun. She turns with a quick motion and blows him a kiss, to which he responds with a wave, and then he turns from her as she continues walking away. Adrien is already there behind him, rifle shouldered.

"Time to go," the boy says. "Who was that?"

"A pretty redhead, as you saw. You ought to run after her."

"When we've thrown them out of Paris. Then I'll have pretty girls and good times."

The bugle sounds the call to arms. Nicolas hoists his sack and his rifle and drags his exhaustion over to where the company is awaiting marching orders.

The streets through which they march are empty, but curtains twitch at a few windows, and Nicolas can see hollow eyes watching him from the shadows. Hands already poised on handles, ready to throw the windows wide and welcome the arriving Versaillais. He is seized with a sudden desire to fire at the squares of glass, to shatter their cold falseness, but the time for wasting bullets is past.

They reach the ruins of the Gare d'Auteuil and walk up the tracks with their wrenched and twisted rails to the viaduct, and they see them: two or three hundred line infantry advancing in two columns on either side of the road.

"Here we go," says Red.

The first salvo cuts down thirty men, who fall with a strange slowness, as if they can't believe it. The others fling themselves to the ground, some of them firing back, and the bullets buzz and whine and smash against the iron girders with a hammering sound. Nicolas can't see anything beyond his gunsight except moving shapes, red trousers dancing in the fog. He doesn't know which ones he's killing, nor if his bullets are the ones that hit them.

For half an hour, from atop the viaduct, the band of comrades pins down the Versaillais or keeps them on the defensive before felling them. Their cries are audible even over the clatter of gunfire.

"Bullets!" cries a fellow to Nicolas's left.

A fistful of cartridges is passed from hand to hand.

"Aim well! Fire true!"

They do their utmost. Below them, the Versaillais fall back, firing. They drag some of their wounded along with them; the men can see others trying to crawl.

"Look there!" cries Adrien.

He points to a soldier who is trying to stand up, supporting himself with his rifle. Adrien fires, and the man is thrown forward by the impact, falling on his face. His arms and legs move slightly in a feeble swimming motion, and then he is still. The boy lets out a shout of joy.

"Did you see that?"

Nicolas looks at his powder-blackened face.

"Waste of a bullet. He was already done for."

"It was my last one."

"All the more reason to save it."

The men call for ammunition, and each of them rummages at the bottom of his pouch for the last few cartridges. An artillery shell whistles past over their heads and buries itself in a garden a hundred meters away, sending up a tree-shaped blast of dirt and fire. Another explodes on the track. Two men tumble down, screaming. A rail is thrown twisting into the air like an enormous serpent.

For nearly an hour they keep their best marksmen at the front of the line, the others reloading the rifles with what remains of the bullets. On the other side, the infantrymen have fallen back. A few fire from gardens, their bullets clanging uselessly off the iron girders of the viaduct. Adrien concentrates, keeping an eye trained on a particular street corner where a soldier appears from time to time to squeeze off a shot. For a moment nothing moves.

Nicolas puts a hand on Adrien's shoulder. The boy's eye is riveted to his gunsight. This time, the ultimate battle is underway. A fight to the death. Head-on. The men out there will give no quarter. *It's them or me*, he thinks. He knows he and his comrades are fighting now with their backs against the wall. He knows the Commune is all but dead, and that the battle for a new world has been succeeded now by a war in which everyone must save his own skin. They can wave their red flags as much as they like, resist the Versaillais forces while shouting *Vive la Commune!* as long as they can, but in the end it will be about surviving the carnage, because that's what's coming. Surviving, if only to have another chance at a coup in a few years, when the terror has passed, replaced by rage and revolt, when a slender sprig of hope blossoms again amid the ruins.

"Kill them, goddamn it!"

Nicolas sees the bullets tear into the wood of the wagon, sending shards flying and striking sparks off the cobblestones all around the infantrymen, who adjust their aim and send their own shots whistling just over the heads of his men like angry hornets. They drop to their bellies, waiting for the volley to pass, because none of them has more than two or three bullets left. Adrien wedges the butt of his rifle into his armpit. Below, in the lengthening shadow cast by a house, the silhouettes of the soldiers crouching beneath the wagon are almost indistinguishable.

"The one behind the big wheel," says Adrien. "He's going to regret coming here."

Nicolas sees his finger brush the trigger, hover over it, and then squeeze. He starts involuntarily at the thunderclap of the detonation. The soldier lets out a cry and crumples in on himself, hands flailing at the ground. The others rush to his aid, undoing his jacket and dragging him to the wagon, then straighten quickly and carry him to shelter at a run. Adrien has enough time to nick one of them in the leg; the man jumps and then hops out of reach.

The men cheer, congratulating the boy. *They won't be back here in a hurry! They've got nothing on us!* Along the railroad line, farther on, the gunfire starts up again and lasts this time for over an hour. Crates of ammunition have arrived from God knows where. They hand it out. Since things are relatively calm here now, a captain asks for volunteer reinforcements for the barricade on the Boulevard Murat. Nicolas, Red, and Adrien step forward and run with a dozen comrades, stumbling over the gnarled crossties, back down toward the ravaged Gare d'Auteuil, which looks like a sinister castle in the fading twilight. There, twenty or so Federates crouch behind segments of the demolished walls, firing in the direction of the boulevard. Shards of plaster and stone explode around them with dry cracks, and they crouch to reload and dart, bent double, through the ruins, beneath fragments of the building's frame dangling like spiders from an invisible thread, changing gun carriages and firing again before falling back and retreating behind the barricade, fifty meters away, that bars the entire width of the boulevard. Nicolas and the others run along the track and down the embankment, letting themselves slide down behind the huge, untidily heaped mass of cobblestones and sacks of dirt. They fire a long volley at the figures advancing toward the barricade, pulling down walls as they go. Then a barrage of retaliatory bullets comes thudding into the sacks with a dull thump, scorching the granite of the cobblestones with a hiss, the mitrailleuse emitting a bizarre grinding noise as it fires. They all hunker down behind the barricade, shoulders hunched, waiting for their opponents to reload, but one fellow gives a cry of rage and stands up, shouldering his rifle, and is flung backward as if he's been struck in the forehead with a mace. Nicolas watches the blood spurt and wonders briefly if he's really seeing what he thinks he's seeing, this scarlet plume—and then he straightens up again, because the others are starting to fire again now that the mitrailleuse has stopped shooting. He's run out of ammunition, so he goes to sit beneath a window looking into a smoke-blackened room, its furniture charred so that it seems to be covered with strange, dark, scaly skin. And then he forces himself to look again at the dead man, to confirm what he thought he saw a few moments ago.

The man is lying on his back amid the spreading contents of his skull. There is nothing left above his wide-open eyes. His perfectly intact nose and half-open mouth, his black, neatly trimmed beard seem simply to be waiting for someone to redo the hair that previously topped them, or to finish modeling the rest of this incomplete wax figure, or to put this broken statue back together. A fellow soldier falls to his knees next to the man, his hands on his thighs, and gazes at the corpse, his face appalled. Nicolas has seen bodies like this before, though, at Courbevoie, and at the Fort de Vanves. Hideous and grotesque forms, blown to pieces, guts spilling out, virtually nothing left of them—comrades they had thought it better to claim had disappeared, to spare their families the sight of them, had instead buried them quietly in the corner of a garden or beneath a tree. That time at Courbevoie, beneath a hawthorn tree. You never completely forgot any of the deaths; they stayed with you forever. Dumoulin, he'd been called. Barely eighteen years old. The artillery shell had fallen at his feet while he was pissing against a wall. And the comrades on the other side of it, teasing him and making fun, had taken bricks to the face. But right now he's troubled by this man, on whom he's just seen death bloom like an evil flower. Dizziness sweeps over him, forcing him to close his eyes.

When he opens them again, he looks for Red and Adrien, doesn't find them. He looks up. The sunset sky is golden overhead, streaked with pink clouds. A bird crosses through this incomprehensible beauty, calling. Nicolas follows it with his gaze until it vanishes behind a tree. He wishes he could stay here and never do anything else, enveloped in this light and the permanent buzzing in his ears, behind this invisible glass wall. He wishes he were somewhere else.

The shooting begins again, some thirty rifles firing without interruption. He sees the gun barrels flashing and sparking. He hears the yells. The mitrailleuse is still out there, in the road, between two overturned carts. Spraying the boulevard with bullets. In the twilight gloom that is beginning to swallow everything up, the men swinging the weapon around to change the line of fire are barely visible. Nicolas fires five bullets in a row, holding his breath with every one, every ounce of his will focused between the bead and the sight and then directed with deadly intent toward the bastards stirring down there. There are a dozen Federates around him, silent, their breathing the only sound other than the clacking of their rifle breeches, all aiming at the four infantrymen maneuvering the volley gun.

One of the four staggers, and the men congratulate each other without ceasing fire.

Shouts ring out behind them. A group of men has just appeared on the corner, about fifty of them, calling out to them and beckoning them over. The Versaillais are hot on their heels. The barricade is about to be attacked from the rear. Adrien dashes toward Nicolas as soon as he spots him.

"Where were you? I was looking for you! Have you seen Red?"

The boy shakes his head, out of breath, unable to speak. He bends over, supporting himself on his rifle.

"The streets are full of them, we can't tell how many. They're coming through the gardens; their engineers are tearing down the walls. They're everywhere; we can't hold them."

Around them, men are gathering their bags and rifles and tending to the wounded.

What about him? They look at the corpse, and for a few seconds there is absolute silence. Even the mitrailleuse that killed him stops firing. Then a volley of bullets whistles past overhead. They have to leave him, Nicolas says. He'll slow them down too much.

"Does anyone know his name?"

"Philibert Vergnaud," a man says. "Of the 68th. We bunked together. A good fellow. I prayed for him just now, because he believed in that kind of thing. I'll tell his wife. She's a brave woman."

They set off. Night falls. In the distance they can hear drums rolling, trumpets blaring, bursts of gunfire. They turn toward the Seine, ending up behind the barricade defending the Quai de Passy; it has been evacuated, too, the wall of cobblestones blown apart by artillery fire. Five or six hundred of them cross the Pont d'Iéna under fire from a battery of guns on a barge that drifts slowly toward them, running through the sprays of river water thrown up by the explosions, soaked in freezing, muddy water. Some of the men fire back over the parapet, but the barge is out of range and the gunners aboard it all but invisible in the darkness.

When they arrive at the Champ de Mars, they find the camp deserted, the artillery park abandoned. A few fires are still burning. There are about a hundred cannons left, half of them unmounted. No horses and carts, no ammunition. Red is already there with twenty other men, standing silently around another man who lies on his side, vomiting blood. Red comes toward Nicolas, limping.

"It's Gallin. You know, the shoemaker from the Rue des Amandiers. They brought him here, but he won't make it any farther."

He gestures at the abandoned guns.

"We could have stopped them with these," he says. "Just look at it. What a waste. Tomorrow they'll blow us to bits with our own weapons."

Nicolas tries to wrap his mind around the extent of the disaster. The Commune falling apart right under their noses, and them fleeing through a city that has already stopped bearing any resemblance to the one they wanted to create.

A group of cavalrymen rides through the ranks; someone gives the order to stop. Guards are posted to monitor the quays, and the men sit down and catch their breath. Flasks are emptied, pipes lit. A few cookies are shared around. But more than anything else, they argue over what should be done. We've got to clear out, and fast! Hell, no! Set up an unbreakable defensive line, with the men and guns we need—but that isn't the problem! It's too late! Where are the plans? Who's making the decisions? It seems that the Central Committee doesn't yet know that the Versaillais are in Paris. Dombrowski has sent a dispatch asking for three thousand men and more cannons. Some of the men take comfort from this; all is not lost yet, then. It's not courage they're lacking, just a few sensible orders and a little organization. Nicolas roams among the clusters of arguing men. He wanders a bit farther, and then it's just night and silence. Some fires are still burning, haloing the rooftops with a reddish glow.

He lingers for almost an hour in front of the École Militaire, where a scant few windows are faintly lit. An occasional cavalryman emerges at a gallop, the clatter of horseshoes resonating for a long time in the deserted streets. When he eventually rejoins the others, he learns that Dombrowski has withdrawn, retreating in an orderly fashion with three hundred gentlemen. La Muette has fallen; all the gates from Saint-Cloud to Maillot are in Versaillais hands. A colonel from the 7th legion tries to assemble the men and organize patrols. Dozens of shadowy figures walk away, muttering, into the night. *I've had enough. I'm going home.* Others form companies of volunteers to go and defend the barricades. Waving a red flag picked up God knows where, they set off, singing "La Marseillaise." They disappear into the darkness, their voices continuing to ring out behind this flag, its color—the color of blood—no longer visible in the night.

Nicolas and Red have managed to convince Adrien not to take part in the desertions. He said it was fucked here. We should be waiting for them farther away, where we can shoot them down with the cannons as soon as they round the corner of a street. Or I'll go and slit their throats myself, tonight, one by one. He waves his bayonet in the air almost fanatically, his face wet with tears. Red manages to grab him by the shirt collar and pin him against an unlit streetlamp. They can hardly see anything in this shifting darkness full of shouts and songs and orders and, sometimes, mocking laughter. He tells Adrien to stop saying such ridiculous things and listen for a minute. They started this together, and they'll stay together. Brothers. Friends. But the boy keeps ranting, and finally he slaps him smartly across the face, which calms him instantly. Now you'll bloody well listen to me. Friends. Brothers. For life. To the death.

"To the death. No," murmurs Adrien. "No."

Night patrol, under a waning moon. They move silently down the Rue du Commerce, rifles loaded, fingers on the trigger guard. At each corner, they stop to glance around. The silence hums in their ears. On the corner of the Rue Fondary, they crouch in a single movement; there, in front of the market hall, is a group of soldiers carrying torches. Other men come and go. They can hear them talking to one another and make out the sounds of clattering and the grinding of metal. Their voices are low in the silence. A horse snorts, and the noise seems so close that they expect to see it rounding the street corner toward them.

"Look," whispers Red.

At the end of the Rue Fondary, to their right, barely a hundred meters away, two sentries appear, looking strange in the moonlight.

"What do we do?" asks Adrien.

"What do you think?"

"We should go for reinforcements and attack them."

"They've occupied the whole arrondissement. We don't know how many of them there are. Probably thousands. And us? What reinforcements? Four, maybe five hundred men? We'll be massacred."

They back away carefully, keeping their eyes fixed on the Versaillais spreading through Paris like a flood that will sweep away all the barricades.

They walk for a long time, picking up a few comrades here and there, wandering in the dark until they reach the first barricades on the Boulevard du Montparnasse. Crowds of women, children, and national guardsmen are milling in the streets behind the redoubts. This area is impregnable, someone tells them. The Versaillais will break their teeth on this barricade if they try to attack. They won't get past, the gunners boast, stroking the barrels of their eight-pound cannons embanked on the Boulevard d'Enfer. Leaning against the wall of cobblestones, two lookouts listen to them with wry half smiles, not taken in, shouldering their weapons and resolutely keeping watch.

17

Antoine Roques overslept a bit this morning. It was the sound of a fanfare out in the street that had woken him, and he wondered for a moment what time it was, for these idiots to be making such a racket. Opening the shutters, he saw a company of national guardsmen parading past to the cheers and applause of the crowd, impeccable in dress uniform, chests laden with ribbons and medals. A horde of children capered around the soldiers, screeching or marching in time with them, sticks over their shoulders to mimic rifles. Twenty musicians walked in front of the soldiers, their polished instruments gleaming golden in the morning light. The drum major, dressed in a comically elaborate red uniform with golden epaulettes, sported an enormous white beard and a large drum that bounced against his bulging belly with every step. He directed the whole spectacle with a martial air, his eyes half-closed, utterly absorbed in his task. Behind him, the trumpets and tubas whined out a "Chant du Départ" whose harmonies were creative at best. Roques watched them recede into the distance, still followed by the mob of shrieking children, curious onlookers massing on the sidewalks to applaud or mock them. When he left the bedroom, they were in the midst of butchering "La Marseillaise" via a series of squawks that could only be the result of a deliberate, concentrated effort to render the song unrecognizable.

Rose had sat with him while he ate a celebratory breakfast. She'd found a bit of brioche at a bakery on the Rue des Marais and had opened their second-to-last jar of strawberry jam for the occasion. She drank a little coffee with him, though not too much, because it gave her palpitations and then she wouldn't sleep at night. They spoke of the children, whom they'd sent to stay with Uncle Charles near Dreux at the end of March, to keep them safe from the horrors of the siege and shield them from what might happen in Paris. The postal service had stopped operating two weeks ago, and they were worried. Of course, Uncle Charles would do absolutely anything to protect his great-nephews. Of course he was responsible, intelligent, well educated, and financially comfortable. But it had been so good to get the two letters he'd been sending every week, with a few lines added by Mariette and the chicken scratch contributed by Bertrand, who could already write his first name even though he was so small. They didn't know any more if it was better to know the children were safe, or to have them with them. They didn't dare talk about what they both feared might happen if everything took a turn for the worse in the coming days. They were quiet, lost in their own dark thoughts. Rose had let out a long, trembling sigh that was more like a silent sob and stood.

"I'm going to go and join them, Antoine. I can't bear to be apart from them any longer. I'm afraid . . . I'm afraid of everything. I've looked into it; I can go by Saint-Denis with the post."

Antoine Roques felt his heart tear in two. He brought a hand involuntarily to his chest as if blood might be seeping through the skin. Rose came closer to his chair and sat back down.

"Why don't you come with me? We'll be with them; we can protect them. What do you think?"

"I can't. I owe—"

He stopped, unable to go on. He didn't know where his duty lay anymore.

"You owe what? To whom? To what?"

"I've made commitments. You encouraged me to do it, remember? You were proud of me for taking on the job. Now I need to see it through to the end, don't you understand?"

"But this is the end, Antoine! It's over, or it will be in a few days; you told me that yourself just yesterday. I've thought a lot about it. We have to get out today, because tomorrow we'll be trapped again."

She'd taken his hands in her own.

"I'm begging you. For our children. For me."

Fat tears rolled down Rose's cheeks. Antoine Roques felt a bitter sob rising in his chest.

"If you die . . ."

"Don't say that."

"If you die, what will become of us? I'll never be happy again. There will always be this empty place beside me."

"I'm not going to die. I have this case to investigate, I told you yesterday. I'm almost ready to wrap it up. I'll finish it and join you as soon as I can. I'll find a way."

She'd risen again, walked to the window, looked out into the street. Roques saw her square her shoulders. She wiped her face with the corner of her apron and turned around.

"So you're going to let me go alone? What will I tell the children?"

He went to her, pulled her into his arms.

"You'll tell them that I love them more than anything in the world. The same way I love you. The three of you are my whole life; you're what gives me hope. I miss them every second. And I'll miss you, and it'll be hard for me. Tell them that what I've taken on here is bigger than me. Tell them what it is, this Paris Commune. It's for them. For all the children of the world. And that means it's worth fighting for, no matter how painful and difficult it is."

They'd clung so tightly to each other that they could hardly breathe. The harsh light streaming through the window threw their embracing silhouettes into sharp relief. They stayed that way for a long time, silent, holding one another, letting tears stream down their faces, buried in each other's necks. Finally Rose detached herself gently and took a step back.

"Go now," she said, gently. "You have a job to finish. And then come to us, as soon as you can."

She disappeared into the next room, and Antoine had decided not to follow her, because he was sure he would change his mind and join her in packing their things if he did.

He went down the stairs still in tears and ran through the streets as fast as he could, hoping his heart might explode and kill him for making the choice he had just made.

Now he is hiding beneath a stairwell along with two armed guards he has ordered to dress in civilian clothing, equipped with clubs. He carries a municipal sergeant's short sword, which he found in a closet in the guardroom, and in his coat pocket is the revolver he never goes anywhere without anymore. Two more officers are roaming the street outside, one of them pretending to be drunk, singing a ditty of his own invention at the top of his lungs. Apart from the cries of a newborn baby, the building is completely silent. It's almost four o'clock, the usual time at which the henchmen of Monsieur Carmon, the building's owner, usually come to extort the rent, raised sky-high despite the decrees of the Commune. They always come on Sunday because they know the tenants will be at home. Occasionally they'll turn up late on a Saturday night, but it's rare. One of them boasted drunkenly in a local pub this morning that he had a job to do this afternoon on the Rue de l'Échiquier, and the information had found its way back to police headquarters.

Roques and his men stand silently amid the smell of piss and rotten cabbage, pressing themselves against the wall.

Earlier this winter a poor woman died in this very recess, of cold and hunger, a wretched girl who sold her bony carcass on the Boulevard de Belleville to feed her three little ones and had been found here, stiff and emaciated, her face and hands almost black. The children had vanished overnight. People said the mother had killed them and thrown them into the canal to put them out of their misery, no longer able to bear their whining and crying, famished and numb with cold in the fireless attic where some bastard had been allowing them to live in exchange for the woman's favors.

The only sounds now are the scratching of mice in the walls, a passing conversation in the street, the occasional burst of laughter from a nearby café.

Roques strains to make out the time on his watch and thinks he can see that it's almost five o'clock. Someone whistles twice. That's the signal.

"There they are."

Four men enter the corridor, their steps determined. The one in front is a colossus whose great height blocks out every bit of light from outside for a moment.

"You two to the right, we'll take the left," he says to his men, turning toward them.

They rush toward the staircase, and just as the last two heavies are about to set foot on the steps, Roques and the two officers shove them with their shoulders and throw them to the ground. A few blows to the ribs with the clubs subdue them soon enough, and they lie there gasping for breath, bawling like calves.

Antoine Roques orders the two other henchmen to come back down the stairs, slowly. *Sûreté Publique, National Guard!* he shouts. He has the sword in his hand, and the two men turn toward him and freeze in shock for a moment, and then suddenly it seems like something is collapsing on him, the ceiling of the foyer, or some huge animal. He is knocked down, trampled on, pinned to the ground, and a hand is squeezing his neck. Opening his eyes, he sees the giant's face, grimacing at the effort required to strangle him. Through his own wheezes and the thumping of the blood attempting to circulate in his head, the erratic pounding of his own arteries, he can hear his men struggling with the third thug. The giant grabs his collar with his free hand and starts striking his head against the stone floor, and he knows that on the third or fourth strike, the back of his skull will cave in. He gropes blindly for something to use as a weapon, anything, a stone or a piece of wood, and he finds the hilt of his sword. A man cries out for help, the giant glances up to see what's happening, and Roques raises the sword and tries to hit out at his attacker; he manages only idiotic little taps, so he tries with the point of the blade, gathering the tiny bit of breath he has left, and the shock of hitting something hard jolts through his fist. He pushes, yelling, and hears a dull crack and then feels softness, as if the blade has sunk into a loaf of bread, and suddenly the grip on his neck relaxes and the saber is jerked out of his hand as the huge man rises up onto his knees, the blade buried deep in his ear, his wide-open mouth emitting a monstrous groan, and then he springs backward, bizarrely, and crumples on the lowest steps of the staircase, his legs jerking with convulsions, his arms extended in front of him as if trying to push death away.

Roques staggers to his feet and sees the enormous body sag, its last breath a thundering wind that makes the whole corridor stink. He slides to a sitting position against the wall, his throat aching horribly, each breath painful, and he coughs and spits, trying to clear his airway, unable to stop glancing over at the cadaver, which has emptied its bladder in death, the air now reeking like a public urinal. The three remaining henchmen are lying flat on their bellies on the floor, their faces bloody, their wide, panicked eyes rolling wildly in an attempt to see what's happening around them. The guards are regaining their breath along with Roques, holding the thugs down with a foot on their backs, their clubs poised above their heads.

Roques looks again at the dead man and can see nothing but the sword jutting out of his ear, congealing blood dripping thickly from the blade's edge. He remembers the crack he felt reverberating through his fist, and he realizes, suddenly, that he killed this man by driving a sword into his brain. He gets to his feet again, panting, his back to the wall, unable to tear his eyes away from the body sprawled on the steps, eyes and mouth open, frozen in the shock he must have experienced when he felt, perhaps, the explosion in his head, even though his mind was already no longer able to understand anything at all.

What was this brute's final thought? Had he even had time to have one? Do people know, in cases like this, that they are dying? One of the men asks Roques if he's all right, and he hears his own voice in a kind of sonorous fog, and he looks at the man through the tears the dust raised by the struggle has brought to his eyes. *Yes, fine, of course, why wouldn't I be? I've just killed a man in a horrible way—not that I know any elegant way of doing it, but yes, I feel perfectly fine.* He gives the worried officer a nod and a hand gesture that seems to reassure him. He feels the back of his head, sees a bit of blood on his fingers, has to lean against the wall again as spots of white light dance before his eyes.

An armed squad of officers comes to fetch the three prisoners, who have to be protected from the crowd drawn by the commotion. Children aim kicks at them; women reach over the guards' shoulders to slap them. The men hang their heads, bloody mucus dripping from their noses, their hair clumped stickily with blood. One of them abruptly lashes out, jumping at a little boy with his shackled fists raised, but a sharp blow between the shoulder blades from a rifle butt shoves him forward, and he goes down on all fours between the legs of his accomplices, who move apart and leave him to struggle to his feet without looking at him. Roques shudders as he sees the corpse being carried past on a stretcher by two groaning, puffing guards, then he steps out of the building, still dazed by the physical altercation he's just endured and by the noise of the crowd thronging around him. He readjusts his shirt collar with its missing buttons, his jacket, his sleeves. When he looks up, there at the front of the mass of onlookers is the pretty brunette woman who impressed him so much yesterday, and he remembers her name immediately: Maria Belmont. She smiles at him, and her big, dark eyes shine with a joy he suddenly yearns to share further with her. He gives her a small wave, to which she responds by fluttering her eyelashes. He wants to go to her, to talk to her, to hear her voice, but the police escort has already started to move, and the men are calling out to him. He looks at Maria Belmont again, repeats her name in his mind. *I would have liked so much to . . . I want so much to . . .* Then he pulls himself together. Rose. The children. *Where would it get me?* He squares his shoulders and turns away from Maria, catches up to his men, shoving down the sentimental melancholy threatening to sweep over him, the words he has read again and again in books over the years ringing in his head all the way to the station.

It's too late to transfer the three thugs to the Prefecture, so he orders them to be locked up in the cells, given something to drink, and allowed to clean themselves up a bit.

Then he goes to splash some cold water on his face and drink a few gulps from his cupped hands before leaving the station again, pausing for a moment on the sidewalk. He rummages in his pockets for tobacco and cigarette papers and busies himself, his fingers trembling, heart still thumping. He closes his eyes as the first puff spreads a gentle glow beneath his eyelids. The street is full of people. It's a sunny Sunday in May. Carefree strollers. Workers in shirtsleeves, national guardsmen out enjoying the fine weather, without guns or military caps, smoking cigarettes, thumbs thrust into their belts. Somewhere an accordion is playing. In the distance, there are the faint sounds of a dance: the polka and the waltz. In the gentle twilight air, Roques manages to reason away his horror and guilt at having killed a man. He would have killed me. Slaughtered me. He was much stronger. It was him or me. He sees the giant's face above him once more, the uncontrolled rage, and he shakes his head to banish the image and looks again at the life happening around him.

There is a man some thirty meters away who's been staring at him, he's sure of it, and who looks away now and pretends to watch a group of children squabbling. The man looks familiar to him; those fevered eyes burning in a face covered thickly with beard, the battered hat set crookedly on his hairy head.

Roques moves in his direction on the opposite sidewalk, calmly, his face thoughtful. He tosses away his cigarette, looks up, sees the man on the other side of the street walking, too, unhurriedly, his hands in his pockets. They reach the boulevard, and the man turns toward the Place du Château-d'Eau, still keeping the same leisurely pace. Roques is behind him, twenty meters away, no more. He keeps an eye on the man's hands in his pockets; there's no way of knowing what sort of weapon he might have in there. He touches the grip of his own revolver but senses that the action is pointless. The man turns abruptly and stands still, watching him approach.

"Well?" Roques says.

"Well, what?"

"We need to talk."

The man clears his throat and spits on the ground.

"'Scuse me," he says.

He smells of stale smoke and sweat. He watches the policeman out of the corner of his eye, head low, his face wary—or fearful, perhaps.

"You're Clovis Landier, aren't you?"

The man nods. "You came and searched my place. A neighbor told me you were asking for me."

"And you—how did you find me?"

Clovis Landier guffaws and shakes his head.

"It wasn't hard. A Commune cop sticking his nose all around the area; it's all anyone's talking about. All I had to do was follow the tracks, as they say."

"Why did you come? It wasn't just to get a look at my face, I imagine."

Clovis starts walking through the crowd of strolling pedestrians again, not looking to see whether Roques is following.

"Can we sit down somewhere? It'll be quieter . . ."

Clovis spots a café and walks abruptly inside, and Roques can only follow him. They find a free table against the front picture window with its little gingham curtains and order steins of beer.

"You're going to arrest me, aren't you?"

"I could. You're an accomplice to kidnapping, maybe murder, too. I don't know the law very well, but that should be enough to send you to La Roquette for a long time, or worse."

Clovis finally looks him directly in the eye, and Antoine Roques can make out traces of the young man he saw in the photographs.

"I'm already dead anyway, so I don't give a damn."

He turns toward the window, parts the curtains, watches the passersby for a moment with curiosity. The waiter brings their beers. Roques pays for them and then leans back in his chair. He doesn't want to rush anything. He knows this man could get up and leave and disappear into the crowds on the boulevard, and there would be nothing he could do about it. He knows—he isn't sure why, but he knows—that arresting him wouldn't accomplish anything. This man has come to give himself up, yes, but not to become a prisoner. Roques would

IN THE SHADOW OF THE FIRE · 279

never have managed to find him. He knows all the back alleys and detours, all the ways to flee and get out of Paris, even with the current situation, to disappear forever. He's given himself up. The same way, perhaps, that you would give yourself up to a friend, or even a stranger on a defeated evening, exhausted from hesitating too long on the parapet of a bridge. All of Antoine Roques's logic, all his reasoning and good sense, are overcome by the desire to know what kind of man is sitting across from him. To know what happened between the day his photo was taken alongside that pretty young woman and the two little boys and today, when he has just all but collapsed, an exhausted and tattered criminal, at the feet of an ad hoc policeman in an insurgent city.

Clovis lets the curtain fall.

"It's strange," he says.

"What is?"

"All those people, outside. They seem happy . . . carefree."

"Maybe they truly are happy and carefree. You don't think so?"

Clovis drinks some beer, sighs, sets his mug back down on the table carefully.

"I find it hard to believe in that kind of thing."

"And I find it hard to believe you came here just to have a beer with me."

"You went through my things."

"Yes. That's my job. I was looking for you because I'm investigating the kidnapping of several young women. And everything points to you being the coachman who's been driving the cab. You fit the description given by several witnesses. A bistro owner saw you in the company of a strange man with a disfigured face, a criminal who killed three men in cold blood the other day in a bar on the Quai de Jemmapes, where you are well known. So yes, I searched your place, to find out a bit more about whom I was dealing with. Would you like to file a complaint?"

Clovis smiles sadly. "And did you find anything interesting?"

He leans across the table, his eyes shining. Roques hesitates before answering, afraid the man will withdraw back into his ragged clothing, or worse, get up and leave.

"I saw the photos."

He doesn't say any more because Clovis Landier closes his eyes for a few seconds, covering his mouth with his hands. Finally he opens his eyes again and says simply, his voice a near-whisper, "And?"

"You looked happy. Much happier even, I'm sure, than those people you were just watching out the window."

"I was."

"What happened?"

Clovis Landier shrinks back in his chair.

"We've got to get that girl out of there."

"She's alive?"

"The man you're looking for is called Henri Pujols. He locked her up in a cellar at 15 Rue des Missions, in the 7th arrondissement. Part of the building was shelled and collapsed. The cellar's underneath the rubble."

"Then she's dead."

"No. Only the upper part of the building fell. The whole ground floor is still standing."

Roques stands up. Clovis looks up at him, still seated.

"Now?"

"Tomorrow it'll be too late."

Out in the street, people are shouting. *Aux armes!* Everyone to the barricades! The waiter dashes to the glass door and pushes it open to step onto the sidewalk, and noise floods into the café. Other customers are leaving the café now, too. Clovis stands and glances out the window. A man passes by on the other side, shouting:

"The Versaillais have entered Paris!"

The cry is echoed all over the boulevard, taken up by hundreds of voices.

Antoine Roques elbows his way through the curious onlookers massed in the café doorway and shoves his way through the unmoving crowd, all these necks straining for a better look, as if infantry regiments are about to appear around the corner. Children, go home now! Louison, look after your little sister. Where is the National Guard? The Central Committee? Idiots! Where are they? At the Point du Jour, at La Muette. They're fighting at the Porte d'Auteuil. "Ah, finally!" says a man to his neighbor. "Now we'll see what we see!" They won't get far, says another man. Paris doesn't belong to them anymore. The people won't let them take it back!

A distant bugle sounds the call to arms.

Roques is almost running when he is brought up short by a woman loaded down with children, trying to gather the rest of her brood. Someone bumps into him from behind; he turns and finds himself face-to-face with Clovis.

"I'm coming with you."

Roques takes him by the arm.

"Come on."

In front of the police station, fifty national guardsmen have gathered. A sergeant is shouting orders, checking equipment, distributing ammunition.

"Where's Barnois?" Roques asks the sergeant.

"Dunno. No one's seen him for three days. I'm his replacement. Chapot, Auguste Chapot. But everyone calls me Chassepot."[15]

"You should see his bayonet!" jokes a soldier.

---

[15] Chassepot: A breech-loading rifle used by the French army in the late 19th century.

"It's not a bayonet; it's a saber!" says another.

Everyone laughs loudly.

"Where are you headed?"

"Porte Saint-Martin; that's the rallying point."

"I need five or six men."

"No chance."

Chapot jerks his chin at the men lining up, ready to march.

"That's all that's left of my company. Fifty-four men, thirty-five rifles, no more than ten cartridges each. I have to find my captain so we can organize a bit. I answer to him and nobody else."

The sergeant turns his back on Roques and gives the order to march. The column of men recedes into the distance. The news doesn't seem to have reached the street here; people are joking with the passing soldiers. A few girls flutter their handkerchiefs, laughing.

Roques goes into the police station, and the clatter and clamor of voices fall on him like a ton of bricks. There are around thirty of them gathered in the lobby, even pushing their way behind the reception desk, some of them wearing National Guard caps but most in civilian clothes, antique pistols thrust into their leather belts and bayonets in leather scabbards hung from their shoulder straps, making them look like a band of warriors, all of them talking and yelling in an indistinguishable melee of voices. They are shouting for weapons to be distributed to protect the area; for the prisoners who were brought in a short time ago, the ones extorting rents for the bourgeois, to be punished; for a new Sûreté Committee to be elected, because the current one is clearly incapable of protecting the people from profiteers.

A dozen guards are facing the crowd down, doing what they can to keep them away from the cells. Roques elbows his way through the mass of people. Someone grabs him by the shoulder.

"Well, well, look here, it's Citizen Roques! Where has he been, eh? Never around when he's needed!"

The man bawling these words in his face is wearing a sort of blue Phrygian cap with a red badge pinned to it. He is still gripping Roques's shoulder with one large hand. It's Jacquet, a loudmouth from one of the local social clubs.

"At least I'm needed occasionally," retorts Roques. "That's the difference between you and me."

Two men guffaw loudly, and Jacquet lets go, his face darkening with anger.

It takes a good five minutes of shouting to calm the crowd down a bit. Roques climbs onto a chair and explains that there are only service weapons here at the station—that is, three rifles in total, no more, and that they'll have to ask at legion headquarters[16] if it's guns they're after.

"What did I tell you all?" one man says. "We have to go to the barracks at Château-d'Eau. We're wasting our time shouting pointlessly, as usual."

"The people have to be able to discuss and debate," argues another. "Speaking our minds and arming ourselves—it's the same thing!"

Some cheer at this remark, while others protest. The crowd is almost on the point of another brawl. Roques is forced to raise his voice again, his throat burning painfully.

"As for the prisoners, you'll have to trample me to get to them. The Commune has never, in my recollection, adopted the law of an eye for an eye, or administered justice without due process. That would be a return to tyranny, which is exactly what we're all fighting against!"

---

[16] The National Guard was organized into twenty legions, one per arrondissement, divided into varying numbers of battalions according to the population of the arrondissement.

There is an approving rumble. Jacquet keeps his thumbs tucked into his belt, his stance martial, but he nods in agreement.

"These people will be taken to the Prefecture tomorrow for additional questioning, and my report sent as well. Until then, they are under my protection. And if it's my resignation from the Sûreté Committee you want, you'll have it as soon as the assembly next gathers. But right now, get the hell out of here and go do your duty as citizens."

The men stream toward the exit, grumbling. A small group lingers, speaking in low voices. Citizen Jacquet gives Antoine Roques a military salute.

"Get yourself to the barricades!"

"I'll be there even if they don't need me!"

When the room has emptied, one of the guards, Batiste Pelloquin, an old-timer and veteran of '48, comes up to shake his hand.

"You're not too bad at this, on my word! I could tell just when they were gonna give in. I know some of that lot; their lives won't be worth much as far as MacMahon's infantrymen are concerned!"

Antoine sees Clovis sitting on a bench, filling his pipe. In the dim light of the lobby, he has transformed back into that inscrutable figure muffled up in his tattered clothing, only his hands moving, shoving the pipe between his bearded lips.

"I need three or four men for an urgent mission, but I don't know where to get them anymore. You should stay here in case things turn bad. Keep your rifles near you and wait for the shift change."

"The next shift should have been here five hours ago. We haven't seen a soul. Same thing happened last Sunday."

Just then the front door is flung open to reveal a breathless Loubet.

"What's happening? So this is it? They've entered Paris?"

"By the Porte de Saint-Cloud," Roques says. "That's all we know."

Loubet looks at Clovis, who hasn't raised his head and continues to puff on his pipe, unmoving.

"Who's this?"

"I'll explain. We've got to go. I need you. Do you have your gun?"

"Of course. You going to tell me what's going on?"

"I'll explain everything on the way. We're going to the 7th, to free a woman trapped in a cellar."

Roques turns to Baptiste Pelloquin. "We'll need a crowbar."

The old man disappears into an adjoining room. They hear him rummaging around, opening cabinets, iron clanking, and then he returns brandishing two iron bars.

"These'll take out even the sturdiest locks!"

Clovis has risen. He takes off the odd greatcoat he is never without, unwinds the gray scarf engulfing his neck. He seems larger, taller, in just his tattered jacket. He is wearing a roomy worker's cap, its brim pulled low on his forehead.

The three of them set off. Loubet goes first without asking questions, but he turns around from time to time, keeping an eye on Clovis. When they reach the Boulevard Saint-Martin, he approaches Roques.

"I think I understand. He's the cabman, right?"

Antoine nods. Two artillery wagons rattle past them. In front of the Porte Saint-Martin, a human chain is adding cobblestones to the barricades. There are hundreds of people: men in shirtsleeves, some in their Sunday-best coats and shoes, national guardsmen from deskbound companies. Some women, filling sacks with earth. An officer perched on a table is directing the operation, his saber in his hand, but no one seems to be following his instructions.

"He came to give himself up earlier. I was on his trail yesterday, and he found out."

"And?"

"And we talked. He told me where this woman, the one who was taken from the boulevard two days ago, was being held. She's trapped in a cellar on the Rue des Missions, under the rubble of a building."

"When, and how, are you planning on arresting him?"

"He wasn't always what he is now. He had a wife and children. He was a happy, good-looking young man."

"That doesn't explain—or excuse—anything. You haven't answered my question."

"And I haven't finished asking all my own questions yet. Patience. Right now he's valuable backup."

They are forced to slide through the narrow defensive passage in the barrier. Two guards stop them and ask where they're going. They show their officially stamped passes, signed by Rigault.

"And him?" The soldier gestures at Clovis, who doesn't flinch.

"He's with us."

The man scrutinizes Clovis's face from beneath the brim of his military cap, then nods.

"If you say so. We're closing this whole place off in an hour. Not sure you'll be able to get back through. And people get pretty nervous at night . . ."

"We'll make a detour," says Loubet.

"A detour, eh?"

This hadn't occurred to the soldier. He thinks about it, then glances questioningly at his comrade, who shrugs.

"Suit yourself," he says finally, handing back their papers.

They make their way to the middle of the intersection, its surface bare earth now that all the cobblestones have been torn out, amid crowds of children playing among the soldiers and earning perfunctory kicks and slaps from the men they're bothering. A dozen cannons stand in a row, guarded by stone-faced Federates with rifles across their chests. The Boulevard Saint-Denis is barred by a wall three meters high, pierced with gun slits and topped by a red flag. Loubet pauses and turns in a circle to take in the full extent of the fortifications.

"Very impressive," he says. "But they'll find a way past and then surround them."

"You seem almost excited about that," remarks Roques.

"No more than you. I'm just observing, that's all. The improvisation, the lack of a cohesive plan. They'll get past, and they'll wipe us out. Like heroic wisps of straw."

Roques doesn't answer. The nearing of the decisive confrontation and the mission they must accomplish this evening make him despise Loubet's defeatist attitude and banish his own doubts and hesitations. It seems to him that all these people who have risen up, ready to fight, all this ferocious resoluteness, can't possibly be vanquished.

Clovis threads his way through the fevered crowds without visibly reacting, as if he's a stranger in this world, and Roques feels as if he is unaware of anyone but himself, solitary and singular even in the midst of all this noise, all these people.

They turn down the Rue d'Aboukir, which is strangely calm, sinking gradually into a greyish twilight, and they hasten their steps, paying no attention to the men gathered on the Rue Chénier ahead of them, a dozen national guardsmen and three armed civilians with red belts around their waists. Roques recognizes Jacquet and gives him a wave.

"Seize them!" orders a sergeant.

The guards run toward them and corner them in an entryway, bayonets drawn, ready to skewer the first person who breathes the wrong way. Loubet explains that they're with the police and starts to put his hand in his pocket for his papers, but a blade is thrust immediately beneath his chin.

"Stop right there, Citizen!" commands Roques. "We've just told you who we are."

But the soldiers don't move until Jacquet comes over and nudges between them.

"Who are you? Traitors. That's what you are. Traitors who refuse to transfer prisoners in the pay of the bourgeois in a timely manner, who refuse to give weapons to the people, who conduct extravagant investigations instead of ensuring the safety of an arrondissement whose assembly entrusted you with that responsibility. You think you're heroic cops out of some threepenny novel, but really you're nothing but Vidocqs, criminals turned policemen, and it's us you answer to! And moreover, at the very moment barricades are being built all over the city, and the people are showing their determination and courage at every turn, you're running off!"

"May I ask what right you have to stop us?" asks Roques.

"The right of the people in arms, who have no intention of allowing themselves to be taken advantage of by suspicious puppets like you. The time for hemming and hawing and compromising is over. The battle is upon us, and we can't leave anyone behind who might shoot us in the back."

He speaks with his hands on his hips, chest puffed out, his Phrygian cap pulled low above his eyes. He turns back toward his men, seeming quite pleased with himself for what he's just said, and then suddenly he notices Clovis and looks closely at him.

"And just who is this? Don't tell me he's in the service of the Commune!"

"He's assisting us," says Loubet.

Jacquet guffaws, and the two other civilians with him smile knowingly.

"A snitch, in other words! That's what you call them, isn't it?"

He pushes his face into Clovis's. "Your name?"

"Clovis Landier."

"Profession?"

"Coachman."

"Where's your coach?"

"I sold it."

"And you . . ."

"My horse died."

Clovis speaks the words in a near-whisper, almost a moan, his voice low and deep. They could have been his last words, as if he had said all there was to say.

Jacquet is silent, his mouth half-open, scrutinizing the impassive face whose skin is startlingly pale, almost gray, beneath the thicket of beard and hair covering it. Clovis's pale eyes, unblinking, the pupils dilated in the twilight, bore into Jacquet like two invisible nails that seem capable of penetrating his brain—and this loudmouth, the blowhard that is Jacquet, standing almost on tiptoe to make himself just that much taller than the other man, can think of nothing to say and drops his gaze, looks away and then back at those eyes that seem to be the only source of light in the darkness of this late evening. Clovis stares back so imperturbably, so unwaveringly, that Antoine Roques finds himself wondering if the man is still breathing.

"Take them away!" Jacquet finally bawls, backing away abruptly from Clovis as if the man had a gun pointed at him.

Roques and Loubet are stripped of their weapons. Their hands are tied behind their backs and they are marched to a barricade on the corner of the Rue du Caire and the Rue Saint-Denis. Fires and torches cast their quivering glow on the façades of the buildings. Groups of men talk in low voices; others are sitting or reclining next to piles of rifles. Behind the redoubt, a café has been commandeered to serve as both general headquarters and an aid station. A small man, his military cap tilted over one eye, his mouth consumed by an enormous mustache, asks who they are and sighs that there's nowhere to keep them, then muses aloud that the cellar might do. They are bundled through a trap door behind the counter.

"Don't drink it all," says Jacquet mockingly, and lets the trap door fall shut.

They find themselves plunged into complete darkness, and for a moment they don't dare move, their nostrils assailed by the choking smell of cheap wine and saltpeter, and then they make out a faint light coming from a window. For the next five minutes they apply themselves blindly to the task of undoing the loosely knotted binding tied by the national guardsmen; once their hands are free, they grope around in the dark, bumping into barrels and crates, stepping in empty boxes. Roques manages to pry a rotted board off the window, and more weak light filters into the cellar, affording them a better look at the pigsty in which they're trapped.

"Look," says Loubet. "I found this."

The glass chimney of an oil lamp gleams in his hands. Clovis approaches, rummages in his pockets, pulls out a box of matches. All three of them heave a sigh of relief at the welcome light.

"We've got to get out of here," says Roques.

Loubet mimes applause.

"Excellent idea. I was thinking the same thing. Now we just have to do it."

Clovis raises the lamp above his head and takes a few steps toward the back of the cellar.

"There's a door here."

They examine the panel, the worm-eaten wood crumbling beneath their fingernails.

"We need to dig around the lock."

Clovis goes to the crates of empty bottles, breaks one and returns to the door, which he attacks with the jagged edge, using the bottle's neck as a handle. Roques and Loubet follow his example and get to work.

For an hour they take turns around the lock, digging, scratching, scraping. Their glass blades break more than once.

But it's only the door's surface that is decayed. Soon enough they reach an inner core of pale, hard oak, managing only to scrape away a few splinters.

Roques sits down on a crate, out of breath, one hand bloody.

"Shit. We'll never get through. We're fucked."

"There's this, but the noise will bring them straight down here. And I'm not even sure it will work on such hard wood."

Clovis pulls a revolver out of his pocket.

"Where did you get that?" asks Roques.

"It belongs to Pujols. There are five bullets left."

"Who is Pujols?"

"The man you're looking for. The one I've been driving around for months."

"You have to give us the weapon," says Loubet. "Let me remind you that—"

Clovis hands him the revolver.

"Use it well, Monsieur l'Inspecteur. I know exactly what I have to be ashamed of—certainly better than you do, because I haven't told your colleague here everything. As for what I have to reproach myself for, I believe, with all due respect, that you're in no position to judge me . . . nor any man, I think."

His voice is dull and flat as always, his diction precise.

Loubet checks to make sure there are indeed five bullets in the chamber and then drops it into his pocket.

"Where did you learn to speak that way?" Antoine Roques asks.

Clovis turns to him, and at that very moment the lamp's flame flickers, twisting, and goes out.

"At the bar. I spent two years as an attorney in Amiens."

They are in darkness again, and the silence that falls as they wait for their eyes to adjust is paralyzing. Clovis's words resonate in Antoine Roques's head. He can't understand how a man could fall so far, sink into the night and live as a homeless reprobate, without any hope of ever finding his way back to the light. He can't imagine that kind of despair. He's familiar with the kind the Romantic poets pour out on the page; he's read the confessions of the century's angst-filled writers with their bottomless disappointment at the real world's failure to live up to their ideals, who are yet so quickly consoled by other ambitions. He knows the grief, the sorrows, the miseries that doom people to permanent, hopeless entrapment in their own lives: the appalling poverty in which the working class is mired, the slums, the grime, the labor that exhausts and kills, the children exploited and beaten like animals, the women mistreated everywhere at every turn, ignorance, illness, all the misfortunes that plague the humblest members of society. His own heart often lurches and swells with indignation at the endless litany, the helpless knowledge that whirls around and around in his head, seeking an outlet.

The Commune, at least, would have been a light in the darkness of the miserable days and years endured in their bleak lives. It would have shown the people that a spark existed, a flame that could be fed to burn more brightly. An ember long dormant, quivering beneath the ashes, that could be stirred back to life. A torch that must be carried through the desert, sometimes even to the blind who didn't want it.

But this man, whose stooped silhouette is gradually becoming visible in this darkness dusted with specks of light—this man has known a different life from that in which the common people are mired: the brightness, the easy happiness of the petit bourgeois. Roques can't understand why he couldn't summon the strength to find them again. His fall is a mystery, his sojourn among the damned of this day and age resembles nothing so much as a self-inflicted punishment. Something has broken him, and he is holding the pieces of himself together, upright, with an effort that drains away the rest of his will.

"Don't be too impressed. All of that belongs to the past; not to me, not anymore."

A fresh hubbub has arisen in the street outside. They can hear a cannon rolling across the cobblestones, its metal wheels grinding and squealing. Shouts. They're directing the gun's placement.

"That woman is still there," says Clovis, "and we're here."

"You're trying to redeem yourself, is that it?" asks Loubet.

"Not at all. My debt is enormous, and I'm insolvent. Let me come with you, free that girl, and then you can do whatever you like with me."

Roques listens to the conversation, at a loss for anything to say. All he wants is for Loubet to shut his trap; the man clearly doesn't understand a thing. For a moment they're all silent, listening to the noise outside. Then Roques pulls up a wooden crate and sits down on it, leaning back against an old piece of furniture. Fatigue settles heavily on him, pressing on his neck and shoulders. He wants to lie down and sleep, with the slender, crazy hope that in the morning they'll be able to get out of here. He thinks of Rose, who must already have left Paris by now, and he doesn't know anymore what the hell he's doing here, shut up in the darkness, prevented from carrying out the very mission that made him reject the happiness that was within reach.

Loubet and Clovis imitate him and sit down, turning up their jacket collars, arms folded across their chests, heads hunched, drowsing in the coolness rising from the beaten-earth floor.

Antoine Roques dreams of his children. He sees them running toward him through a sunlit field and holds out his arms, but they don't get any closer, and he can't tell if they're smiling or grimacing with anxiety and effort, and the steps he takes to reach them sink into soft sand that gives way beneath his feet, exhausting him. When he wakes up, thinking he might have called out their names, he can't remember where he is for a moment, and then he realizes, and looks around for anything they might have missed, a crack in the wall that might have widened while he was asleep, some tool they could use to force open the door. He hears the other two breathing deeply, snoring lightly, so he closes his eyes again and murmurs his children's names, *Rose, Rose, I'll come back, you'll see,* and he sees the lovely face of Maria Belmont going past on an empty street, her dark hair tumbling over her shoulders.

18

He has no idea what time it is. The sun has disappeared behind the ruined building, and the sky is the soft blue of a spring afternoon. He doesn't move for a moment, sprawled on his back, closed up in his own stiff, heavy body, hard as the wood used to make recumbent effigies or sarcophagi.

He can't hear the rumble of the cannons anymore, or see dark clouds of smoke in the sky. He smells burning here in the courtyard and then remembers the explosion that devastated the building, the flames licking at the walls and the woodwork. Suddenly he remembers everything. The girl trapped in the cellar, the struggle with Viviane, the explosion as he was coming down the stairs. Clovis and his dying horse. Clovis atop the pile of rubble. The stone he'd thrown at him, faster and sharper than he would have thought possible. He remembers the shot that finished off the horse.

He wonders how such a wreck of a man, a being reduced to such a crude existence, all but wordless, hairy as a monkey, like one of those monsters used to scare children, the kind their parents tell them hides in cellars or attics, roaming at night with heavy footsteps, making floorboards creak and doors rattle—how such a creature, so deeply attached to the nag that pulled his cab, could have demonstrated the aim needed to hit him squarely in the forehead with a block of stone. And, above all, how he could have suddenly been overcome with scruples, with remorse, about that girl buried in the cellar under tons of debris. He who had never made even the mildest comment, hesitated for the briefest instant, done anything at all that might have betrayed reluctance? Hadn't he helped him subdue the shrieking harpies more than once? Hadn't he gotten him out of a tight corner not once, but twice, by retrieving his sawed-off shotgun from beneath his box seat? Only yesterday, with the sudden quickness he sometimes showed, he'd shot that national guardsman, who hadn't seen it coming. It didn't make sense. Since January, he'd been present for every bit of their grim business, at any hour of the day or night. Without enthusiasm, maybe, but with consistency, loyalty, efficiency.

Pujols remembers their first meeting, as he was coming out of a rag-and-bone man's house in La Chapelle; he'd stumbled across Clovis's hansom cab roaming the neighborhood as if he had any chance of picking up anyone but a knife-wielding lowlife who, as payment, would pick his pockets at best and slit his throat at worst, or a thirteen-year-old whore off to ply her trade on the boulevard, or who might ask to be driven to the fortifications so she could slip through a gap and sell her arse to the Prussians. He'd climbed into the cab after having given his address and then immediately regretted it, wondering suddenly if this might be a trap set by a team of cat burglars who would rob him two days later, or bandits lurking in wait for his descent from the carriage. He had flicked open his knife and clutched it in his lap for the whole journey, ready to slice in half the first person to show his mug at the coach door. But in the end, all had passed quietly, and the cabman, whose name was Clovis, had given him his address and the means to contact him at virtually any time. The following week, seeing as the residence of his landlady, Viviane Arnault, remained undisturbed, as did the apartments of the respectable petit bourgeois men and women who lodged in the building, Pujols had gotten in touch with Clovis.

He thinks back on the past months now as he slowly

regains the use of his body, moving his fingers and hands and then his feet and legs, turning his throbbing head slowly left and right despite feeling as if he's wearing a solid lead helmet against which every beat of his heart clangs like a hammer blow. He pulls himself to a sitting position, and it feels like his head might fall off and thud to the ground like a cast-iron cannonball with his own face, contorted with pain, smeared across the round surface. He touches his forehead and feels an enormous bump split by a large cut. His face is surely swollen, as well, because he can feel his skin stretching painfully when he moves his jaw, and he can barely open his right eye, the one whose brow bone was broken last year. He looks at his fingers, sticky with blood, wipes them on his jacket, and forces himself to breathe calmly, to slow the panicked thumping of his heart.

The tumbled ruins of what was once his building rise up in the back of the courtyard, with its eight apartments and its wide, bright staircase, which he can still see standing on the third floor like the inner spiral of a shattered snail shell, the interiors of the rooms bared by the collapse of the façade, their floorboards sloping toward the emptiness, vomiting their furnishings into the courtyard, their mangled ceilings sagging above living rooms still laden with sofas and armchairs, dark wooden bedsteads still flush against the walls beneath crucifixes and paintings and even shelves of still-intact porcelain ornaments, their whiteness indifferent to the surrounding chaos, and everywhere the great blackish smears from the fire that didn't have time to carbonize everything. His eyes devour these private interiors like a burglar with the power to see through walls, wondering if there might still be a few costly baubles to loot, however inaccessible. And he fantasizes for a few moments, Henri Pujols, of the advantage it would give him to be able to see through things, or people, why not: he wonders if he would be able to see their thoughts forming in their skulls, or to anticipate those thoughts and use them to his own benefit.

He stands up and waits for the walls to stop swaying and the ground to stop rocking before he takes even the smallest step. Then he turns to the hansom cab and the dead horse between the shafts, its lips pulled back on its big yellow teeth. Near the cab he finds the bag he packed earlier, stooping to pick it up and feeling as if his leaden head will cause him to pitch forward and sprawl flat on his belly like the drunken dog he saw when he was a child back home in the village that a few jokesters, even drunker, had forced to drink, and that had staggered through the square howling with terror, stumbling every few meters over its own wobbly paws. It had been found the next day lying beneath a tree, drooling and convulsing, and some charitable soul had ended its misery with a rifle shot, undoubtedly because the joke had gone on long enough. He checks to make sure everything is there—jewelry, money, knife—and then goes around to the other side of the coach, starting a bit when he sees the dark heap crumpled in a corner. Madame Viviane is lying slumped against a door, her chin on her chest. Pujols can't see her face very well as it's covered by the disheveled mass of her hair, so he ventures closer to her and realizes that her chest is rising and falling slightly with her shallow breathing. He nudges her calf with his foot to get a reaction out of her, but she doesn't move, only emits a faint groan. He crouches down and shakes her by the shoulder, lifting her hair to see what she looks like because he remembers striking her yesterday when she was getting in his way, clinging to him like a bundle of brambles, and he sees her torn cheek, a tattered flap of flesh vibrating a bit with her breathing. Blood has run down her neck onto her bodice, and her swollen nose is blue all the way up to her forehead. He can't recognize the face from before, with its lovely light eyes, that pleased him so much the day they met, when he had rid her with kicks and slaps of a group of thieving children who'd been trying to grab her basket of shopping. Her grotesquely puffed lips part over teeth blackened with dried blood, her crooked jaw giving her the look of a congenital half-wit. He reaches for his knife to finish her off, telling himself that death might make her look a bit more dignified, that eternal rest will relax her pain-twisted features, but she opens her eyes and gazes at him pleadingly, trying to say something but managing only to drool bloody saliva, her throat rattling. He stands up, his head splitting, his face burning from the inside with liquid fire as if his blood has turned to molten metal.

The street where Gantier lived is in shadow when he reaches it, the sun already setting. It doesn't take much effort to imitate the staggering walk of a drunkard, muttering curses. He sees a woman and her two little girls cross over to the other side of the street to avoid him, hears windows closing as he passes. He goes into the building and almost immediately comes upon the corpses of the two national guardsmen he and Clovis killed yesterday. Their weapons have been taken, and they've been stripped of their bullet pouches and shoes. He undresses with effort and quickly pulls on the trousers with their red stripe and the tunic, which he cinches with the cartridge strap and the leather belt. The breast and neck of the tunic are stained with blood, and he tells himself that it will only make people believe more easily that he's wounded. He pulls the military cap carefully onto his injured head, and he's sorry he doesn't have a mirror so he can see what he looks like.

Back out in the street he pauses for a moment, unsure of which direction to go; then, hearing the noise of a crowd to his right, he decides to go that way. Two streets along he sees men and some women grouped at the foot of an enormous barricade, and he starts calling for help, exaggerating his limp. People run toward him, two guards and a woman exhorting him to be brave, and he lets himself slump to the ground with a pathetic groan. When he feels hands and arms lifting him with words of comfort, his view of humans is confirmed: they are either kind and stupid, full of vain hopes and childish naivete, or they're corrupt bastards, vicious and perverted. And in either case, they are so easily taken advantage of, so quick to follow the slope down to the precipice, where all he has to do is wait for them.

MONDAY, MAY 22ND

19

They're dancing. Bodies pressed together, they glide among the other couples, brushing past them and sometimes twisting to avoid them in the heat of this dense, supple, serpentine crowd with its sudden turns and nimble steps. Faces pass near, smiles flash, gazes linger. On the platform, in front of a red curtain, the musicians are vague shapes in the tobacco smoke and the shifting light of the chandeliers. These sonorous silhouettes move to their own music. The three violinists sway in a single movement; the pianist is a hunchback bent over his keyboard. The accordionist wipes his forehead with his sleeve, his instrument bulging in front of him like an enormous belly.

A slow waltz. The buzz of conversation dies down to quiet murmurs. Cheeks are pressed to chests, eyes close, the dancers whirl a bit clumsily.

I could feel your hand resting on the small of my back, our fingers interlaced, sticking together with perspiration, and I didn't take my eyes off yours; you smiled and smiled, and sometimes your face turned serious, and when I asked you what you were thinking about you said nothing, just what we were doing right now, and what we would do next, and you held me a little closer, and I felt you against me through my dress and my petticoats, and I wanted to feel you even more, without anything between us. Or maybe you told me you didn't want this to be the end of our story, that sometimes you were afraid, you didn't want anything to separate us—did I understand? Of course I understood, but personally I wasn't afraid. I hadn't been afraid of anything at all since the moment I met you. I felt as if I'd finally arrived somewhere. Not the way you arrive to unpack your things and sit down waiting to grow old—no, more like when you're at the quayside, or on the platform of a train station, and you see the train coming in the distance. Or in port, about to board a ship for a great voyage. Once you spoke to me about America; you'd read stories of Indians and hunters there who roamed the woods, of an immense country where so many people landed every day, and you showed me engravings in magazines, and we said that maybe one day we'd go, we'd leave Europe behind us, watching it recede into the distance with our elbows on the rail of a ship, and it made me cry because I thought about them all, the dear ones of my childhood that I might never see again, and I cried, too, remembering the filth I'd be leaving behind, that I might even be able to forget, with you, thanks to you.

You talked to me about the sea, but I only knew the coast and the misery that haunted it, the boats smashed to pieces and the dead washed up on shore after the storms, so of course it scared me a bit, you know, like when you're near a bad-tempered dog that's sleeping; you've known it for a long time, this dog, but you hardly dare move or even look it in the eyes because it always returns that look with a shifty stare. But if the sea can take us so far away, I think I can find it beautiful, and sit and gaze at it the way we would at a world wonder.

We often talked while pressed against each other in our little bed, the duvet covering us like a great sleeping animal in the February cold, remember? And then later, with the Commune came even bigger dreams, and we weren't afraid of anything anymore—well, you were, actually, you were always worried that everything might go wrong, that we'd be separated, that one of us would be killed . . .

Caroline sits up; her head spins and her gut twists, and her dry tongue sticks to the roof of her mouth, so she finds the pail and scoops up a little water in the hollow of her hand, drinks three or four mouthfuls that she can barely swallow. She doesn't know if she's been talking to herself or if she's been thinking so hard of all these things that they're ringing in her head, spreading out into the silence. She looks for the bright crack overhead and finds it, begs some mysterious power to widen it and make the roof of the cellar collapse, but of course nothing happens. She even wishes that an artillery shell might fall on her prison and destroy it; too bad, too bad if I'm underneath, but at least the sky will be overhead, and I'll die, if I have to die, in the light of day and not in this black tomb.

She gropes for the handle of the bucket and makes her way to the door and starts digging at the beaten earth again. She managed—yesterday? An hour ago?—to reach the other side, and the simple idea of this piece of metal moving in open air was intoxicating, feeling to her like a victory full of promise. Through this mousehole she has made, she thinks she can feel a slight flow of fresh air on her palm, so she brings her mouth to it and inhales greedily, then goes back to digging, wondering how long it will take to get even her hand through the opening, but she knows that if she doesn't do this, if she simply lies waiting in the darkness of her prison and the fog of her memories, she will die—mad, perhaps, surprised by the nothingness at the bottom of her vision-filled torpor.

I'll die alone. Without you. No one will know, and I'll disappear without a trace, leaving nothing but a skeleton someone will find in a few months and toss into a mass grave, and you might look for me for a while before getting used to my absence, but I hope you'll think of me once in a while because I don't know, otherwise, if anyone will remember I existed. They were so angry with me in the village when I left to find work in Paris, my sisters and my brother, who couldn't understand me leaving our dead behind, our parents who had worked themselves to death, plagued by debt, the two little ones carried off by fevers, the shack where we grew up crammed together like sardines in a tin—still happy, though, because we loved each other, we loved each other—I don't know any other way to say it, even in the bad times, when the soup was mostly water and no one smiled around the table, no one spoke or even looked up from our plates, even in those moments there was something that kept us together and made words pointless, perhaps, because sometimes talking doesn't accomplish anything, especially when you can't find the words; it was like a big hand was holding us all in the cup of its palm, in its warmth.

I never explained why I left. Not even to you. I'm sure no one would have believed me if I told them what happened to me on those evenings during harvest time when I was fifteen, and all these years of fear every time I saw them, at the market, at church, and the way they glanced at me, smirking and nudging each other. My father would have killed me and then killed them; I have no doubt. I swear I'll tell you about it if we're ever together again, but I believe I'll never be rid of my self-loathing, the dirtiness I have inside me that never leaves me, that even you and your gentle words and your caresses and all the pleasure you have given me have never been able to cleanse away.

I'm digging beneath this door, and I don't know if I'll manage to make a hole big enough to get out of here; I'm digging, and I don't know if I'm thinking out loud or if I'm just talking here alone like I've been driven mad with fear, already dead to the rest of the world.

She lies down, out of breath, her heart pounding wildly. All is whiteness around her, a whiteness like a thick fog that her mind has created, that absorbs all images and suddenly prevents any memories from forming. So she closes her eyes for a bit of shadow, but everything is still white, and she doesn't know any more if she's sinking into the void or if the void is hollowing her out from the inside.

She cries out. Hearing her own voice, even without an echo, does her good and drives her back to her feet.

20

A house blows up and then collapses, blocking half the road with its debris, and soon gray phantoms appear in the cloud of dust, crouching in corners and kneeling behind blocks of stone or sections of wall and opening fire, and for a moment the men on the barricade keep their heads down, letting the bullets whistle past over their heads or ricochet off the wall of cobblestones like hail. Nicolas feels a tug at his sleeve, and Adrien pulls him toward the entrance to a building and kicks open the door. Red follows, demanding what the hell they're doing, and the three of them climb a staircase to a transom that casts a bluish light on the top-floor landing. They break through a door and enter a small apartment that smells of floor polish, its gleaming parquet floor creaking beneath their feet, and they walk carefully among the furniture almost on tiptoe, like visitors who haven't been given house slippers upon their arrival.

Two windows overlook the boulevard. They open them carefully and then cock their rifles and kneel on the narrow balconies. Red stays just behind them inside with the ammunition and the third rifle so there will be no pause in the firing.

"Don't miss them, okay? Because when they spot you, they won't leave you much time. We need to get the job done quickly."

Nicolas rests the tip of his rifle in the wrought ironwork of the balcony, just beneath a pot of dead flowers hung from the railing. For a moment at least, the Versaillais won't know where the shots are coming from. As long as the smoke from their barrels dissipates fast enough. That detail has never occurred to him before.

Since the five barricades guarding the Place d'Enfer fell, wiped out in an hour, infantrymen have been swarming into the area, looting all the buildings. There are shouts and gunshots. Windows shattering. Only a little while ago, on the corner of the Cité d'Enfer, some of them were seen throwing a man out a third-story window and then coming out of the building pushing three women and four children ahead of them, whom they lined up against a wall. One of the women shouted, weeping, that they were nothing but murderers, vandals, looters, and that at least the Federates didn't behave like that. A soldier plunged his bayonet into her throat, and when the children flung themselves on her body, screaming, and the two other women came forward with fists raised, they shot the whole group and finished off anyone who was still moving by slaughtering them as if they were the straw dummies used in military exercises. This account had been given by a sharp-shooter assigned to somehow cover the retreat. Alone, hidden behind a wagon, there had been nothing he could do. He had spotted the adjutant commanding the group, a small red-headed man with a spectacular mustache, and promised himself he'd put a bullet between his eyes at the first opportunity.

The fires raging in the gutted apartments are sending stagnant, hazy smoke out into the airless street. There is not the slightest breeze. The soldiers progress slowly along the walls, hurrying from porch to entryway. For the moment, things aren't too bad. Around thirty men lie on their bellies amid the rubble of the demolished house, firing continuously toward the barricade, which responds in kind. The men swear at each other between salvos. A boy climbs atop the barricade and throws a stone at the infantrymen, who burst out laughing and aim their guns mockingly at him. A big man in shirtsleeves, bullet pouch strapped across his torso, grabs the child by the belt and pulls him backward, tossing him to the ground, shouting, "Careful, you little idiot!"

An artillery wagon stops on the corner of the boulevard, and five or six men jump out of it to unhitch and maneuver the gun. They roll it fifty meters away while others heave ammunition crates out of the wagon. There are a dozen of them around the cannon, including one officer, undoubtedly a lieutenant. Nicolas can't quite make out his stripes. The lieutenant has drawn his saber, and the silvery glint of it helps Nicolas draw a bead.

He sees one of the men heft an artillery shell and lift it toward the mouth of the cannon. He's directly in front of Nicolas; he doesn't need to move to keep the man in his line of fire. He aims at the man's shins, settles the rifle butt firmly against his shoulder, and at the exact same moment another shot rings out somewhere else in the street, so he pulls the trigger and watches the soldier crumple slowly, still holding the shell, as if the six kilograms of iron have suddenly become too heavy for him. Another of the soldiers goes over to him and bends down, and Nicolas jumps at the shot fired by Adrien: the infantryman falls heavily, thrown under the barrel of the eight-pounder. For a moment the Versaillais freeze, crouching, surely stunned. Two or three of them take refuge behind the cannon. Red reloads, taking their rifles, and just then the Versaillais officer stands up, waving his arms, exhorting his men to be brave. "The stripes," says Adrien. "Let's both get him." They take advantage of a fresh exchange of gunshots in the street to open fire.

Nicolas absorbs the shock of the recoil and can't see anything but the flash of the saber and the man spinning bizarrely as if dancing in some comic opera, then falling. The Versaillais retreat, abandoning the cannon, carrying their dead and wounded, and disappear into a corner of the cemetery.

"What do we do now?" Adrien asks.

"We wait. If we go after the ones down in the street, we'll be spotted right away. At least we've taken the cannon out of the picture for now. It's an eight-pounder, fires shrapnel."

Shouts of joy drift up from the street. The soldiers are withdrawing, step by step, firing to cover their retreat. A man climbs onto the barricade, waving the red flag, and is thrown backward, the cloth enveloping him, a bullet hole in his throat. His comrades cry out and rush toward him. The man clutches at his neck and struggles as blood streams between his fingers. Three or four guards shoot at the soldiers in retaliation, wounding two of them. The others flee at a run, backs hunched, stumbling.

Silence falls again. A few shots sound in the distance; there is a rumble of cannon fire. Behind the barricade, in the crossroads, a crowd of curious onlookers is gathering. Women and men of all ages. A few parasols open. People strain their necks and stand on tiptoe. The buzz of their conversations reaches Nicolas; even from here he thinks he can hear their satisfaction at seeing the Commune finally attacked, their impatience for it to be quashed once and for all. Four women bring food wrapped in dish towels. Men jump down from a wagon to retrieve the dead man and carry him away on a stretcher.

"A mitrailleuse is what we need," remarks Red. "We can't hold them for long. They're going to bring in the artillery, and we'll scatter like a flock of sparrows."

He sits down on the balcony, his back against a shutter, and fills his pipe. Adrien rolls a cigarette with shaky fingers.

"You all right?" Nicolas asks.

The boy nods. After the first puff he lifts his chin proudly, exhaling smoke.

"Why wouldn't I be? What better place is there to be than on a balcony in the sunshine?"

"There, what did I tell you," says Red.

Another cart pulls up on the corner of the boulevard, pulling two artillery wagons. The cannon is quickly maneuvered into place, the unhitched wagons placed defensively around it. Nicolas and Adrien get back into firing position.

"Artillery!" bellows Red. "A twelve-pounder!"

The men on the barricade take aim. A sergeant orders them to hold their fire. A plume of smoke descends on them, driven by a gust of wind. Fire crackles in the destroyed building, beams cracking as they split. The people in the crossroads scurry for cover like a bunch of chickens.

The Versaillais are manning the cannon now, protected by the two wagons. Nicolas draws a bead on a soldier and fires. Adrien pulls his trigger, misses, swears.

"This is pointless. Nothing we can do against a cannon."

They fire two more bullets and then leave the balcony. On the way down the stairs they hear the first artillery shell explode, then shouts in the street outside. Windows break with a crash. They emerge into a suffocating cloud of dust and smoke. The shot was too long. The shell has struck thirty meters behind the redoubt. Figures wave their arms frantically and run in all directions. Nicolas narrowly misses colliding with a body stretched out on its back, its face torn off by the blast. The brain is visible through the shattered forehead. He stumbles aside to vomit, but there's nothing in his stomach, so he simply lets the spasms shake him, bent double.

"Come on!" someone shouts. "Rue Vavin!"

The men shoulder their bags and gather their cartridge pouches, helping friends limp toward the Rue Delambre. A second shell explodes behind them and pulverizes the barricade. Cobblestones thud to the ground around them, on top of them, and the men fall, their faces bloody, knocked unconscious, and their comrades grab them and drag them away. Red is hit in the back and thrown forward onto his hands and knees, the breath knocked out of him. Nicolas tries to lift him up, but his strength is gone, his mouth still filled with bile. A stranger in civilian clothes, coat and tie, comes to take Red's other arm. "Let's go," he says. "You can't stay here." They heave Red to his feet; Red coughs and swears but after a few moments is able to walk unaided. The man walks away, straightening his top hat. *Thanks*. There is an answering wave in response to Nicolas, who never even saw the man's face.

Windows are pulled shut on the Rue Delambre as they pass. The call of a bugle sounds farther on and then stops. There are around a hundred of them hurriedly crossing the deserted Boulevard du Montparnasse, their flag draped over the shoulder of a sergeant who urges the men to pick up the pace. There is a rattle of machine-gun fire from near the cemetery, then two terrible explosions. Men begin running toward the train station. Someone shouts for them to come back, to stay and fight. Red pretends to aim his gun at them.

"Bunch of cowards! They're running like scared rabbits! I'd like to shoot them like rabbits!"

Nicolas puts a hand on his shoulder.

"Come. I honestly don't know what's keeping me from joining them."

His friend looks at him appraisingly, astonished. Adrien, who has been watching the others flee, turns toward them.

"What do we do?"

"For life, to the death. Isn't that what we promised each other?" Nicolas says.

"I don't believe in promises anymore," says Adrien. "You two bastards are all I've got left, so I'm sticking with you. Dead or alive!"

There are no more than twenty of them left now to scale the barricade on the Rue Vavin, outstretched arms helping them climb back down the other side of the cobblestone wall. A captain strides toward them, two revolvers stuck into his belt. He welcomes them with a wide, bright smile, as if they're guests at a banquet.

"We can certainly use you. It's going to get messy around here. I hope some of you are good shots? We need snipers in the buildings. I don't have enough men."

Adrien and a large bearded man step forward. The officer assigns them to two buildings on the corner where the street meets the boulevard. Red decides to go with Adrien, to reload for him like they did earlier on the balcony, and Nicolas, watching the two of them walk away, suddenly feels a vast hollowness in the pit of his stomach. *Be careful.* A child's laughter makes him look around, and he isn't sure if he said the words aloud or simply thought them, so he shakes off the torpor that has come over him, his legs heavy with exhaustion, his back knotted with pain as if weighted down by a cross.

There are two cannons lined up in battery formation. The gunners manning them are seated on crates of artillery shells. Ten men are on guard duty, their rifles resting in front of them. The street is one enormous, milling throng, talking, shouting, arguing, inventorying ammunition. A mess girl moves from one group to the next, distributing flasks, one for every three men. They joke with her, laughing, asking if the flasks are full of cheap wine, and she says the Central Committee has promised to send them a crate of Bordeaux that evening. "Then *vive la Commune!*" bawls out one rogue, draining his flask of tepid water without letting its neck touch his lips. An artillery shell falls somewhere in a courtyard, and everyone hunches their shoulders, the conversations now mingling with the sinister rumble of a building collapsing. A few roof slates fall and smash with a sharp noise.

"There they are!"

They spy the Versaillais soldiers lying in wait on the corner of the Rue Delambre and behind the abandoned barricade on the Boulevard d'Enfer, and soon enough a mitrailleuse is brought in. Nicolas sees the soldiers' rifles lining up, aiming; their red caps are only just visible, but there are around fifty of them, and behind them he can make out the rest of the column, waiting. The roof of the building on the corner of the Boulevard du Montparnasse blows apart, and debris rains down on the men at the same time as the first volley of gunfire strikes the wall of cobbles, hissing and scratching against the stones. Nicolas hits the ground in a fetal position, protecting his head with his arms like the others, who swear and shout and twitch in confusion, striking out at anything that falls on them. Then one of them gets up, bellowing, and wedges his rifle against the spokes of a wheel that has crashed to the ground nearby. He fires, reloads, and the others join him in letting fly one salvo and then another. The cannon roars, and they all watch as the shell eviscerates a building behind the Versaillais firing line. A gunner adjusts the backsight, and the shot blows off a corner of the barricade, and for a moment there is a confused melee among the Versaillais that makes the men shout with joy. The second cannon fires a volley of shrapnel, and Nicolas thinks he can hear the blast tearing down walls, eliciting screams of pain from those Versaillais bastards.

"We need to counterattack while they're down," says the captain. "There aren't enough of us, damn it. Where are the reinforcements? We've got to hold them off, but for how long?"

There is an explosion behind them. A façade collapses. Then another, farther on. Chunks of walls, windows, furniture. A piano topples onto a heap of debris with a jangling, discordant crash. The building's residents swarm out into the street, clearing it as best they can. They pull a corpse from the rubble, an elderly man who offered his services as a shooter this morning but was rejected because his hands trembled too much and his laughing blue eyes were almost sightless. He has stopped trembling now; he'll never see anything again. Two men in civilian clothes, unarmed but wearing leather military belts, carry his body away; it is so thin as to appear weightless, like a wooden puppet with a bloody head.

They can't see the cannons that were used to destroy the street. A reconnaissance mission will have to be launched. Nicolas volunteers himself to the captain, who refuses. Too risky.

"But—we could . . ."

"No, goddammit, I said no! What good would it do? They're farther along the boulevard, on both sides of the street, and they'll get us in a pincer movement! What do you think you're going to do? Attack them with three men?"

A volley of machine-gun fire makes them drop to the ground. The captain clutches his right shoulder. He looks at his fingers, red with blood.

"It's nothing, nothing. A cut."

The cannon retaliates fruitlessly. The captain goes over to it. Impossible to maneuver the guns in battery formation. The Versaillais withdraw to the boulevard. The mitrailleuse's two gunners crouch behind the shield. Three guards remain standing, monitoring the enemy. The others sit down, take off their caps and wipe their foreheads, count the remaining ammunition. We're still all right, but for how much longer? How many attacks can we fend off? Nicolas looks at them, their dirty faces bent over their powder-blackened hands, busy cleaning a gun or filling a pipe, exchanging rapid, indistinguishable words that draw the occasional nervous laugh. Someone taps him on the shoulder and holds out a flask. "It's cool," the man says. "It'll do you good." Nicolas holds the water in his mouth for a moment before he swallows it, and again the memories rush back, the glare of sunshine during the harvest—he can only remember the sunlight at first, and then the details take shape little by little: the wagons, the yoked oxen, men working in the brightness. He closes his eyes and can see it all. The goatskins;

the bottles of wine the little ones like him always wanted to taste, too, seeing the adults happily drinking deep draughts; the strong scent of the wine; the sharp, slightly nauseating taste of it that stayed on the tongue.

The blast of the explosion is so violent that it chokes the entire width of the boulevard with an immense heap of debris. Stones, beams, and shards of glass rain down on the barricade. The men get up white with dust, checking to make sure nothing is broken, wiping away the blood trickling from cuts and scrapes. Nothing serious. They dig in their pockets for their handkerchiefs or untie the scarves around their necks to clean themselves up a bit, and they gaze up at the building that has just blown up. The captain inquires about the number of wounded; voices answer him from the dissipating cloud of dust.

Nicolas has stopped breathing. He doesn't have the time. Or maybe the desire, not now. He goes into the foyer of the building, his mouth and throat filling with dust, unable to see anything beyond his outstretched hands, groping in the suffocating darkness. He doesn't see the staircase until he trips on its lowest step, and then he creeps up it one step at a time, his legs stiff, clinging to the banister, looking up at the ragged holes from which flames billow. He crosses a landing where one intact door has remained closed, a transom above it letting in weak daylight. Across from it, flames growl, licking toward the staircase as if still unsure of whether to climb it. On the floor above, an old woman in a dressing gown waits on the threshold of her front door, disheveled, a nasty cut on her forehead streaming blood. Behind her in the devastated apartment, the golden light of sunset glows through the blasted-out façade. "Someone will have to tell my daughter," she says. "I won't be able to come for dinner with her this evening. Would you mind taking the message? I'll write down her address for you, wait a moment." She disappears into the apartment,

closing the door gently behind her, and Nicolas waits obedi-
ently for her to come back for a few seconds before coming to
his senses and continuing his climb.

The narrow staircase is choked with stone blocks and
debris. A few clouds have appeared in the blue sky visible
through the ragged holes in the roof. He has to thread his way
between sagging beams to reach the landing. He calls out for
Adrien and Red, but his voice is faint and weak, as if smothered by the disaster. He goes into an apartment in which the
walls facing the street are almost completely gone. What
remains of the ceiling is no more than a scattering of ragged
slabs and cracks. He steps over fallen chairs, skirts an overturned sideboard smashed in half. Everything is gray and
white with dust; nothing seems to be in its proper place.
Paintings lie scattered here and there as if some thief, in a
hurry or surprised in the middle of a job, has abandoned
them. Only a small, oval wooden frame, still hung on its wall,
its glass cracked, remains to pay tribute to some grandparent
in an elaborate uniform.

Someone moves in the next room. Something falls to the
floor. Glass breaks. Nicolas has to heave aside a large sofa to
get in.

Red is standing against a wall, covered with blood and dust.
He is holding a motionless body in his arms that Nicolas thinks
is a child at first. Red is weeping, his shoulders shaking with
sobs. He's weeping, and when he sees Nicolas standing in the
doorway, he moans, in a tiny voice that doesn't seem like it
should come from such a large and powerful body:

"I tried to get it out . . . but I couldn't . . ."

Nicolas doesn't understand. Doesn't want to understand.
He steps closer, to force himself to stop denying the truth of
what he's seeing. He touches Adrien's face with his fingertips;
he looks like he's asleep, his mouth open. A jagged piece of
iron protrudes from the back of his head, red with blood.

"I didn't dare pull it too hard," Red says. "We probably shouldn't touch anything, don't you think?"

Nicolas watches Adrien's eyes, thinks he detects a slight quiver in the lids. *He's going to wake up. He's going to come back to us, and we'll take him to a surgeon who'll remove this from his head, because that's obviously what knocked him out. That's it . . . we'll take him to that Doctor Fontaine . . .*

Caroline.

Dizziness sweeps over him, and he shuts his eyes. He grips the back of an armchair to steady himself, and he's surprised by the unexpected feel of the soft velvet against his hand. Outside, the shooting starts up again. Three blasts from a cannon close by shake the ruins of the building they're in, causing even more plaster to fall and smash, a stopped clock chiming pointlessly.

"We've got to get out of here. Come on."

Nicolas tugs at Red's arm; he doesn't move at first—resists, even—and then gives in and reluctantly allows himself to be led. They carry Adrien's body down the stairs with groans of effort and sorrow. Nicolas doesn't know any more if he's out of breath or if grief is suffocating him. "Careful, we mustn't—" says Red. When they aren't looking where they're stepping, to avoid any misstep, they watch Adrien's head lolling back as if dragged downward by the metal shard buried in it.

They emerge into the street amid the hissing of bullets and the shouts of their comrades. Two or three faces turn briefly toward them and then back to the battle. They hurry away; they aren't sure exactly where they should go with their dead friend and his broken skull, but they carry this necessary burden with a sort of pride in doing this for him, taking him somewhere calm where they can talk to him quietly so as not to disturb his newfound rest, where they can wash him, wipe the blood and grime from his face, restore the boyish good looks that must have pleased the girls and would doubtless have gone on to break many more hearts. Yes—they have to take him somewhere safe from the noise and clamor, and they're determined to do it, stumbling in the rutted street, tripping over scattered cobblestones. Nicolas turns back to look at the barricade at the exact moment an artillery shell explodes just in front of it, flinging three men backward in a burst of wood and granite fragments; he doesn't hear any of them cry out, probably because the distance between them and him has become impassable. He shakes with rage and horror, but he knows he isn't coming back. Something in him has broken, something he can't name. Not his courage, but his fervor. His trust in the future the people of Paris wanted to create. Like Adrien, they'll die by the thousands, bombarded, shot, massacred by the bourgeois's army of bastards. Him, too, undoubtedly, because he will not desert. He won't leave the embattled city. He'll continue to fight out of despair, bound by rage alone. But he doesn't want to die without finding her, seeing her again, holding her hand, caressing her cheek. He realizes, suddenly, that happiness exists and that he has met it. It looks like a young brunette woman with a thoughtful face and serious eyes, a musical laugh and a slightly husky voice that murmured in his ear for hours, her body pressed against his on those cold and hungry winter nights when they thought the bad days might finally be at an end.

A small café at the junction with the Rue Notre-Dame-des-Champs has been transformed into an aid station. Two women come out to meet them, their sleeves rolled up, their hair covered by gray scarves. They look at Adrien's body, nodding. "Poor boy," one of them says. They lead Red and Nicolas inside, where a dozen men are lying on the floor. "Put him here."

They set Adrien gently on three tables pushed together, careful to turn his head to the side so as not to drive the piece of iron in any deeper. Nicolas shudders at the idea, and he can hear Red breathing hard with effort, or maybe with sorrow. One of the women brings a pail of clear water and some rags. She starts soaking them in the water, but Nicolas stops her.

"No. We'll do it. He's like a brother. We promised each other. For life, to the death."

So they wash him. They're afraid to scrub too hard, to do any more damage to him, but they work diligently, and the dead young man's face brightens and pales, and his hair is combed back to reveal his boyish features. Red stops, sighs, catches his breath. When they've finished, they step back from the table and contemplate the results of their work.

"You'd think he was my son. Look at him. He looks like a sulky little boy. I never believed he was really eighteen."

Nicolas wipes the sweat out of his eyes. It's hot. There are flies. He bats them away, waving his hand to clear the air of their vile, squalid buzzing, and covers Adrien's face with a cloth.

"We can't leave him like this."

One of the wounded men approaches, limping, his torn trouser leg flapping around his bandaged right leg.

"I can do it, if you'll allow me. I've done it before, patched up the dead. It's the living I don't know how to fix. I've seen it done plenty of times, too. Go on, now, you don't need to watch."

The man bends over the dead boy's head and takes the metal fragment between his thumb and index finger and pulls gently, as if removing a large splinter from a child's finger, and tosses the thing away. Then he quickly presses a rag against the wound, because things start to flow that Nicolas hardly has time to glimpse. Nicolas doesn't know, at that moment, what a man is, if it all comes down simply to this jumble of guts and blood and brains that can be scattered by war, to this soft machinery that can be destroyed in any number of unimaginable ways. He looks at Adrien's face, and the reality hits him and knocks the breath out of him: his friend isn't there anymore. This body isn't him. Adrien was something other than this. He doesn't know the words for it. He's never thought about these things before.

"Should wrap this," says the man quietly.

A woman approaches with a strip of cloth undoubtedly cut from a sheet and hands it to Nicolas. They bandage Adrien's head slowly, with gentle, careful motions, as if they're afraid of waking him up. Now the thick, unruly hair that gave him the air of a rebellious, slightly wild little boy is hidden. His face below the cloth, so smooth and peaceful, looks like that of a girl, or a young prince.

"I think that's better," says the ad hoc medic.

He rests his palm gently on Adrien's chest.

"That artillery shrapnel is merciless. I've seen young men cut clean in half."

"What's your name?" asks Nicolas. "I'm Nicolas. Nicolas Bellec."

He shakes the man's damp, sticky hand, and a shudder passes through him.

"Jean Carpentier."

They move away from the body and head silently for the fresher air outside. Red is there, leaning against the wall, smoking a pipe.

"What do you see in the future, Bellec?"

Nicolas doesn't answer right away because another terrible explosion has just sounded from the barricade. He feels his heart swelling with rage and sadness.

"The National Guard's going to push back these rabid dogs and chase them back to Versailles, and in six months the Commune will be law all over the country, and we'll proclaim the social republic of the proletariat."

"I didn't see it happening that quickly, but in general I agree with you. We can be confident in the future, I believe."

Red has turned back and looks at them, startled at first.

"Don't you agree, Red? Victory springs from the barrel of a gun, right?"

Nicolas has had to force the words past the weight of grief heavy in his chest. He feels weak, utterly drained.

His friend shakes his head with a sad smile.

"Sure . . . especially if that gun belongs to a Versaillais infantryman. Better to try and laugh at it all, if you can manage it."

An aid-station nurse approaches them.

"You should go and lie down," she says to Jean Carpentier. "Your leg will start bleeding again and get infected."

"Leave me be, Marie. My comrades and I are discussing the future. We need to think about making plans."

"If you want to have a future at all, you'd better be careful with that leg. It's not a pretty sight. And as for the future, I try not to think about it that much. I'm not sure I have enough tears left."

A man cries out from inside the building, asking for someone to come. The woman goes back in, dragging her feet.

The gunfire has ceased for a moment. They can still hear the rumble of cannons in the distance, but the street around them is suddenly full of conversations, people calling to one another. The voices are loud because everyone is deafened, their ears ringing with the endless clamor, shouting because their throats are too hoarse for normal speech.

"I'm going," says Nicolas.

"Where?"

Nicolas explains. The Sûreté delegate in the tenth arrondissement, his investigation into the kidnapping of the girls—and Caroline. Everything Lalie told him. The cabman they're trying to find, with time passing, and war everywhere.

Red has picked up his rifle. He unlocks the breech, cleans it, takes a cartridge from his bullet pouch and loads it. Jean

Carpentier has sat down in a chair, his wounded leg stretched in front of him.

"I can't do this anymore. I have to find her. Otherwise all of this will have been for nothing."

"But Adrien, he—"

"Adrien is dead, Joseph."

"Joseph? Fucking hell, that's the third time you've called me that. I don't like it, at all. And you know what? Joseph is dead, too. The only one left now is me, Red, national guardsman of the 105th federated battalion. I don't even know who Joseph is anymore, that respectable metal polisher who always walked the straight and narrow, endured that dead-end life mapped out for him since he was a kid, who sweated blood and tears to raise two children and buried a third, only a baby, who died of hunger in February. I'm not going back to that, Nicolas. I'm going to go out and take as many of those Versaillais bastards with me as I can. And if I run out of bullets, I'll slit their throats with a bayonet or a fucking penknife before they take me. At least my Léonie and the little ones will be able to be proud of their papa."

Nicolas looks at his friend, who has never made such a long speech all at once, and he knows why he loves the fellow. He's had many of the same thoughts—but still he wants to hold the woman he loves in his arms every night as she falls asleep and every morning when she wakes up, when she's still pouty and languid and soft against him, and to have children with her, two or three of them, children he'll spoil and hoist onto his shoulders and play games with, to watch them grow up and become more and more beautiful, like promises finally kept. He wants to have these happinesses before he dies, tangible and real. But he doesn't know how to say any of this to Red, because right now his burly friend is wiping with dirty hands at the tears streaming down his cheeks.

"I do understand how you feel," Red finally manages to say.

"You're young, and you haven't seen much of life yet. Maybe in a few years we can talk again about all this, if we see each other again. If I had a girl like your Caroline, lost all alone in this hell, I think I'd go after her too, and I'd blow up the whole city to find her."

"I don't feel like I'm deserting, though," Nicolas says. "Because everything the Commune has tried to do . . . it's the future it will all count for, and what we've just been through— despite all the suffering and all the death—has been the best time of my life. Because of Caroline, too. I'm not choosing between the Commune and her. Both of them, for me, are what make life worth living, you know?"

Red nods. He forces a smile to his exhausted lips and then puts his hand on Nicolas's shoulder, squeezing it.

"Find her, dammit."

He lets go and turns away abruptly, walking toward the barricade, and Nicolas stands in the middle of the street, more alone than he's ever been in his life.

Carpentier rises from his chair and limps after Red, calling for him to wait, and the two of them walk away together, one with a heavy tread as if a crushing load has suddenly settled on his shoulders, the other dragging a foot, holding his companion's arm, gesticulating wildly as he speaks.

Nicolas briefly considers leaving his rifle and bullets under a table and then thinks better of it, shouldering the weapon and tightening the strap. He might well have need of it on some street corner while he searches for that cop in the tenth arrondissement. Resolutely, he doesn't turn around even when the battle resumes in the distance, even when two huge explosions rip through the air behind him. Ten times he stops, ten times he's overwhelmed with self-loathing for abandoning his comrades to the bombardment, ten times he repeats Caroline's name, and he turns down the Rue Notre-Dame-des-Champs almost at a run, on legs barely able to carry him.

21

The morning has passed without anyone seeming to give them a second thought. They've hammered on the trapdoor, shouted through the cellar window, demanded to speak to an officer, but to no avail. They've gotten hungry and thirsty; they've pissed and shit in corners like zoo animals, and like zoo animals they've paced in circles, slumped in resignation, protested again, and finally fallen silent, exhausted by the dreadful night just past.

When Antoine Roques opened his eyes in the morning, he was sure the fatigue lying on him like a dead animal would make it impossible for him to get to his feet. He emerged from sleep bit by bit, as if crawling out from the squalid rubble of some demolished hovel, his whole body aching from the uncomfortable night on the cold, hard floor, his mind poisoned by the nightmares that his dazed awakening did nothing to dispel. He got to his feet and caught a glimpse of blue sky out the window, heard voices calling to one another and hurried steps in the street. Clovis was sitting on a crate, his face in his hands, unmoving.

"Are you asleep?"

"Of course not."

Loubet *was* still asleep, or trying to be, tossing and groaning, so they kept their voices down, evaluating their chances of getting out of there anytime soon, and then sinking back into the dismal silence of their dark thoughts. Then Loubet had sat up suddenly, groping for his revolver, calling out, "Who goes there?" and the other two couldn't keep themselves from smiling at his alarmed face and the sheepish expression that came over it when he realized he was a prisoner—he, a police officer—in the filthy cellar of a tavern.

Outside in the street now, a crowd is milling and shouting. Roques listens to the profusion of voices for a moment, distracting himself by picturing the faces that go with them. Then his daydreams lead him gently toward the children and Rose, and his throat tightens.

It's around midday, perhaps, when the trapdoor opens and they hear a clamor at the top of the wooden staircase.

"You've no right! They're Versaillais spies!"

"Shut up, you fool, or I'll pack you off to the Prefecture. You, down there! Come on out!"

Roques rushes over. He's recognized the voice of Captain Colin of the 138th, the battalion stationed nearby that assisted him in the search for the spy Courbin. The officer's bearded face is thrust into the opening at the top of the stairs, flanked by two of his men.

"Bloody hell! Get out of there!"

They climb the stairs two at a time as if the trapdoor might slam shut again at any moment and capture them for good. Jacquet, the swaggering loudmouth who arrested them yesterday, is there too, held at bay by a guard.

"One of the boys told me you'd been arrested yesterday. He was part of the patrol but didn't dare say anything because Citizen Jacquet showed a document issued and signed by the Prefecture. I came as soon as I could. If I didn't have more important things to do, I'd give this dolt a good right cross in the face and throw him in prison!"

He goes to Jacquet and seizes him by the shirt collar.

"Now get the hell out of here before I change my mind. Go help carry stones to the barricades, if you're so anxious to serve and prove your loyalty to the Commune."

Jacquet has gone white. He holds himself very stiff and upright, his eyes downcast, lips clamped tightly together. His expression is falsely contrite. Scheming. When the captain lets go of him, he takes a few steps toward the door, glances over at Clovis, and pauses for a moment, then leaves.

"Snake," says Roques.

He grasps Colin's hands in his own. "Thank you for getting us out of there. They'd have let us die in that hole."

The captain pulls back abruptly, seized by a sudden idea. "When was the last time you ate anything?"

Roques feels his stomach twist at the words. Loubet, hearing them, takes a step toward Colin as if he were going to hand them a plate then and there. Only Clovis doesn't move, his gaze fixed on the crowd of women and children and national guardsmen outside.

In a canteen at the end of the street, a surly-faced woman dressed entirely in black serves them bowls of stew and a slice of fresh bread each. She brings sausages and a bottle of white wine they waste no time emptying. They let themselves relax in their chairs as they clink their glasses together, each of them feeling an ache of happiness in his heart, images of spring flashing through his mind, memories of open-air cafés. Clovis smiles faintly, his eyes lowered. Then they eat greedily, noisily, voraciously, not talking too much, and afterward Captain Colin asks them where they were going yesterday, after the fighting had begun.

Antoine Roques tells him the story, explaining everything. Introduces Clovis as an invaluable informant. Loubet darts a hostile glance at him that the captain doesn't see, then returns to his food.

"All that to rescue a woman who's probably already dead?" asks the captain.

There's a silence, then Clovis rouses himself. "It's no different than wanting to save the Commune today."

Colin nods and looks closely at Clovis, his face solemn.

"There's not much I can say to that. You've got a point. We're retreating at every turn. A few barricades are still holding under the bombardment: the Rue Vavin, the Rue de Rennes. But for how much longer? How many hours? The Versaillais are destroying everything around them to get through. They'll raze Paris to the ground before they let the people have it. And they'll kill everyone to take Paris back. So yes, thinking we might still have a chance to save the Commune today is a bit like believing you can save a dying person with prayer even though there's no God. A bit like that woman trapped beneath tons of stone."

"It's called hope," says Roques. "It has nothing to do with the logic of comfortable minds. It makes me think of these fires that keep burning even in the rain."

"But you," says Clovis, "you have your children, your wife. That's where your hope lies. I, however . . ."

"I have a wife and children, too," says Captain Colin. "And I'm here, talking to you, instead of holding them close, and in an hour or a day I'll be with others, under fire. I'll fight to live, not to die. I don't particularly feel like sacrificing myself, you know; I'm thirty-two years old, and there's a lot of happiness I'd still like to experience—but it seems to me that sometimes we have to rise above our own little lives. I don't know you, but maybe that's what you're trying to do, going to look for this woman."

Clovis gazes at him unblinkingly, his eyes very bright. At last he nods, almost imperceptibly.

A national guardsman rushes into the café, breathless, and heads straight for the captain. He seems annoyed not to find Colin alone and hesitates, shuffling his feet.

"You can speak, Fargot. These are comrades."

The man takes a deep breath and grips the edge of the table. Colin pours him a glass of water, which he empties in a gulp.

"It looks . . . it looks like the Versaillais are bypassing Paris, going through Clichy and Saint-Ouen. The Prussians are letting Clinchant's army through. He'll be at the Porte de Clignancourt by tonight."

"They want to attack Montmartre from behind," says Captain Colin. "Who knows about this?"

"The Central Committee's been informed by dispatch. It's La Cécilia who's taken the matter in hand. But it's panic. Anyone who hadn't already fled is leaving now. Seems the cannons on the Butte haven't even been mounted on carriages."

Colin half rises, both fists on the tabletop.

"Come on. With La Cécilia, anything is still possible. As long as there are fighters left to fight."

"The National Guard's been like snow in the sun for two weeks," says Roques. "Too many losses. Incompetent officers. People have lost confidence in them. And it's gotten even worse in the past few days. Valiant armchair warriors like Jacquet and even a few elected officials have asked me to arrest the deserters. I caught a few of them, but then what? I'd have to throw them in jail by the hundreds! And for what motive? It makes no sense. And all those respectable people in the street, spitting in their faces and slapping them when we took them to headquarters. Things like that make you realize that the mob has nothing to do with the people. Anyway, I released them that same night, poor devils, telling them we were counting on them to defend the Commune. Of course they swore to me on their children's lives that they'd be there at the first roll call, and then ran off as fast as their legs could carry them."

"The people don't understand anything," says Loubet. "Except force."

Roques is about to reply when there's a commotion in the street. A mitrailleuse is pushed and pulled past by half a dozen men, escorted by a pack of curious, shouting children. Captain Colin stands, puts on his cap, rebuttons his tunic.

"I'd better be off, Citizens. I've just seen a mitrailleuse go by that no one asked for. Gunners and ammunition should be right behind it, I hope . . . Come with me."

They leave the café. Colin has dug up a rifle and a revolver for them along with twenty cartridges each and has cobbled together a makeshift safe-conduct pass with the battalion's stamp and his signature. Now he bids them good luck.

Everywhere the streets are full of the same hubbub, the same shouts and songs, the same clanging of crowbars prying cobblestones from the pavements. The people have come out en masse to work on this vast construction site without a foreman, where a red flag is planted atop a simple heap of cobbles here and there, scalable in three bounds by children, the way a carpenter adds a roof ornament to crown his work. Thirty rifles behind the heap and defiant, resolute faces. They won't get through. Occasionally the terrible sounds of the battle can be heard when the wind carries them through the streets like a gust of icy wind, and people sniff the air, trying to catch a whiff of something other than the plumes of smoke borne on the wind from the west, but they can't sense the summary executions, the systematic bombardment of streets held by the Federates, the barricades buried beneath the rubble. They can't sense any of it, just that things are going badly.

They're going to have to pass through the line of fire into the area occupied by the Versaillais army. They pick their way through the winding maze Paris has become, doubling back again and again. Sometimes they're allowed to cross over a defensive barrier or creep along a wall, hunched beneath an overturned cart; at other times they're searched, their papers checked suspiciously, squinted at and scrutinized and turned over, only to be waved onward with a weary or irritated gesture, to go and get themselves killed someplace else—because they're leaving the fortified part of the city now and heading straight for the combat zone. Cannon muzzles peek out of embrasures here and there; makeshift firing posts have been set up in the windows of attic rooms. Roques stares at all of it with a mixture of astonishment and alarm. How many of the Federates are left to hold all these streets and squares? Two or three thousand? They say MacMahon's army is forty thousand strong. They say the Prussians have released ten thousand prisoners to fight for the Versaillais. He begins to feel the weight of the rifle on his shoulder strap, and it strikes him that it won't be of much more use against the oncoming frenzy than if he was carting around a block of wood. He feels overwhelmed, small and insignificant in the middle of this battered city, suddenly oppressed by the verticality of the buildings around him as if they might tumble down at any moment, and he lifts his eyes to the sky, searching for a glimpse of its azure calm, and finds dark curls of smoke wafting by instead, blurring together and separating slowly and then drifting lazily toward the fragile, cut-off encampment the people of Paris are building for themselves.

The Rue de Rivoli is choked with smoke. Firefighting wagons plunge into the pea soup in the direction of the Tuileries, their horses at a gallop, skidding on the cobblestones. Roques catches sight of flames licking behind windows here and there. National guardsmen perched on the high barricade stare at the fire, stunned and frozen. An artillery shell explodes on the roof, and a shower of slates rises and falls like a dead tree brusquely shaken free of its charred leaves.

"The Louvre's on fire," says Loubet.

Roques feels his heart clench, realizes he's trembling, and isn't sure whether it's out of rage or fear.

"Come on," he says. "We're running out of time."

They cross the street, followed by Clovis, who seems unwilling to look at any of the destruction, his head down in the acrid smoke.

There is music at the Hôtel de Ville, brass instruments and

a bass drum playing "Le Chant du Départ" while the crowd sings along. Women and children, with red flags fluttering above them. For a moment, the chorus of voices drowns out the noise of the explosions. Some distance away, a few gentlemen in top hats are watching the battalions reforming. Horsemen bearing dispatches come and go, shouting to clear a path among the clumped onlookers, their horses' chests knocking aside anyone imprudent enough not to get out of the way, the animals snorting and shying and pawing the ground before backing off, alarmed by the cries and the sudden gestures, anxious to get away.

They don't linger amid the clamor, hastening their steps along the Seine. The quayside is full of people strolling who pause now and then to look at the fires burning in the distance. The dull rumble of the cannons is endless. As they near the Place Saint-Michel, they hear the distant, heavy rattle of machine-gun fire.

"They've reached the Croix-Rouge," says Loubet. "We'll never get through. We'll be stopped at the first guarded street corner."

Clovis pulls a neatly folded sheet of paper from his pocket. "Maybe this will help."

Loubet unfolds the document and reads it, his eyes widening in astonishment.

"Where did you get this?"

"The fellow I've been carting all over Paris for the last few months was lodging with a woman whose brother is a Versaillais officer. He had him prepare these papers in case she had any trouble with soldiers or the police when they came back. She had one for herself and one for him, under the name Henri Pujols. He was very proud of it. He was hoping to get through the lines and make his escape. I took it from him after I knocked him out. Look at the signatures. There's even an official watermark."

Antoine Roques takes the sheet in his turn and reads it. It's a safe-conduct pass signed by General Clinchant, with an official stamp and signatures. He gives it back to Clovis, who tucks it into the lining of his jacket.

"Wouldn't do to have a national guardsman search me and find this. We'd be set for the firing squad."

"And if the Versaillais find my pass signed by Rigault, they'll line us up against the wall, too."

They set off again down the narrow streets, which are clearer now, the sky above them like a bright ribbon. The cannon fire dies away for a moment, and all they can hear is the sporadic clamor of rifle shots and, in this deceptive calm, that muffled, almost harmless-sounding crackle makes it seem like everything could start up again at any moment, that this isn't the end of anything. On the Rue des Quatre-Vents, Roques pauses in front of an open bar-café with a few tables and chairs set outside. He would love to sit down for a moment, elbows on the table in front of a mug of beer, and think quietly about Rose and the children, about what he has lost and what he is looking for. Decide whether to push on, or to go back home. Clovis and Loubet have stopped, too, and are gazing at the improvised terrace with that dreamy look people get sometimes when they're completely overcome by fatigue. A man is sitting at one of the tables, wearing a red armband, his legs stretched out in front of him, eyes closed. A glass of absinthe sits on the table in front of him next to a shapeless hat. He opens his eyes and looks at them, taking in their frayed, wrinkled clothes, their drawn faces, the rifle strapped to Roques's shoulder, and greets them discreetly with a tilt of his chin. Two other men are playing dominos silently a few meters away, their eyes glued to the game, their moves quick and decisive, their black slabs aligned in front of them like tiny fences, and it seems as if nothing in the world could distract them. Roques can see their starched white shirt cuffs peeking out from beneath the sleeves of their worn smocks. One of them wears a gold signet ring on his ring finger.

Roques jumps when an immense explosion makes the cobblestones quiver beneath his feet and dislodges a few poorly installed windows, which fall and shatter on the ground. A chimney topples over and smashes in the middle of the street. One of the players glances up at the building façades and then returns to his dominoes. His companion hasn't budged, hunched imperturbably over the game; he simply nods, as if approving the renewed bombardment.

"Come on," says Clovis. "We'll have a drink later."

The three of them start walking again, heaving the same sigh of regret. On the Rue Saint-Sulpice, the air vibrates around them with each explosion, windows bursting into needle-sharp fragments that rain down on the pavement like knife blades, crystalline daggers glittering in the scant light, and roof slates plummet straight down like hatchet blades to smash at their feet, so they quicken their steps, keeping their eyes on the heights of this gorge where invisible assailants seem to lie in wait for them.

In the square, in front of the church, which has been transformed into an aid station, the wounded are being loaded onto an omnibus and wagons for evacuation. No one talks much. A man with his head and eyes bandaged groans as he climbs onto the running board. Roques approaches a woman who has just helped the man aboard and is catching her breath, one hand resting on a horse's neck.

"Are you taking them to the hospital?"

The woman gapes at him as if he's just fallen from the moon.

"No one knows where to take them. Far away from here, in any case. Because it'll all be over around here by nightfall. Varlin and his men can't hold the Croix-Rouge for long . . . same with Lisbonne on the Rue Vavin . . ."

She breaks off to stare at Loubet and Clovis, a short distance off.

"What are you doing here, all of you?"

Roques decides to tell the truth because he can't think of a lie. And because maybe the time for lies is over.

"We have to find someone on the Rue des Missions."

"The Rue des Missions? That's behind Versaillais lines. They've occupied everything from Montparnasse to Les Invalides, been there since yesterday evening! You'll be arrested and shot. They're not taking any prisoners, you know."

"A woman is trapped under a collapsed building. We have to get her out of there."

"Let the dead rest in peace. We have enough to do with the ones who aren't gone yet . . ."

"It has to do with a promise I made."

The woman bursts out laughing, wiping her hands on her apron. "A promise! You don't say!"

She repeats the word under her breath a couple of times, as if she wants to remember it, then walks off toward the church without looking back. The omnibus rattles off, creaking, the heavy clatter of its wheels making the ground vibrate. Roques watches it maneuver down the narrow street, the horses walking carefully, shards of glass crunching horribly beneath their shoes.

They leave the square just as fifty Federate fighters arrive and sit or sprawl on the ground, exhausted, drinking from their canteens. The men are silent, their gazes vacant, taking off their caps and running dirty fingers through their hair. A clamor of voices rises from somewhere up ahead, of joy or perhaps confusion, and then the sharp rapping of a mitrailleuse. The smell of smoke. They run and burst out onto the Rue de Rennes, which is in flames toward Montparnasse. A barricade is engulfed in smoke, fire leaping in the windows of the buildings above the combatants' silhouettes. A roof rises as if it's being inflated and then hollows out and collapses, exhaling a monstrous breath of embers and sparks. A child might well believe that dragons are hiding in this war-torn city, that they've come to destroy it and build their own lairs atop the ruins. Roques doesn't believe in dragons, but he is afraid of the gigantic monster scattering its thousands of fire-demons throughout Paris. Rifle bullets whistle over their heads, and they duck buzzing swarms fired from mitrailleuses.

Loubet grabs Roques by the arm and pulls him to the other side of the street. Clovis runs after them, and the three of them huddle in a recessed doorway just as a hail of bullets thuds into the façade near them, peppering them with fragments of stone. They stand still for a few minutes, catching their breath, pressed against each other like little boys caught in a sudden shower. Finally the gunfire seems to die down for a moment, so Roques steps out of their refuge and back onto the Rue du Vieux Colombier. He feels something trickling down his forehead, raises a hand to it, looks at his bloody fingers. A cut, slightly swollen, that's beginning to hurt now. He didn't feel anything when it happened, beneath that rain of rubble. He presses his handkerchief to the wound and keeps going, clutching the strap of his rifle in his other hand. He feels heavy all of a sudden, his ears full of a hissing sound and heavy thumps, his skull buzzing as if an army of insects has invaded it. He's startled when Clovis appears right at eye level in his field of vision and says, hoarsely:

"We might not get out of this alive, but at least we will have done what we had to do."

The man keeps pace with him, a half smile on his face, and suddenly Roques feels some of his strength return.

22

They'd carried him through a carriage entrance and carefully laid him down near other wounded people, with soothing gestures and reassuring words he couldn't remember ever being directed at him before. Pujols tried to remember his mother taking care of him when he was sick, like that time he got sunstroke because his father had made him keep watch all day over the flock in a high meadow in the bright sun, a sun that was fierce and hot even in the morning, the still air seeming to grip him with burning hands, preventing any movement; even the dogs, their flanks heaving, whined with every breath, the cows lying like statues posed in the glaring landscape. There had been fears of a bear attack, so he hadn't dared go down to the stream and had huddled on a rock beneath his straw hat with his gourd of lukewarm water. They'd carried him down from the hillside nearly unconscious on the back of a mule. His mother had bathed his forehead with ice water and made him drink, but he couldn't remember even the briefest words of comfort from her, the slightest caress. They'd put him to bed earlier than usual, and the next morning at dawn, his father had come to shake him awake the same way he did every day, grumbling and shuffling his slippers on the flagstone floor of their shared room.

Four women were bustling around this entryway. One of them, a young redhead, had approached him and asked which battalion he was with, and if it was hard going, and he feigned a spell of weakness and a faulty memory to avoid answering her

338 · HERVÉ LE CORRE

questions, so the girl smiled at him, pressing a damp cloth to his swollen forehead and his battered face, probing with her fingertips the terrible injuries that people had been so shocked by for months, the broken eye socket, the half-closed eye, the sunken features. He'd given her his usual war story, not Sebastopol anymore but Sedan in the Ardennes, and hand-to-hand combat, and the two Prussians who attacked him with the butts of their rifles, and he felt her shiver, kneeling next to him, his hand in hers, and he gave himself up to this exquisite pleasure that was so new to him, this extorted solicitude, this young body so close to his own that made him grow hard despite the migraine throbbing in his skull and his fear of being unmasked and lined up against a wall by these imbeciles, despite the gunfire in the streets, the explosions, and the thundering crash of buildings collapsing.

But imbeciles they were, otherwise they wouldn't have fought, one against twenty, for some misty idea of equality and brotherhood, so misty as to blind them, to focus them all on supporting and assisting those weaker than themselves, unable to conceive of trickery and betrayal. Pujols would have laughed at them, a deep belly laugh, if he hadn't been afraid of being revealed for what he was.

When the girl had moved away, promising to be right back, he felt a pang in his heart, bitter and furious, and he leaned against the wall to look around at the wounded Communards, whining unceasingly or lying immobile and silent, some of them staring wide-eyed at the nothingness that seemed to wait for them. They brought him food, a slice of bread and a piece of sausage and some wine that was nothing like the cheap swill so often served in Paris, and he even allowed himself the luxury of a brief nap, lulled by the milling, disorganized generosity people were showing there despite the war being waged against them.

Now he is on his feet, swaying slightly, his head feeling as if it's caught in a vise, every pulsebeat throbbing painfully, but as he gazes at the poor devils lying on the ground around him he feels better because at least he's whole, because no pool of blood was spreading beneath him while he napped just now, because he has no doubt that he'll emerge alive from this defensive camp whose makeshift fortifications are already crumbling beneath the artillery's assault. He isn't here to triumph or die, like he saw on a red banner hung from a pair of shutters, but to escape and stay alive. That, for the moment, is the focus to which his whole philosophy of life has narrowed—and in truth, it doesn't differ much from the one he's always tried to follow.

A man nearby lifts his head, a bloody dressing over one eye and a nasty-looking cut running the whole length of his face down to his jaw. His blond hair is pushed back and clumped together with clotted blood. He's extremely young, Pujols realizes, and he finds that defiled fairness disturbing.

"Where are you off to in that state, Comrade?"

Pujols looks at the rictus in which the boy's injury has frozen his face and then into the single wide eye with its reddened eyelid.

"I need to move."

"That's how you end up with a bullet or a piece of shrapnel in you. Look, it cost me an eye and part of my face. Kind of like you, actually. We could be brothers!"

Pujols stiffens. These people and their brotherhood, really . . .

"I'd be surprised."

Now the young man gets to his feet as well. "What the hell! Easier to see from here, anyway," he says. "And I only need one eye to aim a rifle at those Versaillais bastards!"

"What about the bullets? And the shrapnel? I thought . . ."

The boy brings a hand to his bandaged face. His fingers are trembling.

"I'm eighteen years old, and like this. They used to say I was handsome, and the girls loved to dance with me, to let me slip an arm around their waist and lead them away from the bright lights of the dance floor . . . and now? What do I have left to hope for? Half-blind and stitched up like a pirate in a comic? Who'll want me now?"

He winces with pain and bows his head, one hand cupped over his ruined eye, and leans back heavily against the wall.

"Christ, it hurts!"

An aid-station nurse comes over and takes his arm.

"Come now, Théo. You should rest. We're waiting for a wagon to take you away from here. A surgeon will take care of you soon. Would you like a little drink?"

She hands him a flask that he immediately uncaps, drinking greedily. She takes it back from him gently.

"Not too much, young man. Leave some for the others."

She strokes his cheek. The hand at the end of her strong arm is white and delicately veined with blue, her fingers very slender. Théo takes it and presses it to his face and then lets go and straightens up as if revived.

"Good God—we must be off!"

He heads out, swaying at first and then striding firmly.

"A rifle!" he shouts. "A rifle! I've only got one eye left, but it's the good one!"

He turns back toward Pujols and motions him over.

"Come on, you big beanpole! Show yourself at the barricade; that'll strike fear into those dogs' hearts!"

Pujols would dearly love to make him shut his trap, this one-eyed loudmouth. He's going to draw attention to him, and questions, and maybe suspicions. Some of the guards are already turning toward him, looking at him curiously and then returning to their duties, indifferent. He decides to go along with this Théo, who has neared the battery guns on the Rue de Sèvres. The two gunners are in the midst of reloading, closing

the breech, and then one of them rests his hand on the handle
that fires the shell, the other surveying the street from behind
the cannon's steel shield.

"Will you let me do it?" Théo asks the first gunner.

The man looks him over, eyes half-shut, then shrugs.

"It's not a toy," he says. "You've got a rifle; put it to good
use."

"I've given an eye. You owe me this in return."

The man takes a better look at him, exhaustion evident in
his face. He sighs.

"In return? There's no exchanges here, my lad. No one's
asked anyone to give anything. Especially not an eye, an arm,
or a leg. You're supposed to stay whole and alive."

Suddenly the young man collapses on the sandy surface of
the street, pitted where cobbles used to be. The shot rings out
at the exact moment he falls, and the men around him flatten
themselves to the ground. Another bullet smashes into the
ground right in front of Pujols, raising a plume of dust and
sand. He crawls to Théo's side and sees the crater blown in the
side of his head, just above his ear. The blood pulses before
each fresh gush, and Pujols stares, breathless, at this life struggling and fading, the bright crimson so quickly absorbed by
the earth. He looks at the single eye, still open, the eyelid
twitching rapidly as if the boy has just heard some startling
announcement, the lips moving, trying to utter one last thing,
perhaps, into the great encroaching silence.

Then the astonishment disappears from the eye, the blood
stops flowing, the mouth stops moving.

"In the window, over there! Third floor!"

Bullets whine past, striking sparks from the heaped cobblestones or thudding into the ground around them. Pujols pulls
the rifle from beneath the young man's fallen body and finds a
few cartridges in his haversack. He runs to the barricade, loads
and cocks the weapon, steadies it on a parapet consisting of a

wooden beam thrown across the cobblestone wall. A dozen others come to flank him on either side.

The two mitrailleuse gunners are trying to turn the cannon, but nothing is happening.

"Someone should invent machines you can maneuver the way you want! These ball cannons are useless!"

The men scrutinize the façades, weapons aimed. Pujols thinks he sees something move: a curtain, maybe, fluttering at an open window. He steadies his arm and rests his finger on the trigger. He doesn't feel the migraine anymore, only a sense of excitement he hasn't experienced in a long time. Even the sessions with the photographer, even the extravagant luxury of widespread thighs and powerful members rutting vigorously in every available orifice, even all that debauchery in which he'd often participated—just a few quick fucks in the endless escapades of a bunch of libertines—had never made him feel this tension gripping his entire body, every ounce of his strength concentrated in a dense knot in his chest like a fist, tightly controlling every one of his actions, down to the slowed beating of his heart.

Then the sniper appears and crouches, hidden behind the metalwork of the balcony. Pujols knows his bullet has a fifty-percent chance of ricocheting off the wrought-iron scrolls. He wedges the rifle against his body and pulls the trigger, then doesn't move. He sees the soldier's body jerk and then fall. Around him, the men shout with joy. Pujols ignores them, reloads, draws a fresh bead. He tilts the rifle-sight downward, toward the balcony on the second floor. The others have fallen silent and taken up their positions again. They hear a sudden burst of gunfire in the neighboring streets, the cannon booming on the Rue de Rennes.

Pujols isn't listening to any of it. The only thing he hears, thinks he can hear, is the scrape of the curtain being drawn, the creak of the handle being turned, and then the window pivoting open on its hinges, and when the two soldiers burst out at the same time like devils, shouldering their rifles, he doesn't move, fires again, watches the soldier who had risen thrown backward by the impact and then topple over the railing of the balcony. The Federates fire now, too, and the other soldier rises and then whirls, his arms flailing in the air, and falls back into the apartment.

Pujols stands up and looks over the barricade and sees the corpse on the sidewalk, its back to him, lying on its side, and he thinks the legs are still moving, slowly, so he reloads and fires one last shot and watches the body shudder as the bullet enters between its shoulder blades, and then he lets out a groan of pleasure and falls to his knees, exhausted and content, his body drained of all energy the way it is after a good long session between a woman's legs or a savage pounding against her arse, and he can barely hear the others crowding around him, congratulating him, shaking his hand, promising to buy him a drink and asking where he learned to shoot like that. He's still on his knees in the middle of them, head bowed as if in prayer, and he gives himself up to this sensation of exquisite delight that he thought he'd forgotten how to feel, the delight of killing, even if it was with a gun and from so far away. He didn't feel anything when he killed those three nobodies in the bar by the canal; they were hardly even men, just insignificant bipeds on this earth, obstacles in his way, inconvenient witnesses, and he'd killed them the way you kick away a dog barking and nipping at your heels. But those soldiers, engaged in a mission, obeying orders, assigned to quash anarchy and to subdue the restive populace, those valiant infantrymen whom Viviane Arnault—who must be dead by now—always raved to him about, with their courage and selflessness and willingness to follow the orders of the intrepid and elegant officers among whom she counted her brother Ernest, those fierce saviors of their native land—they mean something else, even when dead, at least in the eyes of the defenders of the barricade, who revile them as agents of the bourgeois reconquest. He could feel the power of the rifles, the force of the impact cutting the men down as if they were puppets at a fair, and he feels as if, for an instant, the energy of that iron and fire was inside him, that he possessed it.

He lets the flood of compliments wash over him, and then the men return to their posts because the Versaillais are setting up a battery gun at the end of the street, covering this operation with a fresh volley of gunfire that sends a hail of bullets whistling past. Sitting in a covered entryway, Pujols listens to their strange music like broken strings and smashed-in drums, like an orchestra in full rout, bombarded by pellets of steel.

All that afternoon he goes from one firing station to another, keeping the same rifle because he knows it's better than the others, and on the barricades they begin to expect miracles from him, as if he has the power to stop the Versaillais in their tracks all by himself. The streets are destroyed around him, men falling and dying amid the explosions and the cries and the moans, death gorging itself on torn arteries and drinking its fill of screams, leaving a trail of discarded bodies in its wake, and this war in which he feels invincible because it's not his fight makes him shiver with pleasure. He strolls through the chaos, gun in hand, drunk on fire and blood, without really even knowing what he's doing, without understanding what the men battling here are trying to do.

In the late afternoon, he realizes that the entrenched encampment at the Croix-Rouge crossroads is no longer defending anything but a field of ruins. Versaillais infantrymen creep through the rubble, scaling collapsed buildings and lying in wait atop the debris heaps to fire on the Federates. They can be glimpsed every now and then when the wind dissipates the dust and smoke. Pujols and the men manage to pick a few of them off, but eventually an officer called Varlin, a man who has seemed to be everywhere at once and whose presence alone has the power to restore hope and courage under the artillery fire and showers of shrapnel from the mitrailleuses, orders them to turn the cannon and bombard the ruins.

At nightfall, the firing ceases. There are still a few shots loosed on the Rue de Rennes; two Versaillais shells fired from the bottom of the Rue du Cherche-Midi growl past over the men's heads and blow up a building on the Rue du Dragon, and then the silence is complete, leaving their ears buzzing and ringing. The dust settles, and fires cast their wavering light over the rooftops.

On the second floor of one building that has remained standing, in a living room crammed with gleaming furniture, Pujols eats and drinks in the company of two Federates who have insisted on toasting his achievement of the early afternoon. They unearthed a bottle of cognac in an apartment somewhere yesterday, and now they break it out to share with him. They call each other Jeanjean and Olive, and Pujols tells them to call him Isidore. They're surprised by his southern accent, so he tells them he's from Toulouse, that he came up to Paris on the death of his parents and worked in a factory for a few months, then joined the army to see something of the country. The result: the war against the Prusscos, and Sedan, and the terrible injuries that still give him pain when the weather's damp. The two Federates commiserate with him and tell him a bit about their lives, too. Jeanjean is a roofer, thirty-two years old, married to Linette, and they now have only two sons because their oldest, a daughter, was killed during the siege. Olive is a metalworker. He's only twenty-two years old and is planning to get married in June.

Pujols laughs inwardly. Idiot. What is he thinking? He lets the two men chat amongst themselves, remembering the comforts of home, talking about how wonderful it will be to see their loved ones again, as if the renewed calm were any promise of the future. They talk about Varlin again, Eugène Varlin, the kind of man so lamentably rare in the Commune, not one of those endless talkers or newspaper hacks who have been running their mouths for days now, spouting off about the courage of the people and calling on them to fight; no, he's a real warrior, a man who puts himself in the line of fire, whom people follow out of trust and respect, not simply obedience. Pujols is hardly listening to them, a stranger to their hopes and passions. He nods mechanically when they look at him, *of course, fellows, yes, you're right*—but an idea has suddenly come to him, a way of escaping this trap before he gets shot or bayoneted by some Versaillais foot soldier. He'll have to make a break for it this evening, because he has a feeling that tomorrow these barricades and the high-minded men clinging to them will go down in an onslaught of flame. He knows he can only get outside the barricaded perimeter tonight with the cooperation of the men standing watch. The orders went out just a short while ago: no one enters, no one leaves. Anyone approaching or trying to flee will be shot on sight.

He lets them finish the bottle of cognac, drinking to the health of the bourgeois pigs who were stupid enough to leave it behind. Jeanjean gets up to piss in a corner of the room, swaying slightly and grasping the furniture as he makes his way through darkness that a single candlestick can't quite dispel. He chooses an inlaid pedestal table and hums as he empties his bladder onto its finely worked surface.

Olive slumps in his armchair, his eyes closed, sleeping, maybe.

"What if we paid them a little visit?" Pujols says.

"Who?" asks Jeanjean, coming back, buttoning his trousers.

"The Versaillais. We could take down a few of them by surprise; that would put the fear of God into the others. Take a bit of the wind out of their sails, make them think twice before attacking tomorrow."

"And how do you propose we do that?"

Olive has asked the question without opening his eyes, still sprawled in the chair, his hands folded over his middle. Then he sits up straighter and looks at Pujols. "It would be walking right into the wolf's maw. I'd prefer not to be shot, myself. They must be hiding in every nook and cranny; you saw it yourself just now. There were ten times more of them coming than we could kill."

"I quite like the idea," says Jeanjean. "We could always find a guard or two to rough up. It would be revenge for Théo. I knew him a little; we were both from the 12th arrondissement, near Saint-Éloi. Lived two streets apart."

Pujols gets up. Don't give him time to reflect or think about his wife and brats.

"Let's go, then. The sooner we start . . ."

They pick up their rifles and leave the apartment. In the corridor they hear Olive running to catch up.

"Not without me, fellows. With three of us, we can get even for more of our comrades."

His speech is slurred. In the light of the lamp Jeanjean is holding, Pujols can see his eyes wide open and bright, his skin gleaming.

They step out into the dark, quiet street. A few men are sleeping rolled in blankets on the ground near stacks of rifles.

"Put out that fucking lamp!" hisses a sentry.

Jeanjean extinguishes the flame. A gunshot rings out, the bullet whistling over their heads and smashing into a wall.

"Son of a bitch! That one almost got us!"

"I told you!" says the sentry. "They've got snipers in the buildings. You've got to lie flat on your belly if you want to smoke, or they'll shoot your pipe in half!"

They hear him chuckle softly, pleased with his own wit.

They slip their bayonets into their leather belts. The two men guarding the barricade on the Rue de Grenelle block their way. No one gets through; those are the orders. What the fuck are they doing outside at this time of night anyway, instead of snoozing or taking their turn at guard duty? Jeanjean replies that he's well aware of the order, and he'll tell them everything they've done when they get back.

They can hardly see one another. They huddle closely together to speak, murmuring like conspirators.

"As you like. We haven't seen you. If you're not back by tomorrow morning, you'll be considered deserters, and we won't say anything to contradict it."

"We'll be back, don't you worry, Comrade."

The two guards shrug and sit back down heavily, exhausted.

Pujols takes the lead. He can hardly see where he's walking. The street is a dark trench lit only by the faint, bluish gleam of the star-filled sky. He can hear the footsteps of the other two behind him, shuffling and erratic.

"You sure you know where you're going?"

They've stopped. Pujols turns around.

"Just up here, to the left. Come on. I'm sure they're over this way."

He starts walking again, and he can sense them hesitating before they follow. He slows down; he wants them to get closer. They hear a horse nicker in the distance.

"Over there."

Up ahead, two ammunition wagons are blocking the street. They can see the glow of a watchman's pipe. All three of them stop.

"We can't just go up and ask him for a match and then slit his throat," whispers Jeanjean. "And surely there's another one somewhere nearby."

Pujols feels a hand on his shoulder. Olive presses himself against him, and he shudders in revulsion.

"Get off me," he says.

The man withdraws his hand, but then whispers in his ear.

"You've done this before, right? I've never killed anyone."

"Of course I've done it before. You'll see."

The three of them are bunched up in a doorway. Pujols pushes on the door, idly, and feels the striking plate give way. The door swings open slowly, vibrating on its hinges without creaking. A shadowy corridor stretches away in front of them. Pujols feels a wave of dizziness. The migraine starts to pound behind his forehead again. The two steps he takes make him feel like he's falling.

"Hey, where are you going?"

Pujols whirls and strikes out at the figure closest to him, which he can see only as a black silhouette. He hears the man fall back with a hoarse groan and imagines his fingers scrabbling uselessly at his slashed throat to staunch the gush of blood. The other man leaps back, letting out a cry of surprise. It's Olive, the younger one, who wants to get married in June. Pujols steps forward and thrusts with his blade, which grates against something hard, and when he pulls it out, the man gives a howl of pain so he has to stab again, several times, into the heavy, soft mass into which his bayonet sinks without making the man fall or stopping the distraught cries, sharper now, almost childish, more harrowing with every blow. To finish the man off, he lifts his right foot and pushes and watches the figure sway and then fall on its back, silent now except for its rasping breaths and a few faint moans.

But out in the street, people are coming. A cavalcade. Perhaps a dozen of them. Beyond the half-open door he can see the light of their torches. He turns down toward the end of the corridor, which seems to be the source of the endless blackness outside, and the nothingness startles him and takes his breath away, and he doesn't understand what's happening, so he starts to run, whimpering. The pain grinding at his face from the inside tears him away from reality, and it feels as if every step he takes could kill him. For a few seconds he is no longer of this world, and he doesn't have time to explore this new sensation, because he collides with the bottom of a staircase and collapses on the steps, starts to crawl up them on his hands and knees and then gets to his feet, clinging to the banister. He reaches a landing, considers forcing open a door, then keeps climbing again because the voices downstairs are louder now, *this way; you two stay here; you, go and get the captain and some reinforcements.* The light of their torches is brighter, and they are running up the stairs two at a time. Their shadows come fast ahead of them, disproportionately immense.

Pujols kicks open a door and closes it behind him as best he can, then searches for something to push against it, to block it, but finds nothing. He tries to orient himself, looks for the street, sees it out a window. He wrenches the window up, almost tearing it off; flings open the shutters, which clack against the façade; climbs onto the railing.

Before he jumps, he has time to glimpse, at the corner of the street, a noisy troop of infantrymen arrive at a run, shouting as they spot him.

He prepares to hit the ground as harmlessly as possible, to avoid breaking a leg, and he jumps, holding his breath, and when he sees the soldier's face they're both already on the ground, Pujols on top of the other man, and something twists in his gut and he vomits on the horrified man, who bellows and snivels, spluttering openmouthed in the mess Pujols has emptied onto him.

Pujols wants to let himself fall the rest of the way forward, or straighten up, but he's held in position by the blade of a bayonet at the end of a twisted rifle barrel, buried in his gut. He realizes this as the lamps and torches come closer, as he is dragged backward.

The last thing he sees is the muzzle of the rifle aimed at him. Or perhaps the flash of light that scorches his forehead.

TUESDAY, MAY 23RD

23

They had made their way around the firing line. The empty streets quivered around them. Sometimes the sky caved in, and they had to press themselves into recesses until everything the bombs had thrown into the air had settled back to earth. Roques had torn a strip from his shirt and bound up his wounded forehead. They were on the Rue Saint-Guillaume when cries rang out nearby, a man and a woman begging for mercy, then a burst of gunfire followed by two single shots. They could hear the soldiers talking and laughing, and their footsteps were so loud that Roques really thought they might come around the corner any second. They needed to hide, so they pushed open a set of double doors and began to climb the stairs. They listened at doors to see if anyone was still living there, holding their breath to hear even the slightest creak of floorboards, the faintest squeak of a door. On the third-floor landing, a man opened his door a crack and peeked through, his poorly shaven face anxious. All three of them quaked, their hands already on the grips of their guns, then the man gave them a half smile, amused, perhaps, by how much he'd scared them.

"Come in," he said. "You can't stay out there. A patrol went by out in the street just a little while ago, and they'll be back."

Without conferring, they went into the apartment. The lock clicked behind them, and Clovis spun around and saw the man hanging the key on a nail next to the door.

"Don't worry. I'm not locking you in. You can leave whenever you like, even if I don't think it's a good idea."

He was rather short, dressed in a mauve vest over a shirt with rolled-up sleeves. His thatch of yellowish-white hair fell over his forehead, and he was constantly pushing it back. A large mustache drooped over his mouth. He looked at the three of them standing in the entryway, huddled together like timid children, his face serious. He walked past them and waved toward a large living room full of gleaming dark wood furniture, every wall hung with light-filled paintings of pastoral landscapes. He gestured for them to sit down, and they perched on the edges of the armchairs and sofa, embarrassed, their hands on their thighs, not daring to move. He left the room, and they could hear him opening and closing the doors of cupboards or sideboards, then moving farther down the corridor and murmuring "I'll be right back" before reappearing.

"I've got a bit to eat and drink. It's difficult to stock up on provisions at the moment. Make yourselves comfortable."

"We're filthy, and we stink," said Roques. "We'll get everything dirty."

The man shrugged. "On that note, let me introduce myself. I'm Jean-Baptiste Essartier. I'm hiding out here, too, in a way."

Clovis rose and shook his hand. "Clovis Landier. Forgive me; my hands are dirty."

Essartier took a better look at him, nodding. "The important thing is to have an unsoiled heart."

Roques and Loubet introduced themselves in their turn. An expression of surprise flitted across Essartier's face when Loubet identified himself as a police inspector.

"So they're not all at Versailles! You're preserving your own honor, then."

"There is no honor, so I've got nothing to preserve. Let's just say I'm loyal to a profession, and I don't see any reason not to put myself at the service of this new republic."

"There's a bathroom at the end of the hall. You can all have a shave, if you like. I've got some old clothes that are still presentable and should fit you. I have a feeling that, in the days to come, you'll do better in public if you look like respectable men, as they say."

There was soap, and large enameled basins. They washed and changed. Roques went down into the courtyard twice for fresh water from the pump. Essartier came and went with old clothes and towels like an employee at the public baths. Occasionally he went into a shadowy bedroom with the curtains drawn against the still-bright light of the late afternoon. They could hear him speaking quietly, and then he would come out, shoulders slightly hunched each time, only forcing himself to straighten up after a few steps. Roques surprised him twice during these little forays, and each time the man pretended not to see him. As they sat down at the table to eat, he explained that his wife Juliette was ill and he'd been taking care of her on his own for months.

"She's dying of some disease no one can even find a name for. A sort of weakness with occasional, dreadful attacks of pain where she bleeds for days in a flow that nothing can stop, as if she was trying to expel some terrible monster. I think I'm going to lose her every time, but she always regains a bit of strength, just enough to eat a little something and take my hand in hers and beg my forgiveness."

"What do the doctors say?" asked Clovis.

"Not much. One of them told me to travel with her to the Pyrenees so she could take the waters there, said she would profit the most from that."

"The Pyrenees! That's on the other side of the world!" exclaimed Loubet.

Essartier smiled despite the sadness clinging to his features like a transparent mask.

"Not quite. I'd take her there in a heartbeat, in any case. But she was too weak for a long time, during the siege, to make the trip, and now that she might be able to manage it, we can't get out of Paris."

Clovis gazed at him with sorrowful interest, leaning toward him, unmoving.

"Doctors are dangerous charlatans," he murmured. "Calm-faced murderers."

Roques watched the two of them and felt as if an invisible bridge had formed between them, where their grief and pain met. In the silence that had fallen, he listened to the distant noise of the fighting, and the others listened, too, their expressions suddenly remote.

Then Essartier asked them what they were doing in this part of the city, with the Versaillais encamped on the corner. They looked at one another hesitantly, and then Roques told him everything: the kidnappings of young women, the investigation that had led him to the trail of the guilty party, the building that had collapsed on top of the prisoner, trapped now for almost three days in a cellar on the Rue des Missions. The commitment they had made to free her. The promise they had made themselves.

"Three days, you say? She must surely be dead by now."

"There was a bucket of water," Clovis said. "She'll have had something to drink."

Essartier shook his head.

"I don't understand. You're risking being arrested and shot for the sake of a promise? For a girl you don't know, whom no one even seems to be missing? That's crazy! Brave, certainly, but crazy!"

"You know," Roques said, "Paris is lost. Thiers is sending perhaps sixty thousand men, and we have ten thousand against them—at most. Badly organized, poorly commanded. Barricades have sprung up everywhere with no building plan at all; most will be easily gotten round. Better if some of them aren't bothered with at all. And yet, behind each one of them, there are men—and women, too—sometimes only a handful, certain they'll be able to hold, to push back the enemy. They could all go back to their homes and listen to the Versaillais troops parade by from behind their closed shutters. They would probably be safe there. They'd get to watch their children grow up; they'd live to a ripe and peaceful old age in their own homes, a nice bowl of soup every evening. But they're staying. They're waiting for the onslaught. I don't know if they're brave or crazy. I don't even really know the difference between those two words anymore, given the state of things. All I know is that they're doing what they have to do. What they believe is not only rational, but right. They know how this is all going to turn out. They already know the end of the story. But they still have hope. To win. To get out alive. Determined, otherwise, not to die in vain. That's what's driving us. It certainly isn't rational, no."

Essartier listened to him without looking away, leaning forward, his hands folded in his lap.

When Roques finished his speech, silence descended on them as if each were enclosed in his own dome of glass, shut in suffocating solitude, each of them seeking his own truth in what had just been said. Clovis ran his fingers through the tangle of his beard, eyes lowered, then he began to speak in a soft, almost musical voice Roques had never heard him use before.

"I took care of my wife and children until the end, even after I knew there was no hope. And then I prayed to God for two days and nights, on my knees next to their bodies, for him to bring them back to life. None of that was rational. Despite everything, I'm glad I did it, even now. I renounced both God and man after that, starting with myself. I wanted to stop existing without killing myself, to live my own disappearance. I wanted to watch myself cease to exist. And I almost managed it. There was nothing left of me but a bottomless well of sadness that has never quite dried up, and a few memories I refused to believe. I became almost nothing, almost no one. And nothing, and no one, had even the slightest value in my eyes anymore. Then came the day when I saw that girl buried alive. Buried alive. And I realized I couldn't accept it. She was nothing to me. I'd even transported her there myself; I would have transported any cargo at all, no questions asked. And suddenly I found myself facing an impossible situation, unthinkable to me. She was alive—and buried. Only the dead should be so. And so, since then, I've felt myself coming back to the surface of the dead, stagnant waters I'd sunk into."

Essartier kept nodding and then looked out the window at the twilight falling over the incessant thunder of battle. His eyes shone bright. Roques waited for the tears to fall, but the man got up and went to stand in front of one of the paintings on the wall.

"I think we're all in more or less the same place."

He stood there, unmoving, his hands in his pockets, staring at the painting as if seeing it for the first time. A country road descending toward a tiny village at the foot of a hill. Two women. Sunshine. Harmonious nature. Peace.

"This was before. The time when life had the upper hand."

Roques got up, too, and went to stand next to him.

"Maybe it's the life of tomorrow. Because it will go on. With or without us."

He moved closer, examined the signature.

"Pissarro? Is that someone you know?"

Essartier smiled, still looking at the painting. He ran a fingertip delicately over the brushstrokes.

"Camille Pissarro. He's almost a friend. He painted a sign for my brother's inn in Pontoise. He was utterly destitute, and Pascal used to give him lunch quite often, and I was there at the same time as him a few times. He showed me his studio, and I was mesmerized by this canvas, which I immediately bought from him. *Jalais Hill, Pontoise*, it's called. He's in

London now. He had to flee during the war even though he'd just moved to Louveciennes. Seems the Prussians looted his home."

A noise made him turn. A small crash in the bedroom. Essartier excused himself and left.

When he turned around, Roques saw Clovis and Loubet slumped in their chairs, both suddenly asleep, so he stayed in front of the painting, its light fading with the sun, and he listened in the silence to the sound of movement in the bedroom, the clink of glass and the sound of muffled voices, almost distant, as if coming from another world.

All that night, between bouts of fitful sleep, he kept watch, his ears straining at every movement in the apartment, the steps outside in the street, coming and going, furtive, like those of prowlers or brigands up to no good. He stared almost unblinkingly into the fraught silence, broken now and then by rustling sounds or the horrid crack of a building's framework weakening, and yet, somehow, he didn't see her come in.

She stood in the doorway, still as a statue in a white nightgown that seemed to surround her with a pale halo. A mane of long blond curls tumbled about her shoulders. In the blue-tinted darkness, Roques could barely make out the shapes of the furniture around him, but she, the woman, seemed to repel the darkness of the night. He was sitting in an armchair, his feet resting on a chair, and he only had to turn his head slightly to the right to watch her, and he didn't move at all, either, barely breathing, as if he were afraid he'd knock her over if he exhaled. He heard the two others sleeping, Clovis restless, sometimes groaning softly, and Loubet snoring, peaceful as always. He couldn't see the woman's face very well, but he knew she was beautiful, surreally beautiful, he thought suddenly, and he thought he might be dreaming that the model in a painting he hadn't noticed had come to reproach him, to punish him, perhaps, for not paying closer attention. He watched her approach with the gliding steps of a dancer, her hips just grazing the furniture on either side of her path. She went to the sofa where Clovis slept, stopped, stretched out her hand toward his face, stroking his bearded cheek with her fingertips. Her delicate lips moved, but no sound, not even a whisper, could be heard. She went to Loubet and did the same thing, bending slightly forward, a small pendant dangling at the neckline of her chemise. Roques, who had clapped a hand over his mouth to keep himself from crying out, watched her walk to a window, pressing her forehead to the glass and staying like that, unmoving, looking out into the street as if waiting for someone. Then she lifted a hand and held it in the air for a moment, hesitantly, then let it fall gently back onto the handle.

I must get up. I must speak to her. Roques had begun to lever himself upright, gripping the armrests of the chair, but he suddenly felt as if the weight of his body had tripled, and eventually he gave up, breathless. *I'll frighten her. It could kill her, as weak as she is.*

She came toward him. He hadn't seen her leave the window. Her bare feet made no sound on the parquet floor, padding delicately on the large Persian carpet that covered the middle of the room. When she stopped by the side of his chair, he held out his hand, which she took gently in her cold fingers. She bent over him, and he smelled the scent of woodsmoke in her hair, and a hint of lavender, wafting from the undone collar of her nightgown. She smiled. Her dark eyes, enormous, fathomless, were full of tears. He had never seen a woman so beautiful. So close, and yet so untouchable. He wanted nothing more than to press her hand to his cheek, to warm it up. But when he tried to do it, she drew it back gently.

"No."

He would have liked to say something. Even if only to hear the sound of his own voice, which might have woken him and dissipated this illusion. But he was silent.

In the morning, he doesn't know if he's slept. But since he's waking up, he supposes he must have dropped off for a moment. He sees Clovis standing at the window, in the same place the woman stood last night. He wants to reflect for a moment on it, on what happened. To remember that beauty bent over him.

"The street is crawling with infantrymen. We'll never get through."

"Where's Loubet?"

"No idea."

"Did you sleep well?"

"Like a dead man. Why do you ask?"

"Just because . . . To see if I was the only one staring at the ceiling."

Roques struggles to his feet. The room pitches around him for an instant and then rights itself. He goes to the window, leans toward the glass.

"Careful you aren't seen."

A dozen soldiers are patrolling single file on the opposing sidewalk. Their posture is wary, their rifles at the ready. Some of them scan the rooftops and balconies. There is a sub-officer commanding them. A man in a frock coat and derby hat is leading them, gesturing toward a door, waving toward the upper floors. The sub-officer opens the door and tells his men to enter, shouting orders. He wants everyone inside to be brought out to him. Two soldiers stay with him, standing guard. The sub-officer stares up at Essartier's building. Clovis and Roques fling themselves back away from the window. The curtain hasn't moved.

"They'll be coming for us next," Clovis says. "We'll have to find a way."

"Where the bloody hell has Loubet gone?"

They turn toward the door at the same time. Essartier is standing in the doorway in his shirt, his suspenders dangling

362 · HERVÉ LE CORRE

loose. He sways and grips the doorframe to keep himself from falling, as if he suddenly feels ill. He looks at them blankly, his mouth half-open. It's as if he doesn't recognize them, like he's suddenly come upon two strangers in his home. He wobbles and then pulls himself together, passes his hands over his face, takes two steps forward. Clovis goes to him.

"Are you all right?"

Essartier looks up at him and takes him by the shoulders. "She's dead."

He lets himself fall heavily into an armchair.

"I found her dead just now . . . her hand was resting on the back of my neck. I hadn't wanted to move for fear of waking her. I thought she was cold, so I pulled the blanket up around her shoulders, and that's when I . . ."

The front door closes with a bang. Loubet hurries into the room, breathless.

"They're here. In the stairwell. We can try to get out of here by the rooftops. We'll go back down through another building; we can only hope they won't have gotten to that one yet. I've opened the trap door to the roof; it's two more floors up."

For an instant, Roques can't move. His body refuses to obey him; his mind is unable to comprehend what's happening, frozen with horror. The woman, last night. Her cold hands. The silence that surrounded her, wafting from her like perfume. Already dead?

They hear the soldiers' voices in the stairwell. Shouts, curses. The heavy thumping of their boots. Doors being smashed in.

Essartier vanishes into the back of the apartment. Roques picks up his rifle, makes sure it's loaded, locks the breech. He hands Clovis his revolver.

"We'll wait for them to come in. We'll kill as many of them as possible and them climb onto the roof."

"I have another idea," says Essartier.

He is holding a large pistol in each hand. A saber hangs from his belt. He goes to the door, listening.

"What are you doing?" Loubet asks him.

"I'll leave by the rooftops. You three do everything you can to get out of this and go find that girl in her tomb, if she's still alive."

The door begins quivering beneath the thuds of rifle butts. Essartier throws it open and fires at the two soldiers in the corridor. The noise is deafening, and it seems as if he's fully capable of killing all of them on his own. Through the cloud of smoke thinning around them, Roques sees the top of one soldier's head as he flies backward over the banister and onto the stairs below. The other man clutches at his slashed throat and sinks slowly to the floor. The other infantrymen, five or six of them, freeze on the stairs for a moment, pressed together, covered with blood, petrified. Essartier brandishes his saber at them, wounds one of them in the hand, then makes a run for the stairs. Two of the soldiers seem to shake themselves out of their stupor, and they climb the stairs after him, shouting. Four others now burst into the apartment. Breathless and stunned, they stare at the three weapons immediately leveled at them. Clovis, behind them, shoves his revolver against the back of one man's neck.

"Shut your mouths. Put down your rifles and get on your knees."

The one closest to Roques eyes the barrel of the rifle aimed at his head as if to make sure it's clean. Neither he nor his comrades seems to understand what's happening.

"Do it," says Loubet, calmly. "Or we'll kill you. We don't give a damn. We've got nothing left to lose."

The soldiers set their rifles on the floor and kneel. Clovis collects the guns and puts them in a corner, keeping one. He thumps the men smartly and precisely at the base of their skulls, and they drop like sacks of potatoes. Two shots ring out some distance away. They look at each other questioningly for a moment, then pull off their clothes and choose a man each. Roques decides to keep his own boots because the feet of the soldier whose uniform he now puts on are too small. They strap on rifles and pistols, buckling their leather belts. Suddenly Clovis is stalking among the unconscious soldiers with a knife. He grabs one of them by the hair, lifts his head.

"No," says Loubet. "Not that. Not us."

"Then let's go, now." Clovis says. "Quickly."

They move out into the corridor, their feet slipping on the bloody floor.

"Wait for me," says Roques.

He goes back to Essartier's bedroom and pushes the door open. The scent of lavender rises up and envelops him like an invisible curtain. He goes to the bed where the woman is lying in her white nightgown, her blond hair spread around her head, her pendant lying on her unmoving chest. The same overwhelming beauty. He thinks of the fairy tale, the sleeping beauty. He wants to believe in miracles, in magic. He takes a few steps toward her, until his knees touch the edge of the bed. He stretches his fingers toward the dead woman's lips, then hesitates, afraid of soiling her with the filth of the world vomiting itself all around them.

"I'm so sad," he murmurs simply.

He backs out of the room. *So I'm going to lose everything, even her.*

He rejoins the others, and they make their way down the stairs silently, rifles at the ready, poised to shoot anyone who gets in their way. When they're out in the street, Roques looks up at the closed shutters of the bedroom.

"You all right?" Clovis asks. "What was wrong with the dead woman?"

"Nothing," he replies, forcing the words past the lump in his throat. "She looked like she was sleeping. Just sleeping."

"I felt the same . . ."

"Except that—"

"Look," says Loubet.

Up ahead, the body of Essartier is sprawled on its belly in the middle of the street. They approach it. There are two red splotches on its back. Its head is misshapen, its face turned toward them, eyes open. They stand silently for a few moments.

"We can't stay here like this," says Clovis. "They'll think we're praying over him and get suspicious."

They move away from the body. Roques feels as if he's floating in a fog that muffles sound and dulls sensation. He turns back toward this man who has killed himself because his life had no more meaning. He strains for one more glimpse of those empty eyes and wonders what the last thing Essartier saw was, and he is certain that on those rooftops, pursued by soldiers, she was with him.

Clovis takes him by the shoulder and pushes him forward.

"Come on. We have to leave them now."

He smiles. It's the first time Roques has seen him smile. He feels calmer somehow.

"I have to tell you . . ."

"Of course. But not now. Not here."

Roques looks around, jerked suddenly back to earth from his strange state of illumination. There are other corpses lying nearby, at least a dozen of them, fallen where they stood, shot down on their own doorsteps. People are leaning out of the windows.

"There are more of them!" a man cries from his balcony. "Don't miss them!"

Clovis cocks the hammer of his rifle. "You're the one I'm not going to miss, you bastard," he murmurs. "I don't know what's holding me back . . ."

"Possibly a few shreds of common sense," says Loubet dryly.

They hurry down the street and around the corner. A

column of infantrymen led by three officers on horseback is galloping straight toward them. They freeze, their weapons shouldered. Two or three hundred men, panting and sweating, each one's eyes fixed blankly on the sack of the man in front of him. The column turns down the Rue Saint-Dominique, and the sound of their footsteps is drowned out by an explosion from near the Croix-Rouge crossroads.

Five infantrymen come out of a building, pushing a man in front of them, his hands bound behind his back with a curtain tie.

"What are they doing?" Roques wonders aloud.

Clovis doesn't answer. He walks toward the soldiers and their prisoner.

"We haven't found anything here," he says.

A sergeant stares at him.

"Where are the others?"

"There's no one but us."

The sergeant looks astonished. He looks around at the façades and entrances of the buildings as if a patrol might emerge from them at any second. Roques slips his hand into his trouser pocket and grips the handle of his revolver, wondering which one he'll have to shoot first.

The sergeant looks the three of them over again closely, seeming to hesitate. Behind him the prisoner is blubbering, swearing that he never had even the slightest sympathy for the Commune, that bunch of thieves.

"Come with us," says the sergeant at last. "You'll come in handy."

He approaches Clovis.

"Hasn't anyone ever told you to trim your beard and cut your hair?"

Clovis draws himself up, his rifle standing upright on the ground by his feet, almost at attention.

"The Prusscos released me in this condition a month ago.

They were more concerned about feeding me because those sons of bitches didn't give us anything to eat, and about training me to be a real soldier again. So no one's given much thought to my beard and hair."

The sergeant smiles. This masterly explanation is very much to his liking. He thumps Clovis on the shoulder and winks at him.

"We could do with a few more real soldiers. Come on, show us how you boys deal with prisoners. The colonel's orders are three questions, one bullet."

He pulls his revolver out of its holster and cocks the hammer. His men form a circle, their guns pointed at the bound man.

Roques starts to shake. It feels like his knees might give way beneath him. He tries to meet the other two men's eyes, but their gazes are fixed on the man who has been forced to kneel. He looks at the unmoving infantrymen around them and can see nothing in their dirty, poorly shaven faces except profound exhaustion. Their eyes are dead. There's no doubt that this sergeant suspects something, that he's just waiting for some proof of weakness before he cuts them down.

Loubet steps toward the man on the ground.

"Full name? Profession?"

The man lifts his head and pauses a moment before replying. His face is streaked with tears, blood running down his chin from his split lip. He searches Loubet's eyes as if seeking a reason to hope for a shred of mercy.

"Anselme Rouleau, cloth dealer. I—"

"Quiet. Who else around here is part of the Commune? Tell us with whom you've been plotting against the State."

Anselme Rouleau dissolves in tears and collapses to the ground on his side. He kicks his legs and pounds the soil with his open hand like a child having a tantrum.

"My brother-in-law's the one who reported me. He's my business partner, and he wants the business for himself, with my wife's help. That's why I'm here! He was talking to these gentlemen just now!"

Roques turns to the sergeant. "Is this true?"

"Is what true? That he has a brother-in-law? Yes, that's true. But the brother-in-law is telling the truth. He's an honest man. I said three questions."

Roques watches Loubet pulling his rifle from its shoulder strap, slowly.

"What—"

A shot makes them all jump. The prisoner's head is thrown back, a hole in the forehead. Clovis reloads his rifle. He doesn't look at anyone. He shoulders his weapon and then addresses the sergeant.

"You said one bullet, didn't you?"

The sergeant's astonished gaze moves from Clovis to the body and the stream of blood flowing toward the gutter. He stows his revolver. His men shoulder their weapons.

"Come on," he says. "The neighborhood has to be cleansed of this scum."

They start walking, their feet dragging. No one speaks. They turn down the Rue Saint-Dominique, where a sour-smelling breeze blows cold ash into their faces. A mitrailleuse spits in the distance, causing a flock of startled birds to rise into the blue sky over the rooftops. Roques walks behind the others. He looks up, sees nothing. The night seems to cling to the windows, watching him from behind the glass, and he sees once again the woman lifting her hand toward him. He strains his eyes, glimpsing dark reflections, hollow gazes following him. He doesn't know why he's here anymore, doesn't know what he's come here to find. All he knows is what he's left behind, perhaps lost forever. Clovis is walking just ahead of him, and he reaches out and touches his shoulder. The other man gives him a discreet wave of the hand, telling him to stay calm, not to speak.

24

Caroline saw the sun rise. The fissure in the wall above her head had paled, the light seeping through speck by speck until the bright twisted thread returned. She doesn't take her eyes off it. Her stomach is an empty, crumpled sack, knotted with lancing pain. Sometimes it's as if she's being gut-punched from the inside, causing her to double over in agony. Images from last night's dreams flit through her head again: her father falling from a roof, her mother kneeling over her, here in the cellar, stroking her forehead, murmuring to the little girl Caroline had once again become. She'd jerked awake each time, crying out at the sight of her father tumbling through the void, whispering back to her mother and groping for her in the darkness, opening her eyes to pitch-blackness and suffocating terror, unable to distinguish dreams from reality.

She lies for a long moment stretched out on the damp beaten-earth floor, her back stiff and cold, as if that part of her body has already died. The fighting above her is a dull, unceasing rumble that has become part of the background noise, something she almost doesn't hear anymore. She drifts among her memories, gazing wide eyed on scenes of sun and warmth inside her head, of meadows humming with crickets, of murmuring breezes flattening the oat fields with a huge, invisible hand. It almost seems as if she should be able to capture a few glimmers of all this dazzling light and use them to illuminate the depths that are gradually swallowing her. She feels a tiny glow of warmth spreading inside her.

So she sits up. Every bone feels as if it's on the point of cracking, every muscle screaming like it's about to tear. "Nicolas," she murmurs aloud. The walls swallow her voice. She gropes around on hands and knees for the water pail, quaking with terror at the thought of spilling its remaining contents. She can't hold back a groan of relief when she finds the bucket, and she plunges a hand into it and sucks her fingers, then drinks two mouthfuls out of her cupped hand. Hunger blooms in her middle like an evil flower that's been watered, fists twisting her stomach and pounding low in her gut. She feels she can sense them just beneath her skin, ready to punch through it. A wave of dizziness makes her fall to the ground. She feels the soft smoothness of a parquet floor beneath her fingers. Warm wood. The smell of furniture polish. Daylight spills through a window, and she thinks suddenly that she's been having a long, strange dream and that she's finally waking up, that she'll remember where she is.

When she regains consciousness, she pushes herself up with shaking arms and manages to get to her knees, panting. *I'm going to go mad before I die. That's what happens when you die of hunger. I feel like I'm being devoured from the inside. My stomach is eating me.* She doesn't know if she said the words aloud or merely thought them. She looks up toward the bright stripe on the ceiling. She struggles to her feet, holding herself firmly on her legs, squaring her shoulders, dismissing the pain until she can only feel the gnawing in the pit of her stomach.

When she slips her fingers beneath the door and then manages to get her whole hand through the opening, she feels a faint stirring of fresher air on her skin and presses her mouth to the hole, gulping in a few breaths of the outside. This restores some of her courage, and she starts digging again with the handle of the bucket, which she has twisted into a tool. Hours pass, or maybe only a few minutes. She is nothing but this movement now, this effort. Sometimes she can't even quite remember what she's doing; the action has become almost unconscious, mechanical, driven purely by terror.

It's during one of these blank moments that she hears the dog. A distant barking. There was one in the village that used to bark like that, for no reason, at all hours of the day and night. She remembers how her father wanted to go and toss a scrap of meat laced with rat poison over the fence for it, but the dog's owner had beaten him to it one sleepless night by pummeling it with a spade. She thinks at first that her exhausted mind is playing tricks on her again, so she stops and listens, then calls and taps at the door, and the animal starts barking again, closer now, just overhead; it must have climbed to the top of the rubble heap. She talks to the dog, telling it that it's a good dog, that she's happy to hear this voice from outside. The dog whines and yaps; she pictures it as young and playful, intrigued by this voice whose source it can't identify. She slips her hand under the door again, almost her whole forearm now. She would like so much to feel the dog's wet nose, its warm tongue, like when she was little, with the puppy she and her brothers found behind the church.

She starts digging again, thinking the dog might do the same thing on the other side of the door, but it simply keeps barking, as if to encourage her, and she doesn't feel any more fatigue until the moment she hears male voices. The men call out to each other, one of them saying he's heard a noise, that there's someone under there. The voices are muffled at first, but then they ring out, closer. They chase away the dog, perhaps with a kick, because she hears it yelp, and then a gunshot makes her jump, so she calls out: *Help, help me, please!*

Caroline hears them laugh. *There's a girl under there!* Soon she hears stones being shifted, the men grunting with effort as they clear them. She thanks them, so happy that she starts to weep, the sobs jerking and shaking the empty sack of her stomach, and she lies down to calm her breathing as she listens to the men hurrying and shouting encouragement to one another.

She's startled out of the torpor into which she's sunk by a sudden crash against the door—a fallen stone, perhaps—and then she hears a breathless voice right on the other side, asking if she's still there. The hole she dug is like a fallen crescent moon, its light soft and white.

She leaps to her feet and presses herself against the rough surface of the door, thanking her rescuer again and again.

"Get away from the door. We're going to blow off the lock."

She backs away, against the far wall. The gunshots are deafening, and she shrinks into herself, her hands over her ears.

The blast of light that explodes when the battered door shrieks on its hinges and slams against the wall wrenches a cry from her. She huddles into the darkness, her closed eyelids glowing red, trembling, weeping. A hand seizes her by the hair and forces her to look up. A soldier in shirtsleeves, his suspenders hanging down around his hips, examines her with an expression of mingled amazement and disgust. Through her tears, Caroline makes out the astonished face beneath the brim of his cap.

"I'm not touching her until we've spent the afternoon soaking her in a vat of soap and hooch," he declares.

"Looks like a farmyard sow," comments another man. "Fucking Federate bitch. Someone shut her up in there like it was a pigsty; damned if I know why."

They grip her beneath the arms and lift her up. The midday sun hurts her eyes. They help her to stumble over the heap of ruins that extends all the way to the middle of the courtyard. *I'm alive.* She says the words again and again in her head, her arms feeling crushed by the men's big hands. She isn't afraid. Not anymore. Two blasts of cannon fire ring out close by, maybe even at the end of the street. She shivers, despite the heat of the sun. She keeps her eyes down and can see only the bloodied muzzle of the dog, the soldiers' legs. She can hear their heavy breathing, their stifled laughter. They spit on the ground, muttering in disgust. *Sow. Bitch. Covered in shit. She stinks.* They repeat the words in every sort of tone, from revulsion to astonishment. There are maybe a dozen of them. She refuses to look at them, because she knows what she'll see in their eyes. She withdraws into herself, as if into the last redoubt of a ravaged fortress. *I'm alive.*

They tear off her clothes, hitting her legs with a stick to make her lift her feet so they can pull off her skirt, and she waits, shivering in the sun, her eyes closed.

"Go on, your turn. Do a good job."

The cold water they throw over her makes her breath catch and her knees give way. She stumbles and sways and straightens back up. She opens her eyes to reorient herself and can't see anything through the hair that has fallen over her face. She runs her tongue over her lips to catch some of the water streaming over her skin.

The smell of soap. A sponge. The stick lashes out again, forcing her to spread her legs. She is scrubbed and scoured. She remembers seeing cows washed this way when she was a little girl, before they were taken to the agricultural show. *I'm alive. I'm not afraid.* She repeats it in her head again and again, and she isn't sure if she'll be able to believe it for much longer. She decides to open her eyes, to push away the hair covering them.

A very young man, still a boy, really, is working busily around her. He rinses his sponge in a tub full of water, coats it with soap, bends over and scrubs her thighs, her ankles. His blond hair is short, almost shaven. A cut encrusted with dried blood runs along the side of his skull. His movements are precise, ungentle, dutiful, like those of an apprentice watched by his master. The others are sitting on the ground, smoking, watching the show. A soldier stands nearby, holding a rifle. They've all gone silent now. Two or three of them wear the stupid, vacant expressions of simpletons faced with an electric lamp. The young man might be a prisoner. He straightens up slowly and tosses his sponge into the bucket. He lifts his eyes to Caroline's and then looks away quickly.

"There," he says.

The soldier nearby shoulders his rifle and lifts Caroline's chin, forcing her to turn toward the men. They whistle with satisfaction.

"Fuck! That little detour was worth the trouble!"

"We need to make her eat," says one of the seated men.

"And drink," says another.

They burst into noisy laughter.

"Shall we leave her in the buff?"

I'm alive. The terror drains away, leaving her even more naked than before in front of the men's staring eyes. The nothingness whose edge she's had to cling to for the past two days is no threat to her anymore. It has spit her back out into the middle of this courtyard, handed her over to these stares raking over her body, to these hands that will soon be touching and fondling her. To these bodies that will soon be lying on top of her. She thinks of a knife. She can almost feel its weight, its shape in the palm of her hand. A knife. It's all she can think of. Everything would be all right with a knife.

They make her go into the intact wing of the building. The stairs are covered with stone- and plaster-dust that crunches under the soldiers' boots. They enter an apartment on the second floor, the door of which is gaping open. *Sit there.* She sits on a sofa, in a small living room crowded with furniture. Everything is neat and peaceful, as if the residents will come back at any moment and ask these intruders what the hell they're doing there.

"You. Find her something to eat. She'll have to bear up."

The blond youth vanishes into what must be the kitchen. She shivers. Turning her head, she sees a soldier leaning against the frame of the front door. He's smoking a long-stemmed pipe, his face pensive, gazing into the distance. She hears the sound of rummaging from another room, the bedroom; she can see the dark wooden posts of the bed. A man comes out and tosses her a shirt and a pair of drawers, which she pulls on, inhaling the scent of the clean laundry. Just then the blond boy emerges from the kitchen, venturing a shy smile, saying, "This is all I could find," and handing her a piece of bacon and a crust of hard bread on a plate. "There's wine, if you'd like some." Yes, she would like some. And a knife, for the bacon. Of course. He excuses himself and comes back with the object, which he holds out to her, looking into her face.

"I don't have a choice," he says.

She looks at him more closely, wondering how old he is, and he glances away, fidgeting at his own powerlessness, and goes out.

She gobbles the bit of smoked bacon and soaks the bread in the cheap wine and crams it into her mouth, her eyes full of tears. She sucks her greasy fingers and retrieves each bread-crumb that has fallen into her lap, one by one. The blade of the knife is short and sharp. She slips it into one of her shirtsleeves, which she rolls up a bit to form a sort of pocket.

I'm alive, you bunch of bastards. Nicolas.

But Nicolas is far away. Alive? Goosebumps rise on her arms. Caroline lets herself sink back into the sofa and counts the cannon blasts, her mind blank. She's reached fourteen when two soldiers loom in front of her, their bayonets pointed at her chest.

"Okay, come with us. Now."

She stands up, her arms crossed, the knife hidden in the fold of her sleeve, in the crook of her elbow. They push her toward the bedroom. A steel point pricks her rump. The man behind her laughs.

"Did you feel that? That was nothing compared to what I'm going to put there in a minute!"

Next to the bed, she turns toward them and looks each of them up and down. One of them, a redhead with plump cheeks, is massaging his crotch.

"Take off those clothes and lie down."

She begins trembling, abruptly, as if the floor has started shaking beneath her feet, and she can't stop. She manages to take off the shirt without letting the knife fall and tosses it as close to the pillow as she can. Then her hands fumble at the drawstring of the drawers; she finally manages to undo it, and the cloth pools at her feet. She lies down and closes her eyes. The mattress gives way softly beneath her weight, and she feels sleep tugging at her, feels herself sinking into its depths. *Let them do what they want. I'm already asleep.*

But the hand that grips her jaw to find her mouth, the fingers scrabbling between her thighs, the weight of the body lying on hers and the point of the bayonet beneath her chin, *spread them or I'll slit your throat*, rip away the illusion. She would have liked to leave her indifferent body to them and take refuge in the cavern created by her own exhaustion, not to try to fight this hopeless battle, but the pain and disgust are suffocating her, and she gropes around for the knife.

She feels the organ starting to force its way inside her, like the bayonet pressed to her throat.

"Stand up!"

The voice rings out imperiously right there in the room, and Caroline stiffens, taking the opportunity to put her hand on the knife through the cloth of the shirt. The man sprawled between her legs groans and freezes for a moment, then resumes what he was doing.

"Stand up."

The voice is closer now, quieter.

When Caroline opens her eyes, she sees an officer pressing the barrel of a revolver against the skull of the soldier, who isn't moving now.

"Get up, or I'll blow your head off. I'm not going to say it again."

The man rolls to the side, his legs tangled in the trousers around his ankles, and has to hold on to the nightstand to keep from falling. He pulls up his trousers and tries to tuck his shirt-tails into his belt. The officer holsters the revolver, goes to the soldier, slaps him hard.

"Scum. Get out of here."

Another man enters and comes over to the bed. He, too, is disheveled, holding his trousers up with one hand. He sways on his stiff legs.

"But, Captain, they told us that—"

The captain turns and eyes the soldier scornfully.

"They told you what?"

The man ogles Caroline, who is sitting on the bed, covering herself back up.

"Uh . . . well, that any Red whores we caught, we could . . . uh . . ."

The officer steps closer to the man and sniffs him.

"You stink of hooch. If we didn't have a battle to fight, I'd have you both thrown in jail. Get out of this room and keep your noses clean from now on, or I'll arrest you both as deserters."

The two men shuffle out of the room. The captain turns back toward Caroline.

"Come on. I've got to get you somewhere safe. My men will protect you. I'll find you some decent clothing."

Caroline tries to make out the shadow of duplicity in his handsome, square-jawed face, his blue eyes, the bushy mustache sprouting from his upper lip.

"Why are you doing this?"

He smiles. His eyes rest on her, and she feels naked, offered up, the same way she felt in front of the photographer's black box.

"What's your name? Stand up."

She rises and takes a step toward him. He's breathing through his nose, his nostrils flared as if he's holding back his words, or his anger.

"My name is Caroline Dolet. I was kidnapped by a man and locked in the cellar of this building."

He smiles and shakes his head.

"And I'm supposed to believe this, of course."

She shrugs. Arms crossed, she can feel the knife in the fold of her sleeve. Shouts and orders ring out in the stairwell and the courtyard. The captain gestures for her to leave the room. Three soldiers are sprawled in chairs in the living room, their rifles propped up nearby. One of them has put his feet up on the low table and is asleep, his hands folded on his belly. The hems of his trousers are stained with dried blood.

The captain ushers her into a maid's room on the fourth floor.

"Wait here. I'll look after you."

The lock clicks. Two turns. Caroline opens the window, blinking in the sunlight. She clears her throat because it still feels coated with the sewer stench she's just spent two days and nights breathing in. She fills her lungs with air, thinking it will be clean, but it's the smell of fire and smoke she inhales, the smell of Paris burning. She is suddenly aware of the rattle of gunfire, the dull thudding of a mitrailleuse. She leans over the window's railing. Below, the soldiers are clustered around the body of a woman, prodding her with their bayonets as if they're trying to wake her up.

"Nothing more we can do with her," grumbles one of them loudly. "She's done for."

He lifts the woman's dress and petticoat and uncovers her bare stomach. They all laugh and elbow each other in the ribs and pass around a bottle and cough and spit the cheap alcohol on the corpse.

"Throw her in the cellar where they found the other one," says the captain. "I don't want any trouble with the law."

Two men take the corpse by the feet and drag it toward the rubble heap, its lower body completely nude, its head bumping against the stones they try to hoist it over. Two other men take the arms, and they all lift it over a broken beam, grunting with effort, and Caroline watches them disappear into the hole she climbed out of so recently.

Her heart lurches, and she looks away, then turns back into the room and sits down on the bed. She tries to focus on the fact that she has survived, to convince herself that she conquered her fear of death while fighting for her life in the darkness. She tells herself that nothing the Versaillais might do to her could be worse than that. She stands up, holds herself very straight, puffs out her chest. She pictures herself fleeing on the rooftops tonight, running through the streets to rejoin the Communard fighters. She will have the courage. The strength.

A massive explosion erupts close by, making the walls quiver, shaking loose a bit of plaster dust.

Nicolas. The life we dreamed of having.

She collapses, racked by sobs.

25

He hadn't gotten very far. After thirty minutes, he found himself stopped at a barricade at the corner of the Boulevard Saint-Michel and the Rue de l'Abbé-de-L'Épée, near the Institute for the Deaf and Mute. The noise was tremendous, and no one could hear anyone else in the confusion of shouting and orders and arguing; there were perhaps a thousand citizens reinforcing the defenses, heaving two eight-pound cannons as well as they could over the uneven dirt of the denuded street, their wheels jamming in the ruts. Carts trundled past, loaded with sacks of earth, pushed and pulled by women and children. Thirty men were finishing up with a trench they'd dug twenty yards in front of the barricade, standing in the pit up to their waists. Now and then, heads turned toward Montparnasse and the conversations hushed slightly, as if to let the battle rumble and crash; an explosion slightly louder than the rest made a few people crouch in terror, and then the hive of activity resumed, with its commands and counter-orders and exasperated curses and bursts of laughter, all clashing and mingling without any apparent sense.

Nicolas stood still amid the clamor, his gaze lost above the rooftops, his heart torn in two. His comrades under fire. Red. And Adrien, who looked like a sleeping child. *My brothers*. At the Luxembourg Gardens a drumroll sounded in the foliage and caused a flock of sparrows to flutter noisily into the sky. He shook himself, trying to rid himself of the sadness clinging to him.

He wandered for a moment in the fairground-like commotion, not sure what to do, helpless and useless, then went to lend a hand to the Federate guards carrying crates of artillery shells to the cobblestone barricade. One of the men invited him to come and have a drink with two others, and they went into a little bar-café that they'd forced the proprietor to open before locking him in a storeroom because he wouldn't stop bellowing protests at this violation of his property rights and threatening to have them shot by General MacMahon. The men were still laughing about it as they were served mugs of beer by a boy of fifteen, a slightly too-big military cap falling over his eyes, bustling to and fro behind the counter.

As night fell, there were about a hundred of them left behind the barricade. Nicolas made sure not to be the first one on guard; he was exhausted, his rifle weighing heavily on his shoulder like an anvil, every step an effort.

They ate dinner thanks to a mess woman who had set up her cart in front of an entry to the garden. He recognized Madame Lucienne, still dressed entirely in black, and her sister Rita, still silent, from the Place du Roi de Rome. When he held out his bowl, she touched his arm to hold him back.

"We've met, haven't we?"

"How can you recognize me with all these mouths you feed?"

"The other day, in the Place du Roi de Rome, with the 105th. And there was that boy from Le Bourget, like us. I knew his mother. What is his name again?"

"Adrien," Nicolas replied in a near-whisper.

"Is he here? He was just about ready to come with us and help us make the ratatouille! If I see him, I'm going to steal him away, and we'll go hide somewhere before all of this turns to butchery. Tell him I'll hire him on the spot. As soon as this whole thing is over, we'll open a little café way out in the country, in the middle of nowhere!"

She stood on tiptoe and scanned the line of men waiting to eat.

"I don't see him . . . Must not be too hungry . . ."

Nicolas cupped his bowl of soup in his hands. Beans and bacon rinds. It smelled delicious, but he knew his throat would be too tight to swallow it despite the hunger twisting his stomach.

"He died this morning," he managed to say. "An artillery explosion."

Rita buried her face in her hands. Madame Lucienne held her ladle suspended in the air, frozen mid-pour.

"Who's dead?" asked a guard, waving his bowl in front of the two women.

Lucienne served him and gestured for him to keep moving, to make room for others.

"Don't worry about it . . . just a brave young man. Another one."

She said it with an obvious effort to keep her voice from trembling. She served three more men and then handed the ladle to Rita and went to Nicolas.

"Where did it happen?"

"Rue Vavin. He and a comrade . . . they were lying in ambush in a building on the corner with the boulevard. The Versaillais shelled the building. We got him out and cleaned him up."

"And then you left?"

She said the words without the slightest reproachful inflection, but Nicolas felt something like an electric shock grip his heart.

"He was like my kid brother. He had the courage of ten men . . . never afraid of anything. I used to have a pal like that . . . like a fierce little dog . . ."

He broke off and turned as a noisy quarrel broke out between two guards who shouted insults at each other, gripping one another's shirt collars. Some others pulled them apart, saying they'd do better to save their strength to push back the Versaillais when they showed their ugly faces, tomorrow, maybe. The two brawlers walked away, muttering.

"I've lost too many people I loved, you know . . ."

"I think we're all going through that, a bit."

"I have a sweetheart . . . basically a fiancée. Some bastard took her three days ago—snatched her right off the street—and instead of rushing off to look for her I'm here, fighting to defend street corners and piles of cobblestones, and there are even moments when I don't think about her anymore, when I forget she's in the hands of some criminal, some killer. I don't know . . . maybe I thought that with my friends . . . the three of us, the way we stuck together, that nothing serious could happen, even to her. I don't know how to explain it. As if we could conquer any misfortune."

Lucienne didn't speak. She listened to him with her gaze lowered, nodding.

"But I don't believe that, not anymore. I can't. I was at Auteuil and the Place d'Enfer and the Rue Vavin. And at the Fort de Vanves before that, and the list goes on. Under fire, with all those men falling around me—I got discouraged, yes, but I thought we could still keep all this from happening, push back the infantrymen, regain the ground we'd lost. Maybe I thought that because we'll always be worth more than their gunmen, even if we're dead, because we will have fought for everyone's happiness, the universal republic. For things larger than ourselves. Like we all had the same dream, all together. I can't really put what I think into words . . ."

Lucienne put a hand on his arm.

"Don't worry. We understand you perfectly."

"And now that everything is ruined . . . before it all comes crashing down . . . I just want to see her again. I'd do anything for that. To try to get back all the time I've lost."

"You haven't lost it, the time. You've fought. You've looked death in the eye. And you found two brothers, and that's no small thing. It isn't wasted time. It's a part of the life of a worthy man. Like all of these men, who are hungry and dropping with exhaustion. Do you know what they think about as they're falling asleep? Who they whisper good night to in secret, under their blankets? Who they dream of? It could be that half of them are carrying the same heavy burden as you, and, like you, they're putting it down to pick up a rifle . . ."

The two of them turned to look at the line of silent men waiting to be served in the almost peaceful night, a bonfire crackling nearby. Men were seated around it, stirring the coals with their bayonets and raising showers of sparks.

Nicolas didn't know what to think of what Madame Lucienne had just told him. He stood up mechanically, like an automaton, moving so as not to fall, his head feeling hollow and heavy as a cauldron.

He followed a group of Federate guards bunking down in the entry hall of the École des Mines a short distance away. A white tent had been set up as an aid station. Nicolas stopped and stuck his head through the tent flap. In the dim light, he made out two men sitting very straight and still in chairs, their bandaged hands resting in their laps. A woman was tending to them in the light of a lantern, a nearby table filled with surgical instruments.

"Do you know Caroline, from the aid station on the Rue Lecourbe?"

The woman turned around and looked at him for a moment before shaking her head and going back to what she was doing.

"No," she said, with her back to him. "I don't know anyone with that name."

At the foot of a grand staircase, mattresses had been laid out on the floor. Fifty men were already asleep, snoring, faintly illuminated by a few dim night lamps hung here and there. As soon as he lay down, fatigue pounced on him like a huge, silent animal crouching in the dark.

He wakes up several times in the night, thinking he sees Caroline roaming among the sleepers. He calls out her name. A man nearby tells him to shut his trap. Others stir in their sleep, tossing and turning. He stays that way, sitting up, for a long moment, hoping the apparition might return. *If you're out there, come to me, and we'll leave here together.* Maybe he's murmuring. He isn't sure if he's speaking to a sort of ghost or just thinking too hard. He feels as if she might suddenly sit down next to him, and he's already holding out his arms to press her to him. Then exhaustion overwhelms him again, pulling him irresistibly back down onto his pallet.

The men are jerked from their sleep by a salvo of artillery fire exploding in the gardens and by the dry snaps of rifle shots. They're on their feet immediately in the dimness, frozen, looking at one another without really seeing each other, without exchanging a word of reassurance, and then each man picks up his bag and his gun, jams his cap on haphazardly, and heads out into the deserted boulevard in the early morning light.

Nicolas spends that whole day in the Latin Quarter, moving from one barricade to another. Earthen levees, reinforced by more sacks of dirt. Some heaped cobblestone walls, sometimes guarded by only two men. On the Rue des Écoles, a veritable masonry wall. Two cannons, fifteen or so men seated near stacks of rifles, crates of ammunition all around them. Some women come and go, bringing coffee and fresh bread that a baker on the Rue Thénard has managed to make. Nicolas sits down for a moment and allows himself to indulge in this luxury. There is even sugar. The men talk. They won't cross the Seine, at least not here. And elsewhere? How is it all going? Rue Vavin? Nicolas doesn't dare describe the scene he's come from, or admit that he left his comrades under fire behind him. At the Croix-Rouge? The Rue de Rennes? They're holding up. There are a few handfuls of them left. There's Varlin, and Lisbonne. What about Montmartre? No one knows; they haven't seen anyone. Jules Vallès came through here last night; he almost got arrested. No one recognized him with his beard shaved, exhausted, almost limping, holding on to a woman's arm. He said it wasn't going too well at the Hôtel de Ville, that there was a lot of shouting without anyone really knowing what to do. What the hell else do they know how to do up there? They're just talkers, pedestal warriors. We'll need reinforcements, yes. A boy sets off in search of news. They yell after him to be careful; he responds with a careless wave over one shoulder.

Everyone falls silent as they watch the youth walk away. They listen to the cannon fire. It seems thickest near Les Gobelins, toward La Butte-aux-Cailles. Wroblewski, someone says. *They're holding.* No one speaks. Nicolas tries to estimate how far away from here the shells are falling, compared to what they can hear from Montparnasse. A kilometer, no more. They'll be here tonight.

In the afternoon he heads back toward the Pantheon with two other men, friends in civilian life, one of them a talkative jokester, the other quiet and melancholy. The square is crowded with Federates. Maybe three hundred of them. Two officers on horseback weave through the crowd that bristles with bayonets. Men stop them by grabbing the horses' bridles. Nicolas picks his way through the throng. There is a single piece of information being passed from man to man: Montmartre has fallen. Almost without a fight. Most of the men are staring at the ground, and gradually the noise in the square fades to a muted murmur of voices. People are keeping their voices low as if they're at a funeral. No one dares to meet anyone else's eyes, afraid of seeing his own distress reflected in the other faces. A few voices shout out, calling on the men to fight, to sacrifice, and then fall silent again almost immediately.

"This time we're fucked!"

Nicolas jumps as if stung by a wasp and turns, forgetting to breathe.

Red is standing there, leaning on a crutch, his forehead bandaged. He wraps his good arm around Nicolas, who thumps him on the back.

"Good God, brother! What happened to you?"

"Two bullets. One nipped off a bit of my hide and some hair; the other one went straight through my calf without breaking the bone. And just like that, I'm not good for much anymore, even though I can still hobble around, and they sent me to the aid station here, where there's a doctor. He's against the Commune, but he'll treat anyone, he told me. No questions asked. He cleaned the wounds and stitched me up. And you— what the hell are you doing here? I thought you were already in the tenth, looking for your cop!"

"I'm on the way there. But I had to sleep, and . . ."

"Sleep, you say? What on earth is that?"

Red spots the wheel of an ammunition wagon and limps toward it. "Come on, I've got to sit my arse down."

He sits down heavily and leans back against the spokes, his rifle propped next to him.

"How is it going back there?"

"Badly. They'll evacuate tonight, make no mistake. The situation's unbearable. We'll have to fight here."

"Here? The area's poorly defended. There are barricades you can climb over in three steps. Almost no artillery. The men are slipping away, five here, fifteen there . . ."

Red has let his head drop forward onto his chest. Nicolas shakes him awake.

"Come on, we'll find you a place to get some shut-eye."

They go into the fifth arrondissement's town hall, which is

full of milling people, some of their faces exhilarated, some exhausted, and doors endlessly creaking and slamming. No one pays them any attention. A staircase is being guarded by a man sitting on the steps, his rifle across his lap. When he asks them where they're going, Red simply answers, "To sleep." The guard nods and waves them past nonchalantly. In an empty office, Red lets his crutch fall to the floor, flops onto a sofa, and begins snoring immediately. Nicolas clears some piles of paper off an armchair and sits down near the open window. He has no idea what time it is. The sky is milky, the sun weak. It's very hot. He unbuttons his jacket and undoes his collar. The smell of his own filthy body assails his nostrils, sour and thick. And then the odor of smoke again, and the distant noise of the battle.

He dozes there, amid the sounds of shouts and people calling out, yelling, laughing. The city's voices are all speaking at the same time, telling of their fear and their anger and the hope to which they're still clinging. He doesn't see the sunset, the twilight blanketing him with its blue shadow the way you cover a little boy who has dropped off to sleep, gently, careful not to wake him.

And then there is the sound of drums, rolling and rumbling against the façades of the buildings. Nicolas hears Red getting up behind him, the parquet floor creaking beneath his feet.

"It's time," he says.

All around the Pantheon, the commotion of battle pulls men in groups toward the boulevard. The barricade on the Rue Soufflot is manned by fifty Federates and one mitrailleuse. At the corner of the boulevard, men are loading rifles and wedging them into the heaps of cobblestones, adjusting the sacks of earth. People are running in all directions. Ammunition wagons rattle across the rutted ground. The massive barricade below the Luxembourg Gardens is swarming with people. Guards are being forced to shoo away the curious onlookers who stare as black smoke billows into the air from the fires. The smell of burning fills the air like deadly poison. Armed men shove through the front doors of the buildings lining the square, and seconds later windows are flung open, glass breaks, and they take position on the balconies. Nicolas stays where he is, aghast. He looks around at him at the looming disaster. Behind him, Red says nothing but pulls him by the sleeve.

"You should leave now. Tomorrow it'll all be finished here."

"Come with me. You can't fight anymore, my friend. We can search better together."

"No way. With this damned cripple's kit, I'd draw too much attention to you, even if I change clothes. And I'd slow you down. You'll move faster on your own. I can still be of some use here. I'll load rifles, help maneuver the cannons. They'll bloody well see that I'm still good for something."

Two artillery shells explode in quick succession thirty yards from the barricade. Earth and loose stones rain down on the men. There are shouts. People hurry toward the wounded, carrying lanterns. The darkness fills with quivering lights like fireflies. A hole has been blown in the middle of the redoubt. Bodies move and groan amid the rubble.

"Go," says Red. "Find her and save yourselves, damn it. We'll need survivors to take up the guns again, understand?"

Nicolas heads for the barricade.

"Come on," he says. "They need a hand."

WEDNESDAY, MAY 24TH

26

Roques was barely able to shake off the nightmares that besieged him all night, like rats come to gnaw at him and squeal in his ears, or unearthly spiders skittering over his face. He sat up dizzily on his pallet, his head heavy. Around him the infantrymen were stirring, complaining about the night's brevity and the ongoing lack of women, some opining that a few female prisoners should be set aside for the combatants' pleasure rather than shot or sent to prison. Then came the lewd comments, the bawdy stories, the sickening laughter. "Gentlemen! Manners, please!" shouted a colonel. "You're soldiers, not pigs, so why lust after sows?" The men laughed and cheered. This was clearly an officer who knew how to talk to his men.

Roques doesn't know how the other two managed to get any sleep in this boys' school-turned-billet. In the morning, Clovis was silent, as usual, and Loubet seemed to be keeping a close eye on the comings and goings of the officers. They bolted their pieces of bread dipped in weak coffee spiked with a dash of hooch, and then the sergeants formed their patrols, a dozen men each, heavily armed, with strict orders to shoot summarily anyone who tried to flee: man, woman, child. One officer, a captain or lieutenant, is supervising every three patrols, who are left more or less to their own devices as to how to proceed. There is only one objective: not to leave a single enemy behind the lines. To cleanse Paris after two months of defilement.

Building by building, they hurtle up the stairs at a run, smashing in doors, screaming orders and insults into the apartments, dragging terrified residents onto the landings as they protest their innocence. A few proud souls welcome the soldiers mockingly, staring them down defiantly, unbendingly, giving in only to savage blows from a rifle butt and then straightening back up, faces bloody, heads bashed in, jaws broken, struggling to breathe due to cracked ribs. Then they are shoved down the stairs, sometimes falling, rolling, and getting up with groans of pain, clutching arms or shoulders or hips wordlessly, gritting their teeth or limping. They are herded into groups in courtyards, lined up along the sidewalks, and marched in columns to prison, or a convent requisitioned for the purpose.

If the officer commanding the operation is in a hurry, they are shot. If a sergeant grows impatient, he gives the order to finish off anyone who is resistant or badly behaved. A bayonet thrust into the guts, a bullet in the head.

One soldier finds a Federate uniform stuffed under a bed. The man in the wine-red dressing gown and leather slippers recoils, pressing himself against the wall. Is this yours? *No— yes—I refused to enlist. Look, it's brand new. Never worn.* The soldier stands up, shoves the jacket into the man's face. A draft dodger, eh? Is that it? He smells the man's hands. No scent of gunpowder. He smells like chicken, too, says the soldier. Come on, we'll take him.

Roques escorts the blubbering man down the stairs. "It's true," he says. "I never wanted to be part of this farce. The Communeux are a bunch of thieves. If I could have, I would have gone to Versailles, too. But my father-in-law insisted I stay, to look after the apartment and the family business. And now I'm done for. So much for honesty. You obey the *pater familias*, you refuse to get mixed up with the rabble, and you end up in this mess. Take me to your colonel; surely he'll listen

to me, at least." Roques doesn't answer. He has been sleepwalking for the last three hours. Sometimes he thinks he's
going to wake up and emerge from this nightmare. Out in the
courtyard, a dozen curious bystanders are encouraging the soldiers to get on with their task of public cleansing. *Oui, monsieur*, public cleansing! The way you get rid of pests! "Could
be a little rat poison would 'elp," someone suggests. Everyone
guffaws. When the prisoner Roques is charged with guarding
enters the courtyard, the crowd falls silent. All eyes turn to
him, boring into him. *Really, now, gentlemen! You know me!
You know I wouldn't . . .* They all look away. "Can you really
ever know a person?" says a man in a top hat.

Roques doesn't know what's keeping him from taking his
rifle and opening fire on this group of respectable Parisians.
Undoubtedly the fact that his chassepot only shoots one bullet
at a time, and in the time it would take to reload they would
scatter like the rats they're so desperate to rid Paris of, or perhaps swarm on him and tear him to pieces. He watches the
wretched man begging for his peers' compassion, and he wonders if the few cartridges left in his revolver might not help
these model citizens reach a consensus. He listens to the faint
sounds of the battle raging in the distance, and he wishes he
were there right now, behind a mitrailleuse, or lying in wait at
the window of some mansion to kill as many of them as possible, to watch them falling, thrashing on the ground, crawling
away before the coup de grâce; to hear them howling in pain.
War is the only scenario left between these people and the
populace. No compromise is possible. He watches them now,
only a couple of meters away, hateful and haughty and ready to
sacrifice this imbecile the way you shrug off a dead weight, but
so well dressed, their vests neatly buttoned, gold watches in
their gussets, just below the heart, so polite, speaking so evenly,
capable of sending one of their own to his death the way
wolves tear apart the weakest member of the pack.

How stupid he was, two months ago, in the exhilaration and rush of the early days, to accept the police duties that have led him here, forcing him to scheme with the enemy, to ape them in their lowest, most despicable acts—this hunting of human beings, these summary curbside executions, urged on by informers and slanderers, the embittered and the jealous, pointing at windows and giving apartment numbers and murmuring names quietly as if they don't want their voices to be recognized, professing their passion for the Republic and their dedication to law and order before slinking back into the shadows, smug or terrified, puffing out their chests or hugging the walls. The sergeant comes back down the stairs and out into the courtyard now, asking who the blubbering man is. The situation is explained to him, and he eyes the man in the dressing gown and says, "Put him with the others." The prisoner is shoved through the double-door entrance to the courtyard. "But I know Communeux! Real ones," he babbles. "Wait! The concierge at number 56, and his wife! And the wine merchant at number 63! Everyone knows them!"

The sergeant sends some men to verify this. His captain will be pleased. Personally, he doesn't give a damn. He's in the army because in the country village he comes from, near Le Mans, he and his brothers were dying of hunger on a four-hectare tenant farm. This mess with the Republic and the Commune and Reds and all that hot air—let the Parisians worry about that. All he knows is that he has a full belly, and some months he can even send a little of his salary back to his parents. He was just telling this to Roques in the stairwell. *It might even be*, he'd said, as he broke down a door with the butt of his rifle, *that they were right to revolt. Who knows?*

Now the man in the dressing gown is forced to climb into a cart where a dozen prisoners are already seated. He'll be taken before a military court. Maybe he can prove to them that he's just an honest, ordinary bastard. The cart rattles off, pulled by an immense, placid horse and escorted by six soldiers dragging their feet.

In the afternoon, the search operations over, Roques follows his patrol to a billet that has been set up in a school. Near the Croix-Rouge and the Rue de Rennes, the battle rages incessantly. They come up against a column of perhaps a thousand men, marching up the Rue du Bac toward the Seine, followed by ten massive guns pulled by horses. The clattering wheels of the enormous cannons make the ground vibrate, the echo of the soldiers' rhythmic footsteps reverberating endlessly in the distance. Seeing so many men and guns flooding into Paris, Roques is more convinced than ever that the Commune has mere hours left. As the last of the cannons files past, he feels someone put a hand on his shoulder. It's Clovis, whom he barely recognizes: with his newly shorn hair and neatly trimmed beard, he looks like a young man with large, sad eyes and an anxious brow.

"Holy smokes, what happened to you? Did you have a fight with a barber?"

"Almost. He'd helped recruit a battalion, but they wouldn't let him enlist because of a gimpy leg. The opinions he used to express in his salon were well known. He was informed on by his landlord, who must have wanted his shop front back. I told the others I'd deal with him, so they left me alone with him. Awfully trusting after my display yesterday. I said I'd set him free if he'd give me a demonstration of his art, asked if he could make me look human again, so I'd draw less attention. I fired two rifle shots into a mirror and left. Told him he should hide until nightfall and then go and find a safe place."

"What about us? Should we wait for nightfall, too?"

"Where is Loubet?"

"Haven't seen him."

"Where are we in relation to the Rue des Missions?"

"It's that way. Maybe thirty minutes' walk."

They go into the courtyard of the school, where two hundred men are sitting or lying down, grabbing a quick meal or smoking, talking about their morning. There are frequent exclamations and bursts of laughter. Some listen seriously, or with astonishment. It sounds like a bunch of hunters recounting their exploits.

They approach a field kitchen where a tall beanpole of a man with disproportionately long arms serves them a sort of stew. It has a strong smell, of onions and garlic mostly. He serves them in two dented tin bowls.

"You're lucky, fellows. It's all happening so fast that we've had trouble getting the mess wagons through. Weapons and ammunition are priority, they're saying. So us with the supplies, we go last. Anyway . . . the sooner it's finished, the sooner we can all go home. Though I thought things would be even tougher—we're gutting them like trout! The National Guard hardly even exists anymore, nothing but headcases and fanatics left on the barricades—and there'll be no quarter with that lot, of course. This will clean the city of some of its filth, I dare say!"

They sit down near a group of silent, exhausted men smelling of tobacco and sweat. One of them turns to Roques:

"Where the hell did you come from? I've never seen either of you before."

"Must not have been looking, then," says Roques. "I've never seen you before, either. You get here tonight?"

The man shrugs. "Who gives a fuck anyway?"

Clovis rises and signals to Roques. "Come on. I don't want to disturb anyone."

They walk away. Behind them, the soldier mutters insults and vague threats to alert the police.

"We're attracting attention," says Roques. "We're going to have to make a decision soon."

"What about Loubet?"

"There he is now. That nasty business we couldn't avoid

this morning gives me an idea. It might give us a better chance of getting past the checkpoints and the sentries more easily. I've heard that the colonel—you know, Monsieur Three-Questions-and-a-Bullet—is named de Faverolle. He's set up a command post at the Babylone barracks. We're going to take him a prisoner, a well-guarded one."

"All this to find a dead woman. I wonder if . . ."

"I'm asking myself the same thing, and a few other questions besides. But what the hell, I want to finish what I started. I'd like for all this to have some meaning."

Loubet comes over to them, his expression conspiratorial.

"Our cover will be blown by this evening. The sergeant's suspicious. He was suspicious from the beginning, even if what Clovis did reassured him a bit. He just asked me the name of our captain; I did a bit of side-stepping, and he let me go. But they'll arrest us in an hour at most."

"Fuck the captain. I've got the name of the colonel. Follow me."

They leave the billet laughing and horsing around, feigning drunkenness, beneath the indifferent gaze of the sentries on duty, and then hurry away down the sidewalk, ducking between two wagons.

"Get out of that uniform," Roques instructs Loubet. He doesn't seem to understand, opens his mouth to protest.

"You're going to be our prisoner. We're taking you to Colonel de Faverolle at Babylone barracks. It's the only way to get through the checkpoints."

Without another word, Loubet shrugs off his jacket and rumples his clothing a bit.

"Reason for arrest?"

"You helped a suspect escape."

"Fine. But you'll need to rough me up a bit. An arrest has to be rough. It's an unwritten law, but it's the one the police are best at obeying."

Roques looks at Clovis, who shakes his head. "I killed a man this morning. I think that's quite enough for today."

Without warning, Roques delivers a smart blow to Loubet with the grip of his revolver. The other man cries out in surprise and pain and topples to the ground beneath the hooves of a horse, which shies away. He gets to his feet, slightly dazed, his forehead cut and bleeding.

They set off. Every street corner is manned by exhausted soldiers trying to stay out of the blazing sun. For the most part, they don't give a damn what's bringing these two comrades and their prisoner this way. Once a duty officer bars the way and demands an explanation, his rifle at the ready, bayonet threatening. Roques feeds him their line about prisoners and colonels. The grunt eyes Loubet, his mustache quivering with scorn and hatred, as if he might skewer him then and there.

"We'd better go," says Roques. "The colonel doesn't like waiting."

"Oh yes, the colonel," the man says. "I know how we could save him some time . . . but I suppose orders are orders."

He steps back and lets them pass. The three other sentries, who haven't budged, laugh and tease their compatriot.

"Atta boy, Pénicot! You'll make corporal in the end! Don't pay any attention to him, fellows. For him the Commune is Satan's kingdom, and he dreams of wiping out every one of his henchmen. Sees himself commanding a platoon, delivering every single coup de grâce himself. Even had his rifle and bayonet blessed by a priest last week!"

Roques looks back and sees Pénicot, his weapon still held at the ready, watching them walk away, squinting, defiant, obstinate. All the rest of the way down the street, until they turn the corner, he can feel the infantryman's gaze boring into his back.

When they reach the Rue des Missions, Loubet puts his uniform back on, ducking into a doorway to readjust his gear.

"How should we do this?" he asks.

Clovis squares his shoulders, hefting the heavy rifle.

"I'll go. Wait for me here. I'll have a look around and come back. I know the area a bit; I want to make sure there's no danger."

Roques opens his mouth to protest, but Clovis silences him with a gesture.

"I know the premises. And it's up to me to repair the damage I've done, if I can."

Roques doesn't speak, lets him walk away.

"What if he doesn't come back?" asks Loubet.

"He'll come back."

"That man's a criminal. He participated for months in the kidnappings of those girls. He says he was obeying the orders of a killer, but how do we know that's true? You're taking him at his word just because he came to turn himself in, but we've seen that before, these fellows who think they'll get a lighter punishment if they turn their cronies in."

"The man's in the process of struggling back up to the surface of humanity. We should let him swim as best he can."

"Pretty words like that don't change people. Nothing does. We are who we are. Virtuous or vicious. Straight or twisted. I don't believe in the power of words, myself. Or in atonement, or redemption. When there's a worm in the fruit, you have to throw the fruit away."

Roques listens to him, watching the street. A novelty merchant stands in front of his boutique awaiting customers, who are still thin on the ground. Two elegantly dressed men walk past, gesturing extravagantly. One of him spins his walking stick between his fingers.

"Human beings aren't fruit. You're wrong about it all."

"I'm speaking from experience. Twelve years as a policeman will help you understand a lot of things. I've crossed paths with dozens of these people whom you'd have sent straight to heaven without confession and who've just massacred their wife and children or slit an old woman's throat for the sake of ten francs. Sometimes we'd find them slipping around in the blood, covered with it, and they'd start crying and whining; to listen to them, you'd think they had more to complain about than their victims. I remember the woman we went to find at work, to tell her that her three children had been killed, beaten to death with a hammer; a neighbor lady had discovered them by chance. She was gentleness itself. Grief incarnate. The face of an angel. We had to stop her from slitting her own throat with a kitchen knife. I was still green, still fairly new to the job, and the sight of that mother throwing herself on the bodies of her children, screaming, cut me right to the heart. We suspected the husband, who had gone off somewhere to sleep off a cheap wine hangover; we found him still drunk near the Porte d'Aubervilliers. But that paragon of respectability, who hadn't been the last one to tickle the ribs of his children and their mother, had a solid forty-eight-hour alibi: he hadn't left the sleazy bar where we found him passed out in some girl's arms. And as it turned out, the mother contradicted herself in her statements, and we found out she was the one who'd done it, killed her little ones. She ended up confessing to the whole thing."

"Did you ever find out why she committed an atrocity like that?"

"There is no 'why.' Trying to understand something is already making excuses for it, and there's no possible forgiveness in a case like that. She should have been sent to the guillotine, but the court decided against it, probably because people are still far too reluctant to execute women."

Roques doesn't know what to think anymore. He doesn't doubt that the human soul is capable of infinite darkness, of insane desires for destruction and death, of irreducible malice. He doesn't deny the impossibility of shining any light into those depths, of excusing or forgiving them in any way. But he also knows that some people live an inhuman existence where every day is torture, where life is an eternal punishment that doesn't atone for anything, and that it's easy to forget that, even when one belongs to the same human race. With a shudder, he remembers the implacable coolness with which Clovis killed that man this morning, and his silence during the hours that followed. "What do you want me to say? It was that or be shot, with these badly disguised Federate mugs of ours." Neither he nor Loubet had known what to say to that, but each of them had remained shut up in his own bubble of silence, uncertain and uneasy.

"Makes you think, doesn't it?"

"Of course . . . but I . . ."

"And you—you really believe that the Commune, that a social revolution, will make people better by allowing them to live with more dignity, is that it? You believe that humans are basically good. You think that even the worst criminals can always improve, that universal happiness as decreed by some Central Committee, some Convention, will put an end to the filth humans are capable of. I've read all the literature, too. I even wanted to believe it. But reality is a stubborn bitch, Roques. It'll kick you in the arse as soon as you start to relax. Look around you. Listen to your illusions being blown to smithereens by the bombs. Look at your incompetent leaders, your golden-tongued orators who are suddenly at a loss for words, just like the National Guard is finding itself without soldiers or commanders. That's reality."

He pauses, almost breathless, looking at Roques, his expression serious and without irony. He shakes his head, chagrined.

"Frankly, I'd have preferred it to succeed, this whole farce. If only to make those bourgeois bastards pay, knock their fat asses down a few pegs for good. Because those sanctimonious know-it-alls, who put on their Sunday best and go with Madame to mass and then unzip their trousers in the whore-houses during the week, they have their defects, too, made presentable by their fancy educations. I've seen a few of them in my time, too, in their well-protected little nooks and crannies. Men who only like little girls, no older than eight, or little boys. We'd put the fear of God into them; we'd say we were going to tell their wives everything; we'd threaten them with the worst punishments justice can mete out . . . but there was always someone to absolve them of these venial sins, often a priest or even a bishop, who were sometimes in a position to know *exactly* what they were talking about. That's when it wasn't a police commissioner ordering us to look the other way, or acting on Monsieur Claude's orders,[17] setting the case file aside for him in case it might prove useful later on . . ."

"I don't understand . . . why did you stay? Why come this far . . . why risk your own skin?"

"To see. Just to see where this rebellion would go. I quite enjoyed watching the bourgeois world turned upside down in the space of just a few days. The top hats, the detachable collars, the silk vests, the buckled shoes, running away like a herd of goats when a dog barks from behind the fence. Paris without police, delivered into the hands of the people. I was sure it would turn into a free-for-all immediately, an orgy of throat-slitting—but no, the streets became noisier, but safer, too, people singing all the time, and drinking a fair bit, too. I liked it. I watched it all like I was at a play. But as soon as the Versaillais started to take action, I knew it would end badly, and again I wanted to see how . . . I didn't think it would happen so fast.

---

[17] Antoine Claude, known as Monsieur Claude, head of the Sûreté from 1859 to 1875, well-versed in underhanded maneuvers and other manipulations. Spent several weeks in prison during the Commune and then resumed his duties in the service of the victors.

I knew this new republic was built of cardboard, but I hadn't quite realized it was nothing but a house of cards. It's like with Citizen Clovis. I wanted to see how far he was capable of going to struggle back to the surface, as you put it. I'm watching. I'm trying to understand how this type of person operates."

"I don't know why I'm still here listening to you."

Loubet smiles without malice.

"Because you can't do anything else."

Roques hopes Clovis will be back soon, because he can't bear to hear any more of Loubet's calm, pitiless voice, pouring salt in the wound. Loubet is watching the street, too, as he talks. He's propped his rifle against the wall, his hands in his pockets.

"When you don't believe in anything, it's easy to make fun."

"I'm not making fun. I respect people like you, and those thousands of others who thought a new world was opening up for them at last, and who are dying and who will die on the barricades without a prayer of winning. I'm not making fun, I promise you. I'm just telling it the way it is. But it's true I can't make myself believe we'll ever be able to change the course of things. To vanquish injustice, eliminate poverty, establish equality for all . . . to do that, first you'd have to change mankind, take away the desire to dominate, to take advantage of others, to cause suffering. And I don't think that's possible."

"But it's society that drives people to all that. When you force men to work until they drop just to survive, you can't expect them to raise themselves up, pull themselves out of the conditions they're living in, all on their own. If you spend your life kowtowing to others, nose in the trough, you get used to it. You either turn into a permanent hunchback—or you straighten up and stand tall. That's what happened on July 14th, in June of '48, on March 18th . . . You can't predict it. Why at those particular times, and not sooner, or later? The Commune . . . it's an idea. An idea by which people can raise themselves up. Dream higher. And they'll fight to the death for it."

Loubet nods.

"Not bad. Maybe we're both right, after all. Look, he's coming back. One point for you."

Clovis rejoins them, slightly out of breath. He looks at them with wide eyes, his forehead shining with sweat.

"It's bedlam. There are fifty of them there, doing who the hell knows what . . ."

Roques seizes him by the collar. "The girl?"

"They're looking for her everywhere. She escaped tonight, over the rooftops. Two of the men told me they don't really give a damn anyway, because she belonged to the captain."

Roques leans heavily against the wall, almost slumping to the ground, his legs feeling as if they've given out from under him. As if the exhaustion of the past two days has suddenly thudded down on him like a sandbag on his shoulders that he'd forgotten about.

"How did she manage it?" he murmurs to himself. "She must be exhausted."

"It's that captain, make no mistake," says Clovis. "He must have reserved her for his own dirty pleasures. There are plenty of people like that out there, more than you might think. Pujols was in cahoots with a photographer who dealt in that sort of thing. Imagine what he must have subjected her to, for her to take such a risk."

Seeing that Roques has crumpled against the wall, his head in his hands, Clovis goes to him and thumps him gently on the shoulder.

"Come on. Don't be disappointed. At least she's alive. I'd have preferred to free her ourselves. I'd have liked to open that door for her myself, given her that first glass of fresh water and that first slice of bread, for all those reasons you already know."

"And you think that would have made up for your crime? A glass of water and a crust of bread?"

Roques looks up, jolted suddenly out of the dark thoughts and unforgiving rebukes with which he's been tormenting himself.

Loubet is holding a revolver in his outstretched hand, mere inches from Clovis's face, his finger on the trigger. His expression is one of weariness, or perhaps indifference. Roques thinks he could fire at any second without a qualm.

"Set down that rifle and put your hands in the air."

Clovis doesn't move. He gazes curiously at the policeman, then, sighing, puts his rifle on the ground.

"I should have expected this," he says.

"You didn't free that girl; you won't have been any use in this matter at all. Your role as temporary police assistant ends today, right now. You're my prisoner, and I intend to deliver you to justice, which is about to be restored in its full plenitude and power."

Roques takes a step forward, but Loubet pulls a second revolver from one of his pockets and points it at him.

"You're mad!"

"No. Call me anything else you like, but I'm not mad. Or is anyone mad who doesn't see the world like you do?"

Roques struggles to process the sight of this impassive face, this even voice, this almost pompous tone. Here in front of him, armed, stands a cold-blooded animal, a viper nourished in his own bosom, as the story goes, who is now holding them at the mercy of its venom. In the fable, the farmer kills the snake with an axe before it becomes too dangerous.

He hurls himself at Loubet, rifle butt thrust forward, but the other man dodges and then deals him a fearful blow in the temple that makes him sway and then sag against the wall behind him. Through tears, amid the dull clamor of his ringing ears and throbbing arteries, he sees Loubet, and hears him say that he's not going to kill him because that wouldn't accomplish anything. *Dead or alive, you're nothing, so what's the point?*

When he opens his eyes again, he wonders for a moment where he is, then recognizes the doorway they were standing in, and his whirling mind can't figure out why he's alone. He's even starting to wonder if any of what he's hazily remembering really happened at all—and then a blinding pain shoots through his head, and it all comes back to him, overwhelming him, knocking him flat on his back again.

The sky thunders with cannon fire. He can feel the ground shaking beneath him, reverberating throughout his whole body. He could weep at this whole catastrophe, at his own failure—but deep in his throat there is a burning knot like thirst, and his heart is still beating too fast, pounding with sadness and rage.

He struggles to his feet and sets off down the street rumbling with his defeat, staggering, drunk with exhaustion.

27

He'd come back with wine and flowers. Five or six roses, their stems wrapped in newspaper, and a bottle of red wine from the Loire valley. He also brought glasses. Real wineglasses, light and delicate, maybe even crystal, with gilded etching. And cheese. He came back with all of that, but he wasn't alone.

Another man came into the room with him, a man dressed in civilian clothes, elegant ones, a midnight-blue silk cravat tied at his throat, a gold chain hanging discreetly from the watch pocket of his embroidered mauve and Indian rose vest. He stood stock still in the middle of the room at first, slightly out of breath from climbing the stairs. He looked around, intrigued, without paying the least attention to Caroline, who had sat down on the bed when she heard the click of the lock, and then he sighed and set down the basket he was carrying, extracting from it a box of caramels and a packet of wafers, which he put on a small table.

The captain tossed the flowers on the bed and then set down the rest of what he was carrying, arranging it all on the table as carefully as if he were a butler. Then he hung his cap on the window-latch and turned to his companion.

"Well? What do you think?"

The other man inspected Caroline, his gaze raking over her from head to foot, his lip curling scornfully. She felt his eyes on her as if they were a pair of moist hands touching her, fondling her.

"Have to see."

She started trembling. She was cold. An explosion more violent than usual made her jump, and she dashed the tears from her eyes with the back of her hand.

"Take that off," ordered the captain.

Obey. Buy some time. She stood up, unbuttoned her blouse, let it fall to her feet. A shudder ran through her body. Her heart thumped in her chest, at the base of her throat. She was nothing more than that pulsebeat now. She wondered if they could see her arteries throbbing beneath her skin. She considered covering her sex with her hands and then decided against it, forcing herself to let her arms hang loosely at her sides. She looked from one man to the other, hoping that her eyes didn't betray her terror, that the tears wouldn't fall right then. She wanted to defy them with her gaze, to cow them and their intentions. Not to appear like the humiliated, defeated victim that would excite their thirst for destruction.

The man in civilian clothes approached her. He bore a strong resemblance to the officer, she observed. Brothers, undoubtedly. He'd circled her slowly, grazing the small of her back with his fingertips, and come to stand in front of her again, his face mere centimeters from her own. The man's green eyes didn't blink. Caroline forced herself to focus on the gold flecks in his irises, so she wouldn't look away. His eyes were frighteningly beautiful.

The man slid a hand between her thighs, slipping his fingers up inside her, quickly and deftly, then sniffed them. Licked them.

Caroline had closed her eyes. She tried to focus on something else, someone else, but nothing and no one sprang to mind, her mind obstinately blank, like a pool of stagnant black water. She felt her knees grow weaker and weaker, and she tensed her legs, bracing for the fall.

"They cleaned her up just a little while ago," said the captain.

The man turned around. He took off his vest and tossed it on a chair.

"I'm thirsty. How about some wine?"

The captain uncorked the bottle with his teeth and spit the cork onto the ground. He filled two glasses.

"What about her? This is a party, isn't it?"

"No, thank you," Caroline said, and sat down, not daring to put her blouse back on.

The knife. The idea struck her like a blow from a fist. She had slipped it under the mattress several minutes earlier, near the head of the bed. Too far away. And then what would she do with it? She'd have to attack the captain first, she mused, put him out of commission because he was armed. He was still standing near the window, three meters from her. She'd never have the strength to do it, or the time. And the other one?

The man approached her, a full glass in his hand, and held it out to her.

"Drink. Make a toast with us, or we'll be offended. My name is Martin, and this is my brother Édouard."

She drank a mouthful of wine, and she liked it. She would have liked to eat a few of the wafers, too; she could see the packet on the table. It surprised her to feel these desires, as if part of her, driven by primal need, by hunger and thirst, was acting independently of the fear that still gripped her. The men didn't move or speak, content to sniff the contents of their glasses and sip slowly, so she looked at them more closely. Both of them had the same closely trimmed beard, the same short-cropped hair; they were about the same height. They really looked very much alike, and if not for the different colors of their eyes—those of the soldier, Édouard, were brown—they could have been mistaken for twins. They exchanged a satisfied, knowing glance. They didn't need to speak much, it seemed, to understand each other perfectly.

Martin untied his cravat, letting its two ends hang down his chest like a scarf, and poured himself another glass of wine. Abruptly, he asked Caroline if she knew how to dance. She said yes because she didn't know what else to say, because there was nothing else to say or do, and the two men leaned against the wall on either side of the window, and Édouard said, "Then dance!"

She stared at them, perhaps trying to discern in their expressions the negation of what they'd just ordered her to do, the hint of a twinkle that would have meant they were joking, but both of them met her gaze unblinkingly, and neither of them moved, waiting to see what she would do. She felt cold again and hardly dared to move or even breathe, as if the slightest movement of her body would send an icy wind swirling around her.

"To dance, you've got to be on your feet," remarked Martin, "and not sitting on your arse."

She still didn't move, so he walked toward her, took both of her hands, pulled her to him. He started to sketch the steps of a dance somewhere between the waltz and the polka, pressing his pelvis against Caroline's, and she felt his sex hardening between his thighs, rubbing against her, and the man grasped a fistful of her hair and pressed her face to his chest with a choked groan, his fingers sliding down between the cheeks of her arse.

Crushed against his chest, Caroline broke into tears, and the man groaned words of encouragement, clearly taking her sobs for moans of pleasure. She was being smothered, suffocating, and finally she jerked away, coughing, and spit on the floor. The man slapped her, pushing her down on the bed. His brother approached, unbuttoning his jacket, undoing his suspenders. She saw their two faces leaning over her, backlit, calm and determined, and their tall forms filled her whole field of vision, absorbing all the light from the window. They were like two shadows looming over her, bringing the night with them.

The sound of hammering on the door plunged the room

into absolute silence, dense as a block of granite. No one even breathed, and the noise of the combat outside seemed suddenly stifled by the thick stillness in which the two brothers stood frozen for a few seconds.

Édouard, the captain, quickly tugged his clothing straight and hurried to the door, then went back toward the window to retrieve his cap. When he opened the door, a soldier saluted him peremptorily and said, out of breath, that the colonel wanted to see him right away. The officer had hesitated, starting back toward his brother, and then turned and left, slamming the door behind him.

Caroline took advantage of the moment to retrieve her blouse and felt around under the mattress for the knife. The man had gone to lock the door; now he turned and poured himself another glass of wine, which he sipped, looking out the window.

"It's burning," he said. "I prefer to see this city in flames rather than in the hands of the lower classes. It's a purifying fire. We're cleansing Paris of its vermin. This bodes well. The army is crushing them under the rubble. All these ruins, these streets, will have to be blessed later on, to chase away the stench and the demonic spirits that might still be roaming around. God, who has been fighting evil since the dawn of time, knows we're on his side. Sodom and Gomorrah have been destroyed, and Paris—overrun by possessed souls, contaminated by orgies and drunkenness—might be, as well, if necessary."

Caroline listened to his voice, low and droning, almost a growl, from the state of half sleep into which she had fallen, struggling to wake herself up by moving her legs and pinching her cheeks. When she saw him turn back toward her, undoing his belt, she thought she would never have the strength to fight him off. The knife was so close but seemed impossible to reach beneath the mattress.

The first blow struck her at the top of her thighs, the second in her gut. She curled into the fetal position, shielding her head and face with the pillow. The man panted above her, hitting her mercilessly. Her back, her legs, her arms burned with pain. She bit back her cries to keep from exciting him even more, but when his belt buckle lashed against her ribs she groaned, begging him to stop, and he threw himself on her, his body heavy on hers, forcing her to uncurl from the compact ball she'd made of herself, holding her down with his arms and legs. She felt his moist lips sucking her skin, his tongue licking her back, her neck, and terror ripped through her because he was like an animal mounting her. When he bit her, when she felt his teeth sinking into her shoulder, tearing her flesh, she flung her arms and legs out suddenly, like a big living spring, and he rolled off of her, disoriented.

She saw his half-open mouth, trickling blood, and his face. Expressionless. Staring at her imperturbably. She knew he was preparing to attack her again, and that he was taking his time, savoring the moment.

She let her arm hang over the side of the bed and found the knife, making sure her grip on the handle was sure, and she buried the blade in the man's throat. He fell into the narrow space between the bed and the wall and, struggling to his feet, wrenched the knife out, threw it across the room, and pressed his hands to the wound, blood streaming between his fingers. He took a few steps toward the window, his mouth open wide as if he had a sudden need for some fresh air, and then he fell to his hands and knees before sprawling heavily on his side. Caroline sat, watching his shoulders heave three times, four, and then grow still. She jumped when the man's legs suddenly tensed convulsively, afraid he would get up and come at her again with his torn, gaping throat, his mouth full of blood like a vampire, and devour her alive—but he didn't move again after that, and she sat for a long moment, not daring to stand up in front of this corpse with its back to her.

The sound of orders being barked in the courtyard outside startled Caroline out of her daze, and she got to her feet, slipping on her blouse and buttoning it up to her neck, and went to the table where the brothers had arranged their delicacies. She opened the packet of wafers and gobbled two of them at once, chewing them with her face turned to the sunny window, to the blue sky with its long streaks of black smoke, her eyes full of tears. She ate two more of the sweet cookies and drank the rest of the wine straight from the bottle, and then devoured two pieces of soft caramel that stuck to her teeth, remembering that day at the village fair when she was a little girl, when her mother had bought her the same sweets from a vendor's cart.

Caroline turned over the body of the captain's brother with her foot, being careful not to step in the blood pooling around him like a crimson cloak. His eyes were wide open and staring. He'd wanted to believe, maybe, that the light from the window would keep him alive while he waited for the bleeding to stop. She opened the window and leaned out, clinging to the guardrail as a sudden wave of dizziness threatened to send her toppling into the void. The effort reignited the pain in her shoulder, where that cannibal had bitten her. The sun was already low, its rays bathing the rooftops, gleaming golden between the chimneys. She didn't see anyone. She could hear men's voices, talking loudly, but the words were indistinct and muffled though clearly angry, as if arguing.

A gutter ran the length of the rooftop, under the eaves. A short roofer's ladder hung a bit farther away, perhaps three meters from her. She looked down again. The dizziness had passed. She turned back into the room and began undoing the dead man's trousers, managing to slide them out from beneath the corpse without too much difficulty and then pulling them off completely. She thrust her own legs into them, relieved that the dead man hadn't pissed himself as he was dying. They were far too big for her, of course, so she looked around for the belt he had used to beat her and found it draped across the foot of the bed. She pulled it as tight as she could and buckled it, then rolled up the trouser cuffs. Then she put on the jacket; it was lined with silk, and the softness surprised her. The jacket's tails thudded heavily against her thighs, and she wished she could see herself in a mirror dressed this way. Since her feet were bare, she took the socks, as well, the socks that had belonged to the man named Martin, whom she was glad to have killed. Seeing him dead, knowing that she'd had the strength and the self-possession to bury that knife in his neck to save her own life, restored her trust in herself, and she felt brave, full of courage.

She climbed over the railing of the little balcony, and her legs began trembling as soon as her feet touched the gutter, which sagged slightly beneath her weight. She pressed herself against the slope of the roof, still scalding hot from that day's sun, and took little sliding steps, inch by inch. She wanted to look down, to make sure there was no soldier aiming his rifle at her. Her breath caught in her throat at the idea of a bullet hitting her in the back like a hammer blow and sending her hurtling four floors down, her body racked with agony before smashing and breaking on the ground below. She made sure she had a firm grip on the first rung of the ladder and then climbed the four remaining rungs slowly, her arms suddenly weak, terrified that the whole thing might break loose.

When she reached the wide, flat ledge, she rested for a moment, lying on her belly, catching her breath and trying to calm the furious pounding of her heart. Then she got to her feet and looked at the soot-blackened chaos of the Paris rooftops stretching away into the distance all around her, full of hidden chasms and netherworlds, and she felt like a shipwreck survivor in the middle of an ocean of iron and stone veiled with dark plumes of smoke, their bellies flame-red. It was a world in the process of sinking, perhaps, of devouring itself, to end in charred nothingness. Snippets of ideas came to her, visions, or sensations, rather, but she couldn't force her mind to consider what her next move should be. She simply felt compelled to keep moving, like an animal in flight, instinctively grasping at each moment what must be done in order to stay alive just a little longer.

She walked for a moment along the rooftops in the twilight, her legs trembling. The sheets of zinc squeaked beneath her feet, giving way a bit here and there, and she felt as if they were concealing traps, pits, sinkholes into which she might tumble. Eventually she came upon a half-open trapdoor leading to an attic. Forcing the hatch up, she clung to the edge for a moment and then let herself drop into the dimness below.

Thick, choking dust billowed up around her when she landed, and she coughed, flailing to free herself from the cobwebs that drifted down on top of her. She shook herself and tossed her hair, revolted by the feeling of the wispy, filmy strands sticking to her face and fingers. Brushing the last of the dust off the men's clothing she wore, she turned in the darkening attic and let out an involuntary shriek at the sight of a man standing against the wall, a broad-brimmed peasant's hat on his head, looking at her. She groped in her pockets for the knife that wasn't there and shuddered, remembering the captain's brother wrenching the blade out of his neck. So she clenched her fists, noting the location of the attic door, and inched slowly toward the figure—and then felt a fierce urge to slap herself, because the human shape rising up from behind a packing case was only a mannequin, its features smooth and its eyes blank and empty, terrifying as those of a dead man. Caroline rubbed her eyes, which were filled with dirty tears because of all the dust, and looked more closely.

It was dressed in a sailor's jacket and corduroy trousers patched at the knees, clogs on its feet and a broad-brimmed gray canvas hat on its head. She couldn't tell whether the face was supposed to be male or female. In the thickening twilight, its utter stillness and those eyes, rolling upward, were disquieting.

She turned away from it and looked around at the rest of the room, cluttered with the bric-a-brac typical of these kinds of places: an armoire, three wooden trunks with rusted locks, a few chairs, a large suitcase with a saber hung from it. She remembered the chateau just outside her village, abandoned for years; her older brother Milou had found a way inside. Most of the enormous rooms had been freezing cold and empty, damp and decrepit, but the attic had been a place full of strange wonders they'd spent weeks exploring. They'd forced open doors and broken locks and opened trunks that creaked and exhaled heavy, perfumed scents, sometimes mingled with other smells that had momentarily driven them back from their Pandora's box like a slap in the face, slightly nauseated but impatient, unsure of what to do—before the temptation became too great and they launched themselves eagerly at their dusty, withered treasures.

The door squealed on its hinges and opened to reveal a wooden staircase descending toward a landing bathed in bluish light. She listened, didn't hear any noise. She crept down the stairs and stopped again, straining her ears into the silence for the sound of someone breathing, the slightest creak that might signal an ambush. She pushed open the door of an apartment full of shadows and felt reassured by the darkness inside. She had emerged from a tomb that seemed to have no way out, no end to its depths. The blackness in that place had been absolute, and yet she had come back from it, as if from among the dead. She felt powerful. Invulnerable, even. She walked past the furniture, relying on the dim light that filtered through the blinds. The shapes of armchairs and sofas were distinguishable beneath the sheets covering them; mirrors reflected occasional glints of light like the eyes of animals following her through a dark forest. She explored all of the rooms and found a large kitchen knife, which she clutched tightly.

Finally she fell onto a bed and slept, the knife under the pillow, her hand resting on top.

Cries out in the street awaken her. She sits up, her knife in her hand, her breath short. She goes to a window and opens it a crack. The sound of footsteps. People running. Then two men speaking beneath the window, breathless. "Too bad," says one of them. "He won't get far." They walk away. Caroline peeks through the slats of the shutters. The dark sky is tinged with a reddish glow. She feels a slight, cool breeze on her face. She'll have to get moving before dawn breaks completely.

She crosses the courtyard of the building at a run, her stockinged feet noiseless on the ground. The double doors groan open, revealing the empty street. Off to her right, above the rooftops, the sky is glowing like a forge. The Rue de Rennes is in flames. She turns her back to the inferno and sets off, coming out on the Rue de Sèvres just across from the Hospice des Incurables. The sidewalks are full of sleeping soldiers. The path is crammed with wagons, their harnessed horses asleep with their noses in their feed buckets full of oats. Here and there, men sit unmoving around small fires, their huddled outlines making them look like boulders that have rolled to these positions. She freezes, taking careful note of every movement in the darkness. She doesn't see any sentries, so she darts between two wagons, glances around one more time, and crosses the street. The hospital entrance is unguarded. She moves into an immense courtyard where several coaches are stopped around a garden whose geometric design she can barely make out. Lanterns hang, swaying, in the archways. She retraces her steps and goes down a small corridor to the left, its stone floor gleaming faintly in the lamplight. A wide staircase rises up in front of her. She has started up the steps, her head down to see where she's going in the dimness, when a low voice makes her jump.

"What are you doing here?"

A nun is waiting at the top of the stairs, her hands on her hips. She is so thin beneath the enormous wimple on her head that it looks as if she's about to be carried away by some huge bird of prey.

Caroline climbs a few more steps, and the husky voice stops her again. "What do you want? Answer me, or I'm calling the guard."

Caroline can see the bony face better now, creased with wrinkles, the dull eyes sunken deep in their sockets. She tries to think of something to tell the woman so she'll allow her to come the rest of the way up the stairs because she's had an idea.

"I'm looking for General MacMahon."

She giggles, then forces herself to laugh loudly.

"Yes! General MacMahon, the savior of Paris, and of all respectable people!"

She laughs more loudly still, clutching her stomach.

"Come," says the old nun. "I'll take you to him. Come on, child."

Caroline walks the rest of the way up the stairs, giggling her thanks in a little-girl voice. When she is finally standing face-to-face with the woman and gets a clear look at her face, her heart stops for an instant and she can't breathe. Her eyes are not eyes, but a roving beast that has made its nest in her skull and is pressing against the eye sockets, a viscous liquid without the slightest light, absorbing the darkness and spitting nothingness back out. It's hollow, seemingly vacant, and yet it shifts liquidly like a poisoned pool.

"General MacMahon is here?" asks Caroline, twisting her mouth into an idiotic, demented grimace. "Because I have important things to tell him."

Deep in those hollow eyes, something flares to life. The wrinkled lips open to reveal toothless gums.

"Of course he's here, my girl. I will take you to him. Follow me."

The old woman sets off down the corridor ahead of Caroline, the hem of her gown brushing the floor at each step, her wimple flapping around her like a large set of wings. A door opens suddenly, and a soldier steps out, bareheaded, a pipe in his mouth. He greets the nun and goes on his way. Another corridor and then two doors, which the nun locks behind her with a set of keys she has pulled from some fold in her robes and which dangle, clinking, from her fingertips.

Caroline can't breathe. She forces out a few more mad-sounding chuckles to keep the woman from getting suspicious, but she almost can't muster the breath to do it. Lamps cast yellowish haloes on the walls. The frail silhouette ahead of her seems to fade in and out of the blackness. When she emerges back into the pale light of a lamp, Caroline shoves her in the back and seizes her head in both hands and knocks it against a wall twice. The old woman struggles weakly, her fingers clinging to Caroline like dead branches, and then lets go. Caroline lets her sag to the floor and then starts stripping off her clothing.

The acrid odor of sweat and old piss assails her nostrils, fusty smells rising from the limp body. Caroline peels off her jacket and slips on the robe. She feels as if the stink of it is soiling her even through the shirt and trousers she wears. It reminds her of the goat enclosure at the market where she used to linger, fascinated by the vertical pupils of the animals and the way their yellow eyes seemed to stare back at her through the bars.

She wipes the inside of the wimple, afraid of catching head lice, then puts it on her head, securing it as well as she can. She wonders what she must look like in this ugly, ridiculous outfit, but the old woman, half-bald, wispy strands of whitish hair sticking to her scalp, has begun to move, moaning like an ancient mummy brought back to life after centuries in the tomb. Caroline drags her toward a narrow door that opens into a closet and stretches her out in the back of it between two piles of dirty laundry. She takes the ring of keys and reopens the doors she heard being locked behind her only moments ago, like those of a prison. She goes back down to the court-yard just as two wagons arrive, wounded patients being carried out of them on stretchers. Two more nuns hurry toward the new arrivals, lanterns in hand, and Caroline goes along with them. There are four infantrymen, all of them in bad shape, groaning and writhing. One of them is holding a large wound in his torso closed with his hands; another, an officer, lifts an arm that ends in nothing more than tattered flesh and bone. "Poor child," murmurs one of the nuns.

The soldiers accompanying the wounded have taken off their jackets and rolled up their shirtsleeves, their forearms covered in blood. Without their military caps, they look like butchers who have wandered away from their counters. They carry the stretchers into a room already filled with around thirty men lying on mattresses on the floor. Caroline smells again the odor of bloody, dirty bodies mingled with the scent of bleach. The other stink of war.

She cleans wounds and bandages limbs. In the dim light, no one notices her or wonders at this new face. It's as if her dis-guise has absorbed her identity, as if it has melted and blurred into the noise of groaning and murmuring. A doctor makes his entrance, disheveled and grumpy. He examines the four wounded men, declaring two of them past hope with a careless wave of his hand. The two nuns accompanying him on his rounds cross themselves and gesture to the stretcher-bearers to take them somewhere else.

Caroline doesn't see the sun rise. She realizes suddenly that the bombardment has started up again, and she steps out of the room for a moment to breathe a bit of fresh air and stretch her legs, wondering when they'll find the old lady she knocked out. Behind her, the stretcher-bearers are preparing to set off again. She hears them say that the day promises to be terrible because the villains they're up against don't lack guts, fighting tooth and nail one against twenty, angry as dogs that must be pitilessly put down. "Do your duty without weakness," says a nun. "For God and the Holy Church."

Caroline turns around to watch the soldiers maneuvering the wagons out of the courtyard. She goes back into the sick-room and spies a half-open satchel next to a sink. It turns out to contain a scalpel, a pair of scissors, and some clean linen bandages. There are implements for sewing up a wound, as well, so she puts everything back inside, closes the satchel, hefts it to her shoulder. She steps out into the corridor again and hurries toward the exit. "Sister! Sister? Where are you going?"

She hunches her shoulders. It feels as if her poorly secured wimple is about to slip backward. Her heart pounds at the base of her throat. She tries to focus on walking very straight, without bending or weakening. She saw a tightrope walker cross a wire stretched across a square once, always on the verge of falling, endlessly losing his balance and finding it again. She is walking a tightrope of her own now. She couldn't be any more terrified if she were walking on the endless edge of a razor blade. She can hear shouts from upstairs, the sound of hurrying footsteps. "Help, someone! Hurry!"

"Sister?"

People are coming after her. Large strides. The sound of hems brushing the ground.

424 · HERVÉ LE CORRE

Reaching the street, she breaks into a run. Soldiers are stowing their sleeping gear, packing their sacks, hurrying to carts and wagons. One company is already on the march, led by two officers on horseback. A few infantrymen call out to Caroline, inviting her to have a coffee with them, chiding her for being in too much of a hurry, or too pretty beneath her flapping-wings headgear. She shakes her head and tries to look prim as she weaves through the groups of men. "Sister, I have an injury I need to show you! It's swelling up!" Raucous laughter follows her until she turns down the Rue du Bac, which is lined with wagons guarded by sentries chatting with the women who have come down from their apartments to offer them coffee and cookies. Some of the blinds open, and figures lean out carefully and scan the street, then close their windows again when others come to elbow for space and watch the show.

At every intersection, Caroline must pass guard posts or barricades often manned by policemen. The locals come out to talk to them, bringing them food and congratulating the army on its operations. A few tricolored flags are hanging from balconies, stores are reopening, and people stroll at a leisurely pace on the sidewalks. Caroline explains at each checkpoint that she has been sent to bring comfort to the brave troops fighting on behalf of God. She opens the satchel and shows the guards its contents, saying that it's an emergency, that the wounded are waiting for her. The sentries shrug their shoulders and let her pass, almost hustling her along. It wouldn't take much for them to send her straight to the devil.

On the corner of the Rue de Grenelle, atop the still smoking ruins of a barricade, she approaches a group of people who have gathered in front of the bullet-riddled, smoke-blackened shop front of a wine merchant. Twenty onlookers stand in a circle around four or five bodies lying on the ground. From closer up, it's clear that there are five of them. Federates. She wants to examine all the faces, to be certain, but only two are visible. Nicolas. She doesn't know how long it's been since she stopped thinking of him. She tries to conjure the image of his face in her mind, but she can only make out a smile, a silhouette seen from the back, walking away. This strikes her as a bad omen, and her chest constricts as she's seized by a sudden urge to cry.

A man uses his foot to lift a corpse's arm, lying on its chest, and the limb breaks off and falls to the ground. A woman lets out a little shriek and leaps backward. "Don't be afraid, dear madam. It's as dead as its owner. And that dirty hand won't be soiling anyone else's virtue!" The people laugh. A man in a top hat and pince-nez with the appearance of an academic or a professor at the Sorbonne points with the steel tip of his cane at the brains spilling out of one cadaver's skull. "There's one who didn't have much in his head . . . no surprise he acted like a beast." Murmurs of agreement. A few people chuckle as they lean over the hideous wound. Monsieur has a way with words. Caroline makes her way to the front of the crowd, facing the bodies. The man in the pince-nez turns to her and doffs his hat.

"Too late for extreme unction, sister, though I don't see the point of commending the souls of these miscreants into God's care."

"Do you even think they had souls?" asks another man in a royal blue cravat, nudging the body of a very young man with his foot. "Or simply that bilge leaking out of his head like fromage frais?"

The two men bow to each other like fencers after a match and then shake hands, laughing.

"Ah! How good it is to see life starting up again after these weeks of terror!" says the man in the blue cravat.

"I'll say!" exclaims a large, elegantly dressed woman. "All these layabouts with their caps pulled down over their eyes and their brutish faces and vicious expressions! I didn't dare even leave the house anymore!"

Caroline walks away. Two artillery wagons pass her. The soldiers sitting in the backs of them on ammunition crates gaze at her drearily, disheveled, jolting with every rut in the street. Sporadic cracks of gunfire sound in the distance. Up ahead, toward the Seine, thick smoke from a blazing fire completely blocks the view. The Rue de Lille is on fire. Above the rooftops, the sky has disappeared behind a veil of black clouds. During a brief glimmer of sunlight, Caroline sees a column of infantrymen, maybe a hundred of them, waiting with their rifles shouldered. Three officers on horseback speak to each other, gesturing enthusiastically, as they watch the fire. There are two explosions. Shouts of joy rise from the cluster of troops. A building rumbles as it collapses.

Another barricade forces Caroline to turn down the Rue de Verneuil. Two columns of soldiers making their way along the sidewalks are obliged to scale the massive rubble heap that is all that remains of a ruined building. She follows them over the mountain of broken furniture and shredded paintings still attached to sections of walls. A portrait of a beautiful woman, a bouquet of tulips in her hand. A pendulum suspended in the void, hanging by its spring. Shards of dishes that crunch beneath Caroline's feet. A cast-iron stove standing perfectly upright atop a chest of drawers. She clambers down the other side of the pile, assisted by a soldier who waves to get her attention and holds out his hand. As she passes a gutted storefront, someone calls out to her from inside. A corporal takes her by the arm. "Your timing is perfect. We need you."

A dozen men are lying on the floor. Two soldiers in shirtsleeves come and go among them, leaning over one, comforting another in murmurs. Their wounds have been bandaged with strips torn from shirts and dirty rags. One of them is breathing through a piece of bloody linen laid over his face. When Caroline lifts away the cloth she notices his teeth first, and his tongue, moving in his mouth. She can't quite comprehend what she's seeing. A large part of his face has been torn away. One of his eyes has been crushed into bloody gelatin. The man grips her hand.

"Well?"

The voice from above her makes her jump. The corporal squats down next to her and sighs.

"You see what these barbarians are capable of."

Caroline tries to regain her breath to answer. She just encountered the barbarians ten minutes ago on a street corner, making fun of the dead. She saw them clustered around a group of corpses like crows on carrion. Joking. Cawing.

"He'll need a surgeon," she says. "I can't stitch up what isn't there anymore."

She stands up and looks around at this aid station that has been set up among the scattered shoes and spools of thread and sheets of leather in this cobbler's shop. The corporal leads her to a lieutenant whose thigh has been gashed open to the bone by an exploding artillery shell. Grimacing and pale, the officer thanks her for coming. She wipes the wound with a bit of bleach, explaining that she will have to sew it up. The man visibly gathers his courage, stands up against the wall he's leaning on, closes his eyes, grits his teeth.

Caroline tries to remember what Doctor Fontaine always said, that this was a way for her, as a dressmaker, to keep up her professional skills. She has sewn up wounds at least a dozen times now, but she's never quite managed to think of human flesh as just another kind of fabric.

The man starts to groan at the first prick of the needle. The corporal gives him a rag to bite on.

"Just think of those bastards, Lieutenant. Of all the ones we've crossed off the lists already. In three days you'll be back out there, putting those sons of bitches to the sword again."

Caroline pauses to wipe her forehead on her sleeve. She

doesn't know how she's resisting the temptation to plunge her needle deep into this Versaillais haunch of meat, to make this gunman howl like an animal. She finishes the suture and stands up. The lieutenant thanks her again, sweat pouring down his face, and asks, when the corporal has walked away:

"Is it your religious order that makes you wear trousers?"

He lifts a hand to his holster and then lets it drop again.

"What does it matter, after all . . . the corporal doesn't realize that in three days, four at the very most, all of this will be over. We'll have gotten rid of every one of these fanatics. I might be lucky enough to take part in the great street-by-street, house-by-house extermination of the filth. I suppose you're one of them?"

Caroline kisses the wooden cross hanging around her neck and makes a brief curtsey before moving on to tend the other injured men. For perhaps an hour she bandages wounds, murmuring a few words of comfort to the worst cases, the ones who ask her if God will really be waiting for them in heaven. She expects to hear the lieutenant's voice ordering her arrest at any moment and doesn't dare look at him.

When she leaves the shop, she hears him say:

"Good day to you, sister! My best to your sans-culottes!"

She hurries down the sidewalk. The street is crowded with soldiers and stopped wagons. She reaches the quayside, where the wind blowing over the Seine is laden with smoke. Whole companies are marching toward the Latin Quarter. It feels as if the ground beneath her feet is quivering under the thud of boot treads and the rattling of cart wheels. The barricades defending the bridges have all been destroyed; sparks are still crackling along the shattered carts' wooden shafts and leaping behind the wrenched-off doors of broken furniture piled atop the cobblestone heaps. There are bodies lying on the ground here and there, and even on the demolished barricades themselves, arms flung wide, chests caved in.

The Pont du Carrousel is unguarded on this side of the river, so Caroline starts across it, feigning a limp. On the other side, around twenty soldiers are manning a still-standing barricade, undoubtedly abandoned by the Federates. A sub-officer approaches her, his rifle on his shoulder. He asks her where she's going, and she says that she has to go see her mother, who is very ill. She arrived this evening with the troops, and Colonel Ferrandeau has granted her a few hours' leave. She invents the name on the spot, telling herself that there's no way the strapping fellow now facing her can be familiar with every single colonel in the Versaillais army. He asks to see what she's carrying in her satchel, then orders his men to let her pass.

She walks away with twenty mistrustful gazes boring into her back, exhausted, perhaps, or simply indifferent, watching this petite nun limp away beneath her wimple. Reaching the opposite bank, she passes the still-smoking Tuileries, flames still leaping in some of the gaping windows. It is broad daylight, and yet Paris is in shadow, as if night might fall at any moment. Everywhere there are fires giving off plumes of black smoke as thick as pitch. The streets are empty. A few figures huddle behind the barricades. She looks up at the windows and sees the occasional curtain twitching. Reaching the Place du Châtelet, she pauses, breathless.

This part of the city is caught between two battlefronts: behind her toward the Latin Quarter, and to her left toward La Madeleine. She wants to scream, to weep, to roar in anger and sorrow, but she doesn't feel strong enough to do any of those things, and it would be pointless anyway. The smell of burnt fat and old piss rising from her robe makes her gag, so she shoves open a door and pulls off the outer layer of her clothing and throws the putrid rags as far away from herself as she can, and immediately she feels lighter, cleaner. The wooden cross bounces on the stone floor of the corridor, and she is seized with the urge to smash it, but the sound of a bugle close by draws her back outside. Fifty men and women have just passed the Tour Saint-Jacques at a run, armed civilians and national guardsmen, followed by a mitrailleuse being pulled by a mule.

She runs after them and catches up with them on the Avenue Victoria. A barricade erected in front of the Hôtel de Ville brings them up short. With ten rifles pointed at him, a small man explains that this gun is needed at the Rue Beaubourg, that it alone might almost have the power to break the Versaillais offensive. He waves his arms, his gesticulations growing ever broader and more dramatic, seizing great armfuls of air and then clutching theatrically at his chest, fists closed, almost begging, and the men standing on the barricade listen to him silently, their expressions inflexible or dubious, some of them nodding, some shrugging. They've probably heard this kind of thing from others, too, the same sort of claptrap, promises of radiant tomorrows and victory from the barrel of a gun, exhortations of courage and sacrifice.

Suddenly a window explodes behind them, and then another, and everyone watches the flames leap and dance across the elegant façade, and they all cry out with surprise and rage, some of them burying their faces in their hands, their shoulders shaking with sobs, while others disperse, some even abandoning their rifles and shrugging off their bullet pouches.

Caroline has cried out, too, and now she stands and watches the headquarters of the Central Committee of the Commune burn, watches all of their mad hope rise in smoke and flame above the tiled rooftops and disappear, hundreds of sheets of paper drifting from the gaping, blown-out windows, undoubtedly containing future plans for the city, heroic proclamations calling for the old world to be brought down and the pages of the bad days to be torn out of the calendar, perhaps to be replaced by new names like in the past. She watches, choked by bitter grief, as her youth and all her desires are consumed, the pleasures that have illuminated her nights reduced to mere ashes.

The little man who was arguing for their passage at the barricade now steps forward with the twenty or so women and national guardsmen remaining after the others have dispersed. The Federate sentries let them pass with their mitrailleuse. Caroline walks behind the heavy gun, keeping her eyes on it. They can still bring down some of these butchers before they're killed themselves. Her steps are quick and firm. A little girl takes her hand, almost skipping beside her, looks up at her with large, smiling blue eyes, and asks her why she's crying.

28

All night, those who weren't sleeping had watched the city burn, the sky reflecting the funereal light from the fires back onto their faces. At around midnight, the bombardment had ceased near the Rue de Lille and the Gare d'Orsay, and then the fires had set in, gorging on everything that fell between their crimson-toothed jaws.

Those who managed to fall asleep grunted and tossed uneasily beneath their blankets and opened their eyes wide in the darkness without really seeing anything, then sank back into the bad dream that had awakened them.

In the mild early morning, everyone smelled of sweat and yearned to rinse their mouths and spit out the foul-smelling residue of tobacco and wine. Provisioners brought buckets of water, and they rushed over for a swallow, pushing and shoving one another, almost fighting to fill their tin flasks, drink, and wash their faces. Water was given to the injured, who hung back on the edges of the melee without daring to stick their crutches in, and everyone eventually shared as friends once their throats had been moistened a bit.

Now the morning's repast arrives under escort. A baker on the Rue Laplace has managed to produce a batch of bread, the last one. There's no more flour. The two hansom cabs full of bread have had to be protected from attack by furious citizens claiming that they had more right to it than all those lowlifes getting drunk on the barricades.

The warm crust crackles between Nicolas's fingers. He chews

slowly, letting the taste fill his mouth, and he closes his eyes to enjoy the flood of happy images crowding his mind. He was on watch from three o'clock to sunrise, and now he should be asleep, but exhaustion has made his body tense up and quiver like a cable about to snap. Next to him, Red is savoring the bread, as well, grimacing at each stab of pain in his leg. The aid station on the boulevard was evacuated during the night. Yesterday evening, at the Pantheon, a nurse had sniffed at the wound and put his bandage back on. "It's all right for now. But I'm out of clean linen. You should get yourself to the Boulevard de Sébastopol; there are people there who can look after you. We're waiting on a coach to get us out of here; there's no use in staying. There's nobody left at the Rue Saint-Jacques, or even at the École de Médecine. Come with us; we'll make room for you."

Red had declined. "I'll be all right," he said. "And if we all leave, there'll be no one left on the barricades." The nurse had looked at him in surprise. "What are you planning to do on the barricade with that bum leg of yours? If it starts bleeding again, or gets infected, you'll only be a burden. And between us, one man, more or less, isn't going to change a thing. We'd need whole regiments."

Nicolas was going to say something to convince Red to go, but his friend had walked away, limping slightly, forcing his back to stay very straight, his cap set crookedly on the bandage wrapped around his head.

They finish their bread and drain a flask of water, smacking their lips as if it were fine wine. Nicolas gestures at Red's leg.

"Does it hurt much? What have you done with your crutch?"

Red clutches his knee and shakes his head.

"Dunno . . . I'm all right. Just hurts because it's scarring over, that's all."

"You should have left last night with that wagon they were expecting. You'd be getting treated now."

"Sure. Hide myself away like all those idiots and cowards who abandon their post as soon as it gets a bit tough. What the hell are they doing to do, each of them behind his own little barricade, guarding his own corner of the street? What good is that? It's here we need to wait for them, the infantrymen, before they waltz in. We can buy time for our comrades farther down the line to organize a real defense, get back on their feet."

Two artillery shells explode in the Luxembourg Gardens, throwing up a vast plume of smoke and leaves. Another shell falls near the Senate.

"Look, Montmartre is wishing us good morning," Nicolas says. "Can you believe this? We could have held off the Versaillais forces with our fire, and yet they're shelling us! The ones in command there should be shot, the ones who've done fuck all."

"Yeah, I call that traitorous. But it boils down to the same thing. Have to line them up against the wall."

Nicolas gets up and holds out a hand to Red, who doesn't refuse it. They walk to the barricade on the Rue Soufflot. Red is still limping slightly and ends up leaning on Nicolas's shoulder. They find about fifteen Federates busily cleaning rifles, seated on ammunition crates and chairs taken from some café. A pot of coffee sits in the middle of the circle on a round, marble-topped table.

"Is it hot?" asks Red, reaching for the pot.

"Help yourself, Citizen. Someone's gone for another. There's a woman in the church over there who makes a hell of a pot of coffee."

"Hell, eh?" remarks an old man with a full beard. "That's fitting, considering what we've got in store for us!"

They all laugh without taking their eyes off their work.

The coffee is good. Red and Nicolas sit down and apply themselves to the task, wiping the rifles clean of the residue of

mingled grease and burnt paper left by the cartridges, swab-
bing the barrels, making sure the firing pins haven't broken.
Fifty rifles are already stacked against a wall, clean and ready
for combat.

The old man with the beard, who has gotten up to add
another to the stack, points at the rifles, counting each of them
in turn.

"We'll end up with more rifles than men, if this keeps up,"
he says.

No one answers. Doubtless because they all know he's
right.

"Look, there's the top brass," he says.

The men look up. Some of them get to their feet.

A group of around ten officers, surrounded by a few escort
guards, have stopped at the corner of the boulevard and are
looking at the Pantheon, gesturing broadly. They're speaking
loudly, but no one can make out what they're saying.

"That's Maxime Lisbonne," the old man says. "We'd do
well to listen to what he's saying. He's no windbag, that one.
Ah! And I see Citizen Allemane, too."

He sets off, a rifle on his shoulder, limping slightly. Nicolas
goes after him.

"Do you know all those officers?"

"Hell, no. But those two fellows are famous. If the
Commune had been led by more men like that, we wouldn't be
in this mess today."

"I was at the Rue Vavin, but we didn't have a chance to see
Lisbonne."

"They had to evacuate last night. Same thing at the Croix-
Rouge. Things are falling apart everywhere."

Other men are approaching the group of officers.

"We must withdraw," Lisbonne is saying. "Gather our
troops on the Right Bank, where we still have a solid foothold.
We'll take all the ammunition and artillery we can carry. We

can get omnibuses to transport it all. Better to organize a with-drawal in good order than beat a retreat under fire with no plan, leaving our weapons and munitions. If we start now, we can be on the other side of the Seine by late morning. The men are demoralized; they're abandoning their posts, and we can't do a thing to stop them!"

Allemane shakes his head. He stares at the ground, scuffing the toe of his boot in the dirt. The area around the Pantheon has been turned into a stronghold, he says. There are barri-cades everywhere that can still resist, giving the Central Committee time to gather reinforcements. He mentions La Butte-aux-Cailles, held by Wroblewski. More than a thousand men and artillery that will be on the way here by tomorrow.

Lisbonne shrugs.

"It's hopeless here, Jean. They're five hundred meters away at most, and there are ten thousand of them, if not more! They'll raze the Latin Quarter to the ground if they have to, they'll destroy the Sorbonne, they'll . . ."

A cavalryman leaps off his horse and bursts into the middle of the group, panting for breath and lifting a hand vaguely in the direction of his cap in a hasty salute.

"The Central Committee is evacuating the Hôtel de Ville as we speak. They're withdrawing to the town hall of the 11th. They're ordering all battalions to follow them."

"Why the 11th? It's here that things are happening!"

Lisbonne strokes his mustache with his thumb and index finger.

"My decision is made. I'm leaving this afternoon with my men."

A loud hum makes them all drop to the ground in a single movement. The shell explodes in front of the Pantheon. And then another. The Rue Soufflot is full of crouching bodies all the way to the square, crawling to huddle at the feet of the buildings.

Nicolas hurries toward the barricade, followed by the old man with the beard, who shouts that this is the end, and that they won't take him alive. The guards have taken up their rifles. They stuff their pockets and pouches with cartridges.

"We have to stay in pairs. One to fire, the other to reload. Take four, because they'll get clogged quickly."

Nicolas imitates them. Red has found an empty bullet pouch and is cramming handfuls of cartridges into it.

"Rue d'Ulm!" Allemane cries.

"Go! We'll stay here. They're already in the Gardens."

A little boy comes running, his legs stick-thin, his bare feet bloody. "There's a column marching up the Rue Racine!" he shouts. "And another on the Rue Monsieur-le-Prince!"

Red runs toward the Pantheon, dragging his foot behind him like a dog caught in trap from which he's trying to struggle free. Nicolas catches up to him, and they turn down the Rue d'Ulm. Citizen Allemane is ahead of them, a rifle in his hand, with five or six men. Farther on, beyond the barricade on the Rue de l'Estrapade, a column of infantrymen is spreading out. There are perhaps a hundred of them. Bullets whistle through the air and strike sparks as they crunch against the pavement. They run. The barricade is defended by five men. Across from it, the soldiers continue their progress along the sidewalks. Some others fire from windows. Red fires back, and they hear the sound of glass shattering, then a stifled cry. Red reloads. Nicolas sees a spot of blood bloom on his friend's trousers. Red grimaces and shakes his leg, to shake off the pain, maybe.

"Wait," someone says.

Suddenly, the soldiers throw themselves to the ground on their bellies in the middle of the street and open fire. A sharp rattling sound echoes off the heaped cobblestones, and bullets rebound to strike the façades of the buildings, leaving white gashes in the stone like chalk marks.

The barricade opens fire. Three Versaillais soldiers fly into the air, and others roll on the ground, yelling. They retreat, crawling, leaving behind their wounded comrades who thrash and call for help. Nicolas takes aim at a sub-officer who has foolishly stood up to give orders. He pulls the trigger. The man jumps and then abruptly clutches his neck as if he's been stung by a hornet. He whirls around, and the blood flying from his wound looks like a scarf around his neck for a moment, then he drops to his knees. Another bullet hits him in the back, and he falls facedown on the ground. The others scuttle to safety in the Charité convent.

"Finished him off for you. He won't bother anyone again," Red says.

He sits down, pressing on his calf to stop the bleeding, breathing heavily, his face gleaming with sweat.

"Fuck, I'm thirsty," he says.

Nicolas asks the others if anyone has a canteen. A comrade passes him a nearly empty one. "That's all I have, my friend." Red drinks greedily and then sinks back against a cart wheel leaning on the cobblestone wall and closes his eyes.

"How do you feel?"

Red plucks at his jacket, sniffing the collar. "I stink like I'm already dead. What I wouldn't give for a bath." He sits up straighter and reaches for a rifle, reloads it, reaches for another.

"At least I can still do this," he says.

"Here come some more of them. They've got a mitrailleuse."

The immense weapon approaches slowly, its gunners staying hidden behind its shield. The gunshots begin again from the windows. Thirty soldiers emerge from the convent, shooting at the barricade to cover the gunners' maneuvering. And then the firing begins.

Nicolas lets himself drop to the ground. He can hear the humming of the bullets just before they strike. One of the two men hit flies into the air without a cry, as if yanked backward by the material ripping from his skull. The other man stands still at his gun carriage for a moment, his rifle aimed, before falling on his back.

"Retreat! Retreat!" shouts Allemane.

Nicolas helps Red to his feet. A comrade comes to take the rifles and hoists them onto his shoulders. They run as well as they can toward the Pantheon, pursued by a series of detonations. They don't know if it's their own ringing ears whistling and clanging and roaring under the effects of effort and terror or if the air around them is nothing now but a fiery swarm of bullets. They burst into the square at the exact moment an artillery shell explodes on top of the building above them. The blast of hot air, chunks of stone, and dagger-sharp fragments of glass knocks them to the ground, and they struggle forward on hands and knees, unable to see any farther than their own outstretched arms. Nicolas lifts Red by the collar of his jacket, but his friend is too heavy and falls back down on his elbows, panting.

"Leave me here. It's not worth it."

Nicolas grabs him beneath the arms and carries him, clutching him against his body. For a moment they look like a pair of drunken dancers, swaying and ungainly, then Red grips him and manages to drag his own weight. They head for the Rue Soufflot. Federates are firing ceaselessly from the pediment of the Pantheon. There is a moment when a gust of wind thins the smoke and Nicolas sees the Versaillais emerging from the Luxembourg Gardens and fanning out along the boulevard. Two guns are firing shrapnel at the barricade barring the street, manned by a dozen men. Shards of metal and nuts and bolts shriek through the air, shattering windows and pitting stone. Nicolas scans the chaos for the men who were with him on the Rue d'Ulm and doesn't see them in the confusion of men running in all directions. Crossing the Rue Saint-Jacques, he sees another demolished redoubt, five Federates lying on their stomachs amid the tumbled cobblestones, firing and reloading and firing again. He turns down another street—he can't tell which one it is; he only knows that it goes down toward the Boulevard Saint-Germain. He only knows that, here, the clamor of the battle is somewhat quieter and that the relative calm makes him feel a bit stronger. He holds Red's arm firmly across his shoulders, his friend hopping on his good leg, and he wonders how long he can go on before he falls down and doesn't get up again. "Leave me here," Red says again. "Save yourself. It's over for me. I won't go much farther."

Nicolas leans against a wall so as not to collapse. He can't see anything anymore. It feels like his eyes are exploding from the blinding light, are tinged with red, maybe bleeding. He starts when he sees, through the painful glare, the face of a woman emerging from the wall and then leaning toward him, holding out a small, thin hand. "Come. Don't stay there."

He doesn't know how he's ended up in this crimson darkness, his arm still around Red's waist. "Come," says the voice again; he can hardly tell where it's coming from, like a quivering phantom in front of him that could dissolve into the blackness at any moment. "It's on the second floor."

Red lets out a groan with each step they climb, his fingers clenching Nicolas's shoulder. Once it even sounds like he's weeping. They reach a landing, the floor creaking beneath them, and that familiar little sound abruptly banishes the violence out in the streets. They enter a dark apartment smelling of wax and old paper. And cake. The old lady helps Red stretch out on a sofa covered with a sheet.

"Madame, no . . . I'm so dirty . . ."

"Be quiet," she says, gently.

Nicolas is afraid to sit down in this elegantly decorated apartment. All the shutters are closed. The fighting a short distance away has taken on the air of carnival noise. Nicolas feels a surge of anger at himself for the thought as soon as he has it. He pictures his comrades under fire. Those who have fallen and those who are still hanging on, despite fear or injury. Mitrailleuse bullets begin buzzing in his head again. He looks around, confused, shouldering his rifle.

"Have you decided to stand guard?" the old lady inquires, smiling.

He babbles an apology, not daring to lay a hand on the gun even to put it down, afraid of frightening her.

"Sit down, then."

She walks out of the room with quick little steps. Nicolas sits down next to Red, who seems to be sleeping. He lays a hand on Red's forehead. It's burning with fever. His leg has stopped bleeding.

"You'll see. It's going to be fine."

Nicolas says the words without really believing them. He knows nothing is going to be fine. The old lady is busy in the next room; he hears silverware clinking, pots and pans clanking. He closes his eyes for a moment and feels sleep settling heavily on him, so he gets up again, pinching his cheeks. *Don't fall asleep.* He doesn't know how many hours he has left before he'll be taken, or killed. Killed. He knows how the Versaillais operate. The talk he's been hearing since yesterday is about nothing but executions. Massacres, rather. Any man stopped in possession of a weapon, or even suspected of having one, is being shot on sight. They say some soldiers are opting to use their bayonets for the job instead, or even the butts of their rifles. Playing with the corpses. And women aren't being spared, either. They don't kill them right away, though. Not in the same way. They kill them twice.

Caroline.

He realizes that he hasn't thought of her since yesterday. He murmurs her name to himself aloud, summoning her image, and he sees her in the middle of a group of soldiers. They're tearing her apart. He opens his eyes to dispel the vision and lets his gaze wander around the furniture-crowded room.

The old lady comes back with a white bowl smelling of bleach, a towel draped on one shoulder and a linen cloth over her forearm, like a waiter in a boulevard café.

Red groans with pain when she takes off his shoe. Then she cuts off his trouser leg with a large pair of scissors, peels off the soiled dressing, and begins to clean his leg, which is black from his toenails to just above his knee. A blackish liquid seeps from the puffed-up wound.

"He's feverish. He needs to stay here and rest."

Red opens his eyes and smiles weakly. He holds a hand out to the woman, who places her own thin, frail one in his dirty palm.

"Gonna have to cut my leg off, aren't they? When it hurts like that it's because it's starting to rot. Gangrene . . ."

His voice chokes slightly. He shakes his head, undoubtedly trying to clear it of the distasteful thought.

"Don't talk nonsense, and kindly stop crushing my fingers."

He opens his big fist sheepishly. The woman's hand flutters out of it like a bird.

"What's your name?"

"Guérin. Marie-Jeanne Guérin."

"Mine's Joseph Favereau. But everyone calls me Red, 'cause of my hair."

"And maybe your ideas, too!" She lets out a small, tinkling laugh, and Red smiles widely as she rebandages his wound.

"And you?" she asks Nicolas, without looking up from her task.

"I'm Nicolas Bellec. We're from the 105th."

"My two sons are in the National Guard, too. The older boy, Louis, is a captain in the 58th. The younger one, Jacques, is a sergeant. They both came to see me the day before yesterday, as a surprise. Oh, they couldn't stay long . . . two hours,

IN THE SHADOW OF THE FIRE · 443

maybe . . . but it did me so much good to have both of them near me. And they aren't so very far away. They're guarding the Hôtel de Ville. For now, anyway, they're not in danger."

She falls silent, drooping slightly in her seat. She wipes her hands on the towel slowly, her head down. She tosses the cloth onto a pedestal table wearily and gazes blankly into the distance.

"I want so much for them to come home. When this is all over. Because it will be finished soon, won't it? And it will end badly, of course."

"We have fought. We are fighting. But soon it'll be a matter of saving our own skins."

"It was so beautiful, though, a true republic . . . My husband and I were always in favor of that. If he were still with us, I think he'd be out there fighting and making me worry about him, too!"

She smiles sadly. Her eyes are bright. In the silence of the room, they listen to the sound of the battle raging outside. Red has fallen asleep. He snores gently.

"You should go," says Marie-Jeanne.

Nicolas looks at Red.

"Leave him here. He won't take another step. He must have lost a lot of blood; he can't lose any more. And I'm afraid gangrene has already set in. Look how black his leg is. And the smell. Don't you smell it?"

No, Nicolas doesn't smell anything. He shakes his head. He rises, takes a few steps, incapable of thought. To go, to leave his friend, his brother, behind. He sniffs the air. There is something sweetish in it, slightly nauseating . . .

"I don't know," he says. "My nose is full of smoke and gunpowder. But—"

"Go on, or you'll both be arrested, and me with you. If they only find Joseph, I'll pretend to be a crazy old woman who let in a madman pounding on her door."

Nicolas approaches the wounded man and takes his hand. Red opens his eyes.

"Don't dawdle. They'll cordon off this whole neighborhood, and it'll be too late."

"I'll come back. I swear."

"On Thiers's head, I bet . . ."

They smile at each other. Nicolas feels Red's hand squeezing his own with unexpected strength.

"You might come back, but I'm not sure I'll still be here."

Red looks steadily into Nicolas's eyes as he says this. He adds, "No matter what, I won't be here."

Nicolas tries to think of what to say. He can't let those words fall into a silence where they will reverberate endlessly.

"You won't be here anymore, but we'll find each other. Life will go on, and we'll make jokes again, and have drinks. You'll see."

Red nods. He lifts a hand to his leg and grits his teeth.

"You'd better go now. You're losing time. Listen, outside. They're winning. They'll be on every street corner by nightfall, and then it'll be an enormous bloodbath."

He closes his eyes and sighs.

"I think I'll sleep a bit. I'd like for it to happen while I'm sleeping."

He withdraws his hand, and Nicolas's own hovers in the air for a moment before he lets it drop back onto the arm of the chair. He hears Madame Guérin's light footsteps approaching behind him. She holds out a pouch.

"You really must go. He's right. I've put something in here for you to eat and drink."

Nicolas takes the pouch and grabs the strap of his rifle. The weapon is hard and heavy against his back. He suddenly doesn't remember what he's supposed to do. He feels as if he can't move, like he's nailed to the floor. Marie-Jeanne smiles at him and then taps him on the arm as if to shake him out of his numb torpor. He goes back to Red and crouches next to him.

"Do you realize how much we've been through together, my brother?"

Red opens his eyes. They're very bright in the dim light. From fatigue, of course. And then there's that leg, being destroyed from the inside out by the progressing disease.

"What we believed in, at any rate . . . We had good times."

Suddenly, his big arm comes out and wraps around Nicolas's neck and pulls him into a tight embrace, and Nicolas feels the heat of the fever and Red's heart pounding, and he kisses Red's stubbly, dirty cheek again and again, and his comrade, his brother, does the same, and they know they're both remembering the same thing, the hugs of childhood, the comforting embraces of a parent when they were upset, the moments when they were strong, invincible, because there could be no danger in the shelter of those arms.

"Go on."

Nicolas stands up. Red closes his eyes again and turns his face to the back of the sofa. When Nicolas pauses next to Madame Guérin to thank her, she caresses his cheek, and he kisses her fragile hand.

"Go, my boy. Save yourself. Save yourself."

The street is full of black smoke. He runs, his rifle held in front of him, toward the sound of gunshots coming from the corner of the Rue des Écoles. A mitrailleuse is being fired, off to the left. A dozen men are crouching behind a pile of sacks of dirt, waiting for the volley to end. Bullets thud into the sacks like punches from a fist. Just behind them, five corpses lie in a row, their hands folded on their chests.

"Where the hell did you come from?"

Nicolas hunkers down beside the man who has just spoken.

"The Place du Pantheon. I don't know where I am anymore."

"Did you come here hoping someone would explain it to you?"

"Hey! Look who's coming to visit!" another fellow cries, reloading his rifle.

Two Federates are running toward them, firing their guns. About thirty Versaillais come swarming around the corner of the Rue Fontanes, shouting joyfully. The Federates take down five or six of them, and that quiets down the others, who drop to the ground and aim their rifles.

Nicolas follows the others, who flee down the Rue Saint-Jacques. On the Boulevard Saint-Germain, three men fall. A group of infantrymen is entrenched behind the barricade just in front of them, guarding the intersection. Nicolas crouches in a doorway and reloads. He spots an officer who is commanding the snipers, saber in hand. He fires, misses, reloads, fires again. The officer spins and vanishes behind the pile of cobblestones.

Nicolas runs, bent double, pursued by gunfire. Bullets thud into the walls above his head like hammer blows. He doesn't know where the others have gone. When he raises his head, he sees Versaillais soldiers pouring down the streets in every direction, stockpiling equipment in the Place Maubert. Someone shouts insults down at him from a balcony and then calls out to the soldiers: "Here's one getting away! Over here!" He crosses the road and plunges into the Rue des Anglais. A volley of rifle shots seems to follow him, echoing in the narrow lane. He runs, trips, straightens up, hears shouts, and sees an entire patrol of soldiers advancing in formation down a street to his right, filling up its entire width. He finds the Federates from earlier on the corner of the Quai Saint-Michel, only six of them now, crouching behind an overturned cart and three barrels that must have rolled there God knows how. The men are reloading their rifles under fire from a group of soldiers standing at the entrance to the Petit Pont.

"Only five cartridges left," one comrade says.

"Same," gasps another. "Better not waste 'em."

"We fire and run," suggests Nicolas. "Otherwise we won't get out of here."

The others look at him, surprised, then nod silently.

"One target per man. Left to right."

For a moment they hold their fire, simply letting the bullets buzz past overhead or thump into the wood of the barrels.

"On my command," says one man.

They get ready, settling themselves as best they can.

"Fire!"

A single, terrible explosion sounds, and the men across the street fly backward and hit the ground.

They cross the quay right under the noses of a fresh column of soldiers arriving at a run. At the entrance to the bridge they jump over dead bodies, shoving aside those who are still alive with their feet and the butts of their rifles, and run, yelling like a band of boys fleeing after having broken a window or swiped some fresh fruit from a shop front. As they head down toward Notre-Dame they stumble, no longer shouting but coughing and gasping as they pass the National Guard barracks, which are still burning, spitting plumes of smoke and showers of sparks as their blackened walls cave in. They make their way onward, doubled over by the blasts of hot air gusting out of broken windows. Nicolas tries to catch his breath and straightens up when he hears three gunshots in succession ring out from the bridge just behind them. A burning pain pierces his shoulder, and he is thrown forward as if he's been punched in the back. The towers of the cathedral seem to turn upside down, the sky whirling above him, cloudy and low, striped with trails of black smoke. He tries to gulp in some air and despairs of ever taking a clean breath again, and then he sees his comrades on the ground around him, flat on their bellies, rolling into position to return fire.

"Don't move," says one of them, a very young man he hasn't noticed before. "We'll get you out of here."

Nicolas realizes he hasn't really looked at their faces. He doesn't know what they look like, these men with the pack nipping at their heels. He realizes that all their faces, including his own, must seem interchangeable. Right now they have almost ceased to be people, really. They're simply big game being tracked, combatants caught short of ammunition, vanquished insurgents. Their loved ones have undoubtedly given them up for dead, are weeping even now at the thought of never seeing them again, carried off in the whirlwind of what will soon be called History.

He wants to lift his head and look more closely at them, these anonymous men who are just like him, but the sky pitches again and nausea grips his stomach, and he feels himself falling into a deep hole as if the ground has suddenly turned into a yawning, bottomless chasm beneath him.

THURSDAY, MAY 25TH

29

Antoine Roques was arrested on the first street corner by the captain with whom he'd been on patrol that very morning. Pointing his revolver at Roques's forehead, the man accused him of espionage and promised rapid punishment. One soldier had stunned him with a blow of his rifle butt; another tried to get him back on his feet with a vicious kick to the ribs. He leaned against the wall to catch his breath, wiping the blood from his forehead with his shirttail. Of the seven or eight men surrounding him, only one had a rifle aimed at him. The others merely sighed or shuffled their feet, impatient, maybe, or just exhausted. One of them shoved him forward, and they walked at an unhurried pace through streets choked with broken glass and slate roof tiles, collapsed chimneys, sheets of paper, clothing, and shoes.

The cavalry barracks on the Rue de Bourgogne had been hit by several artillery shells that destroyed the living quarters but left the stables intact. Roques was thrown into a stall, where he tripped in the darkness over a man who pushed him away with a foot, grumbling. He sat down on the damp floor next to another man whose legs and arms were folded, his head slumped on his chest, apparently asleep. His eyes growing accustomed to the dim light, Roques saw that there were six of them in the stall, including three Federates, one of whom had a bandage wrapped clumsily around his head and eyes, his face covered with blood. He sat very straight, his legs stretched out in front of him, his hands on his thighs.

The man sitting next to the bandaged Federate stared at Roques, his eyes wide and bright in his soot-blackened face.

"You're an infantryman; what the fuck are you doing in here? You mouth off to an officer? Didn't button your spats properly?"

The third Federate, on his other side, elbowed him and muttered at him not to talk to strangers, especially enemy ones. He shrugged and shifted to a more comfortable position, leaning forward.

Roques felt a bolt of pain shoot through his head. He closed his eyes, lifted a hand to touch the still-moist wound with his fingertips, the blood dried in his hair. Each pulsebeat in his arteries threatened to puncture his temples.

"No, I'm not from Versailles. It's just a disguise. My name is Antoine Roques. Delegate to the Sûreté Publique in the 10th arrondissement. I belong to a deskbound company of the 86th."

"You don't say. And of course we're supposed to take your word for that?"

"Do whatever you like. Considering where we all are right now, I couldn't care less."

"I don't much care, either, to tell the truth. Still . . . what were you doing out this way? You're a long way from the 10th."

Roques didn't feel like telling him the whole story, but he would do anything to escape from the dark ideas beginning to swarm into his mind like an insidious infestation and told himself that a bit of conversation might distract him for a few moments.

There was a sudden thump on the side of the stall.

"Shut your mouths in there, or I'll come in and shut them myself with my boot heel!"

The man sitting next to Roques was startled out of his torpor and straightened up a bit.

"The soldier's right," he said. "Some of us would like to get some sleep, believe it or not. I'll need a clear head tomorrow to present my defense in front of the judges. I have nothing to do with the lawlessness and thievery of the past few weeks, nothing in common with any of you. I'm an honest man. I've always respected the law."

The door suddenly flew open, and the guard entered, bellowing, and shoved his bayonet beneath the chin of the man who was just talking.

"You going to shut it, or do I cut out your tongue?"

The self-proclaimed honest man shrank back against the wall. The Federate sitting across from him snickered softly beneath the battered brim of his cap.

Soon enough, all was quiet again. The Federate held his hand out to Roques, murmuring, "Noël Dumartin, 58th battalion."

In the dreary silence that fell again, Antoine Roques tried to force down the terror rising in him. In a day or two he would be dead. That possibility had never really occurred to him before. He'd been afraid over the past several days, but at no point had he been conscious of being on the edge of nothingness, leaping over it with a bound the way you jump over a puddle, without really being aware of the abyss he'd just avoided. Was it really possible that everything was going to end? It was inconceivable, obviously. Even people who believed in a god, who thought they had a place reserved for them in heaven, greeted the sight of approaching Death with horror and prayed for just a little more time on earth, even though they should, by rights, be embarking on this new adventure with curiosity.

He would never see his children again. He would never be able to tell Rose what he couldn't explain to her when she decided to leave Paris and he chose not to go with her. He would have abandoned them all twice. Once by letting them leave without him, and again by dying, shot and tossed into a mass grave.

He pictured his little ones at every age they'd been, remembered the warmth and weight of each of them against him. The way Mariette threw her arms around his neck and hugged him so tightly. The way Bertrand laid his head on his chest, as if listening to his heartbeat.

Rose's voice, her smile, her big dark eyes, the Roman nose she hated. Her skin, her breasts, her buttocks, her sex. The pleasure they'd always given each other, even during the darkest hours of the siege, despite hunger and anxiety.

He'd lost it all too soon. And he was about to lose it again, forever.

Grief had replaced terror. He forced back the tears making it hard to breathe and turned his eyes toward the door with its small rectangle of night, lit by the fading gleam of day, the silhouette of the guard with his rifle pacing back and forth in front of it.

Exhausted by the pain, he must have slept.

A noise wakes him up, confused, and he smells shit and urine. The dawn light is milky outside, and he sees the body of the wounded Federate lying crumpled, head slumped on its chest.

"It's over for him," says Noël Dumartin. "Better that way. Did you sleep?"

"Yes, but I didn't mean to. You?"

"Same thing. I wanted to stay awake, guess it won't be long before I never open my eyes again."

Roques's blood runs cold at the words, but he's also feeling the stirrings of a faint, mad hope with the new day. The hope that he might still live. He imagines calling the guard, or doing something to provoke his sudden entrance, rifle at the ready. He pictures himself seizing the weapon, disorienting the man, disarming him. He's sure Citizen Dumartin will help him, if only by keeping the other man from shouting. Then, the rifle in his hand, he'll cross the courtyard, clearing a path with the bayonet, take down an officer to get his revolver. He'll run out in the street and scream fire, take advantage of the general confusion to hide in a building. He'll wait for days or weeks, trying to survive alone, or even holding the occupants of some apartment hostage at gunpoint. He tries to remember the layout of the barracks but can recall only the long, painful, stumbling walk here. He'll have to take Dumartin along with him, he thinks, because he'll know what to do.

The door opens, and two policemen step back and order them out of the stall. They all get up, some of them groaning with the effort. The dead man sags slowly to the side, his back catching on the rough wall. Then Dumartin turns back toward the far end of the stall and undoes his trousers and starts to piss. The other Federate imitates him. Roques does the same thing, relieving himself in the exact place where he was just sitting. The two civilians, the so-called honest man and another, a youth who hasn't said a word and has slept, or pretended to sleep, this whole time, wait by the door.

They step outside. In front of the other stalls, more policemen are collecting the other prisoners. Three officers on horseback watch the proceedings from the center of the courtyard, each holding a revolver.

There are around fifty prisoners in all. Shuffling, hacking, coughing. Roques is in a kind of daze. The only thing left to do is leap on one of the officers, seize his gun, and be cut down. At least he'd die fighting. Having tried something. But his legs tremble, and he feels completely sapped of strength.

They are herded past the stables and into a guardroom where they sit down against the back wall facing around fifteen soldiers who stand in front of a set of double doors. A sergeant steps forward, his thumbs hooked into his belt.

"When your name is called, get up and follow the guards. Keep quiet. You have no rights here."

The prisoners grumble and mutter. Some start to cry. Roques is sitting next to Dumartin, who stares ahead at the boy sitting in front of him, sobbing.

"We've got to get out of here. We have to focus on that."

Roques has murmured the words, hardly moving his lips. The other doesn't react, so he's about to repeat himself, but Dumartin cuts him off. "I heard you. There's nothing we can do here. As soon as we're judged, that's the moment to try. They aren't shooting people here. I haven't heard any gunshots since yesterday. We have to wait for the transfer."

Roques catches the eye of a soldier about to advance on them. He drops his gaze and falls silent.

They don't speak for hours. At around noon, two policemen pick six men at random by pointing at them.

"Me, too?" asks Roques.

"Yes, you, too," one of them says. "Why not you, too? Doesn't matter anyway, you're all going in."

Getting to his feet, he squeezes Dumartin's shoulder briefly. "See you soon, Citizen."

Dumartin doesn't answer. He doesn't look up.

In a large room, a former mess hall that still smells of burnt fat, three officers sit behind a table. A four-sconce candelabrum sits in front of each of them. One of the men, on the far left, is bent over a large notebook, a pair of spectacles perched on his nose.

"You, step forward!"

A man moves, barefoot and limping, toward the chair serving as a witness stand. He is wearing a tattered shirt stained with blood on one shoulder and Federate uniform trousers. One of the officers looks up at him.

"Full name?"

"Dupré, Alexandre."

"Where were you arrested?"

"Rue Racine, yesterday afternoon."

"Were you fighting?"

"Of course."

"What do you mean, of course?"

"It was a duty and an honor for myself and all my comrades."

The officer nods at the man taking notes. Two policemen come for the man and march him out of the room, twisting his arms behind his back. A door creaks and then slams behind them.

"Next!"

Roques walks toward the chair. He eyes the three military types scribbling things on sheets of paper. They dip their pens with precise gestures, wiping them carefully on the rim of the inkwell. They look like office clerks at work, silent and efficient. Their boots are impeccably clean, the black leather shining with a bluish gleam.

Roques's confused mind tries to focus on these details. The gold buttons. The regiment number embroidered on the collar. Then the one who seems to be in charge of questioning looks up.

"Full name?"

"Roques, Antoine."

"Where were you arrested?"

"Rue Dupin."

"Were you fighting?"

"No. I was—"

"Just answer the questions. What were you doing in this quarter, where heavy combat was taking place?"

"I was doing my job."

"Which was?"

"Which was to find a young woman who had been kidnapped and imprisoned by a criminal. Her case and two others were brought to my attention at the police headquarters of the 10th arrondissement, where I was the delegate to the Sûreté Publique."

The officer leans back and crosses his arms, his expression suddenly interested, a nasty smile on his lips.

"May I ask who vested you with this . . . authority?"

"The committee that elected me."

"So you were entrusted with police duties, if I understand you correctly?"

"Yes."

"Who made up this committee?"

"Citizens from the arrondissement."

Roques pictures the smoky room, hears again the noise, the clamor of voices, the shouting. The laughter.

"Why are you smiling?"

"I was smiling at pleasant memories."

"What pleasant memories? Of the Commune? You do know that this ridiculous charade is virtually at an end, don't you? You realize that you stand accused of high treason against the nation, as well as murder and other crimes? Do you know the penalty you're facing? That should wipe the smile off of your face, shouldn't it?"

Roques chooses not to let himself be intimidated by this brass hat. He forces himself to smile again. He doesn't know if he'll have the strength or the courage to do much more of it in the hours to come.

"Yes, pleasant memories of those days, those weeks. I was happy, in a happy city. And I feel I've done my duty as a citizen."

"What duty?"

"To keep my peers safe. To prevent thefts and abuses of all sorts. To help those weaker than myself."

"You're a policeman? Are you even slightly qualified to hold that position?"

"I'm a bookbinder. I learned a few basic things from an inspector who stayed here after refusing to follow the commissioner and the rest of his colleagues to Versailles."

"His name?"

Roques hesitates, then decides to name the bastard who betrayed him.

"Inspector Loubet. Aristide Loubet."

The officer leans toward his colleague, and they exchange a few words.

"This criminal you spoke of, did you arrest him?"

"No."

"Do you know where he is now?"

"I have no idea. He's probably dead."

"What is his name?"

"Pujols. Henri Pujols."

"And this young woman, did you find her?"

"Yes. But when we got there, she'd already escaped. Your men had freed her. But then she got away from them. She'd been held at 15 Rue des Missions. Some of your men were billeted there."

"Easy enough to check."

Roques restrains himself from shrugging. *Check it, then, you son of a bitch. As if the truth mattered to you. You're going to line us all up against the wall and be done with it. So let's finish up here.*

The judge-officer exchanges glances with his associates, then snaps his fingers. A policeman approaches and hands him a sheet of paper, which he stamps, the noise echoing horribly in the high-ceilinged space.

Roques is pushed outside with a rifle-butt jab in the kidneys, but as his hands are being tied behind his back, he can't keep from looking up at the sky, at the dark, puffy clouds fighting the blueness that remains. There are a dozen men here in the courtyard, disheveled and sometimes bloody, being watched by the same number of soldiers. One of them, a sub-officer, gives the order to march, and they are hustled out of the barracks, their captors shouting at them to walk faster, and they are hurried through streets full of idle soldiers smoking or eating, clustered at tables in front of cafés, waiters serving them beer and wine. From the windows come hateful shouts. *Shoot them right here, right now! I want to watch! Thieves! Trash!* A bourgeois man in a blue vest, his cravat undone, comes out of a building with a shoe in his hand and uses it to strike the man in front of Roques, who wobbles on his feet and then straightens his back, upright and stiff, as if nothing had happened. The policeman pushes the vengeful man away gently. *Calm down, now. We're dealing with them.*

Roques can't think of anything at all anymore. He just wants it to be over now. He tries to imagine the place where they'll shoot them. The wall. Bullet holes left over from previous executions. Blood, maybe. He's in a sort of permanent stupor. Dizziness threatens to bring him to his knees with every step. He doesn't know if he's afraid. He doesn't know if he's feeling sadness or regret at having to die without seeing Rose and the children again. Possibly he is already beyond the feelings that make up everyday life, the feelings which, along with the moments of happiness and joy and hope that carry us along—and all the disappointments we force ourselves to rise above—define our existence.

He realizes that they're going down the Rue de Rennes. Military convoys pass by en route to the battle, the constant rumble of which he can hear behind him to the east. Wagons and artillery. Columns of soldiers marching steadily. The hulk of the Gare Montparnasse looms up in the distance, sunlight glittering sharply on its broken windows. Roughly a hundred prisoners are waiting in the forecourt; they've been allowed to sit down, and they huddle together in clusters, staring blankly into the distance. The police push Roques and the nine others with him into the midst of this herd, the soldiers guarding the crowd barking at them to get to their feet. Papers and instructions are exchanged, regulation salutes given, and then the prisoners are kicked and prodded with rifle butts and bayonet points until they form a column. They are forced to walk down the gravel-strewn Chaussée du Maine, which is almost completely blocked at one point by the ruins of a collapsed house. The battle that raged here was quick and brutal, ripping off a few roofs, smashing several walls, and blowing up two or three houses before moving on to where the serious fighting was about to begin.

A crowd has gathered at a crossroads in front of the remains of two gutted storefronts. There is shouting at the prisoners, insulting them. Women rush at them, armed with broken pieces of wood or parasols. Men hurl obscenities at them and strike them with their walking sticks. The prisoners hunch their shoulders. Federates who have withstood volley-gun fire for hours on end allow themselves to be beaten and cursed like donkeys. Still, one strapping young man rebels, seizing a man by the collar of his frock coat and lifting him off the ground, then smashing his nose with a single head-butt. The man yelps and falls on his arse. Two soldiers step in, hammering at their mutinous captive with their rifle butts. Other prisoners lift him up, shielding him with their bodies. Before a free-for-all can break out, however, two more soldiers take aim, fingers on their triggers, and the men fall back in line.

Roques feels someone touching his hands.

"Don't move. Don't turn around. I'm untying you. We all have our hands free, except for you lot. Shouldn't be that way."

He rubs his freed wrists and murmurs a thank you without daring to turn, unable to see the face of his benefactor. He asks where they're being taken.

"Bloody Versailles, that's where. We're special cases, they

told me, otherwise we'd already be lying dead against a wall or behind a hedge in the Luxembourg Gardens."

"Versailles? But this isn't the way. Why Luxembourg?"

"Where have you been?" another man asks. "It's a real slaughterhouse over there. We heard the execution squads firing their guns until ten o'clock last night, and it started up again at seven this morning."

"Whether it's Luxembourg or Versailles, sooner or later . . . Anyway, they'll lock us up for the night at Issy, I'm sure."

"Shut your traps!" shouts an infantryman passing their part of the column. "By God, you've got nothing left to say!"

They fall silent. The only sound is the heavy thump of boot heels on the cobblestones and the crunch of broken glass beneath their treads.

Roques thinks about the Luxembourg Gardens. He and Rose went walking there a few times with the children. A pang seizes his heart; a knot forms in his throat. He's almost relieved to feel these things, though; he thought his heart was already dead. He rubs his hands together and rolls his shoulders, trying to relax the tight muscles.

"It's not even worth trying," murmurs the voice behind him. "I've thought about it, too, and so have a lot of the others, I'm sure."

My little ones. Rose. I can't bear it.

Suddenly something is happening up in front of them, something that causes them all to look up. Policemen shouting, ordering everyone to clear the path. The column stops. The guards crane their necks, staring up toward the end of the street, standing on tiptoe, asking each other what the hell is going on.

If he believed in anything, Roques would mutter a prayer of thanks to what some people call Providence. To his right, a narrow street leads away among small houses and gardens.

He'd only have to run forty meters and jump a fence to lose himself among the sheds and vegetable patches.

Antoine Roques runs. He dashes along the beaten earth, leaping over ruts. He feels no fatigue. *Look at me. I'm doing it. We're going to have a fresh start.* He smiles. If he had enough breath, he'd laugh out loud. *Don't be sad, my dear ones.* He can see all three of them, clear as day. Their astonished faces, their outstretched arms.

He hears shouting behind him. They must be ordering him to stop. He jumps to the side, vaults over a gate. A bullet buzzes past his ears. Leaping, he sees a rosebush to his right, leaning toward him, laden with enormous red blossoms.

The sudden impact he feels in his temple strikes him down and, in an instant, he is no more.

The wobbly planks of the fence he was trying to jump quiver beneath his dead weight. From where they stand guarding the column of prisoners, "La Marseillaise" explodes from the soldiers' mouths like a bomb.

30

The man is alone on the stage, lying on a blue velvet sofa, a cushion beneath his head. He wears a black vest over a white shirt with the sleeves rolled up. Arms folded on his chest, he's asleep in the half-light beneath the rafters. At his feet, out in the audience, rows of empty seats stretch away. There are perhaps twenty men sitting there, most of them slouching in their chairs, looking for all the world like bored spectators—ill-mannered, even, in their indifference—except for the bandages wrapping their heads, or the makeshift crutches propped up beside them. Storm lanterns have been hung beneath the balconies. Weak light from the boulevard outside filters in through the doors. In the aisles, other men lie on stretchers or improvised pallets. The occasional cry or curse rises from this audience of pain.

Caroline straightens up from the bedside of a patient whose remaining stump of a thigh has begun to bleed again, massaging the small of her back and wiping the sweat from her forehead with the back of her hand. The air is heavy, hot, and damp, and thick with a sweetish odor that sticks to the back of her throat, faintly nauseating.

They set up the aid station early this morning behind the barricade blocking the boulevard at the entrance to the Place du Château-d'Eau. The wounded have poured in from all over the city, coming via the Boulevard Saint-Martin and the Rue de Turbigo, brought by exhausted Federates in a few hansom cabs and even handcarts. They all tell the same stories of fearsome combat and desperate resistance. Of one against ten, against twenty. Of fleeing beneath a hail of bullets, saving their own skins at the cost of abandoning artillery and ammunition. Of leaving behind dead comrades and their last shreds of hope. The Versaillais are spreading through the streets like a monstrous flood, submerging the barricades and drowning them in blood.

Caroline looks up at Doctor Servin, asleep on the stage after a night of operating in a café on the Rue Réaumur before being forced to evacuate under bombardment. Caroline can't stop thinking about all that blood. Buckets full of blood. They didn't want to leave all the amputated arms and legs there to rot, so they'd piled them all onto a couple of sheets and taken them to Père-Lachaise this morning, where the gravediggers had spent all of yesterday digging pits. Just to be ready, said the foreman, since this is where everything always ends up. He'd laughed when he said it, like a creaking door. Still, said Paulin, one of the three boys who'd carried those pieces of dead courage to the cemetery, he buried them with a kind of gentleness, carrying them to the edge of the grave as if they were small children.

The other women here in the aid station are doing much the same as Caroline, standing up and stretching their backs, wiping their hands on their dirty aprons, giving the closest comrade a sad smile and then glancing at the stage where the doctor is still dozing. For a moment, nothing and no one moves. The injured men seem to have been soothed by their clean bandages and neatly stitched wounds, and by the few reassuring words the nurses have found to give them. The bowl of soup and slice of bread for those able to swallow. It's almost totally silent. Even the battle seems farther away.

Caroline goes to sit down in one of the red armchairs whose neat rows she somehow finds calming. The seat squeaks when she sits down on it. She leans back in the chair properly, nestling between its soft arms, stroking the soft velvet with her fingertips. This is the first time she's ever set foot in a theater. This one stands on what they used to call the Boulevard du Crime; people used to throng the theaters along here to watch dramas full of murder and be deliciously frightened. She's heard about the crowds of playgoers, where bourgeois Parisians slummed it alongside dancers and entertainers and the hoi polloi. There were even magicians who could make someone shut inside a trunk disappear with a wave of the hand. *Presto!* Gone! And freaks of nature: two-headed calves, a man born without arms who would paint your portrait with his feet, a bearded woman, terrifying twin sisters with only a single pair of legs between them. Caroline would have loved to see all that. Wearing a dress she'd made in secret out of leftover scraps of rich cloth and pieces of ribbon and odds and ends recovered here and there in the workshop. How elegant it would have made her feel to sit down in one of these armchairs and shiver at the make-believe horrors and scream too loudly at the fantastical murders being committed onstage, only to watch the victim get up and bow to the audience at the end of the show, a knife still jutting out of his back. How she would have loved to weep hot tears at the tragic fates, the stories of orphaned girls abused by their guardian and then miraculously reunited with the mother they'd believed dead. To marvel, to shudder, to sob. That's living. That's what makes a heart beat. These plays that soothe the pain of reality.

Her heart is beating now—thumping madly at the sight of these men lying here, filthy and suffering, dazed, unconscious, or numb with despair, oblivious to whatever the coming hours might have in store for them. Thinking, perhaps, of their loved ones, wondering if they'll ever see them again, or if their lives from now on—mutilated and disfigured as they are—will even be worth living.

Two men in National Guard uniforms abruptly dash into

the room and ask to speak to the person in charge of the aid
station. Three women step forward and talk with the men in
low voices. Caroline gets up. The new arrivals' faces are covered in sweat. One of them has a gash running the length of his
forehead, encrusted with blackish dried blood. The aid-station
nurses point to the stage, where Doctor Servin sits up on his
sofa, rising immediately when he sees them. They pick their
way among the wounded men toward the stage. Some of the
injured men sit up, as well. *What's happening?*

The doctor steps down from the proscenium. Caroline
approaches with the other women, their gazes absent, their
eyes very bright.

"You have to leave this place," says one of the Federates.
"There are infantrymen three hundred meters away, on the
Rue de Turbigo. The barricade can't hold more than another
hour. They've brought in a mitrailleuse, but it won't be
enough. They're coming around behind the Prince-Eugène
barracks as we speak. The quarter will be completely overrun
by nightfall. They massacred an entire aid station yesterday at
Saint-Sulpice. The wounded, the nurses, the surgeon.
Everyone."

Doctor Servin looks from one of the men to the other,
aghast. He darts a glance around the room, his gaze lingering
on the balconies, and then his eyes come to rest on the women
standing frozen, waiting for a decision.

"What am I supposed to do? I have a dozen nurses here for
almost a hundred seriously wounded men. A third of them
have had limbs amputated. Twelve only last night. And where
will we go?"

"Belleville. They've gone to get an omnibus that was trans-
porting ammunition to the Bastille. It'll be here soon."

"Good."

The two men leave again, almost at a run. Relieved, maybe,
to leave this place with its stink of death.

"Try to get the ones that can stand up on their feet," the doctor says. "I'll see about how we're going to manage with this omnibus."

The women disperse among the pallets. Five of the injured men have already risen without help and are swaying on their feet, afraid to take even one step. Others have woken in their chairs and are looking around, distraught, like spectators forgotten there by the rest of the audience after a show.

Caroline hurries toward a man on the verge of falling and slides herself beneath his arm. He straightens up, grimacing, and limps with her toward the exit uncomplainingly, teeth gritted. His trouser leg has been cut away to the upper thigh, which is wrapped in a large bandage. She can feel the dampness of his sweat-drenched armpit against the back of her neck. *I'll be fine, I'll be fine*, he repeats to himself in a murmur, leaning heavily on her. They reach the sidewalk just as the glass in the theater doors explodes. Bullets smash against the façade, sending slivers of stone flying. The windows of the surrounding cafés shatter. The men manning the nearby barricade unleash a volley of bullets in response; there are twenty of them, firing endlessly into the Place du Château-d'Eau. They gesture to one another at the windows of the barracks from which the Versaillais are pelting them. Two artillery shells explode in front of the barricade on the Boulevard Voltaire; another demolishes the upper floors of a building on the corner of the Avenue des Amandiers.

"We need people to carry stretchers!" shouts Joséphine, a nurse who is supporting two barely conscious men with her powerful arms unaided.

Someone comes to help her get the men seated on the ground and then runs into the theater. Two old men arrive, each of them with two bags strapped across his chest.

"We've brought food and drink. They wouldn't let us enlist, but we'll show them we can still be good for something!"

A group of men is coming up the boulevard toward the Place du Château-d'Eau. They are carrying rifles, revolvers thrust into their belts. Behind them are thirty Federates pulling a mitrailleuse.

Caroline helps her wounded patient to lean against a wall. She advises him to sit down so he doesn't get hit by a bullet, but he says again that he'll be fine and thanks her. As she turns to leave, he seizes her arm, holding her back. *Take this*. He pulls a revolver from beneath his jacket.

"And just what am I supposed to do with that?"

He insists. "There are five cartridges left. Don't waste them."

"No. Keep it."

The man refuses to take the weapon back, so she sets it down next to him with a stammered *Thank you, just the same* and hurries away. Glancing back, she sees him slide to the ground against the wall, his eyes closed.

The omnibus arrives, drawn by two exhausted horses. It stops around fifty meters away, and the cabman climbs down from his seat and takes shelter behind the coach.

A gaggle of young boys dashes up, eight or nine of them; Caroline doesn't have time to count them because just then a fresh hail of bullets smashes into the walls and pavements, and she is forced to flatten herself to the ground. The boys don't flinch. They beg for rifles, arguing with a sergeant who orders them to get down and then go home.

"This *is* our home. Don't bother giving us stupid advice. We want to fight."

Tiredly, he gestures at a few rifles propped against a row of barrels. Boxes of ammunition on the ground near them. The kids rush for the guns and load them. One of them, a tall blond boy, cries out as he's struck by a bullet. He sways on his feet, his torn throat gushing blood, then collapses slowly as if determined to remain standing. His friends stare at him for a few seconds, horrified, then lean on the sacks of earth and open fire.

Caroline makes three trips between the theater and the omnibus almost at a run, her arms tense and straining beneath the weight of the stretchers, unable even to crouch under the whistling bullets. Back inside, she leans on a chair, out of breath, her heart feeling like it's about to explode. The mitrailleuse starts firing outside. There is a commotion in the lobby. "Help! Hurry!"

She summons what's left of her strength and courage from somewhere deep inside, between her gut and her heart, and rushes toward the cries.

31

The bullet is still lodged beneath his shoulder blade, and every movement feels to Nicolas like a knife churning his innards, its point lancing toward his chest. In a small bar transformed into an aid station, a gangling, probably drunk fellow called Célestin, who claimed to know how to bandage horses and had sewn up a few wounds near Sedan, washed the bullet hole out with cheap hooch and stitched it tightly so it wouldn't leak, he'd explained. He said he'd learned how to do it in the war from a lieutenant-colonel, a surgeon by profession, who'd assigned him the tasks of cleaning and sewing while he carried out endless amputations in a neighboring tent.

Every time he shoulders his rifle, with every effort he makes to release the bolt on the cocking lever, the knife twists again. It bleeds a little too, of course, beneath the bandage Célestin applied so tightly, "Like for a horse, see? That won't budge anytime soon."

He isn't afraid anymore. The bullet he took could have killed him instantly before he even realized he was dying. Now he's expecting the next one any minute, but he'll do everything he can to avoid it, to stay alive, even though right now he isn't quite sure what the point of life will be, once they've lost this battle for good, their hopes destroyed for years to come. But he knows that it might all be over for him at any time, and he doesn't understand the indifference he feels at the thought of death. All he knows is that what they are doing here, all of them—the few that are left, anyway—has to do with making them pay, those others, for every meter of ground they're recapturing. And maybe with ensuring that someone who comes after them, some posterity, will know that for two months in Paris, in the spring of 1871, there existed a feeling of hope so beautiful that people were ready to die defending it.

Here he is, Nicolas Bellec, on this Thursday the 25th of May, behind a barricade, on the corner of the Rue de Lyon. His every thought, every feeling, has narrowed down to the breadth of the cartridge he has just loaded into his rifle, this tiny piece of lead that will, if all goes well, end up buried in a Versaillais soldier's skull.

He is jolted out of his thoughts by the sound of creaking and bumping coming from around the corner. All the men assume their positions. A flask of well-watered wine is passed around; it's tepid and sharp-tasting, but it moistens their mouths and throats, helping them swallow without moving their heads too much.

A cart trundles slowly around the corner. Nicolas can see the red-clad legs of the soldiers creeping along behind it, sheltered by its bulk. Then the cart begins to pitch and sway, finally collapsing in the middle of the street.

"Wait," says a Federate who was a captain but tore off his stripes this morning, deciding that the foolishness of rank served no purpose now. "Wait," he repeats. "Don't waste your bullets."

Almost immediately, a mitrailleuse is shoved into view, maneuvered by four or five men, and hauled into battery position. The first volley erupts into the street with a terrible roaring clamor, and the Federates throw themselves down behind the barricade, their hands covering their heads as shards of wood and granite and burning lead rain down on them. The man who used to be a captain straightens up to glance at the scene, and his cap flies off and he staggers backwards, the top of his skull shorn off. The young man next to him lets out a cry and stares at the corpse on the ground, the cobbles behind its head covered with a spreading lake of blood. Nicolas, crouching between two overturned barrels, watches the street fill with soldiers. Lying on their bellies in firing position, they are clustered behind the shield of the mitrailleuse, firing over the top of the cart and through holes in its bottom that they must have cut out in advance.

"Gerfaut! Your shot!"

A short, sturdily built man in shirtsleeves positions himself behind a sort of arrow-slit and shoulders his weapon. Two other Federates crouch next to him with more loaded rifles, ready to hand them to him. Gerfaut is completely still, his expression intent, stretched nearly flat on his stomach. Bullets continue to whistle past overhead, smashing into the piled cobblestones with a hard snapping sound.

"Well? What are you waiting for?"

"Shut up," mutters Gerfaut.

The sound of the shot is barely audible over the mad clamor of the unceasing fusillade. Nicolas sees Gerfaut's shoulder absorb the recoil. He fires again, six more times. His comrades reload the guns.

"You've gotten three of them. There's one more of the dogs behind the mitrailleuse."

The gunfire stops—but it isn't followed by silence. Their heads are full of ringing and buzzing noises, their faces still tense, almost grimacing, their eyes half-closed, their shoulders hunched like shell-less turtle men.

"What's that?" asks Gerfaut, still in firing position.

The men risk a glance over the top of their makeshift rampart.

A child.

A very little boy, six or seven years old at most, is standing in the middle of the road, looking left and right at the combatants from each camp. He is bare-legged, dressed in a shirt that reaches his knees. He must have come out of the building behind him, with the broken windows and wide-open door. He darts a glance to either side again and then sits down.

Then the calls start. The warnings. Don't stay there. Come over here. Where's your mother? Go on, little one. Gotta get out of here. Those men over there are the bad guys; they'll hurt you.

Nicolas and the others can see the infantrymen standing up behind their defenses, waving their arms. Some of the Federates have climbed up on their own barricade and are clapping their hands, trying to get the child's attention.

For a moment, it's a free-for-all. A sort of yelling competition. There's even some laughter. The two sides wage a battle of gestures. Keep away from those brutes over there; they'll shoot your house full of holes. Watch out for the firing squad. At Versailles they eat little children; the ogre's called Adolphe Thiers.

Gradually, though, the shouts, the exclamations, the rude remarks taper off. The little boy doesn't move. He's found something on the ground: a pebble, maybe, or a stray bullet. He's playing with it. Or, rather, he isn't playing. He passes the object from one hand to the other over and over, tirelessly repeating that single movement.

Nicolas hears the shot and sees a few sparks erupt from the ground in front of the child. An infantryman shouts again, *Get out of here, you little bastard!* Another gunshot rings out. A puff of dust rises very close to the boy. A few of the Versaillais soldiers laugh; others seem to be protesting.

"I see the shooter," says Gerfaut. "I'll teach him to enjoy things like that, the piece of shit."

Nicolas sets down his rifle and begins to climb over the cobblestones.

"What the hell are you doing? Come back here!"

His comrades keep their voices low, as if they're trying to

avoid drawing attention to him while he walks slowly out into the street.

All of the Versaillais soldiers have risen from their crouching positions and are watching him. Three or four aim their guns at him.

"Don't get any closer, you son of a bitch!"

A dozen paces at most separate him now from the little boy, who continues to toy with whatever he's picked up off the ground. When Nicolas is a mere six feet away, the child lifts his head and stares at the sky. He doesn't look at Nicolas. His gaze slides over him without stopping, passes right through him, lost in some unknowable distance.

"Come here."

Nicolas stoops down and holds out his good arm. He expects the boy to do the same thing, but he doesn't move, his gaze still on the sky, darting around constantly until Nicolas wonders if the child might be blind. He picks him up, and the boy struggles with sharp little grunts, pushing away the arms holding him and butting his small head against the confining chest. Nicolas feels as if he's holding a feral kitten. He walks quickly back toward the barricade. Behind him, the Versaillais have fallen silent.

The explosion steals his breath as if he's being smothered, and he finds himself lying at the base of a wall beneath an avalanche of bits of wood and stone shards. He's curled himself into a ball, the child underneath him, so tiny now that Nicolas thinks for an instant that fear might have made him shrink, like in those fairy tales where lying makes noses grow. He gets to his feet and sees, through the cloud of dust beginning to resettle, his comrades standing up, bending over those who are still on the ground. There's no need for words. They seize their weapons and the remaining ammunition and run toward the Place de la Bastille. Three casualties remain lying in the dirt, bloody and gray with dust.

The child is weightless in Nicolas's arms, clutching his jacket with one tiny fist. To the left, the two cannons on the barricade barring the Rue Saint-Antoine fire by turns. A building is in flames on the corner of the Boulevard Beaumarchais. Men are evacuating the barricade there, four of them pushing and pulling an eight-pound gun toward the Rue de la Roquette. Nicolas continues toward the boulevard.

"Where are you going? Not that way; it's going to collapse!"

He turns around and sees one of his comrades from the Rue de Lyon, who is part of the group heading for la Roquette.

"Can't be helped!"

He is forced to stop running because his legs are screaming in agony. In front of him, the building's chimneys topple onto the roof of the neighboring house, crushing its roof, clumps of bricks smashing on the pavement. Nicolas makes a detour, the child still clinging to him, and for a moment the noise of the battle recedes as they move away down the boulevard. On the corner of the Rue des Vosges, a woman's voice calls out to him, and he looks around for her, finally spotting her in the doorway of a shop.

"And just where is the defender of the Republic off to right now? What have you got in your jacket there?"

Nicolas approaches the shop. It's a laundry, giving off a lovely scent of clean linen and soap.

"We're setting up an aid station," the woman says. "The others will be back soon. Whose child is this?"

Nicolas explains. Tells her the whole story. The woman clucks sympathetically at the brave little soldier in his arms.

"I don't know about brave," says Nicolas. "I'm not even sure he realizes what's happening, the danger he's in. Or maybe he's seen some terrible things that made him like this . . ."

The woman reaches out to stroke the boy's curly hair, but her hand has barely brushed his head when he shrinks from her, pushing her hand away.

"Oh, dear. Well, leave him with me, anyway. He'll be better off here than with you, dodging bullets. Where are you going now?"

"Belleville, I think. I'm going to stop at Château-d'Eau, see if I'm needed there."

"You're needed everywhere. Alive, most importantly. Keep that in mind."

He passes her the child, who clings to him and then struggles in the woman's arms. She cuddles him against her breast and kisses him despite his thrashing protests.

Nicolas leaves them. He can still feel the warmth of the little body against him. He hurries down the nearly deserted boulevard, past people watching and waiting on their doorsteps and out their windows for whatever comes next. A man spits at his feet. Another invites him to get himself shot. Two young girls call out to him from a balcony and then burst into laughter. He hears the sound of mitrailleuses exchanging fire somewhere off to his right: the Boulevard Voltaire, he thinks. He runs, but exhaustion brings him to a halt after only a few meters. The stabbing pains have intensified in his shoulder, and he can tell the dressing is soaked with blood. In the distance, the Place du Château-d'Eau is a gigantic cauldron of fire.

An omnibus is parked on the street in front of him. Wounded patients are being loaded into it, men and women hurrying busily to and fro. They're evacuating an aid station set up in a theater. He approaches the scene. The barricade a mere thirty meters away is fully engaged, bullets striking the façades of the buildings. The square is full of heavy drifts of dark smoke.

A girl turns around. Her thin face is nearly swallowed up by her blue checked scarf.

Nicolas's heart stops. Her breath catches.

Caroline.

32

They stare each other, just to be sure. Nicolas ventures a smile. Caroline comes toward him. She gestures at the bloody bandage on his shoulder.

"What's wrong?"

"It's nothing."

He seizes her hand and kisses it. She pulls it away, shaking her head.

"Move it, Citizen!" Two stretcher-bearers trudge past carrying a weeping man with an amputated leg.

"Come."

She takes him by the hand. She wants to slip her arm into his, but she can't. This isn't a lovers' stroll in the park. The words refuse to form in her dry throat. What can she say to him?

Nicolas pauses for an instant as they enter the lobby of the theater. The elegant woodwork, the gilding, the deep crimson of the armchairs hold him spellbound, and he wonders how such a beautiful place can still exist at a time like this.

"No more patients; take him back outside," says Doctor Servin, packing his instruments into a satchel.

"Yes, but it's him, it's . . ."

The doctor looks up at her, glances over at Nicolas.

"Bring him here. And you, let me have a look at that. And put down your gun. I may be a doctor, and by no means on your side, but I'm still less dangerous than those soldiers they've unleashed against you."

He unwraps the bandage, picking out the stitches that have come loose, and cleans the wound.

Caroline hasn't let go of Nicolas's hand. Exhaustion threatens to overwhelm him. He wishes he could just lie down here, against her, and sleep. Nothing else. And when they woke up, they would tell each other everything.

"I'll need to extract the bullet. It went through the shoulder blade but didn't have the momentum to come out the other side. I can feel it here, under the skin. What do you think?"

Nicolas agrees. He is so tired. He lets himself sink into the chair.

The doctor takes a scalpel and a pair of pliers from his bag. He cleans Nicolas's skin with bleach and makes the incision quickly and cleanly.

Caroline turns her head away. Nicolas groans and crushes her fingers in his own.

"There it is," Servin says. "Look."

He shows him the bullet, held in the pliers, then lets it drop to the floor.

His wound rebandaged, Nicolas stands up and waits for the room to stop whirling around him. Doctor Servin has disappeared. Caroline is standing there, very close to him.

"Are you all right?"

He nods. "I've been looking for you, you know."

She caresses his cheek.

"I know. We lost each other."

They hear shouting, and then a commotion in the theater lobby.

"We have to get out of here," Caroline says.

He puts his filthy shirt and jacket back on, picks up his rifle, makes sure there are still a few cartridges left in his pouch.

They emerge onto the boulevard. A woman tells them the Versaillais are coming up the Boulevard Voltaire. The mitrailleuse at the barricade has run out of ammunition and ceased firing. Dead bodies with dirty, contorted faces are lined up on the pavement like they're sleeping.

So they run. There are perhaps twenty of them hurtling through streets studded with makeshift barricades guarded by men who have no idea from which direction the enemy will come. On the Boulevard de Belleville, hundreds of men, wagons full of ammunition, and artillery guns wait for officers and barricade commanders to finish arguing over them. Battalions in full flight stagger into the square, twenty or thirty exhausted men with haggard faces, sometimes led by a corporal. "All dead," they say. "What can we do?" A few Commune leaders with red scarves around their waists stand on chairs and read aloud martial declarations urging the people to take up arms and repel the enemy. No one listens to them. Some furious men tell them to take up arms themselves instead of prattling on. There's no lack of weapons; all they have to do is pick them up.

The rumble of bombardment sounds from every direction. Fires cast a pall of choking smoke over the chaos.

Caroline and Nicolas dash from one group to the next, not speaking, sometimes clasping hands so as not to lose each another. On the Rue Rébéval, they find a small bistro open, smelling of soup and wine. There are some national guardsmen in full uniform, their weapons propped up against their chairs, sitting silently with glasses of white wine in front of them. The *bistrotier* approaches and offers them bowls of vegetable broth and some cheese. He's a tall, austere man with an enormous mustache. He shuffles back toward the kitchen, returning quickly with a small tureen and two bowls.

"There you go, lovebirds," he says as he sets everything down. "That will fill your bellies."

And then some hard bread and the cheese. And wine, because there is no more water. *Wine, then.* They thank him.

The man remains standing by their table, his face somber, watching them ladle out the soup.

"This is all very sad indeed," he says. "Who'd have thought it would end this way?"

Nicolas looks up at the man's sorrowful face and doesn't know what to say. He asks how much they owe, and the man shakes his head.

"Nothing at all. Or whatever you want. I'm closing tonight, going to lend a hand on the Rue de Puebla. There are still some soldiers there; we should be able to make them suffer a bit. Give them something to remember us by."

"And after that?" asks Caroline.

"After that? I'll do the same as everyone else: I'll try to save my own skin, if it isn't too full of holes. Or I'll hide out for a couple of weeks in a ditch somewhere, or cross Prussco lines. They say that, toward Bagnolet, you can get through at night, by the Porte de Ménilmontant."

"Do you know where there might be a room to rent around here?"

"Yes, a bit farther on. A widow. Old lady Charpentier. A building with blue shutters, the only one on the street. She won't give you any trouble."

Someone calls out to him, so he wishes them good luck and goes behind the counter to serve two impatient Federates.

They eat greedily, wiping the soup tureen clean and devouring even the bitter rind of the cheese, the hard pieces of bread they didn't dunk in the soup scratching their gums. The white wine flows smoothly down their throats, going to their heads a bit in their exhausted state.

Outside, they hesitate on the doorstep of the bistro, wondering what time it is. The sky is dark, full of large charcoal-colored clouds. They decide to return to the boulevard in search of news. Dombrowski is dead. The Luxembourg Gardens are an abattoir, firing squads at work from morning to night.

Everywhere the Versaillais are searching, arresting, shooting. The streets are clotted with corpses. Blood. The gutters of Paris are running red with blood.

Rage and chaos.

The crowd has grown. Some people wander aimlessly; others form groups and volunteer to go make a stand against the enemy. Some loudmouthed onlookers bawl in protest and stoop so far as to shove and jostle the Federates trying to assemble. Nicolas steps closer to an officer who is addressing a group of some fifty men. The Place du Château-d'Eau has been overcome. A column is already marching up the Rue du Faubourg-du-Temple, intending to meet the infantrymen head-on and hold the barricade on the Rue Saint-Maur. The officer sets off; some of the troops follow him. The others discuss what they should do. March toward Père-Lachaise and strike the Versaillais attacking the Bastille from the rear. A sergeant explains that his brother-in-law is there, a good friend, a brave man. Twenty men head off down the boulevard singing "Le Chant du Départ."

Nicolas clutches the strap of his rifle as he watches them leave.

"My God, look at them," he says. "They're ready for more. They have so much pride!"

"And you?" Caroline asks. "Are you ready for more?"

"I wish I were—but I can't take any more. I don't know what difference it makes."

They pass an ammunition wagon guarded by two men seated on crates. Nicolas pauses and hands his rifle to one of them.

"Here—I found this."

He empties his pouch of his last six cartridges. "And these."

The man looks at him, surprised, glances at his wound, clutches the cartridges in his hand. Then his gaze shifts to Caroline.

"I understand," he says, with a smile. "We have to save what can still be saved."

They nod at him and walk away.

"Take care of yourselves!" the Federate cries after them. "My name is Marius Meylan! La Marseillaise's husband!"

They turn around and see him standing there, brandishing the rifle with a wide smile. Caroline blows him a kiss, and Nicolas waves again with his good hand. Their hearts are heavy. Then Marius sits back down and turns his back. They start walking again and, without speaking, turn down the Rue Rébéval. They find the widow's house easily, thanks to its blue shutters.

The widow comes to the door quickly, opens it a crack, and eyes them, her face stern. When Nicolas explains that the owner of the bistro gave them her address, she lets them in and leads them down a narrow hallway.

"This is it," she says, opening a door. "It overlooks a small courtyard. You can even get out to the Rue Vincent if you cut between the houses. Anyway . . . there's water in the pitcher, and there's the basin and a piece of soap. The last tenant left weeks ago, but I always keep everything spick and span. I'll be in my kitchen downstairs if you need me."

They thank her, saying it's very nice. Nicolas asks how much it costs.

"Nothing if you're from the Commune."

She goes to the window and looks up at the sky.

"It's going to storm tonight. That'll put out the fires."

She closes the door softly behind her, and they don't even hear her footsteps in the corridor as she walks back down the hall.

They make themselves comfortable and stretch out on the bed. The room is dark, smelling of clean linen and woodsmoke. They lie silently for a moment, their eyes on the damp-spotted ceiling. Then Caroline takes Nicolas's hand and brings it to her lips, then kisses him gently. Nicolas pulls her to him and kisses her forehead, her nose, her lips. She responds in kind, and they lie entwined for a long while, sometimes letting out embarrassed little giggles, as if it's the first time. Their hands grip each other's hips and shoulders. They press their bodies together until they're overheated, and then they unbutton the necks of their shirts, their lips seeking out hidden bits of skin, the hollow of a collarbone, the base of a throat.

They don't speak. This needs to come first. Only this, because they know without saying it that they don't feel capable, yet, of anything else. Not yet. Their minds revisit the days they've just been through, and each of them shivers, and their throats tighten even as their lips try to find the way back.

Later, after they've slept a little, in the lightning-streaked night, they talk. Caroline doesn't dare tell everything; she feels too dirty, too tarnished. Nicolas can't quite find the words to express his grief at losing the two brothers he'd found. Neither of them can always see, in this darkness that unites them, the tears that both are allowing to fall.

They sleep badly, but they're content. The rumble of thunder mingles with the endless cannon fire. The rain patters and streams and overflows. The wet noise of it makes them thirsty, so they drink water from the pitcher, dripping it everywhere and laughing. They sleep holding each other, fully dressed. Each is woken by bad dreams, the ones they'll never tell, and drifts back to sleep in the other's arms.

The nasty weather raging outside doesn't frighten them.

FRIDAY, MAY 26TH

33

The sound of someone pounding on the front door of the house penetrates the terrifying nightmares into which they've both strayed, and they wake up, reassured at first as the bad dreams dissipate. But it seems as if the door's about to be smashed into splinters, and they hear shouts of "Open up! In the name of the law!" and then the widow calling that she's coming, and the noise of a key rattling in the lock while she explains that it needs to be oiled, and that an old lady like herself sometimes has trouble getting out of her house, all while the soldiers grumble and threaten and hammer on the door, the rain falling on them undoubtedly doing little to help their moods.

Caroline opens the window and climbs out onto the ledge while Nicolas listens from behind the door to the old lady protesting at the intrusion, swearing that she lives alone and hasn't seen anyone for days. Then she cries for help and then shrieks with pain, begging for mercy. Caroline seizes Nicolas's hand and drags him out into the little courtyard while he sputters with blind rage.

"They're beating her, damn it! They'll kill her!"

Caroline doesn't say anything. Without weapons, alone and on the run as they are, they can do nothing but flee like game being hunted. They weave between the wooden sheds and the cobbled-together lean-tos built onto the backs of houses, sometimes containing dogs that bark and hurl themselves against the rickety doors. Rainwater gurgles in the gutters and streams down the tar-papered boards of the roofs. They run silently through this soaking-wet labyrinth until it spits them out onto a deserted street of disjointed cobblestones, lined with single-story houses and gardens enclosed by ramshackle fences. The smell of cold ash floats in the air beneath a low sky.

They stop beneath an archway to catch their breath. They listen to the fighting start up again, its noise somehow muffled by the thick layer of clouds and the pouring rain. Nicolas imagines the last few barricades dissolving, washed away by the downpour or the streams suddenly overflowing, nothing but dikes of sand erected against the storm. He wishes he were with the others. He knows he wouldn't miss a single shot, that the Versaillais would fall by the hundreds, that they wouldn't get through—no, they wouldn't, and there would still be hope of repelling them. His mind thrills for a moment at the thought of heroic combat, of decisive action, of daring counterattack. As if the outcome of the battle depended solely on individual courage, on strength of will. Courage, daring, and—yes—heroism, why not: he has seen them at work. He has watched the fear in his comrades' eyes disappear in the span of a blink when they decided to stay, to hold on beneath the onslaught of lead and fire, or when they rose up above the rampart to shoot. He has also seen young men die when they'd hardly had time to live, and he pictures Adrien's serious face as he spoke of the future like a promise he seemed to be making himself, one he was determined to keep.

How he wishes Adrien would show up right now, running breathlessly through the rain, Versaillais infantrymen in hot pursuit. They'd find a way out of this, the two of them. He imagines the boy's ghost rising up beside him, thinking that maybe he dreamed all of it—the deaths of his friends, the Versaillais attacks, the crushing of the Commune in blood and chaos—and that he'll wake up in a barracks any minute and everything will still be possible. He wishes that kind of magic were real. Or at least that he could believe in it, like children do, could still hope for improbable joys.

Caroline shakes water from her hair. She is shivering in her man's jacket, its collar and shoulders soaked through.

"We need to move," she says.

Nicolas emerges from his reverie and takes her arm. They start walking again, hunched beneath the rain in the gray light of early morning on this deserted street. Up ahead, on the Rue de Puebla, the fighting suddenly resumes. They hear the crack of two rifle shots. An artillery shell explodes, then another. Nicolas turns around, slows down.

"Come on," says Caroline. "It's no use going that way."

She pulls him away. The fusillade continues. Crossing another street farther along, they hear shouts. A gunshot. They break into a run.

"Where do you think you're going?"

The voice is deep and strong, almost commanding. Nicolas stops, blinking the rain out of his eyes, looking for its source, and sees an old man standing in his doorway, leaning on a cane. He wears a peasant's hat, his blue eyes gleaming brightly below its wide brim, and a flowing oilcloth greatcoat that reaches down to his feet.

"S'not wise to be out in the streets at such an early hour," the old man says.

"Why do you say that?"

"Well, because of the rain, naturally!"

He lets out a sharp little laugh that shakes his whole body. Caroline tugs at Nicolas's sleeve.

"We're wasting time. Let it go."

"And time is something you don't have a great deal of left, my dear mademoiselle, is that right? And yet so young!"

The man walks toward them, his steps light and agile, twirling his cane—which he clearly doesn't need—like a

490 · HERVÉ LE CORRE

sergeant major. He stops in front of Caroline and looks her over with his laughing eyes.

"How lucky that I came out this morning; here I am meeting a pretty girl. But enough of this polite chatter. I know a place where time doesn't matter, where you can wait for better days. In your situation, at any rate."

He pauses as three artillery shells explode a short distance away, toward the boulevard. The humid breeze blows smoke through the street, heavy and thick as autumn fog.

"They'll destroy this city before they let you have it," says the man, sniffing the air.

"What do you mean by all this talk of time?" demands Nicolas.

"There's a cemetery at the end of this street. Belleville Cemetery. An ancient place where many good souls have found their final rest. My parents, my daughter, my wife. Clotilde and Ninon."

He breaks off, blinking rapidly, the blue of his eyes momentarily mixed with gray. He shakes his head.

"It isn't used much anymore. Perhaps because it's a bit too full, I don't know. But go there. There are some funerary monuments you can hide in. And try to find the caretaker, that old nut. Gustave, he's called. He'll help you. We fought together in '48, and again in '51. We're too old to fire a gun now, and perhaps age and the sorrows of life have made us believe a bit less in all that, too. But believe me, my heart has beaten louder over these past few months. And Gustave's, too, he told me. He almost wept over it, the old fellow. I'm sure he's poured his heart out to a few of the dead in his garden, as he calls it. He has his favorites, who have the same ideas he does, who agree with him—silently, of course. I've forbidden him to wake up my own loved ones. If they came to visit me, silent and ethereal, I wouldn't know what to say to them. Ghosts are of no use. I prefer memories."

Caroline nods in agreement. She feels the same sorrow. She smiles at the man, and he stretches out a slightly unsteady hand to touch her cheek. Then he gathers himself, squares his shoulders. His eyes regain their light, brighter than the gray day.

"The devil take melancholy . . . This is about you saving yourselves. Tell Gustave that Simon sent you. Do tell him that. It'll please him."

Nicolas thanks him, shaking his hand. The man bows comically to Caroline, doffing his hat and gesticulating extravagantly. A group of Federates passes them almost at a run. There are perhaps twenty of them, their clothing disheveled, carrying guns. They're exclaiming loudly, shouting for vengeance. They run up the Rue de Belleville and hesitate at a crossroads, unsure of which direction to take. *This way*, one of them cries, and they disappear. Gunshots ring out, and the sound of a bugle. Voices call out; others respond. The quarter seems to waken suddenly with a start.

Nicolas and Caroline start walking again through the rain, which is coming down even heavier now. She turns back toward Simon, still standing behind the thick veil of the downpour, and blows him a kiss, to which he responds with another bow. She wonders if he might be a former actor, and thinks again of the Theatre Déjazet and Doctor Servin. Of the night spent tending the wounded, soothing those who were going to die, and knew it, and chose not to believe it. She takes Nicolas's arm and presses herself softly against him, and he feels that if they stay close together like this, nothing bad can happen to them. He hunches his head down into his shoulders and quickens his steps, seeking to get farther away, as quickly as possible, from the war seething around them, being waged against the people of Paris and all their hopes, because he's ashamed of deserting them this way, and of being glad to do it.

The cemetery gate creaks dully on its hinges, and they pause, transfixed by the tree-lined path stretching away from them, leaves trembling in the wind, and by the neat rows of tombstones above which the sky seems lower, the rain colder. They press closer to each other and start moving again, spotting the caretaker's little house with its white shutters. They knock on the door and wait, listening for the sound of movement inside. A cat watches them, sitting in the doorway of a small shed crammed with tools.

They turn away and walk along the pathways, through the silence sheltering beneath the trees and among the graves, the shouting of the crowds and the thunder of the bombardments making the sky quiver, and even the raindrops themselves seem to shake. Eventually they come upon a row of those funerary monuments the bourgeois love to erect, probably to prove their dominance even in death. The doors and iron gates of the monuments they check remain stubbornly closed—but then one of them opens with a dreadful squeal. Caroline strains her eyes into the darkness of the tomb, nauseated by the odors of mold and saltpeter and even a faint stink of putrefaction that makes her recoil. She feels as if, once this rusty door is closed on them, it will never open again, and it won't matter much if there are two of them in this blackness, if a grave yawns open beneath them and swallows them up.

"Come on," Nicolas says, holding his hand out to her. "It's big, and we'll be dry."

She shivers, remembering the cellar where she thought she would die, and fear pierces her heart like a needle, stealing her breath. The cold seems to penetrate her very bones.

"It's not the same," he says. "Look, there's light."

He points to a cross shape cut into the wall, narrow as an arrow-slit, that lets in a bit of daylight. Caroline steps inside and immediately huddles on a stone bench. She shudders as she hears the door closing with a dull scraping noise. *I'm among the dead. I'll never get out.*

They take off their jackets and drape them over stone

crosses. Then they wring out their shirts, shivering, half-naked, and put them back on, the cold fabric making them gasp. They rub each other down to warm up: their backs, shoulders, bellies, chests, arms, thighs. They make sure to leave no part of their stiff, cold bodies untouched, but caresses are the furthest thing from their minds. There is no tenderness in the motions; they're even savage, in a way, in their determination to chase away the iciness clinging to each other's skin.

Both of them yearn for a fire. For a blanket draped over the shoulders, for thick socks that reach up to their knees. For a bowl of hot soup, a bit of fresh bread. A bed. It all seems like unimaginable luxury now, utterly unattainable, as they sit pressed against each other in this tomb with its stones green with moss, discolored, and icy cold. They don't dare speak of it aloud though, neither of them wanting to pain the other, to make things even more difficult for her companion in misfortune, his companion in these evil times.

They don't dare speak of *that*, either—of their inability to feel again that delicious shiver that ran through them when they were near each other, before. They both feel as if something inside them has died, something they can't name.

Caroline knows that it was another woman who emerged from that cellar, perhaps leaving her childhood, her youth in the darkness behind her. She doesn't know if part of her matured or rotted as she lay in that hole, feeling herself near death. She couldn't find the words to try and explain all of this to Nicolas last night. She wonders if she'll ever find them. And if it would be of any use.

Nicolas, too, has lost some of his vital strength. He can't manage to shake off the sadness lying heavy in the depths of his mind like sludge in a pond, rising up and clouding everything when the surface is disturbed by the tiniest nothing. He tells himself it will pass. He wants to believe it. He touches his wound through the bandage and is surprised that it doesn't hurt, but he knows that in the future this scar, whenever he touches it, will revive other pains.

They think all of this without saying anything, amid the frightful clamor of battle all around them. They have no idea what time it is. The rain has tapered off slightly, but the day doesn't seem to be brightening. Caroline glances up from time to time at the pallid light filtering weakly through the cross, looking for any hint of the reemerging sun.

They doze off occasionally, waking with pounding hearts, always anxious, the rain pattering softly, continuously on the roof. In the evening, they hear a crowd shouting, crying out with hatred, letting off a flurry of rifle shots. It's close by. They get to their feet, on high alert, listening for the sounds of people entering the cemetery. But the silence that abruptly falls again is absolute. They huddle together, hardly able to see one another.

Night falls. They slip on their jackets, waiting, passing the time by trying to imagine what they'll do tomorrow, starting from the assumption that there will be a tomorrow. They hear the gunfire start up again, then stop, then erupt once more before dying away.

It's in this renewed silence that they start suddenly, both of them crying out. The iron door has been flung open, and a man is standing there, a lantern in one hand, a rifle in the other.

"Come out of there. I knew I'd find you."

They emerge shakily into the drizzle. They can't make out the man's face beyond the glare of the lamp.

"Go. That way."

"It was Simon who told us—"

"I know."

Their ankles twist on the uneven surface of the path. Weak light gleams through a window. The man steps in front of them and pushes open a door.

"Go on in."

He shuts the door behind them and throws the bolt. Caroline and Nicolas make a beeline for the fire, kneeling in front of it, warming their hands near the flames.

"Take off those rags and hang them to dry. I'll give you something else to wear. I've got a few old things left that I've had for far too long."

They turn to look at him, at his long, bony face, his hollow cheeks scantily covered by a scraggly beard.

"Don't stay on your knees like that, nothing divine about this fire. There's no God here. Or anywhere. Take a chair. I'll bet you're hungry. I'm Gustave, by the way."

They shake hands, and Nicolas pulls up two chairs. The wooden seats creak beneath the weight of their exhaustion. The man sets about cooking them an omelet. His back to them, busy at the stove, he explains that they'll have to wait until dawn, because that's when the Prussians are least vigilant. They've brought in reinforcements to keep fugitives from getting through. They can be seen patrolling from the fortifications. It seems the bastards have set up heavy artillery in front of the Fort de Vincennes.

"We'll leave here tonight, and then wait near a blockhouse until sunrise."

"Why are you doing this?" Caroline asks.

"Because there's nothing else I can do. We'll get out through a gap in the wall made by the bombardment during the siege. We'll have to walk."

"Then we'll walk."

They eat, and talk a little. The old man is silent for long stretches, nodding, looking from one of them to the other with a disconsolate expression, grieved that things have gone so terribly wrong.

"You still might see it one day, the universal workers' republic. We were almost there. We can't lose every time, don't you think?"

They don't know what to think anymore. They don't have the strength now to imagine some bright future, and the anger inside them makes their hearts pound—but so does their exhaustion, and the thought of the forced walk ahead, with no end in sight.

"We just have to hold on, one day at a time," Caroline says. "We'll think about the future later."

She stands up, stretches, and rubs the small of her back. Gustave brings some old blankets and spreads them in front of the fireplace. They lie down, their bodies stiff and heavy. As they fall asleep, it finally occurs to them to exchange a smile.

SATURDAY, MAY 27TH

34

Gustave wakes them up with a gentle nudge of his foot. Nicolas thinks blearily for a moment that a captain has come to rouse the company for battle, then sees the three-sconce candelabrum above him, its flames quivering. The embers of the dying fire shift in the hearth with a soft crackle, and Caroline can't resist going to warm her hands again. The clothing Gustave gives them smells of dust and woodsmoke. Caroline is nearly swallowed up by her patched frock coat. They share a pleased glance.

Outside, the night is cloaked in fog. They can hear the eaves dripping. Gustave calls the weather a happy surprise.

"The fugitive's cloak," he says.

He walks ahead of them with quick, firm steps. He carries his rifle on his shoulder, supporting himself with a strong, gnarled walking stick. They can barely see the houses, the empty spaces of the gardens. The cobblestones gleam slightly with some mysterious light the overcast sky has managed to radiate in spite of everything. Gustave pauses at the corner of a street and listens. They can hear men talking in low voices. A faint metallic sound. Clinking. The scrape of shoe soles on the ground. Soldiers.

Gustave signals to them, and the three of them cross the street, bent low. Nicolas remembers the night battles with his comrades. He puts his hand on Caroline's shoulder. She turns to him, pale and hollow-eyed, her features drawn.

They reach the foot of the ramparts. Near a blockhouse

there is a breach, a mass of fallen stones. All they have to do is climb over it.

"We'll wait here."

Gustave sits down on a rock, his rifle across his chest. They huddle in a sort of niche, the two of them pressed together, facing him. They all gaze out into the fog-choked night with its silence full of strangled cries, of imminent explosions. A dog barks. Then another, farther away, answering the first. Then silence again. Nicolas lets his mind wander and imagines the two animals' throats slit by the soldiers whose approach they'd betrayed.

Caroline dozes off. She dreams that she's still lying in the depths of the cellar and that suddenly the ground lifts up and a corpse rises, groaning, struggling against the earth covering it, and it's her father who sits up and turns toward her, but she can't see his face very well; she knows it's him, but he keeps turning, and it's so dark, and when his face finally appears it's a hideous mask, moaning and begging, and she cries out and wakes up, terrified.

"It's all right," Nicolas murmurs.

She gasps for breath, slapping at her cheeks.

"Did I scream loudly?"

"No. It was like you'd gotten tangled in a spider web."

Gustave stands and looks out at the thinning fog.

"Time to go."

They walk along a rutted path, past the ruined barracks at the base of the fortifications. A slight breeze stirs the haze and lets it settle again. They quicken their pace without discussion, afraid of being spotted. Caroline occasionally touches Nicolas's hand.

Eventually they come upon a mass of dirt and stones. The rampart has been severed in two, eviscerated, and now they must climb over this heap of rubble. Gravel trickles down behind them, large pebbles that make a worrying amount of noise. They let themselves slide down the other side and land on their bottoms in the mud in the midst of a still whiteness, thick as cream.

They trudge through puddles, climb over little hillocks of earth, skid on patches of clay, finally reaching a gravel road. This area has been completely abandoned by its residents, its woods cleared and flattened during the siege. Nicolas explains that they must walk three meters apart, to make the sentries' task more difficult. So they press on as if each of them were alone, the fog separating them making them feel even farther apart. All around them are fields they can't see, exhaling a strong, almost warm scent.

Gustave crouches down. They imitate him.

"There," he says.

Up ahead, they see the dark mass of a house. A farm, maybe. They can hear people speaking German.

"Head right. Take off your shoes, or you'll get stuck in the mud."

They slip their shoes off, shivering as their feet sink into the soaked earth, and follow the line of furrows with their shoots of young wheat. The mud is up to their knees; they are forced to wrench their legs upward with each step. Caroline falls on her side, and the ground gives way beneath her hand when she tries to get up. Nicolas pulls her to her feet.

"I can't go on," she murmurs.

Nicolas supports her, and they stagger along, gasping, stopping occasionally to catch their breath. Gustave is creeping along almost on all fours ahead of them. Finally they reach an embankment planted with hawthorn. They pause there for a few moments, scraping off the mud coating their feet, and put their shoes back on. There is a road on the other side of the embankment. They don't dare sit down, for fear they won't be able to get up again. Gustave takes a canteen out of his sack and hands it to Caroline. It's water cut with a little bit of plum brandy. She's never tasted anything better in her life.

The sun is up, and the wind is growing stronger. It stirs the fog, lifting it bit by bit.

"Bagnolet is that way," says Gustave. "An hour's walk."

The road is paved, and they make quick progress. Nicolas turns back to look at Paris in the distance, from which intermittent cannon fire has begun rumbling again. His heart clenching painfully, he forces himself to time his breathing with his steps. Gustave turns down a narrow sunken road hidden between two hedgerows.

"They'll help us in the village. I know a good fellow. Rosteau, he's called. I helped him bury his parents two years ago. He's become a friend. He runs a bistro behind the church—it's where people go when they're avoiding mass."

The path climbs a hillock and crosses a wide road. Gustave motions to them to hurry up. The fog is lingering at ground level in the fields, and a light drizzle has begun to fall again.

A cry of *Halt!* A patrol, off to the left. Gustave shoves Caroline and Nicolas, who roll down the slope before they know what's happening. They see the old man shoulder his rifle and fire, then toss the gun aside and run from the other side of the path out into the road. A shot rings out, ripping through foliage and shattering branches overhead. Gustave is still running. They hear the Prussians shouting. Nicolas drags Caroline into a flooded ditch. They crouch low in the water. The soldiers pass on the road, a dozen of them, perhaps, and continue on in pursuit of the old man.

"Let's go."

They pull themselves out of the water, clinging to the brambles, and pull and tug each other back to the path, running as best they can. Two gunshots make them stumble, but they straighten and see the patrol catching up to Gustave, who is crawling, then pulls himself to his feet, then falls again.

They dodge a low dam and drop to their bellies in the mud, creeping forward on all fours, sometimes weeping with exhaustion or laughing for no reason, when suddenly they are able to walk upright for a few moments. They reach the first houses of Bagnolet in the rain and come upon a woman who stops to watch them pass, covered in mud and probably a frightful sight, like something out of a nightmare.

"Come," she says. "You can't stay out here; the patrol will be through soon."

She leads them to a stable, where three cows eye them placidly. In the back, a big horse paws the ground. It's warm. They sink into a pile of straw.

"Don't move," says the woman. "You're safe here. I'll be back."

At around noon, she returns with a tall girl who looks with horror at these two creatures that have seemingly emerged from the earth like the living dead risen from their graves. They are each carrying two buckets of hot water. They scrub Caroline with a big piece of soap and dry her with a piece of woolen cloth. She lets them bathe her as if she's a child. The women don't speak, simply asking her to lift her arms or a leg, to close her eyes when they wash her hair.

They don't dare look at Nicolas, who washes in a corner, his back to them.

They spend the day wrapped in oversized shirts full of holes, sleepy and silent. Exchanging touches every now and then as if to verify that the other one is really there, alive, and that all of this is real. Once, a Prussian patrol enters the farmyard. A soldier gabbles a few words in broken French about fugitives being sought. Shot, he says. *You'll be shot!* The farm wife responds that she hasn't seen anyone, of course not, not in this weather. She has something for them. They hear a great commotion in the henhouse and the screeching of a chicken, which she hands to the soldiers. "Good chicken," she says. "Good for soup tonight!"

A man comes to the farm at nightfall. He's called Maurice Rosteau. The news of the death of a man named Gustave, who shot at a patrol, has made its way around the village. He wants to continue what his friend started. They dress themselves in some old clothing. Later, they'll be shocked by their own appearance.

They leave the farm in a daze. Allowing themselves to be led, drained of all strength of will. They thank the woman, whose name is Victorine. Crossing a street, Nicolas pauses and looks off toward the west. There, in the distance, Paris in flames casts a reddish glow into the low sky, like a bloody breath.

Caroline's hand squeezes his shoulder.

"We'll come back," she says. "We'll come back."

SUNDAY, MAY 28TH

EPILOGUE

The others are dead. He took the remaining cartridges from their pouches. During a lull in the shooting, he loaded nine rifles. He carried some of the bodies to the ruined shop front of a haberdashery, laying them out there as best he could. He wept as he did it. He hadn't thought himself capable of tears anymore, and yet he sobbed as he lined them up, forcing himself to cover the crushed faces and gaping skulls with military caps scattered here and there. Then he dug a shallow hole behind a kind of arrow-slit between two heaps of tumbled cobblestones. He spread a blanket on the ground in the hole and stretched out on his belly in firing position.

He is wearing a red armband. He's in his shirtsleeves, covered with dirt and blood, his poorly shaven face black with gunpowder. There's a cut on his forehead and a gash on his right cheek. His age is impossible to tell.

He waits. He is alone amid the ruins of the Rue Ramponneau.

Just a little while ago, after their attack, the Versaillais withdrew to the Boulevard de Belleville, taking their cannon but leaving the mitrailleuse in battery formation in the middle of the crossroads. He squints down his rifle sight, aiming the gun at one street corner and then the other.

They come back, moving along in the shelter of a wagon. A soldier appears and plants a tricolor flag in a heap of rubble. *Give yourself up, you pathetic wretch!* the others shout. *You're the last one; we'll leave you alive!*

They laugh.

He doesn't tremble. He fires. The recoil thumps against his sore shoulder. The flagpole breaks, and the piece of cloth falls into the mud.

A volley of bullets passes over his head, rattling like hail as they strike. He reaches for another rifle. Lines up the shot. Another flag is being waved above the wagon. He holds his breath and pulls the trigger. Missed.

Another rifle. He barely aims. The flag falls.

The soldiers laugh. "You son of a bitch! No respect for the flag. We'll rip your guts out!"

For a moment, nothing moves in the silence that falls over the quarter. No gunshots. The dead are beyond speech, and those who will die fall silent.

He shatters the pole of the third flag with a single shot. The soldiers have stopped laughing. "Well?" an officer shouts. "What the hell game are you playing?"

The man rolls and crawls to a corner. He pulls his wallet out of his pocket and takes out two photographs, which he looks at for a long time and kisses before slipping them deep into his trouser pocket. A pretty blond woman smiling beneath a tree. A couple posing, their faces so happy, two little boys with serious expressions seated in front of them.

He dodges into the entrance of a building. He knows there's a passage there, at the rear of the demolished courtyard.

Fifteen minutes later, a hundred soldiers attack. They climb over what remains of the barricade, firing bullets into the dead, killing them again with bayonet thrusts. Drunk with rage.

A captain finds the wallet. He opens it and pulls out a law degree, folded into a small square, in the name of Clovis Landier.

They say five hundred men combed the quarter, house by house, rummaging through every heap of ruins, with the sole aim of capturing the insurgent who took on an entire company alone, desecrating the flag three times.

The dead on the barricade, identified by terrified witnesses, did not include his body.

One might assume that, having found his soul again, he lived to travel a long road with his beloved ghosts.